NIGHT KILL

A Novel by R.L. Edinger

Author's Note:
This is a work of fiction.
Names, characters, places, and incidents either are the
product of my imagination, or are used fictitiously, and
any resemblance to actual persons, living or dead, events,
or locales is entirely coincidental.

Published by
R.L. Edinger
819 27th Street
Two Rivers, WI 54241

Cover & book design by R.L. Edinger,

ISBN-13: 978-1461099895
ISBN-10: 1461099897

Printed in the United States of America

This book is dedicated to…

My family for their love and support with all the hours
I spend on the computer, thank you.

And those who continue to be loyal fans of
Andrew Knight; you have my many thanks!

Acknowledgements...

A person would think that of all the pages to be written in a book, the acknowledgement pages would be the easiest of all to do; trust me it is not! How do you thank the people who have been an inspiration, supported, or contributed to the completion of this book? The following is my attempt to put into words my thoughts and the way I feel.

The first person I would like to thank is my wife, Linda. She's the one who has been the most patient, understanding and supportive through not only the process of this book, but the previous ones. She is also the one who keeps reminding me that there is more to life than writing. Somewhere along the way, this next person and I ran into each other. Renda and I met on the website, gather.com, and through time have become good friends. Renda has been an inspiration, supportive, and a true friend I have ever known; even though we have never met face to face. Besides me, she has been the most passionate about my stories.

Through Renda, I met another person that has been a part of this book. It is her sister Kay. I would describe Kay as the head Cheerleader for the Andrew Knight Fan Club. Kay continues to lead through her enthusiasm and positive attitude. On a side note, Kay was the winner of a contest I had sponsored on gather.com. It was a contest to submit a character idea for this book. The character Kay submitted for the book is Kara Sadler. So, keep an eye out for this very interesting and pivotal character I created from Kay's submission.

Finally there are two more people I would like to thank for the part they had in this book. The first is Holly. I met Holly through a game we both enjoy playing on facebook The game is Kingdoms of Camelot and on the game Holly (Lady Toughcookie) and I met because we are part of the same alliance. So when I put out a request for someone to proof the French words in the book, Holly graciously and willingly answered the call. She has done a wonderous service for me and I thank her greatly. The other person is Pastor Henry Koch. When I could not find anyone on facebook that was fluent in German, I turned to my coworkers. I asked around if any one knew of someone fluent in German. After several attempts, they suggested calling Pastor Koch. After introducing myself to him, I explained what I needed. Just like Holly, Pastor Koch graciously accepted the task. He even took the time to explain to me his written corrections, as well as to me which were spoken. It was a great moment for me.

In closing I would like to share with you that writing this story has turned out to be more than I expected. It has turned out to be a life lesson as well. I have found out that there are people out there who are willing to take a chance on someone they have never met before. Thank you my wife and soulmate Linda; Renda, Kay, Holly and Pastor Koch. You have been an inspiration to me as well, and forever more will be a very important part of my life.

Foreword

I have always been an avid reader. From the time I can remember, I have had a love for books and a wide array of genres. According to my current mood or mindset, I will pick up a book to take me away...to foreign lands, different times, or to just meet "new" people. At times, I may be in the mood for a good historical read, other times I may be in the mood for a good horror, and then there are times a romance calls to me. Either way, reading is a fantastic past time and a great hobby. There is always an adventure to be had and lands to be explored. After reading a good book, I enjoy writing book reviews. Writing the reviews allow me to share my thoughts about a writer and story with others. You can never be too young or old to establish a love for books, to allow yourself to be whisked away.

Somewhere along the way, R.L. and I ran into each other. I began reading his articles (or posts as they have become to be known on Gather). He would post blurbs on his various books and I would read them with interest. Being introduced to R.L. and his writings online has been something of an adventure in itself. What started as an online acquaintance has evolved into an endearing online friendship. We "met" at the website Gather.com, which started out for writers and has since evolved into more of a social site. Regardless, there are still writers and artists who remain members on it. Finally, one day, I decided to pick up one of his books, which happened to be the second book in this series, *The Forgotten King*, I was hooked and purchased the first and third books in the series. During that time, R.L. and I would exchange thoughts through emails. It grew into ideas and our relationship continued to grow from simple author/reader to an endearing friendship. I am thankful to know him.

Having the opportunity to read all three of R.L.'s books, *Journey into the Knight, The Forgotten King*, and, *Into the Fire Storm*, has offered me a look into the life and adventures of Andrew Knight. The characters have come alive and now I feel as if I know them personally. To expound a bit more, each of these books offer intrigue and suspense while allowing you to trail along and try to solve the mysteries. Trailing along beside Andrew Knight and trying to unravel the mystery is part of the fun as far as I am concerned. One thing I particularly liked about *Journey into the Knight* is it is actually a collection of smaller stories. This was a plus because it allowed me to read the selections while waiting at doctor's appointments and other places. I used the time to try to figure out the "who done it" before reading the rest of the story. What makes a book or story even greater is when you feel you are pulled into the story line and actually "there", or when you feel the emotion of the characters. A good book pulls you in, holds you there...allowing you to experience the whole effect. So far, R.L.'s writings have done just that and I greatly enjoy following Andrew along on his "journeys".

It has been an honor to come to know R.L. With the passing of time, R.L. and I have shared our different thoughts on various things, including writing. It has been interesting to witness the evolution of this new story *Night Kill*. I have found R.L. to be a wonderful inspiration and he is supportive, kind, and intelligent. There are many authors I admire and seek out their material to read. One of those is R.L. Edinger. When I was first introduced to his work online, I was not sure if I would like it or not...but being the reader I am, I decided to try it. From the first few pages, I was enthralled with R.L.'s main character, Andrew Knight. I devoured one book after another and was ecstatic to learn there would be a fourth book in the Knight series. As an added bonus, I was thrilled my sister won the character contest R.L. held. It was interesting to see how R.L. weaved her character into the story. As I have mentioned before, I am honored to have seen R.L. "in action" and watch this book progress from an idea into an amazing story. Somehow, R.L. weaved his magic again in *Night Kill*. I am honored to be allowed a "sneak peek" of this new, upcoming novel. In it, the characters seem to evolve together, creating a captivating dance and alluring the reader. Compared to the other stories R.L. has written, I have found this one to be more intense, showing a deeper, darker side of the main character. R.L. seems to allow Andrew to come more alive in this later story, becoming more "human" by experiencing the darker side of life, making mistakes like those that we all do, and trying to fight "good and evil". Although the previous three books are very good and you would be missing out if you do not read them, I feel this new book is one of R.L.'s best thus far. This is going to be a great addition to my growing library and will certainly be to yours, as well as the other three books.

A little teaser ~ in this new story, members of the Higgins family are murdered, save one...Storm. Her missing boyfriend, Wyatt, is immediately suspected of the brutal murders. The intensity of the search for the truth brings Andrew into the depths of vampirism, allowing his dark side to surface. Will he survive it all? Will those close to him survive? Only the pages hold the answers. Come along on this journey if you dare. You will not want to miss this newest story in the series.

Happy Reading...Enjoy the Journey!
-Renda Brooks

Introduction

What if a gothic tale of vampires were married to a classic murder mystery thriller? So what if there were such a book?

The idea for this book actually came from a question my oldest daughter asked me one day; why don't you write a story about vampires? Well, did she forget that I write mysteries were the first question on my mind? Probably not, so I gave her the benefit of the doubt. I responded that it would have to be a mystery. Now this raised some more questions in my mind. First of all, how would I be able to marry these two very distinct genres? Second would the story line be strong enough to hold the interest of the reader? And finally, would I be able to pull it off? So once more it was off to the internet to do some more research.

I started with the Vampire genre. Vampire literature covers the spectrum of literary work concerned principally with the subject of vampires. Okay, well that was pretty straight forward I thought. I mean, there have been countless books about vampires. I've even read some like Bram Strokers 'Dracula' and watched movies like 'Interview with the Vampire'. And yes, I admit that I have watched the 'Twilight movies'. I mean we have been fascinated with these undead creatures since the beginning of history.

The next area of research was the mystery genre. Now this was familiar ground to me, but nonetheless fascinating. In my research I found a definition of the mystery/crime genre I want to share with you. Mystery fiction is a loosely-defined term that is often used as a synonym for detective fiction or crime fiction— in other words a novel or short story in which a detective (either professional or amateur) investigates and solves a crime. Sometimes mystery books are nonfiction. The term "mystery fiction" may sometimes be limited to the subset of detective stories in which the emphasis is on the puzzle element and its logical solution (cf. whodunit), as a contrast to hardboiled detective stories, which focus on action and gritty realism. However, in more general usage "mystery" may be used to describe any form of crime scene fiction, even if there is no mystery to be solved.

Okay, now we have our two different genres, how do you bring them together? Well, you need a story, a plot, and a mystery that revolves around vampires. That seems easy enough, right? It could not be a true vampire story about the undead, for after all it still had to be a mystery. It had to be rooted in the vampirism culture of today, and yet be true to my roots in the mystery culture I grew up with.

So to get a better understanding of this whole vampirism culture, I had to do some more research and want to share what I found out with you. A Sanguine (or Sang) is a vampire that feeds specifically off of the blood of others, and cannot achieve satisfaction through any other feeding methods. Psychic Vampire (psi vamp) is a vampire that feeds directly upon the vital energy of a being, and cannot achieve satisfaction through the intake of blood. Psi feeding methods can be long ranged or up close. Hybrid vampires are a vampire that requires both blood and vital energy to satisfy its needs. So basically it is person who cannot adequately sustain their own physical, mental or spiritual well-being without the taking of blood or vital life force energy from people. I also found out there are also is autovampirism. Let me explain further.

Clinical psychologist Richard Noll proposed a term for clinical vampirism and named after the very fictional Renfield character of Dracula fame due to his eating flies, spiders and various other behaviors in belief that he requires/craves their lifeforce the syndrome is said to be a pathological and delusional disease 'fetishistic and compulsive' and for the most part affecting males.

Now that I had a better understanding of this culture, what was next? When you have vampires, you must also have vampire slayers, right? So what is a vampire slayer? A vampire hunter or slayer is a character in folklore and works of fiction, such as books, films, and video games, which specialize in finding and destroying vampires, and sometimes other supernatural creatures. A vampire hunter is usually described as having extensive knowledge of vampires and other monstrous creatures, including their powers and weaknesses, and uses this knowledge to effectively combat them. In many works, vampire hunters are simply humans with more than average knowledge about the occult, while in others they are themselves supernatural beings, having superhuman abilities. A well known and influential vampire hunter is Professor Abraham Van Helsing, a character in Bram Stoker's 1897 horror novel, <u>Dracula</u>.

I had all the elements to move forward; the vampires, the vampire hunters, and of course yours and mine favorite Private Investigator Andrew Knight. But the one thing I did not have was the story. With all of this information and prior experience, what kind of story was I going to write? They say that you need to capture the reader's attention in the first chapter of the book, or you will lose their interest. Okay, so that was simple enough, right? Let me see, vampires and vampire hunters, hmmm? Well of course it was simple. In the first chapter I had to have some vampires killed, right? <u>Night Kill</u> puts forth a fantastically thrilling effort with just such a story.

The story <u>Night Kill</u>... In the snowy, quaint countryside, a loving family gathers in their home to celebrate the much anticipated winter solstice. Finishing touches are being made for the arrival of the rest of the clan. Suddenly, the Higgins family, are attacked one by one and murdered in cold blood. The only survivor of the brutal attack is the couple's daughter, Storm. The authorities suspect Storm's boyfriend, Wyatt, immediately. Evidence found at the crime scene brings the authorities to this swift conclusion. The clan's council of elders set forth governing laws and expects everyone to follow them. Several months earlier, Wyatt, was excommunicated for violating these laws. Wyatt's mysterious disappearance has added more chaos only making things worse! Wyatt's mother, Nedra Collins, and the family priest pay a visit to Private Investigator Andrew Knight. Andrew is informed of details of recent events and the fact that Wyatt is being treated by Psychologist, Claudie Straussman, for a mental condition. Nedra hires Andrew to find her son before the authorities and prove his innocence of the murders. Immersed in the Gothic world of modern-day vampires, blood feasts and a ritualistic killing, Andrew becomes drawn in and discovers his dark side. Things get even more sinister as the newly elected County Sheriff shows her contempt for Andrew. She loathes Andrew's involvement in the investigation. Things only intensify in the search for Wyatt and clues to the Higgins murder as their relationship becomes more confrontational. Andrew and ultimately the reader will be shocked by the truth as the solution to this mystery is revealed in the final two chapters.

It is my hope that the reader will enjoy this book. So what are you waiting for?

—R.L. Edinger

NIGHT KILL

A Novel by R.L. Edinger

Chapter 1

The shimmering moonlight danced across the fields of white which were etched with black shadows of forest trees. The cold winter night lay still with nary a breath of wind, or sounds from the forest creatures.

A dark manor at the end of the long, winding road, quietly nestled, seeming snug and warm, waited for those who had been invited to come safely inside.

Natasha, and her husband Jonathan, were putting the finishing touches on their dining room table. While Jonathan arranged the place settings, Natasha lit the candles and dimmed the lights. Tonight they were celebrating the winter solstice. Soon their guests would arrive to partake of the rituals set forth by the clan. It would be a celebration for both kindred and those whose life blood was freely offered for the taking.

The doorbell interrupted as it announced the first guest to arrive. Natasha told her husband she would get it and that he should finish with the settings. She excused herself and left the dining room to go answer the door.

Natasha brushed aside the tussles of her long, flowing auburn hair. She paused briefly in front of the hall mirror to check her looks. Satisfied, Natasha walked up to the door, and grasped hold of the knob. She flung it open with dramatic flair, though not necessary, but it was just her way.

A lone, hooded figure greeted her with silence. Sadly, Natasha never had time to ask who they were, or to react. A single sharpened wood arrow ravageously pierced her body. Natasha stumbled back a bit, but was able to catch herself against the wall. The hooded figure had already loaded a second arrow in the crossbow. Natasha was about to cry out, but the second arrow struck next to the first! The force of the blow sent Natasha crashing into the hallway table.

Jonathan heard the crash, and immediately flew out from the dining room and into the hallway. He saw his beloved lying amongst the splintered, broken wood and remnants of a shattered vase. He rushed to her side, knelt down, and drew her close to him in his arms. Jonathan's mind screamed as he gazed upon the lifeless, bloody face of his wife. He howled out his agony at seeing the twin arrow shafts protruding from Natasha. Jonathan gently laid Natasha back down whilst he brushed her lips with one last kiss. Suddenly Jonathan caught a glimpse of something moving in the shadows of the front porch. He stood and turned to face the shadowy figure.

Jonathan took a step towards the shadow. He saw that the person wore a hood.

"Coward," Jonathan hissed. "You murdered my wife. Why do you hide your face from me? Let me see who you are, so that when I kill you I will see death on your face."

Jonathan exploded at the person, who at the same time reached beneath their long, black leather overcoat. Jonathan felt the sharpened points of the three throwing stars strike his chest. He torn them away and kept going. The hooded figure leapt into the air and with a round house spin kick, slammed a boot heel into Jonathan, whom tumbled to the snowy ground. Jonathan stood defiantly and spat blood from his mouth to the ground.

"Do you think you're fast and strong enough?" Jonathan cursed. "Or smart enough to take on me and not some poor defenseless woman?"

Jonathan charged again and lunged into the air; however, the hooded figure was ready and leapt again, this time drawing two blades of sharpened steel. As both came together in a mid-air death dance, Jonathan winched as the blades struck him without regard in the chest, back and neck. Jonathan plummeted back to the snowy ground in a heap. The hooded figure instead landed back down without as much as a sound.

Jonathan rose to his knees and looked up at the hooded figure. He brushed aside his blood-matted golden hair. Jonathan felt his life ebbing away. The hooded figure stood in front of Jonathan forming an 'X' with his two swords.

"Let me see your face," Jonathan coughed.

The hooded figure took the two swords in one hand and with the other removed the hood. Jonathan's eyes drew open wide and before he could utter a word, the hooded figure struck!

Peter was in the kitchen finishing up with the tray of appetisers. He was listening to his favorite tunes on his Ipod. He liked to pump up the volume. Oh sure his parents complained that he was ruining his hearing, but he didn't care. His mother told him to have plenty of nourishment for the blood partners. Peter was glad that the rest of the clan was going to be here tonight. The winter solstice was the one gathering that he looked forward to every year, unlike his sister.

Peter walked from the kitchen into the dining room. His parents weren't there. Where could they be? Peter tuned off his Ipod and removed the ear buds. That's when Peter heard his father shouting at someone. Peter put down the tray and sprinted out into the hallway.

"Mother!" Peter cried out. He rushed to her and knelt at her side. "What the hell?" he was shocked upon seeing the arrow shafts. She felt so cold to the touch. Peter trembled as the realization of his mother being dead finally hit home. Peter lay her back down and continued outside. Just as Peter stepped onto the porch, he saw his father hit the ground. A darkened figure stood with his back to Peter. He heard his father ask to see the person's face, which they did. Peter watched in horror as the figure replaced the hood and without remorse, killed Jonathan. "No!" Peter bellowed. He flashed his fangs and tore off in the figure's direction.

Peter hadn't gotten far when the first throwing star slammed into his neck. He stumbled to his knees, but quickly recovered. Peter went on, but was hit with two more throwing stars with lethal force in his chest. Peter flashed his fangs and ripped them out. He crouched down and sprang forth. Peter did a forward hand flip and with both boots drove the figure to the ground. Peter instantly spun around and grabbed the figure by the collar. His eyes reflected the rage in his soul. Peter threw the figure against the tree not far from them. Peter retrieved one of the swords as the figure dropped.

"Nice blade," Peter said running his finger tips across the unsharpened surface. "Its now time for you to die." The hooded figure had loaded his crossbow while Peter was preoccupied admiring the sword. Peter raised the blade and rushed to strike, but was hit instead with the arrow. Peter dropped the sword as the arrow perforated the flesh of his chest. Peter tumbled face down in the snow, driving the arrow further in.

The hooded figure rose and walked over to where Peter lay, and bent down to retrieve the sword. There was one more left.

Storm was chilling out in her bedroom. The music from her boom box was blaring and she chatted away on her laptop. Her parents complained all the time that she could never hear them or what was going on downstairs in the house. She thought it was best to stay out of the way as her parents made preparations for the winter solstice. Like the rest of the coven, to her parents this was a really big deal. She on the other hand, wasn't as traditional as the rest of the clan.

Storm noticed the time on her laptop screen. It was nearly 9:30 p.m. The rest of the clan and the blood dolls would be arriving soon. She did wonder though why her mom hadn't come up to get her. Her mom was very strict about being there when the rest of the clan arrived. So, Storm shut down and put away her laptop on her night stand. She bounded of the bed and over to the boom box which was on her desk by the wall across from the door. Her back was to the door when she heard it open. Not bothering to turn around Storm just said, "Yes, I know mother." Storm jerked and felt an uncomfortable pressure from her chest. The force from the pressure slammed her against the wall. Storm couldn't speak as she collapsed backwards. Storm heard a sound like when you snap a twig, and everything went black.

Storm awoke to the sound of her heart beating in her ears. She tried to stand, but was too weak. She looked at the front of her blouse and noticed the strangest thing. A wooden tip was protruding out. Storm started gasping for air, but only blood spittle flew from her mouth. She couldn't call out for help. Tears rolled down her cheeks smearing the dark eyeliner she wore. With every bit of strength she had, Storm lay down and pulled herself towards the door.

Storm took a short break when she reached the open doorway of her room. When she looked back, Storm saw a trail of blood. She didn't have time to panic; she needed to find her parents. With new found strength, Storm made her way to the stairs. How would she get down now? Since the arrow tip was in front, Storm decided to lie on her back and slide down the carpeted stairs. She would use the banister posts to hold onto. Storm died a little more inside and the pain nearly caused her to black out, but she managed to roll on her back. With only the strength in her arms and hands to help, Storm started her painful trek down the stairs. "Keep going," Storm spoke words of encouragement that only she could hear. She strained with all her being to keep from sliding down unchecked, which meant certain death. For what seemed like hours, even a day, Storm finally came to rest leaning against the last step!

Her heart was beating slower now and Storm rested for a little. The hallway was dark except for the moonlight peaking inside with very little light. Storm saw a dark, huddled mass lying motionless in a broken pile of the hallway table. She sniffed back the tears and started to drag herself towards it.

When Storm reached the broken table and shadowy mass, she saw that it was her mother. With hardly any breath left and unable to cry out loud, Storm still wept. She pulled herself up closer to her mother. Storm saw the arrows and her mother's blood stained face. What kind of monster could do this? They had done nothing wrong to deserve this kind of pain. Storm grimaced as she bent down and kissed her mother goodbye. Storm knew she needed to get help. She touched her mother's cheek one last time and started to crawl towards the open front door.

The night air was bitterly cold and it made her shiver. Storm scooted this time down the front porch steps. That's when she saw her father. He was dead. The snow was stained with his blood. Storm crawled to him and when she got there, laid her head on his chest. His body was cold and his life-force gone. Storm grieved knowing that only the shell of the man she knew as her father remained. Storm felt weaker now, but she had to continue on. She searched the darkness around looking for any hope. Storm saw car lights winding their way up the driveway. She could relax now and feel at peace. Storm lay back on the cold, snowy ground. She couldn't feel any of it at all, but a thin smile of satisfaction drew across her face. Storm closed her eyes.

There was no more shimmering moonlight, but instead a sea of red and blue flashing lights. The stillness of the cold winter night had been broken by approaching sirens.

A dark colored sedan came to a sudden stop once it had reached the end of the driveway. Its lone occupant jumped out with flashlight in hand.

Sheriff Delsmann ducked under the yellow crime scene tape. Feeling chilled, she zipped up her blue parka.

"What have we got here," she asked while taking in the overall horrific scene.

"Two male victims," the CSI technician answered. He pointed in the direction of the house. "There is a female victim in the hallway. The fourth, a teenage girl, has already been transported to Bayport Memorial. She's stable but in critical condition."

Sheriff Delsmann knelt down next to the technician. In all her years as a detective in Chicago, she had never seen anything this horrible.

"The first victim is a male in his late forties," the technician said. "He has slash wounds on the chest, back and neck. It appears they may have been caused by sword of some type. He also had some puncture wounds from those throwing stars we found on the ground."

Sheriff Delsmann stood up and walked over to the younger male victim. The technician joined her. They knelt down again.

"This victim is in his teens," the technician said.

Sheriff Delsmann grasped hold of the boy's shoulder and carefully rolled him over.

"What the hell is going on here?" she gasped upon seeing the arrow in the boy's chest.

"There's more," the technician said. With his gloved hand he lifted the boy's top lip.

"Fangs?" Sheriff Delsmann said.

"All four victims have vampire fangs," the technician explained.

"You said the older female victim is in the house," Sheriff Delsmann answered.

"Yes," the technician replied.

"Make sure you get everything we need," Sheriff Delsmann ordered. She rose to her feet and immediately headed for the house.

Sheriff Delsmann walked up the front porch steps and into the house. Another CSI technician was collecting evidence in the hallway. Sheriff Delsmann saw that the female victim had two arrow shafts protruding from her chest and was lying amongst a broken table and vase. Sheriff Delsmann continued on down the hallway and up the stairs. She walked into the daughter's bedroom. A third technician was collecting evidence from the area next to the bed. He was bagging splintered pieces of an arrow shaft.

"What have you found thus far?" she asked.

"Just these broken pieces of arrow and this blood stain on the carpet," he replied.

"Is this where they found the daughter?" Sheriff Delsmann asked.

"No," he replied, marking the evidence bag. "She was found outside next to her father and brother."

"She managed to get outside after being shot!" she exclaimed.

"It appears she dragged herself," he answered. "There's trace evidence on the stair railings and carpeting there."

"Just make sure you go through the room thoroughly," Sheriff Delsmann said. She left the room and headed back down stairs.

When Sheriff Delsmann walked down the steps, she stopped briefly to examine the blood stains on the railings. She had a sense of admiration at how brave and determined the wounded girl had been in her trek to get help for her family. Sheriff Delsmann continued down to the first floor and entered the dining room.

An eerie feeling came over Sheriff Delsmann when she saw the empty chairs surrounding the elegantly decorated dining room table. The silverware was still wrapped lovingly in white linen clothes. The bone china and crystal glassware stood in patient silence waiting to be used by guests that would never arrive. A sense of sadness washed over Sheriff Delsmann as she took in the hopeless and despair in the room. There were no signs of the killer being in this room. She moved into the kitchen.

Just like the dining room, there were no signs of the killer being in here. Sheriff Delsmann opened the refrigerator. There were several food trays ready to serve. Bottles of wine had been placed in the cooler, chilling to perfection but none would ever be opened and consumed. She closed the refrigerator door and walked to the oven. Sheriff Delsmann opened the oven door and could see the carefully prepared roast and potatoes that were now just a dried out mass of muddy colors. Sheriff Delsmann closed the oven door and left the kitchen to go outside again.

As Sheriff Delsmann stood on the porch she surveyed the area in front of the house. She flipped on the flashlight and walked down the steps. Sheriff Delsmann walked slowly around the exterior of the house. She was looking for clues. The only footsteps thus far were her own. When Sheriff Delsmann got to the back of the house she noticed a back door. As she walked up to it, Sheriff Delsmann saw boot prints in the snow. With her flashlight, Sheriff Delsmann followed the boot prints until they disappeared at the edge of the surrounding woods.

"Send a deputy to the back of the house," Sheriff Delsmann spoke into her radio.

A few minutes later, a deputy joined her. Together they took off in the direction of where the boot prints were headed.

Sheriff Delsmann and the deputy drew their weapons and stepped into the dense woods. Slowly and painstakingly, they traversed through the forest thicket. Sheriff Delsmann felt her heart beating wildly in her chest. She didn't really like the darkness nor the fact that at any given moment something or someone would jump out at them. It was never like this back in Chicago. Even with all the things she'd seen working as a detective on third shift, it still wasn't as white knuckled as right now.

The boot trail eventually led them to a road about a mile from the house. The road was smooth and showed no signs for tire tracks. If they had a vehicle waiting here, there was no way to know what kind it was, or even how long it had been here.

"Let's head back," she ordered. Somewhere in the blackness of the woods a tree branch snapped. The sound echoed throughout the quietness. Instantly both of them realized they weren't alone. "Douse the lights," Sheriff Delsmann hissed. Sheriff Delsmann and the deputy killed the lights and crouched down behind the snow embankment. They waited in complete silence. The only light was from the moon directly above them. Once her eyes were adjusted to the darkness, Sheriff Delsmann could make out the silhouettes of the trees intermixed with the moonlight. At first she thought her eyes were playing tricks on her, but Sheriff Delsmann swore one of the trees was moving.

A few yards away, a shadowy figure strode confidently from the woods and onto the road. Sheriff Delsmann and the deputy crouched down further as the shadow looked in their direction. Neither Sheriff Delsmann nor the deputy moved. Apparently satisfied, the shadowy figure started walking down the road.

"We need to get this guy," Sheriff Delsmann whispered.

"But we don't have backup," the deputy protested.

"We're both armed," Sheriff Delsmann said. "Plus we have the element of surprise."

"Yes M'mam," the deputy answered.

"We go on three," Sheriff Delsmann said clicking off the safety of her weapon. The deputy did the same. "One, two, three," Sheriff Delsmann counted. Slowly, cautiously, they rose to their feet and took off after the shadowy figure.

Sheriff Delsmann and the deputy must have had fortune smile on them and now they were just a few yards away from their suspected killer.

"Now," Sheriff Delsmann commanded. They immediately lit up the suspect with their flashlights and pointed weapons at them. The person had a loaded crossbow held in place with a sling over and around their back. They were dressed all in black. A hood covered their entire head so the sheriff and her deputy couldn't see their identity.

"Sheriff's department," Sheriff Delsmann barked. "Put your hands where we can see them. Do it now!"

The shadowy figure stood, not moving at all.

"Put your weapon on the ground and step away!" the deputy shouted. "We will shoot if you don't comply."

Again, the shadowy figure did not move.

"What the hell is this?" Sheriff Delsmann looked at the deputy.

The Shadowy figure whipped around and with blinding speed sent his deadly reply. The deputy was the first to hit the icy road bed as the throwing stars viciously buried themselves in his chest. Sheriff Delsmann turned and ducked but still two others shredded her parka and dug deep into her back. Sheriff Delsmann shrieked from the burning pain. She turned around, faced the suspect, and somehow managed to fire off several shots. She watched mortified as the bullets struck but the shadowy figure remained standing.

"What the hell are you," Sheriff Delsmann stood defiantly. She pointed her weapon and fired three more times. The shadowy figure stumbled this time and dropped onto the road. Sheriff Delsmann checked on her deputy. He was okay, but badly injured.

"We have a deputy injured," Sheriff Delsmann called on her radio. "We also have a suspect down. Send a couple of squads now." She reloaded her weapon and looked over at the suspect; who was gone!

"Where are you?" Sheriff Delsmann whirled in all directions with her weapon ready to fire. Her wild-eyed search turned up nothing.

"Over here," a voice finally said.

Sheriff Delsmann spun in the direction of the voice. She pointed her weapon, but it was too late. The arrow drove itself with unrelenting desire into Sheriff Delsmann. She flew several feet backwards landing softly now in the pillowy snow. Sheriff Delsmann could hear a death rhythm in her ears. The pressure in her chest was crushing and she couldn't breath.

"Next time we meet you die." The shadowy figure announced, turned and walked away.

Sheriff Delsmann tried to reach for her shoulder mike, but the pain was unbearable. All she could do was watch in silence as the person faded into the darkness. Talia breathed slowly and closed her eyes.

Chapter 2

Andrew came into the four season room trying to balance the tray with beer, snacks, and cell phone. He put the tray and cell phone down by the edge of the indoor hot tub. It was really nice to have an indoor hot tub since they remodeled the four season room this past summer. It sure was a lot better than freezing your butt off going outside in the snow and cold if you wanted to take a dip in the hot tub.

Andrew tossed his robe and towel on one of the wicker chairs. The soothing waters of the hot tub really felt good as Andrew slipped into it. He opened an ice cold brew and took a long, slow swig. It hit the spot perfectly. Andrew grabbed his phone when it started buzzing. It was a text message from Megan.

"Conference is okay," Andrew read aloud the text.

"I felt the baby moving during dinner."

"Miss you and the baby terribly. When you coming home?" Andrew texted back. He took another drink waiting for Megan's reply. His phone buzzed.

"One week. Miss you too. What are you doing?"

"I'm in the hot tub with a beer, but no one to share with." Andrew typed. He pressed the send key. Andrew opened the bag of chips and had just put some in his mouth when his phone buzzed again.

"LOL," Andrew read Megan's text. "Better be alone or you're in big trouble."

"No worries. Better get some sleep. Text me tomorrow." Andrew replied. He hit the send button.

"Luv you. Later." Megan texted him back.

Andrew closed his phone and set it down. Andrew grabbed some more chips. As he was chewing away, his phone buzzed.

"Doesn't she ever sleep," Andrew laughed. He flipped open his phone. It was Maggie and Sam.

"What's up?" Andrew answered the call. He listened to his aunt. "I'm just sitting in the hot tub drinking beer and trying to relax," Andrew replied. He paused and then said, "How's the weather in Arizona? Is Sam bored yet?" Andrew laughed at his Aunt's reply that Sam was indeed bored, but was enjoying the nice weather. Andrew listened some more. "No I'm not working on any case right now," Andrew said. "I'm just trying to get some rest that's all, nothing more." He finished off his beer. "Yes, Megan's in Chicago for a national newspaper conference." Andrew told her. "The baby is doing fine." Andrew opened another beer. "Yes, I'll have Megan call you when she gets home," Andrew promised his aunt. "I love you too," Andrew answered before closing his phone. He didn't want anymore interruptions, so Andrew powered off his cell phone. Andrew tossed his phone on one of the wicker chairs. He put the beer down and reclined back against the cushioned edge of the hot tub. Andrew inhaled and exhaled deeply as he let the soothing waters take over. Finally, there was peace and quiet.

Andrew heard the doorbell announce the arrival of a visitor and his quiet time vanished completely. Andrew grudgingly rose out of the hot tub and grabbed his robe. According to the clock on the wall it was almost eight thirty. Who would be so bold as to disturb his quiet time? The office was locked up for the night and none of his clients knew his home address. So who could it be?

Andrew left the four season room and walked through the foyer to the front door. He already felt chilled and drew his robe closed even tighter. Andrew opened the front door.

He saw a woman with wispy blond hair dressed in a nurse's uniform carrying a briefcase. He didn't know her, but of course he did recognize the man with her. It was Father Michael, his parish priest. The old priest wore bifocals and had much less hair than Andrew remembered.

"Andrew," Father Michael smiled at him. They embraced briefly. Father Michael, in return, introduced the woman with him. "Andrew this is Nedra Collins."

"Nice to meet you," Andrew said, shaking her hand.

"Mister Knight?" Nedra blurted out, "I want to hire you to find my son."

"We need to explain," Father Michael apologized. "Do you have a moment?"

"Please come in," Andrew said. "Go sit down in the family room while I go change."

Nedra and Father Michael went to the spacious and nicely decorated room as Andrew went upstairs to change. "So much for peace and quiet," Andrew grumbled as he went into the bedroom. He quickly took off his wet trunks and robe and threw on a pair of jeans and sweat shirt. He slipped on a pair of leather slippers and went back downstairs.

Andrew joined his guests in the family room. He sat down on the sofa. Nedra and Father Michael were already seated in the chairs in front of the fireplace.

"So tell me all about it," Andrew settled back.

"Two weeks ago my son's girlfriend and her family were attacked," Nedra said.

"That was the Higgins family in the news, right?" Andrew interjected.

"Yes," Father Michael answered.

"What does that have to do with your son?"

"My son was a member of the Ravenclaw coven," Nedra explained. "The coven consists of five clans. There are, the Higgins, Drakes, Bristols, Hancocks, and Moores. The leader of the coven is a man called Vlad Ravenclaw. Wyatt was excommunicated because he violated the governing laws of the coven. My youngest son Chad is your average sixteen year old. His girlfriend Amber is from the Bristol's family."

"Did you say coven?" Andrew interrupted. "Were they witches?"

"No, vampires," Nedra answered.

"Did you say vampires?" Andrew was taken aback.

"They perform blood rituals," Father Michael explained. "They drink human blood from donors. The church has never condoned this type of behavior.

Since the murders, the rest of the Ravenclaw coven has gone into hiding. Vlad Ravenclaw believes that the clan is the target of a secret society of vampire slayers."

"I'm sorry but would you like something to drink?" Andrew suddenly remembered his manners.

"Some coffee would be nice," they answered.

"I'll be right back," Andrew excused himself and went to the kitchen.

"You said he would help," Nedra looked worriedly in the direction Andrew had gone.

"Andrew is a good man," Father Michael answered. "He's also the best private investigator I know. He will find your son, trust me."

Andrew returned a short time later with a serving tray with a coffee carafe, cups and cream and sugar. He set it down on the coffee table and quickly served up some for his guests. He then served himself and sat back down.

"While I was in the kitchen, I came to several conclusions," Andrew took a sip from his cup. "First of all, I don't believe you've told me everything. Second, from the tone of urgency in your voice I get the sense that you feel your son is in danger. And lastly, you believe that your son, Wyatt, is involved somehow with the attack on the Higgin's family."

"My son suffers from Renfield's syndrome," Nedra finally confessed. "He was receiving psychiatric treatment for the condition."

"I'm not familiar with Renfield's syndrome," Andrew said. "Who was his psychiatrist?"

"Okay," Nedra drew a deep breath. She explained, "Renfield's syndrome, also called simply Renfield syndrome and traditionally known as clinical vampirism. It is a mental disorder used to describe an obsession to drink blood."

"When did you first notice it in your son?"

"When my son was young, he fell off his bike and scraped his knees," Nedra further explained. "He put his hand on the injuries to stop the bleeding. When I got there I saw Wyatt licking the blood off his hands. As soon as Wyatt saw me, he immediately stopped." Nedra stopped to finally take a drink from her cup. Andrew picked up on the sadness in her voice as she continued, "When Wyatt reached puberty it became worse, almost a sexual arousal with him whenever he saw blood. He also was cutting himself."

"Is that when he met the Higgins girl?"

"Yes," Nedra replied. "That's when he met Storm."

"So they brought him into the clan then, right?"

"Yes," Nedra said. "Jonathan, Natasha, Peter and Storm inducted Wyatt into their clan. There were others that also joined. Wyatt told me that they had agreed upon to follow the laws set forth by the coven. The members of the coven would carefully screen those who were willing to be blood donors for the coven."

"So what happened next?"

"He couldn't control his urges and sought out blood from those outside the coven," Father Michael answered this time.

"So he was excommunicated," Andrew surmised. "There's more, right?"

"Let me explain," Nedra said. She first asked for a refill, which Andrew obliged. She took a long, slow drink of her coffee before continuing, "After Wyatt was excommunicated from the coven he hooked up with a supposed vampire slayer by the name of Night Blade."

"What I heard from other parents whose kids are involved in this vampirism," Father Michael replied, "Night Blade is trained in the martial arts, and various forms of weapons. He or she has been rumored to be responsible for several deaths."

"Can they identify this Night Blade?"

"According to the kids, Night Blade wears a full head mask," Father Michael answered. He also asked for a refill of coffee, took a quick drink and went on to say, "After Wyatt hooked up with Night Blade, he was trained to be a vampire slayer. It's also rumored that Night Blade arranged a permanent blood doll for him."

Andrew sat there and mulled over all that he had learned. His head was reeling with all kinds of questions and weird thoughts. Andrew couldn't fathom that people were actually like this. He knew about the Goth culture and that several sub cultures branched off from it, but vampires?

"Who's in charge of the investigation?"

"Sheriff Delsmann," Nedra replied. "She and one of her deputies were also attacked the same night as the Higgins."

"Interesting," Andrew mused while sipping his coffee. "Well then, you've got yourself a private investigator."

Nedra jumped up and rushed over to Andrew. She bent down and threw her arms around him in a tight hug which almost made him drop his cup. Andrew's face flushed.

"Okay, okay," Andrew said patting Nedra on the back. "You can let go now."

"I'm sorry," Nedra apologized and sat back down.

"Stop by the office tomorrow and I'll have you sign the papers," Andrew said standing up. Nedra and Father Michael followed suit. Andrew walked them to the front door. They said their good byes. Andrew closed the door.

He immediately went to his office and turned on the computer. As soon as it was up, Andrew typed in vampirism. The search engine came up with more than three million hits. He was shocked to say the least. Andrew clicked on the first one.

"Sanguine (or Sang) - a vampire feeds specifically off of the blood of others, and cannot achieve satisfaction through any other feeding methods," Andrew read aloud. He quivered at the thought that people actually drank human blood.

Andrew continued, "Psychic Vampire (psi vamp) is a vampire that feeds directly upon the vital energy of a being, and cannot achieve satisfaction through the intake of blood. Psi feeding methods can be long ranged or up close. Hybrid vampires are vampires that require both blood and vital energy to satisfy their needs." Andrew turned on the printer and sent the information to it. He next typed in Renfield's syndrome. Once up, Andrew clicked on the link and started reading it. "Renfield's syndrome is traditionally known as clinical vampirism, though not currently categorized as a mental disorder used to describe an obsession to drink blood.

The term was first coined by Richard Noll, and is named after Dracula's insect-eating assistant, Renfield, in the novel by Bram Stoker," Andrew shook his head. Things were really getting near the edge of bizarre here. For him things were black and white, good or bad, right or wrong, there were no gray areas. Of course it was possible that he would have to open up his mind when it came to this vampirism subculture. Andrew continued reading; "People who suffer from this condition are primarily male. The craving for blood arises from the idea that it conveys life-enhancing powers. According to Noll, the condition starts with a key event in childhood that causes the experience of blood injury or the ingestion of blood to be exciting. After puberty, the excitement is experienced as sexual arousal. Throughout adolescence and adulthood, blood, its presence, and its consumption can also stimulate a sense of power and control. Noll explains that Renfield's syndrome begins with autovampirism and then progresses to the consumption of the blood of other creatures." Finally Andrew searched for a description of 'blood doll' to have a better understanding. Within minutes he found a multitude of hits. Andrew selected one and read, "A blood doll is a mortal who freely lets vampires drink from them. Frequently found as members of subcultures such as the Goths, blood dolls seek a perverse thrill from the 'kiss', but their tendency to actively seek out vampires to give it to them means that they unwittingly walk a very thin and dangerous line with their lives." Andrew shuddered at the thought that people were actually willing to do this. He had read all he needed to. Andrew sent the information to the printer, shut down the computer, and headed off to bed. The first order of business tomorrow would be to touch base with a courtesy call to Sheriff Delsmann. Hopefully she would be able to help him by providing answers from the investigation. Andrew flipped back the covers and climbed into bed. He recovered himself and after finding that 'comfort spot', drifted off to sleep. Soon Andrew was snoring away some where off in a deep sleep.

Sheriff Delsmann walked into her office with the morning paper and a cup of coffee in hand. She sat down at her desk and put the coffee cup down. Sheriff Delsmann grimaced a little when she opened the paper. The reason was, splashed across the front page were the words 'The Vampire Murders'.

"Great," Sheriff Delsmann lamented. "Just great!"

She folded the paper up and tossed it into the recycling bin. Sheriff Delsmann spun around to the credenza where her computer was and turned it on. While waiting, she stood up and glanced out the window down at the street in front of the building. A red AC Cobra came to a stop in one of the parking spaces. She saw a well dressed dark haired man get out with a briefcase. He quickly jogged across the street and into the building.

Andrew stopped at the service window in the lobby of the sheriffs' department building. The deputy on duty recognized Andrew.

"Good morning Mister Knight," she said.

"Good morning," Andrew answered. "I have an appointment with Sheriff Delsmann."

"Here's your visitors pass." She smiled and handed him the clip-on ID badge.

"Thanks," Andrew said, as he clipped it to his lapel. She buzzed him in.

Andrew took the elevator to the fourth floor and when the doors opened, he exited into the large detectives' room. Usually the guys in the division greeted him with smiles and handshakes. They were always glad to see him, but today it was different. There were no smiles or handshakes. All of the guys looked grumpy, and grudgingly as they were doing their work.

At the far end of the room was the office of the sheriff. Andrew had worked with the previous sheriff, Sheriff Ackerman, for several years. He didn't know what the current sheriff was like. Andrew had done some checking on her before he came here today. Sheriff Delsmann, Talia, had been a detective with the Chicago police department for twenty years. She was a highly decorated, police officer.

Andrew knocked, and immediately opened the door. The woman seated at the desk looked to be close to his age or a bit younger. The slender African American woman with straight black hair motioned for him to come in. Andrew did just that and strode up to her confidently and they briefly shook hands.

"Please be seated Mister Knight," Talia gestured to one of the chairs in front of her desk. "Would you like some coffee?"

"Yes, that would be nice."

"Could you bring Mister Knight some coffee," Talia buzzed the intercom.

"So tell me what I can do for you," Talia settled back and unbuttoned her dark blue blazer. "Or is this just a courtesy call?"

"Direct and to the point," Andrew smiled.

When the receptionist entered with his coffee, she smiled and said, "Good morning Mister Knight."

"Good morning Jenny." Andrew smiled back. She was the only one smiling.

"Please leave us alone, Jenny," Talia seemed to chastise her.

"I've been hired by Nedra Collins to find her son, Wyatt," Andrew announced.

"Well as you know I cannot share any details of our investigation," Talia replied harshly. Andrew detected a note of disgust in her voice as well. She went on, "All I can say is that Wyatt Collins is a person of interest."

"I can get a look at the crime scene?"

"No," Talia shot back. "Besides I don't see how it will help you locate the boy."

"Is there evidence linking him to the crime?" Andrew asked. He continued, "What about professional courtesy?"

"I cannot comment on the DNA evidence. And you are here to tell me about professional courtesy?" Talia retorted. This time there was no mistaking her disdain for him. Talia opened her top desk drawer and plopped a manila folder on top of the desk pad. She put on her reading glasses and began, "Andrew Phillip Knight. Born in Bayport, attended the Bayport school system. Graduated from Washington High School and went on to attend Mount Richmond Community College." Talia paused to take a drink and draw a quick breath.

She continued reading, "Graduated with honors and law degree. Instead of going into law practice, joined the Preston Detective agency instead as an investigator. You graduated with a degree in private investigation, an expert in all types of weapons, multilingual, and efficient at several forms of martial arts. Your success rate in solving the cases you work on are well, quite phenomenal." Talia closed the folder and put her glasses down. The look on her face concerned Andrew greatly. He was not ready for her next barrage.

"So tell me Mister Knight, where were you when the Higgins family was attacked?" Talia began her unexpected interrogation.

"What!?" Andrew was taken aback.

"You're trained in martial arts; you're efficient with all types of weapons. One of the types used was throwing stars. And according to my information throwing stars is sometimes your weapon of choice," Talia started ticking off each item she listed on her fingers. "Did someone hire you to eliminate the Higgins family?"

"I'm not going to dignify that with an answer," Andrew growled back.

"I'll be honest with you Mister Knight," Talia said leaning forward, placing her folded arms on the desk. "I have never liked private investigators. I feel you and your fellow colleagues tarnish the work we law enforcement professionals do." She unfolded her arms and pointed a warning finger at Andrew, "If you go anywhere near the crime scene I will have you arrested for obstruction, tainting an ongoing crime scene, and any other charge I can come up with! Do I make myself clear?"

"Perfectly," Andrew said as he rose from the chair. Andrew walked up to the door, opened it, and before leaving, said, "I thought you would be professional enough to work together on this case. But apparently I was wrong."

"Good day, Mister Knight," Talia's voice was icy towards him.

"Good day, Sheriff." Andrew answered and slammed the door shut.

As soon as Andrew left, Sheriff Delsmann got on the phone and placed a call, "This is Sheriff Delsmann. I want you to double up the security at the Higgins house." She paused as the person on the other end must have questioned her decision. Talia continued, "Because I believe that a private investigator by the name of Andrew Knight will try and get a look at the crime scene. If the deputies see any sign him, Knight is to be arrested immediately." Talia hung up the phone. She was very upset and slammed her fists on the desk. Talia had a feeling that Andrew Knight was going to be a problem.

Andrew walked briskly to the elevators. He was not in a very good mood. Andrew pressed the button for the elevator. With each passing second he had to wait, Andrew was becoming more pissed off. He was not use to this kind of treatment from the authorities. For some reason Sheriff Delsmann had it in for him even before he could make a good impression. The other thing that really pissed him off was that she had the guts to accuse him of murdering the Higgins family!

When the elevator finally arrived, Andrew stepped inside and waited for the doors to close. He was about to press the lobby button, but stopped and glanced down at his visitor pass. Andrew smirked and instead pressed the basement button. The reason he did, was that all the files from every case the department worked on or currently was working on, were stored down there.

The elevator doors had barely opened, when Andrew jumped out and hastily walked to the records department. When he opened the door, Andrew saw a friend of his sitting at the main desk.

Darcy looked up when the door opened. It was Andrew Knight. Darcy had always had a crush on him since the first day she met him. She straightened her uniform top and smiled as Andrew approached.

"Hey Darcy," Andrew smiled sitting down on the edge of her desk.

"Hi Andrew," Darcy answered. "So what can I do for you?"

"Listen Darcy," Andrew leaned closer. Darcy thought he had the nicest looking green eyes. "I'm working on a case and I need to get a look at the information from the Higgins investigation."

"I'm sorry Andrew," Darcy pulled back. "We have orders from the Sheriff not to share any of that information with you." Andrew walked around to Darcy's side of the desk. He pulled her and the chair away from the desk and swung Darcy to face him. Andrew got down on one knee and leaned in closer.

Darcy's face flushed and her heart started beating a bit faster.

"The woman I'm working for asked me to find her son," Andrew explained and peered directly into Darcy's blue eyes. "I need those reports to help me understand what happened at the Higgins house and provide me with a start on this case." Andrew drew his face and body even closer to Darcy. He knew she had a crush on him and he was going to use every tool available to him to get the job done. Even if that meant he had to flirt with Darcy to get his way.

"But," Darcy protested.

"Please," Andrew begged with sad eyes.

"Alright," Darcy finally gave in. She surprised them both when she gave Andrew a sudden kiss on the lips. Darcy's face turned red again, and she pushed her chair away and back to the desk. Andrew rose to his feet, his face was red too. Darcy logged into the file with the information from the Higgins investigation. Soon she had the files up and pressed the key to send them to the printer.

Sheriff Delsmann had just finished logging off her computer. When she stood up to leave, Sheriff Delsmann saw that Andrew's car was still there.

"Damn it," Talia cursed. She went to her desk and picked up the phone. "This is Sheriff Delsmann," Talia said. "I want you to get down to the records department immediately." She stopped to listen to the person on the other end. She continued, "Andrew Knight is still in the building and I think he is down there trying to get information on the Higgins case. Stop him at all costs. He is not to leave the building!" Talia slammed down the receiver. She knew Andrew was going to be a thorn in her side, just like all the other private investigators she had dealt with before. No regards to the law. Talia opened the right bottom desk drawer and took out her clip on holster with service weapon. She clipped it to her belt and rushed out the door. Talia wanted to be the one to see the surprised look on Andrew's face when he was arrested for tampering with an ongoing investigation.

Darcy went to the printer and gathered all of the papers she had printed for Andrew. She returned to her desk and put them in a large manila envelope. Andrew thanked Darcy with a hug. Darcy held onto him a bit longer, drinking in his scent. She let go. Andrew opened the outer door and was just about to step into the hallway when he saw the elevator doors open. It was Sheriff Delsmann and several deputies. Fortunately, he ducked back in the records room before they saw him.

"We have company," Andrew looked at Darcy.

"I'll get fired," Darcy complained.

"Don't worry," Andrew reassured.

"There is a fire exit," Darcy suggested.

"You have a key, don't you?" Andrew asked.

"Yes," Darcy remembered. "I can unlock this door."

Darcy used a key to unlock the door and then opened it. Andrew peered inside the unlit stairwell.

Sheriff Delsmann and the deputies with her, burst into the room. The deputies immediately secured the room while at the same time, Talia walked up to Darcy, whom was sitting at her station.

"Where is he?" Talia barked accusingly at Darcy.

"What are you talking about?" Darcy replied when she looked up calmly from her computer screen. "I'm alone." Talia wasn't convinced.

"If we find Andrew Knight anywhere in here," Talia said sternly. "You will be fired."

Talia surveyed the room. The only way out was the emergency door, but the alarm hadn't sounded. "Did you unlock the door for him?" Talia further accused.

"Like I said Sheriff," Darcy answered. "I am alone."

Talia walked over and used her key to turn off the alarm and open the door. She looked over to the two deputies. "Watch her."

Talia left the door open to provide enough light to see by as she started up the stairs. But the further she ascended, the less the light helped. Talia used the handrail as her guide in the total darkness. Eventually, Talia got to the door. With both hands, she opened it.

The bright sunshine blinded Talia when she stepped onto the roof. She was blinded for a few minutes as she had turned away from the open doorway. When Talia opened her eyes again; she drew her weapon and approached the open door. She stepped inside. Talia searched the stairwell from top to bottom. There was no sign of Andrew anywhere to be seen. Could he have been hiding in the dark? If he was, she didn't hear his breathing.

Talia called down for the two deputies to join her to search the roof. They joined her immediately. All three started to search the roof. Talia and the two deputies checked out every possible hiding place and finally found themselves standing at the short block wall that framed the entire roof. A short distance away was an access ladder. Talia rushed over and climbed up the first few steps. She peered over the edge to see if the emergency ladder had been deployed; it had not! Talia could see the street in front of the station. Andrew's car was still there. Talia scanned the length of the street, searching the shops and Marettti's deli store fronts. She saw Andrew come out of the deli carrying what she assumed to be a doggie bag. It appeared that all this time, Andrew had been in the deli having a meal. Talia cursed and climbed back down on the surface of the roof. She put away her weapon, and with a look of disappointment etched on her face, entered the stairwell and closed the door behind her.

Andrew had just come out of Marettti's deli. He looked up and saw Sheriff Delsmann peering down at him. He wondered if she was trying to figure out how he did it. Andrew turned and smiled at Rachel, who was behind the deli counter. It was nice to have friends in all kinds of places. Andrew waved at her, and she did the same in return. Andrew had scored one against Sheriff Delsmann, but he wasn't finished with her yet. The next place he had to search was the Higgins crime scene. Andrew drove off with thoughts of which friend's help he would need next.

Talia and her deputies returned to the records area.

She walked up to Darcy and roughly grabbed her by the arm. Talia forced Darcy into the chair by the desk.

"What did you give him?" Talia's said through clenched teeth. "You need to tell me, now!"

"I gave him nothing," Darcy defended.

"I know you did." Talia pointed an accusing finger at her. "Either you tell, or spend some time in a cell."

Talia motioned for the deputies with her to place Darcy in custody. They hesitated at first, but when Talia glared at them, they did as requested. Darcy still proclaimed her innocence as she was led away.

Chapter 3

The red AC Cobra came to a screeching halt in the circular driveway. Andrew jumped out and bolted inside the house with his ill-gotten gains. He slammed the door closed behind him and flew upstairs to his office.

Andrew removed the manila envelope from his overcoat. Andrew hung up his coat and sat down at his desk. He immediately opened the manila envelope and removed the report. Andrew started with the father, Jonathan Higgins. He was found dead outside in the front yard. He died from multiple slash and stab wounds. Jonathan had a successful web-based business based on the vampirism culture. Andrew read that Jonathan's business grossed nearly one million dollars last year. Next was Natasha Higgins. She died as a result of severe trauma to the lungs and heart from being struck with two wooden arrows. Natasha had her own catering business with mostly clients that were also involved with vampirism. Peter Higgins, their son, died as a result of an arrow to the heart. He was attending

Washington High School in Bayport. He was in his senior year. He was a straight 'A' student and on the honor roll. The report mentioned that he had a girlfriend by the name of Ashley Matthias. According to the report, they were so far, unable to locate Ashley for questioning. Peter was found lying a few feet from his father.

Andrew pulled the page about Storm Higgins. Storm also attended Washington High School and was in her sophomore year. She was also an honor roll student. The report indicated that her boyfriend, Wyatt Collins, was considered a person of great interest. Again, it stated that they could not locate him. Andrew read about Storm. He couldn't imagine the strength and courage she must have had to crawl from her room to the outside. The report stated that Storm had been shot in the back with a single arrow. Andrew put the report aside for a moment. The doorbell announced an unexpected visitor. Andrew gathered up all the papers of the report and put them back in the envelope. He stood up from his desk and walked over to the bookcase. The doorbell chimed again. His surprise visitor was growing impatient. Andrew hid the envelope and left to answer the door.

Andrew opened the front door and saw Sheriff Delsmann standing there. She appeared more relaxed and happier now, as opposed to her hostility earlier today. Andrew suspected she was up to something and that it had to do with the stolen report.

"What do I owe the pleasure?" Andrew smiled.

"I would like the chance to apologize for my earlier behavior," Talia smiled back.

"Would you like to come in?" Andrew gestured towards the inside of the house.

"Yes, please," Talia replied, still smiling. Andrew did not trust her.

Andrew closed the front door and escorted Talia to the family room. Talia took a seat in one of the chairs by the fireplace. Andrew sat down on the sofa.

"You said something about apologizing?" Andrew repeated.

"Yes," Talia said, clearing her throat. "It was very unprofessional of me to berate you like that, especially not knowing what kind of private detective you are." Talia paused. Andrew could see that she was choosing her words very carefully this time. "Sometimes I'm quick to judge people, so I apologize."

"Apology accepted," Andrew said, smiling. "Do you have some time for coffee?"

"Yes, that would be nice," Talia seemed to force a smile Andrew thought. "But first may I use the bathroom?"

"It's up the stairs and the first door on the right," Andrew said. He left to go to make coffee while Talia went upstairs to use the bathroom.

Talia stopped in front of the bathroom door. She stood there for a minute listening and then she continued down the hallway. Talia was glad Andrew fell for her little rouse about wanting to apologize to him. There was no way she trusted Andrew. She suspected that he did in fact get a copy of the investigation. The question that was foremost on Talia's mind was where Andrew would hide the report. Talia opened the door to the library and stepped inside.

Andrew was in the kitchen getting the coffee maker ready. Once he had put in the filter and coffee grounds, Andrew poured in the water. He put the coffee pot in place and turned on the switch. Andrew walked over to the doorway and bent his head to listen. He knew that Talia didn't suddenly feel guilty about trashing him earlier today. She was here to find out if he had a copy of the investigation, and to find out where Andrew had hidden it. He had to decide how much time he would give Talia before coming to get her.

Talia found nothing in the library other than lots of books. She continued onto Andrew's office. Talia grasped hold of the doorknob and gave it a twist. She opened the door and went inside. There were some tall bookshelves on one wall, a nicely polished wooden desk and a large draped window. "Oh great, more books," Talia groaned. She quickly began her search.

Andrew decided it was enough time. He loaded the serving tray with the coffee carafe, two cups, and cream and sugar. Andrew carried the tray in the family room. He set it down on the coffee table. He went to find Talia.

Talia had searched through all the books tall enough to hide the report. She found nothing. Talia was seated at Andrew's desk. She tried the desk drawers, but they were all locked. She looked at her watch. Twenty minutes had gone by; too much time! Talia bolted out of the chair and immediately left the office. Once in the hallway, Talia now crept at a slower pace. She was now at the bathroom door.

Andrew walked up the stairs and that's when he saw Talia exiting the bathroom. She smiled at him.

"Are you feeling okay," Andrew asked, concerned.

"Yes, I'm fine," Talia assured him. "I was just admiring your bathroom."

"Coffee is ready," Andrew said gesturing towards the family room down stairs.

They walked together back to the family room.

Talia along with Andrew retook their seats. Andrew poured them each a coffee.

"Just sugar," Talia said.

"Okay," Andrew answered. He put sugar in her coffee and handed it to her. Talia took a sip. It was perfect. Andrew fixed his own beverage and settled back against the cushioned sofa.

"So what is the real reason for your visit?" Andrew asked.

"W-What do you mean?" Talia stuttered a bit.

"It is to apologize for trashing me earlier?" Andrew continued.

"Yes, I do apologize for the way I jumped on you," Talia offered an apology.

"Then let's start over," Andrew smiled.

"Let's," Talia smiled as well.

"Do you like living in Bayport?" Andrew began.

"Its quite different from Chicago," Talia laughed. "It's more laid back, quieter. Although I do miss the night life, you know like the blues clubs."

"There's a club down on Water Street called "The Elbow Room," Andrew said. "It's very much comparable to the clubs in Chicago. As a matter of fact the owner, Harlow Grant, is originally from Chicago."

"So are you originally from Bayport?" Talia asked.

"My family is not originally from Bayport," Andrew answered. "My great-great grandparents moved here in the 1800's from New York."

"Say it's getting late." Talia glanced at her watch. "I better get going."

"I'm glad you stopped by," Andrew put his cup down and stood up. "I'll walk you to the door." Talia handed Andrew her empty cup, which he put next to his. They walked together to the front door.

"I'm glad we had a chance to patch things up," Talia said. Andrew opened the door.

"Me too." Andrew smiled at her.

"We'll have to do this again," Talia said.

"Yes, we should," Andrew answered.

They finished their good byes and Talia left.

Andrew closed the door and went back to the family room. He started to clean up, when the door bell rang. Andrew put down the serving tray and went to answer the door. When Andrew opened the door, no one was there! He scanned the area with discerning eyes, but there were no movements in the surrounding bushes and trees. How strange he thought. Andrew quickly closed the door and went back to cleaning up.

Talia was on her way back to the department. She took out her phone and placed a call. After several rings, the person picked up.

"This is Sheriff Delsmann," she spoke insensitively. "Make sure no one; especially Andrew Knight gets a look at the crime scene. Talia listened, and then spoke, "Yes, at all costs." She pressed the end button. Talia thought back to her little chat with Andrew. He was all pleasant and very nice to her, but she suspected that

Andrew was playing her for a fool. Andrew Knight was a lot smarter than he was letting on. But now Talia was on to his little psychological games. She already anticipated his next move. For Andrew that would be to get a look at the crime scene so that he could compare it with the information in the stolen files. After that, logically, Andrew would try and see Storm Higgins at the hospital. Unfortunately for Andrew, the only thing he would find at both the crime scene and hospital would be more security. One way or another, Talia would have Andrew Knight's head on a platter; guaranteed! Talia smirked at her own cleverness as she swung her car into the parking space at the department. Before getting out she said aloud, "Andrew Knight, you're investigating days are over."

The sun was slowly giving way to the night sky. Soon it would be dark. Deputy Nash was sitting inside his nice warm squad at the end of the long, winding driveway. At least he had the easy job while guarding the Higgins crime scene. The other two deputies on duty had to patrol the property. Sheriff Delsmann had given them orders to stop Andrew at all costs from getting a look at the crime scene. Deputy Nash and the other deputies actually liked Andrew, so did the rest of the staff. But for some reason Sheriff Delsmann didn't, and since she was the boss they had to follow her orders.

A tan subcompact sputtered its way up the driveway and came to a stop in front of the squad. Deputy Nash got out just as the lone occupant of the car did the same. It was an older man with a priest's collar and suit.

"Excuse me my son," Father Michael said. "I'm looking for 8275 County Highway T."

"Well Father," Deputy Nash said pointing back to the main road, "When you get to the end of the driveway, take a left and go about two miles. Turn left, that's County Highway T, and you should find it."

"Thank you," Father Michael said. He looked around at the crime scene tape and barricades blocking the driveway. He asked, "Is this the Higgins home?"

"Yes Father," Deputy Nash replied. "It is still an active crime scene and we're guarding it to make sure no one gets inside."

"I see," Father Michael nodded.

"It'll be dark soon," Deputy Nash said. "You had better get going Father."

Andrew crouched down behind a large maple tree. He was wearing winter camouflage. He observed Father Michael talking to the deputy whom was guarding the driveway. A satisfying smile slowly spread across his face. Andrew slipped into the woods surrounding the Higgins house.

Deputy Brown was patrolling the eastern parameter of the property. He stopped to survey the area. With the dense woods and the fading sun, it was hard to see anything further than a few yards. Deputy Brown took his flashlight and flipped it on. He searched the woods with the brilliant beam of light.

Andrew dropped to the ground as the beam of light shone in his direction. As soon as the light passed, Andrew crawled along the snowy ground on his belly. He had only gone a short distance, when the light returned forcing him to cover his face and blend in with his camouflage.

Deputy Brown didn't see anything, so he continued on his patrol.

Andrew watched the deputy walk around the backside of the house. He jumped up and dashed to the side of the house. He tried the window, but it was locked. Andrew spread apart the evergreen bushes that ran along the house. Andrew knelt down by the basement window, it too was locked. He heard footsteps crunching in the snow.

Deputy Brown walked back along his patrol route. He was searching the area with his flashlight, and this time shone it along the bushes by the house. He saw only the dull shades of green, brown, and white, nothing else. Deputy Brown continued on his way.

Andrew crept along the side of the house using the bushes for cover. He paused a few times listening to see if the deputy was on his way back. Andrew did not hear any sounds, so he crept on and was soon at the back of the house. Andrew quickly stood up and walked up the back steps to the door. He tried the door, but it too was locked. Andrew unzipped his jacket and removed a lock pick set. He bent down to take a look at the lock, and selected his tools. Andrew carefully inserted the picks in the lock and a few seconds later had the door open.

Deputy Brown thought he heard something. He quickened his pace as he headed to the back of the house. As he came around the corner, Deputy Brown had his weapon drawn and flashed the light at the back door. Nothing was there.

Andrew relocked the door and was about to move on when he suddenly froze. Someone was jostling the door handle to make sure it was locked. Andrew held his breath and made no sounds. After a few minutes they stopped. Andrew closed his eyes so he could get use to the dark. Although the sun was nearly gone, the yard light would still give him enough light. He couldn't use a flashlight because it would give him away.

The sun had disappeared behind the winter woods now. Deputy Nash was still talking to Father Michael, when he saw Sheriff Delsmann's squad come up the driveway. The headlights nearly blinded them before the car turned and parked beside the other squad.

Talia got out and closed the car door. She walked up to Deputy Nash. He was not alone. There was an elderly priest with him. Talia was not thrilled.

"What's going on deputy?" Talia demanded.

"Father Michael stopped to ask for directions," Deputy Nash explained.

Talia for some reason was suspicious. "Directions to where?" she asked.

"8275 County Highway T," Deputy Nash replied.

"Just a minute," Talia said as she pulled out her blackberry. "I'll look it up for you." She keyed in the address using the GPS application. Talia smiled upon receiving confirmation. She looked at Father Michael, "You said 8275 County Highway T, right?"

"That's correct," Father Michael answered.

"There is no such address," Talia said. She looked at Deputy Nash, and pointed to Father Michael. "Detain him."

"What?" Father Michael protested.

"Why," Deputy Nash asked.

"Somethings not right here," Talia said. She looked accusingly at Father Michael and pointed a finger at him, "You know Andrew Knight don't you Father."

"Yes, why do you ask?" Father Michael answered.

"He's here isn't he," Talia further accused.

"I don't know what you're talking about," Father Michael replied calmly.

"I want Father Michael placed under arrest," Talia ordered.

"What is the charge," Deputy Nash asked.

"Interference with an ongoing investigation," Talia said. She spoke in her shoulder mike, "Deputy Brown, Deputy Miller, this is Sheriff Delsmann. I want you to search the house."

"Why," they responded in turn.

"We have an intruder on the premises," Talia answered. "And his name is Andrew Knight."

Andrew was in the foyer. He was kneeling down next to the broken hallway table and lamp. Andrew carefully examined the broken pieces of wood and ceramic. He looked in the direction of the door. From what he had read from the report, Natasha was the first victim. She was shot while answering the door. Andrew looked at the door before closing his eyes. Andrew envisioned the surprised look on Natasha's face when she realized it wasn't their expected guests. Andrew stood up and walked in the direction of the dining room. He entered the room and looked over the table that was still set for guests that would never arrive. Jonathan was in this room putting on the finishing touches for their guests. Andrew turned towards the doorway. He closed his eyes again. He saw Jonathan rush into the hallway and how he saw his wife lying amongst the broken table. Andrew sympathized with how angry Jonathan was feeling. He would have done the same. But the killer knew this and used it against Jonathan. But why was the killer waiting for Jonathan outside?

Andrew went in the kitchen next. This was where Peter was when his parents were murdered. The music on his I-pod muffled the sounds of them dying. Andrew returned to the dining room. When Peter realized his parents weren't there, he went to investigate. That's when Peter saw his mother. Andrew shut his eyes again. Andrew could picture Peter when he saw the killer murder his father. The rage inside of Peter must have blinded his judgment. Otherwise why would a young man take on a dangerous killer? Andrew reopened his eyes and he surveyed the room one last time.

Andrew returned to the foyer and started up the stairs. He paused and looked over the railing spindles that had dark stains on them. It was dried blood. Andrew continued on his way upstairs and down the hallway to Storm's bedroom.

Andrew opened the door to Storm's bedroom. He walked inside. Andrew scanned the room first, and then walked over to the bloodstain on the carpet. He knelt down to examine it. He was disappointed thus far that nothing provided any new physical evidence. Andrew could feel Storm's presence in the room. He decided to use some of the techniques that Roxanne had taught him. He closed his eyes to focus on that feeling. He took deep breaths, clearing his mind of all the distractions around him. When Andrew reopened his eyes, he stood in the corner of the room as a silent observer; a shadow of things yet to be. Storm was on her bed. The music from her boom box was blaring and she was typing away on her laptop. That's why Storm didn't hear all the noise downstairs. Andrew saw Storm look at the time on her laptop. It appeared that she was late. Perhaps she wondered why her parents had not called for dinner yet. Storm shut down and put away her laptop on her night stand. She bounded off the bed and over to the boom box that was on her desk by the wall across from the door. Her back was to the door when she heard it open. Andrew wanted to scream out for Storm to turn around and lock the door, but she did not. She just thought it was her mom. Not bothering to turn around, Storm just said, "Yes, I know mother." Andrew's heart started to race and his breathing was erratic as the door swung open. He tried to move but couldn't; he was just a shadow. Andrew saw the tip of the arrow in the sheath of the crossbow. Andrew saw the arrow strike Storm in the back. Storm jerked and slammed against the wall. Andrew tried to reach out, but was frozen in place. He saw Storm collapse to the floor, driving the arrow in further. Andrew screamed, but no sound came from his mouth. His eyes were drenched with tears as Andrew closed them. When he opened his eyes again, the room was empty and dark. The killer didn't want to see Storm's face. Either it was someone that knew her, like Wyatt who still had feelings for her. Or it was a cowardly bastard afraid to face an innocent young girl.

Deputy Miller remained posted by the front door. Deputy Brown entered through the back door while at the same time Talia came in the front of the house. They both drew their weapons. Talia didn't say word, but motioned that they would go into the dining room first. They each took up a position on the sides of the entrance to the dining room. Talia counted off to three on her finger and they spun into the opening with weapons ready. No one was there. Talia was visibly disappointed. The next room was the kitchen.

Andrew was finished in Storm's room. He left the room and was about to go back down stairs. He saw a couple of shadows enter the dining room. Suddenly Andrew dropped down on his belly. They were looking for him. Andrew withdrew silently back into Storm's room. He didn't bother to close the door as it might give him away. Andrew couldn't afford to be caught in the house. It would finally give Talia reason enough to have his license suspended, or worse, jail. He walked over to the dormer and slowly opened the window.

There was no sign of Andrew in the kitchen, so they continued by going back to the foyer. Talia indicated they would precede upstairs. She was the first to go followed by Deputy Brown. Slowly, and with caution, they walked up the stairs. First they searched Peter's room and next they went to Storm's. Talia carefully pushed the door open some more. She motioned to Deputy Brown and instantly they stormed the room. Andrew wasn't there!

"Damn it," Talia cursed.

"Maybe he was never even here," Deputy Brown put away his weapon.

"Check the window," Talia ordered just as she noticed it was open. Would Andrew have been so desperate to climb out on the roof? That's what she thought that day at the Sheriff's department building. But he wasn't on the roof then, nor now, Talia suddenly realized. Andrew had hidden somewhere. Talia snapped her fingers realizing that Andrew was hiding under the desk in the records room that day. Talia spun around just in time to see movement in the hallway.

"Let's go!" Talia barked. "He's heading down the stairs."

Andrew leapt to the floor from the last two steps, rolled and stood to his feet once more. He didn't bother to look back and kept on towards the back door. Andrew threw open the front door. The area was clear. He hesitated a moment and could hear Talia and the deputy giving pursuit. Andrew bounded outside and jumped off the top step. He sprinted into the dark woods and swiftly faded out of sight.

Talia and Deputy Brown, weapons still drawn, clamored down the stairs. The back door was already open.

"Hurry!" Talia bellowed.

They quickly exited the house. Talia searched the area with her flashlight. There was no sign of Andrew. She had no way to prove that he was even there. Next time, she would be ready. Next time, Andrew Knight wouldn't get away.

Andrew observed Talia and the deputy as they stood on the back door steps surveying the area with flashlights. When the beam flashed his way, Andrew dove down on the snow and blended in as best he could. It must have been enough, because they gave up and went back inside. They headed to the front of the house.

"Did you find anyone?" Deputy Miller asked.

"No," Talia cursed.

Talia and her men walked up to Father Michael.

"Let him go," Talia commanded.

"Thank you," Father Michael said, rubbing his wrists. "May I go now?"

"Yes Father," Talia replied. "You may go."

"Thank you," Father Michael said. He got in his car and drove off.

"What now?" Deputy Nash asked.

"Keep the area secure," Talia ordered as she walked to her own car. She turned, and with an icy tone said, "If you catch Knight anywhere on the grounds, take him out."

"You're not serious," Deputy Nash choked.

"Don't hurt him," Talia replied. "Just arrest him."

"Yes Sheriff," all three replied.

Talia got in her car and drove off to the end of the driveway and stopped once she'd reached it. Talia looked at her reflection in the rearview mirror. "You look tired," she said. "I know," her mirrored self answered. "What are you going to do about Andrew Knight?" Talia asked, staring into seemingly lifeless eyes. "What do you think?" came back the mirrored reply. "I can't say," Talia said, this time looking away. But an answer did come from somewhere in the dark, "You know what has to be done." Talia didn't answer the voice, but instead drove back to Bayport.

Andrew walked back through the woods to where he had parked. A sudden shiver ran up his back. He spun around, searching the blackened trees. Nothing was there. Andrew couldn't shake the feeling that he was being watched. He had only gone a few more steps but suddenly froze in place. There were fresh boot prints in the snow heading towards the Higgins house. Andrew knelt down to examine them. He could tell from the depth and distance of the tracks, it appeared that the person was in a hurry, almost at a full run. Andrew stood and took off in the direction of the tracks, but he was careful not to be noticed as he kept close to the cover of the surrounding trees.

The moon was finally showing its face from behind the clouds. Its light reflected off the snow, illuminating everything on the ground.

Andrew came to an abrupt stop and silently dove behind a large oak tree. The reason for this was that someone dressed in black was crouched behind another tree watching the deputies patrol the area. Andrew peered from behind the tree to observe them. The person had on a long black coat and a hood covered their head and features. Could this be Night Blade or was it Wyatt. Andrew wasn't sure if they were armed or not. Andrew ducked back behind the tree. Had the person seen him? He waited for a moment and went back to spying. They were gone! Andrew searched the area, but saw nothing. He stood and that's when Andrew heard a branch snap behind him. Just as he stood up, they started to withdraw two swords. Andrew didn't give them time to attack but leapt into the air and hit the person with a combination spin snap kick. They stumbled backwards, letting go of the swords. Andrew rushed, ready to finish them off, but they quickly recovered, jumped in the air and hit Andrew with double round house kicks. Andrew stumbled to his knees and tried to shake off the affect. He recovered and scrambled to get the swords at the same time they did. The two of them rolled entwined in a death grip, each trying to gain control of the swords. It ended with an elbow jab to Andrew's head and they claimed the prize. Andrew jumped up and seeing a thick branch, managed to grab it just as they swung the swords at him. They were relentless, and seemed to grow angrier with each blow Andrew blocked. The attacked escalated as they threw several kicks along with thrusts of the blades. Andrew blocked each with his own counter move, but grew worried as the swords chipped away at the branch. Then with one final horrific blow, the branch split in half! Andrew tossed it aside and reached for his sidearm. His attacker with skilled precision removed the gun from his grasp and flung it some distance away into the snow. Unarmed, he faced his attacker, waiting for the final assault. Andrew immediately drew back as they slashed the blades at his chest. He stumbled a bit and tried to recover, but it was too late. They somersaulted in midair landing behind Andrew and drew the razor-sharp blades across his back slicing open his coat, and punching him in the back of the head with the sword handles. Andrew sunk into the snow face down.

Deputy Brown was on his rounds when he heard noises coming from the woods. He called for Deputy Miller to join him.

"Do you hear that?" Deputy Brown asked as soon as Deputy Miller joined him.

"Yeah," Deputy Miller answered. "It sounds like a fight coming from somewhere in the woods."

"Let's go," Deputy Brown ordered drawing his service piece. Deputy Miller did the same. The two deputies took off in the direction of the noise.

As the deputies arrived, they were horror-struck to see the masked attacker slash Andrew across the back and hit him on the back of the head. They saw Andrew fall face down into the snow.

"Freeze!" they barked, pointing their weapons at the masked attacker. Instead, the person bolted off into the depths of the woods. The deputies shouted another warning. The person continued running from them. The deputies fired, but the person was too far away. The two deputies did not give pursuit; instead they attended to Andrew.

Andrew was not moving. Deputy Miller knelt beside Andrew to check him over. He was expecting to see blood on the back of Andrew's coat. There was none. Deputy Miller took his glove off and slipped his hand into the slashed coat. He could feel the body armor that Andrew wore underneath.

"What is it?" Deputy Brown asked.

"He has on body armor," Deputy Miller answered.

"He's out cold?" Deputy Brown surmised.

"Yeah," Deputy Miller answered.

"Do we arrest him like the Sheriff said," Deputy Brown asked.

"What do you think?" Deputy Miller replied.

The two deputies lifted Andrew up and carried him back to where Deputy Nash was standing beside his squad. When he saw them carrying Andrew, Deputy Nash rushed over by them.

"What the hell happened?" Deputy Nash demanded.

"Knight and some masked person were fighting in the woods," Deputy Brown explained. "We broke it up. The other person got away. Knight was knocked out cold."

"He's cut across the back," Deputy Nash further observed. "Is he hurt?"

"No," Deputy Miller answered. "He's wearing body armor."

"Do we arrest him?" Deputy Brown asked. "You know, like the Sheriff told us to."

"What do you think?" Deputy Nash answered sharply.

"He's done a lot for us and the Bayport cops," Deputy Miller added. He looked at Deputy Nash. "He's even saved your skin a couple of times as I recall."

"Yeah I know," Deputy Nash lowered his eyes to the ground. A few seconds later he looked back up at his partners. He was about to say something, when they all heard Andrew coming to.

Andrew opened his eyes to see Deputy Miller and Brown holding him up. Deputy Nash was standing in front of him. Suddenly things didn't look so great.

"Don't worry," Deputy Nash smiled. "We're not going to arrest you."

"Why is that?"

"You're a good guy, and well the Sheriff is a real..."

"Pain in the ass," Deputy Brown chuckled.

"She'll find out you know," Andrew reminded all three of them.

"Not really," Deputy Nash replied. He looked at his fellow officers. "As far as we're concerned we never saw you, right guys?"

"Right," they answered.

Andrew took a moment to get his bearings and immediately shook hands with all three deputies. He thanked them and took off in the direction of where his car was parked.

The three deputies returned to their respective posts waiting for the relief shift to arrive in a couple of hours.

Andrew walked to his car slowly. He was now certain it was not Wyatt. Whoever it was though, they were very experienced in the martial arts. Andrew finally arrived at his car. He winched a bit as he bent down to unlock the door. Once inside, Andrew stopped to reflect further. Logically, the next thing he would do is go see Storm at the hospital. But a nagging thought in the back of his head warned him that Sheriff Delsmann would be waiting for him. Instead, Andrew decided he would try and local Wyatt. The person that attacked him was of slender build and average height. They wore a mask to conceal their identity and black gloves to cover their hands.

Andrew started the car and shifted it into drive. The tires dug into the snow packed road as the car sped off back to Bayport.

From the safety of the dark woods a pair of eyes watched as Andrew got into his car. It was a disappointment that he had survived. A promise was made that next time there would be no errors and that Andrew Knight would most certainly die.

Chapter 4

"Collins, you're next!" Coach Martell barked while looking at his clipboard.

Chad swallowed hard and looked first at the balding man in the blue and black jumpsuit that held his future in his hands. Chad stepped up to the rope, beads of sweat on his brow. Chad bent his head back following the length of the rope with his eyes to the very top to were the green tape was taunting him like so many times before. This was his last chance to finally make it, or get the only "D" on his otherwise perfect report card. If you gave him a problem to solve in calculus; to write an essay for English, or any other subject in school; Chad would've pass it without any problem.

"Move it Collins," the whole class chastised him this time. Chad jumped up and grabbed on with both hands while at the same time crossing his legs and digging his tennis shoes into the thick rope. Chad shimmied with all his strength towards the top of the rope. He kept telling himself not to look down, not to let the sweat on his forehead keep him from reaching his goal. It took two long weeks to get to this point; two long weeks of all the guys in class making fun of him because he was the only one left that couldn't climb the rope all the way to the top. This was his chance to prove all of them wrong, but also to impress Amber.

Chad's muscles strained with each movement of his arms and legs working together in concert towards the crescendo of his ascent. Finally, and with all his body straining to keep his place, Chad reached out his fingers which were just inches away from the coveted green piece of tape. Chad swallowed hard and for a minute took in the surroundings below. He had the best view in the gym. He could see the girls' class at the far end of the gym and there she was, Amber. She wasn't like most girls he'd dated before. The first time Chad had his mom meet Amber, it was very awkward. Here he was introducing his mom to this girl with short cropped black hair, dark brown eyes, black finger nails and lipstick. She looked more like a vampire than the girl next door. But after they talked for a few minutes, his mom realized that Amber was a very intelligent girl and that the way she was dressed had nothing to do with who she was.

"Collins!" Coach Martell barked again. It startled Chad so much so that he almost forgot where he was for a second and nearly let go of the rope. Chad quickly recovered and with one last effort touched the tape with the tip of his fingers. He'd finally made it! Just as Chad tried to savor his victory, the class bell rang. He suddenly started to slip and the rope became too hard to hold onto anymore. Chad slid down the rope. The friction burned at the flesh of his hands, arms and legs without any remorse. Chad cried and let go of the rope when he was still a few feet off the ground. He landed hard on the padded mat with a loud, painful groan. An explosion of laughter erupted from the group as Chad withered on the mat with his hands tucked in his armpits trying to sooth the pain. Amber saw what had happened and rushed over. She shoved the boys out of the way, gave the coach a sharp look for just standing there too, and then knelt beside Chad. Amber helped Chad to his feet and walked him to the nurses' office.

"Thanks," Chad said.

"I was impressed," Amber answered. "Until you crashed and burned."

"Burned is right," Chad replied looking at his hands. They were red and felt like they were on fire.

"Maybe this will make you feel better," Amber said. She looked around first making sure they were alone and kissed him. Her lips tasted like black licorice. Chad forgot his pain for a minute.

"Better?" Amber asked when their lips drew apart.

"Yeah," Chad answered as they stopped in front of the nurses' office.

Amber walked him inside and after explaining the situation to the nurse; she left to go back to class. The nurse had Chad sit down and took a look at his hands. She got some antibiotic cream and gauze from the cabinet. The moment the cream touched the flesh of his hands, the pain instantly went away. The nurse wrapped his hands.

"I have to call your mom," she picked up the phone.

"Oh great." Chad lamented.

Chad looked in the mirror, but it wasn't the reflection he was use to. The young man in the mirror wore dark clothes and looked very Goth. Chad moved his head to the side to check out his newly pierced ear. Amber gave him a crucifix as his first earring. He picked up and opened the gift wrapped box that was sitting on the edge of the sink. Inside was a pair of fangs. Chad snapped them into place. Chad left the bathroom and walked down the hallway to his room. Today was his eighteenth birthday and Amber was going to take him out to celebrate. She told him to dress Goth because they were going to a special place tonight where she'd planned on giving him an exceptional birthday gift. Chad hoped Amber would approve.

Just as he turned off the lights, the door bell rang. Chad knew it was Amber and flew down the stairs to answer it. When he opened the door, Amber immediately smiled with approval.

"You two have fun," Nedra said brushing wisps of grayish blonde hair from her face as she walked into the front room. She'd just gotten home and was still in her nurses' uniform.

"Thanks mom," Chad replied.

They said their goodbyes and were on their way.

A full moon was rising as Amber and Chad walked towards the abandoned building at the end of the long gravel driveway. They weren't alone; Amber's brother Seth and his girlfriend Gabriel, along with his friend Jazz and girlfriend Melissa were with them.

"You sure this is okay," Chad asked. He'd just noticed the 'no trespassing' sign.

"Yeah it's okay," Seth answered. His hair was thick and black and he had several earrings in his left ear with a beaded chain running to one in his nose.

"Look what we hav' here," Jazz teased Chad and Amber as he flashed his fangs. He went on, "A couple uv baby bats." He was a thin, tall kid with frizzy black hair. His eyes looked more like holes in his head because of the dark eye shadow he wore.

"Knock it off Jazz," Melissa yelled at him. She had more of a Victorian look but still wore the black makeup and hair like the rest.

"Just teasin' that's all," Jazz answered.

"And will you quit using that dumb accent," Seth warned raising his fist like he was going to punch Jazz.

"Okay, okay," Jazz grumbled. He liked the accent.

The six teenagers stood in front of a formable looking wood door. Chad wondered how they were going to get inside. That's when Seth produced a homemade lock pick from his trench coat pocket. They all watched as he easily slid the pick into the archaic lock and with a couple of turns had the door open. Seth put the pick back in his pocket and gave the door a shove. The creaking it made upon opening, reminded Chad of all those old horror movies he'd watched on late night TV. He also remembered that no good came from the people going inside those haunted places either.

The entrance way was very dark, so Seth took his lighter and flicked it on so they could see. Jazz, Melissa, Gabriel and Amber did the same.

The first thing that caught Chad's attention was this painting of a nude woman on the wall next to the stairs leading to the second floor. She was breathtakingly beautiful with her cascading layers of golden blonde hair, and very sensuous with her perfect form. The more Chad stared at it, the more he swore she could've stepped off the wall and joined them. Chad felt it belonged in an art gallery in New York.

"They keep trying to cover the damn thing up," Jazz said all the while copping a feel of the woman's breasts. "They painted over it, sanded it, and used paint remover on it. But it keeps reappearing. How is weird is that?"

"It keeps coming back?" Chad swallowed hard.

"Don't listen to Jazz," Amber reassured him. "It's just one of the stories about this place. They're just trying to scare people away."

"It's true," Jazz started to say, but Melissa jabbed him in the ribs with her elbow. Jazz yelped and backed away. He didn't like it when she did that.

"Time to go upstairs," Seth said as he led the way.

The rest followed. Chad glanced back over his shoulder at the lady on the wall. He could've sworn that at the same moment her eyes turned and she looked back at him.

When they got to the dorm room, the three girls disappeared into the large walk-in closet. They emerged a few minutes later with a dozen large candles and an Ouji Board. The girls set the candles in a large circle. Jazz took out the Ouji board and game piece. Amber lit the candles and joined the rest whom were already seated on the floor.

"What should we ask it?" Melissa said.

"Haven't a clue," Gabriel added.

"I don't know," Chad replied.

"I know, I know," Jazz answered. "I'll ask about my family."

Jazz placed his finger tips on the triangular game piece. He asked, "Who's the next to die from the hands of the mysterious Night Blade?" The game piece didn't move. Jazz tried to force it, but it refused.

"Let me try," Seth pushed Jazz out of the way. He reached in his pocket producing a tatty piece of cloth. Seth took his pocket knife and cut his finger letting a small drop of blood fall on the cloth. Next were Melissa, Jazz, Gabriel and Amber; but when it came to Chad he didn't want any part of it.

"Come on," Seth said. "It's just a game."

"No way," Chad protested further.

"Please Chad," Amber pleaded, nuzzling his neck with a kiss.

It tickled whenever she did that, but it also made him always give into her whatever it was that she wanted.

"Okay," Chad said. He took the knife and nicked his index finger. The sting only lasted a second and soon his blood was mixed with the others. Seth placed it on the game piece and immediately it started moving. As everyone watched the triangle floated across the surface of the game board finally coming to rest over the letter "D".

"D for Death," Jazz said with a howling noise.

"Knock it off Jazz." Melissa hit him in the chest.

"Will you two stop it," Amber said, but then froze.

Then they all heard it.

"What is that?" Chad peered into the darkness just beyond the circle of light.

"It sounds like someone tapping on the window," Seth answered.

"You guys are scaring me," Gabriel said.

"But we're on the second floor," Melissa said.

"I'll go look, you bunch of wimps." Jazz jumped to his feet. He left the security of the light and walked across the room over to the window. All eyes were on Jazz's dark silhouette. There was nothing, and then came the scream. It was a horrible, terrifying scream and Jazz bolted back to them.

"It's after us," Jazz said. His face was white and breath labored.

"What's after us," Melissa and Gabriel cried.

"The Night Blade," Jazz screamed.

"I'm going." Seth stood up. He entered the abyss.

Seth walked over to the window. He peered outside but saw nothing. All Seth heard was the rustling of the branches in the trees; nothing else. He was about to turn and leave when it felt like an icy hand slid across his back finally coming to rest on his shoulder.

"Knock it off," Seth cursed to himself.

Seth returned to the group.

Jazz burst out in uproarious laughter.

Seth had had enough. He rushed over and tackled Jazz to the floor. Seth started punching him repeatedly. Jazz begged Seth to stopped, but he didn't. It took the others to finally drag Seth off of Jazz, who crawled away over to the safety of the window.

"You're crazy," Jazz spouted off, wiping the blood off his lip.

"You're a jerk," Seth cursed back.

"Will you two just stop it?" Amber scolded them.

"I think we should stop." Melissa suggested.

"I agree," Gabriel added, looking at Seth. "We should go to our room."

Everyone else split off to the other dorm rooms, but Amber and Chad remained behind.

Chad sat on the tatty, musty smelling mattress. Amber stood in front of him and slowly unbuttoned her blouse. His eyes were immediately drawn to her lacey black bra.

"I couldn't find anything to buy for your birthday," Amber said removing her blouse and bra letting them drop to the floor. "So you get to have me."

Amber pushed Chad back on the bed and straddled him. They started kissing. Chad's felt as if his heart was going to burst. Amber stripped the rest of her clothes off and did the same to Chad.

"How does that feel," Amber murmured as she felt him enter her.

"It feels warm," Chad answered.

The darkness held on tightly in spite of the sunlight which was poised and ready to take its place. The Sheriff's department had received a report that a group of teenagers had disappeared during the night while trespassing from the grounds at JFK Prep.

Sheriff Delsmann slowly drove up the gravel road as another squad followed closely behind. To her left was a shabby looking trailer. In front was an historic monument of faded brick and broken windows.

Sheriff Delsmann parked her car and got out. There were two people waiting for her. A woman in her late fifties, whom was quite slender, dressed professionally, and her silver hair had nary a strand out of place. The man, whom appeared to be in his late forties with grayish black hair, was wearing a security guard uniform.

"Georgina Rowlands," she said. She pointed to the first man, "This is Tommy Johnson. He is the on-sight security guard."

"Sheriff Delsmann, "Talia replied.

"A pleasure," Georgina answered.

Andrew quietly and carefully negotiated the woods of the JFK Prep campus. After the incident at the Higgins's home, Andrew set up a meeting with Nedra. When they had met, Nedra recalled that Wyatt had told her that JFK Prep was one of the popular hangouts with the younger members of the coven. She told him that sometimes they either came to hook up or perform blood rituals. Andrew had also contacted Peter at the Bayport Police department about information on Night Blade. According to the files, in the past six years there had been numerous reports of teenagers and adults vanishing on the JFK Prep grounds and the surrounding area. All of them were vampires. The only description of Night Blade was that he or she was average height and build. There wasn't very much to go on. The only way to find out who Night Blade was would be by capturing them before someone else were killed. Nedra had called him last night very upset and crying. After Andrew had managed to calm Nedra down, she told him that her other son Chad had disappeared with his girlfriend Amber and some other teenagers. Nedra knew that they were going out to celebrate Chad's birthday last night and that they were probably going to JFK Prep. So not only was Andrew at JFK Prep to find Wyatt, but also the missing teenagers.

He approached the main gravel road that led up to the dormitory building. Andrew quickly ducked down when he saw two squad cars make their way up towards the dormitory. Andrew waited a few minutes and using the trees as cover again, he made his way to where two people were waiting. There were some low, thick bushes not too far, for Andrew to hide. He slipped beneath them unnoticed. Andrew settled in and listened in on their conversation. "Please follow us." Andrew heard Georgina say.

They all walked in the direction of the side entrance.

"We've gone through several contractors, because of," Georgina interrupted. "Oh, how shall I put this? It was because of certain incidents happening on the property."

"What incidents?" Talia asked.

"Well," Tommy jumped into the conversation. "A lot of vandalism being done by kids breaking into the place. There are also strange things happening on the grounds."

"What things?" Talia asked.

"Never mind," Georgina replied.

Talia stopped and turned around. She had a feeling that someone was following them, but she saw nothing.

Andrew used the surrounding cover to trail behind as the five of them walked to the side of the dormitory. He listened with great interest as Georgina and Tommy explained what had been happening on the JFK Prep grounds. Andrew swiftly drew himself up tightly against the wall, blending into the shadows. He did so when Sheriff Delsmann turned back and looked in his direction.

Once they reached the side of the dormitory, a heavy wooden door greeted them which looked ominous and foreboding. Georgina used her key to open the door. Once inside, the painting of a nude woman immediately caught Talia's attention along with her deputies. She walked up to it.

"Who painted it," Talia looked at Georgina.

"I am not sure," Georgina answered. "But we tried to cover it up and it just reappears."

"What do you mean it reappears," Talia asked.

"We've painted over it." Tommy was exasperated. "We even tried paint remover."

"Paint remover?" Talia exclaimed. She ran her fingers gently across it, feeling the brush strokes and imperfections of the wall that made up the beautiful painting. "It looks untouched."

"I have to be going." Georgina glanced at her watch. She looked at Talia. "I have a meeting this morning with another contractor." Georgina handed Talia the keys. "Just lock up when you leave and give the keys to Tommy. If you remember, his trailer is by the main entrance." Georgina was ready to leave the building, when Tommy took Talia aside to speak to her privately about something.

"Just watch out," Tommy warned. "There are some strange things going on here." He glanced at the painting of the woman. "They say the ghost of one of the founders, Father Oswald, roams the building and surrounding ground. They say he punishes those who desecrate this place. I've seen him myself; a man wearing a tatty hooded robe." Tommy laughed.

The two of them left Talia and her deputies alone.

Once they were gone, Talia gave her instructions.

"I'll search the dormitory. You two search the surrounding grounds. We'll meet up in an hour at the cars."

As soon as her deputies departed, Talia ascended the stairs leading to the second floor of the abandoned dormitory. She walked down the hallway and stopped at one of the dorm rooms. Talia turned the doorknob and entered the room.

The dorm room was plain looking. The walls were faded and the paint was chipping. There were several cracks in the ceiling. Only a single partially boarded up window provided very little light in the room. The remnants of melted candles were on the floor. Talia thought it was very strange for six teenagers to simply disappear. In the corner was an old mattress; it was of no importance. There was no evidence that the youths walked off or were forcibly removed. Talia noted some of the buildings were interconnected as she drove up the main road of JFK Prep. The only one connected to the dormitory was the St. Ambrose Chapel. She headed back down to the first floor. It was still dark inside the dormitory, so Talia flipped her flashlight on.

Andrew was about to move, but froze as the two deputies exited the dormitory. As soon as their flashlights came on, the deputies began their search of the surrounding grounds.

Andrew left his hiding place when they disappeared out of sight. He immediately headed to the side entrance. The heavy wooden door creaked when Andrew opened it. He stepped inside and turned on his flashlight. Andrew shone it on the painting of the woman. She seemed to stare right through him. Andrew shuddered. He was about to head up to the second floor, when the glow of an approaching light appeared at the top of the stairs. Andrew ducked back outside and slowly closed the door.

Talia heard a low creaking noise as she stopped at the top of the stairs. She shone her light at the door, but no one was there. Talia blew it off as nothing and descended the stairs. Talia continued her search of the first floor of the dormitory. She was looking for any kind of footprints, or signs of someone being dragged. Talia saw none. Just ahead at the end of the hallway was St. Ambrose chapel.

Andrew felt the coast must be clear by now, so he went back inside. He immediately headed up stairs and walked down the hallway. Andrew stopped at one of the doors. He turned the knob, opened the door and stepped inside.

The dorm room was plain looking. The walls were faded and the paint was chipping. There were several cracks in the ceiling that spread across it like spider webs. Only a single, partially boarded up window provided very little light in the room. The remnants of melted candles on the floor reminded Andrew of a bizarre-looking birthday cake. In one of the corners was a tatty mattress. It must have been left over from the time when the dorm rooms were used by students that attended the school.

Andrew walked over and knelt next to the mattress. He examined it closely. It was stained with bodily fluids. Andrew removed a small magnifying panel from his coat pocket. He leaned down closer to the mattress, but found nothing else. Andrew put the magnifying panel away and was about to stand up, when he noticed it. The 'it' was the fact that the dust outline around the mattress had been disturbed ever so slightly. One wouldn't have noticed it unless they were where he was right now. More importantly, it meant that someone had flipped the mattress. Andrew carefully lifted up the mattress and shone his light on the back side. It was stained with blood, not weeks, months or years old, but fresh blood. Whoever was on the mattress was bleeding.

Andrew set the mattress back down and stood up. He searched the rest of the room for more blood spatters. The weird part was that there were none. How could that be? If the people on the mattress had been bleeding, how could they have been carried from the room without leaving some kind of blood evidence behind? Where did they hide the bodies? There were a dozen or more questions running around in Andrew's head. He decided to continue searching the rest of the grounds for Chad and the others.

As Talia neared the chapel, her flashlight caught a hooded figure dressed in black standing ready to enter the chapel.

"Hey you there!" Talia shouted. She broke into a full run, but the person quickly slipped inside slamming the doors shut behind them. Talia hit the doors to open them but was stopped instantly! She stumbled backwards landing on her butt. Talia cursed and immediately rose to her feet again. She tried the door. As Talia suspected, it was locked. She had to find another way inside. So she backtracked outside and ran down the pathway to chapel. Talia found a side door. She grabbed the door knob and gave it a twist. It opened! Talia withdrew her gun and stepped inside. She had just taken a few steps toward the center of the room, when the door slammed shut. Talia spun around and shone her light at the door. No one was there. Talia turned her attention back to the search.

She was in a study, a priest's study. The wooden desk was badly weathered, and the leather chair cracked with stuffing coming out. Both were covered with a layer of undisturbed dust. She was about to enter the sanctuary, when Talia felt a blow to the head. She crumpled to the floor and was out cold.

Andrew followed the first floor hallway up to the doors of St. Ambrose Chapel. The doors were locked. He would have to find another way inside. Andrew backtracked and went outside.

Andrew found a side door. He grabbed the door knob and gave it a twist. It opened! Andrew withdrew his gun and stepped inside. It was a priest's study. The wooden desk was badly weathered, and the leather chair cracked with stuffing coming out. Both were covered with a layer of undisturbed dust. Andrew walked around the desk when he saw scrawled in the dust the words, 'Gewalt wirkt Gewalt'.

"Violence equals violence," Andrew repeated aloud in this time in English.

As Andrew turned towards the sanctuary door, he saw Talia lying on the floor out cold. Andrew knelt down and made sure she was okay. He rose to his feet and was about to enter the sanctuary, when he heard approaching footsteps. It must be the deputies, so Andrew beat a hasty retreat into the sanctuary.

When Sheriff Delsmann didn't show up at the prearranged meeting spot, the deputies decided to go find her. After searching the dormitory and since the inside door was locked to the sanctuary, they had to find another way inside. That's when they found this door.

With weapons drawn, they stepped inside. It was an office. Once inside, they found Sheriff Delsmann lying on the floor unconscious. They knelt down and revived her.

Talia awoke a bit groggily. She was surprised to see her deputies.

"Where did the masked figure go?" Talia asked looking around the room.

"We saw no masked figure," they replied.

"We need to search the sanctuary," Talia said, finally standing up.

"Are you okay enough to do that," one of the deputies asked worriedly.

"I'm fine," Talia insisted. "Let's go."

Andrew stood, staring in awe at the majesty of St. Ambrose Chapel. Even though the pews were covered with years of dust and showing signs of decay, Andrew imagined the day they were still brightly stained and filled with the faithful. He felt sad that all of the stain glass windows had been smashed, forever obliterating the dramatic scenes depicted of the passion of our Lord. While researching JFK, Andrew read that Father Oswald and the other priests whom founded this former seminary were from Germany, so that might explain the words written in German. But how did this tie in with the attack on the Higgins family or the missing teenagers for that matter. There were still just too many questions. What Andrew needed were more answers. Andrew started towards the main doors of the sanctuary when he heard the door to the priest's study open. He immediately dropped to the floor and started to crawl along on his belly beneath the pews.

Talia stepped through the open doorway first with her gun at the ready. Seeing that things were clear, she motioned for the deputies to follow. All three stared in awe at the impressiveness of the sanctuary. Despite the years of wear, it still had a certain sense of spirituality that couldn't be explained.

Talia led the way towards the altar, but froze suddenly in her tracks at the sound of creaking. She spun around just in time to see one of the massive wooden doors in the back of the sanctuary open just a bit. But no one was there. Talia motioned for the deputies to follow as they went to investigate. They had only taken a couple of steps when the door closed again. Was it a ghost or something more human? Talia wondered. The three of them continued towards the back of the sanctuary. Along the way Talia noted that it looked like someone had crawled along the dusty floor on their belly.

"Knight!" Talia bellowed. The deputies were taken aback by her sudden outburst.

"What?" they answered.

"Andrew Knight is on the grounds," Talia answered. She pointed wildly at the closed doors. "It was Knight who I saw going into the sanctuary dressed in black wearing a mask. He must have been back to make sure we wouldn't find the missing teenagers."

"We saw no one," the deputies replied.

"We need to find Andrew Knight and arrest him," Talia screeched.

Andrew rose to his feet once the door closed. The sun was just peeking at the horizon. He started walking along the path that led back to the main dormitory. It was a bit chilly and he could see his breath. The hairs on the back of Andrew's neck bristled when the sound of the heavy wooden doors creaked open. He turned around and saw Talia along with the two deputies. Their gaze immediately rested upon him. He had been discovered! Andrew took off running down the path that led to the wooded acres on campus instead of the one to the dormitory. He needed to find a hiding place fast.

Talia and her deputies had just exited the St. Ambrose Chapel when she saw Andrew walking up the path towards the main dormitory. He stopped and turned around to look back at them. When he saw them, he took off running towards the woods.

"After him," Talia took off. The deputies followed.

Andrew had a few minutes head start, hopefully it was enough time to escape or find a place to hide. Unfortunately the woods were sparse and the snow not deep enough to blend in. Andrew practically flew down the winding path and soon came to a small kidney-shaped lake. The woods were thicker at the far of the lake, where there was some open water. There was no other way to go, but across the ice. He started across and had not notice the partially snow covered sign that read 'Danger-thin ice'.

Talia and her deputies were just coming around the last bend in the winding path that led them to a small lake. She was about to give pursuit, when one of the deputies grabbed hold of her coat and yanked her back. Talia shook free and shot him an angry look. He walked over to the sign and brushed off the snow. The sign warned of thin ice. Talia turned and watched Andrew, who was about half way across the ice. A satisfying smile slowly spread across her face.

"Hey Knight!" Talia shouted above the wind.

Andrew stopped when Talia called out his name. He turned around to look.

Talia cupped her mouth and shouted, "There was a sign that warned of thin ice!"

Andrew heard her. This was not good.

"Don't move," Talia shouted. "We'll radio for help." Talia turned to one of the deputies. "Call the local fire department and see if they have water rescue equipment." The deputy immediately did so.

Andrew couldn't risk being arrested. It would seriously impact his investigation. More over Sheriff

Delsmann would certainly come up with some charges to keep him in jail for a long time. Either way she would have him arrested. Andrew looked at Talia standing there all smug. He gave her a salute and headed across the ice.

Talia's mouth dropped. She couldn't believe what Andrew was doing. The idiot was continuing across the ice. Was he so desperate to get away from her? Talia almost couldn't watch and was about to turn away when they all heard it. It started out low and soon came to a thunderous sickening cracking sound. The ice was giving way. Talia rushed to the edge of the lake and stopped.

"Don't move!" She screeched. It was too late. They all saw the terrified look on Andrew's face as the ice split open and swallow him up. He was gone in a matter of seconds!

Talia tried to go after him, but the deputies restrained her.

It seemed like an eternity before the local fire department emergency crew arrived. Talia was pacing back forth, impatiently waiting for them to get their ice gear on and airboat ready to go. An overwhelming feeling of remorse suddenly washed over Talia. She never imagined that her lust to have Andrew put away would have ended this way. It was no longer a rescue mission, but a recovery one.

Leslie was still wearing her fuzzy slippers and bathrobe. Her ash blonde hair was swept up and held in place with a red banana clip. She finally had a day off from work at the hospital. On those days it was always her turn to make breakfast.

Leslie had just finished whipping up the scrambled eggs when her daughter Hannah threw open the kitchen door and rushed inside. She was all flushed and panting to catch her breath. Hannah brushed her brown hair out of her eyes.

"Mom," Hannah gasped, trying to catch her breath from running.

"What is it?" Leslie asked.

"I...I was feeding the horses when this man came stumbling into the barn," Hannah finally blurted out. "He looked at me and just fell down in the hay."

"What?" Leslie stammered.

"His lips were blue and his clothes looked wet," Hannah said.

"Show me," Leslie said. Before they left, Leslie grabbed the portable defibulator from underneath the sink. She had bought just in case there was ever an emergency and for the fact that they lived out in the country far away from the hospital in Bayport.

When they got to the barn, Hannah led her mom to where the man was laying in the hay on the floor. He wasn't moving.

Leslie knelt down and put her cheek over the man's mouth. He wasn't breathing. Leslie checked for a pulse. There was none. "Go call 911," Leslie immediately ordered Hannah. She took off like a shot back to the house.

Chapter 5

The airport courtesy van turned into the circular driveway. There were already several cars there. The people from those cars were waiting for the single passenger in the van to arrive home from her trip.

Megan recognized Lisa's car along with two unmarked squad cars. Megan saw Lisa, Peter, and another woman whom she didn't recognize waiting for her. She started to panic and it was hard to catch her breath. Something was wrong. Something was wrong about Andrew. Megan started to cry just as the van pulled up along side the other cars.

Lisa walked briskly up to the van and slid open the side door. She saw that Megan was already crying. Lisa grasped hold of Megan's hand and helped her exit the van. Lisa looked at the Peter and Talia with a nod to retrieve Megan's luggage. She held on to Megan, whom was trembling uncontrollably with tears just streaming down her cheeks.

"Let's go inside," Lisa insisted. Megan just nodded.

Lisa opened the front door and walked Megan into the family room. She had Megan sit down on the sofa. Lisa grabbed a box of tissues from the fireplace mantle and brought them with her back to the sofa.

Peter carried Megan's luggage into the foyer and set it down. Talia followed closely behind him. Soon the both of them joined Lisa and Megan in the family room.

Lisa had her arms around Megan, whom rested her head on Lisa's shoulder. From time to time she dried her eyes, but the tears kept coming.

Peter looked at Talia first, then said, "Um, uh, Megan we have some bad..." Peter couldn't finish he words. He broke down. When Lisa saw her husband, the usually tough guy crying, she started crying too.

Talia sighed deeply. It was up to her to tell Andrew's wife what happened.

"Missus Knight," Talia began. "I'm here to inform you that your husband is..." Talia paused. How could she tell Andrew's wife that he died while begin pursed by her and her deputies. She didn't force him to do it. Talia pressed on, "That your husband fell through the ice on the lake by JFK Prep. He was there because..." Talia stopped again to collect her thoughts.

"Why was he there?" Megan finally spoke. Talia glanced at Peter and Lisa. The looks they had on their faces told Talia it was up to her to answer, not them.

"Two deputies and I were at JFK to investigate the disappearance of six teenagers on the property," Talia explained. "We were just coming out of the dormitory when Mister Knight was spotted. He took off running."

"Why did he run?"

"I had issued an arrest order," Talia answered.

"Why?"

"Mister Knight had interfered with a previous investigation," Talia said in her defense. "The orders were if Mister Knight were caught anywhere on the premises of a Sheriff's department investigation, he would be placed under arrest."

"Why?"

"As I said, he was interfering," Talia answered. She was angry at being questioned by Megan. It was Knight who was breaking the law that day, not her. How dare his widow have the indignation to question her? Talia shot back, "We gave pursuit and Mister Knight chose to invade us by going across the lake. He was unaware of the sign warning about thin ice. It was not our fault. We broke off the chase. Mister Knight chose to continue."

"Why?"

"Why do you keep asking me why?" Talia growled.

"Why are you still here?" Megan screamed back. Talia found no support from either Peter or Lisa. It was strange at how, in a room full of people, one could be so alone. She rose to her feet. "I'm truly sorry." Megan did not answer, but sought out instead, the comfort of Lisa's embrace.

Talia walked out of the family room and the house. She got in her car and slammed the door shut. They hadn't recovered Knight's body as of yet. According to the fire department, the lake at JFK Prep was a spring fed and 30-40 feet deep at the center. With the depth and freezing temperatures of the lake, Knight would only have minutes to get to land and possibly survive. Even then, hypothermia would set in and he'd be dead anyway. Although Knight had shed his coat and he may have been a good swimmer; he would have to get on land and find a way to keep from freezing to death. It sounded too impossible to even believe that Knight could do that. Since they couldn't locate Knight's body, Talia had sent a request to have special imaging equipment brought in from the State Crime Lab. Hopefully they would be able to find the body. Unfortunately, it would be weeks before the equipment would arrive, since it was being used by another law enforcement agency in Marathon County. So for now the search for Knight's body would just have to wait. Talia knew it was rather morbid to just sit by and do nothing, but what else could she do in this case? Talia started the car and drove out the circular driveway.

Leslie tore open the man's icy shirt. She figured that he must have fallen through the ice on the lake at JFK Prep because it was the only water near her horse ranch. He was in great physical shape and that was probably the only reason he made it this far. She opened the kit and attached the pads and wires as shown by the directions. Leslie turned on the power and waited for it to charge. As soon as the screen indicated it was ready, Leslie hit the button. The man's body convulsed for a several seconds and then lay still. Leslie felt for a pulse, still none. Leslie charged it again. She stopped to look at the open barn door. There was no sign of Hannah or the sounds of sirens. When the unit was fully charged, Leslie hit the button again. Again, the man's body rose from the lifesaving charge and quickly fell again. Leslie checked, still no pulse.

"Damn it," Leslie said. If it didn't work next time, she would start CPR. There was no way she was going to let this handsome stranger die in her barn. Leslie charged the unit again and when ready, hit the button. This time he gasped for air, his eyes opened and started coughing. He closed his eyes again. Leslie felt for a pulse. There was one and his was breath was shallow. Leslie got up and grabbed some horse blankets. She returned to the man and covered him up. Hannah finally entered the barn.

"I called 911, Mom," Hannah announced.

"Good honey," Leslie hugged her daughter.

They heard the approaching sirens.

The first responders swarmed the barn. They checked the man's vital signs and stabilized him. They wrapped him in a thermal blanket to maintain his core body temperature. With one swift movement, they had him on the gurney and ready for transport to the hospital. Hannah hung onto her mom tightly as they wheeled the man out of the barn. They followed behind and watched them load him into the ambulance.

"Is he going to be okay mom?" Hannah asked, worriedly.

"I think so honey," Leslie answered.

The ambulance took off with sirens blaring as it headed to Bayport Memorial Hospital.

Megan was sitting in the family room. She was paging through their wedding album, looking at photos of her and Andrew. Her bottom lip trembled and her eyes welled up with tears. Megan closed the album and tossed it aside. She grabbed some tissues just as the doorbell announced a visitor. Megan got up and went to answer the door.

When Megan opened the front door, she saw Chloe, whose eyes were red from crying. They quickly rushed into an embrace and didn't let go. What didn't help was that they started crying again. Several minutes later, they parted and Megan led Chloe inside the house. They went to the family room. They sat down next to each other on the sofa. Chloe saw the wedding album.

"Why are you torturing yourself," Chloe asked holding up the album.

"I really don't know," Megan muttered.

"Any news about Dad's body yet?" Chloe stuttered a bit. It felt surreal to even ask. How could his life just end like that, drowning in a lake? She had read all his case files and was amazed that he had survived all of those dangers. And he died because of an accident?

"Did you call Maggie and Sam?" Chloe asked.

"Lisa called them for me," Megan answered. "They will be here tomorrow."

"What about Father Michaels?" Chloe said, blowing her nose.

"He's coming over later to discuss the memorial service," Megan replied.

"I still can't believe he's gone," Chloe sniffed. "I...I finally just got to..." Chloe broke down sobbing. Megan put her arms around Chloe and held onto her.

Doctor Granger and his team were waiting for the ambulance to arrive. They had everything ready to treat the patient's hypothermia. Now it was just a waiting game. They did not have to wait too long.

The ambulance pulled into the drive-thru portico of Bayport Memorial Hospital. The crew unloaded the patient and rolled him into the emergency department. Doctor Granger and his team took over moving the gurney into room two.

Leslie and Hannah arrived a few minutes later at the hospital. Leslie wore a heavy winter coat over a pair of jeans ripped at the knees and a cardigan sweater. Hannah was also dressed with her favorite down coat, jeans and pink turtle neck. Both had on matching brown winter boots. Leslie parked her car in the employee parking lot and after getting out, they both headed for the emergency department. When they got inside, Leslie with Hannah in tow, walked up to the check-in desk.

"Hi Janice," Leslie said to the nurse on duty.

"Hi Les," Janice answered. "I thought you had off?"

"Yeah I did," Leslie answered. "But the man they just admitted was from my place."

"The cute one," Janice replied.

"Yeah him." Leslie searched the admitting charts.

"He is in ER Room Two," Janice informed her.

"When can I see him?" Leslie bit her lip." "I...I mean to make sure he's okay."

"As soon as they put him in a regular room," Janice said. She noticed the nervousness in Leslie's behavior. "I'll let you know as soon as he gets in a room."

"We'll be back." Leslie led Hannah that away.

One of the nurses's hooked the man up to the monitor for his vitals. Another started an IV as Doctor Granger removed the thermal blanket and checked the man over. Fortunately there were no external signs of frost bite. Another nurse checked the man's clothing for identification. She didn't find any. Doctor Granger placed a call to the Bayport Police department to inform them that they had an unidentified male and to send over a detective to talk to the man. Thirty minutes later they had the man stabilized and moved him into a regular room.

Detective Salerno was the investigator on call that afternoon at the station. She took the call about the unidentified male patient. Lindsey gathered her briefcase with the papers she needed to interview the man, along with a camera.

Leslie and Hannah were just finishing up eating some lunch, when they heard the page. She rushed over to the cafeteria phone and called the emergency room desk. Leslie listened and quickly thanked Janice for giving her the room number. Hannah smirked as she watched her mom straighten her hair and adjust her sweater.

From the cafeteria they took the elevator to the third floor. Once they had gotten off, Leslie and Hannah headed down the hall to room 322. The door was slightly open. Leslie felt nervous and her hands were sweating. Hannah let go of her mom's hand while making a yucky face. She had never seen her mom this nervous before.

Leslie exhaled deeply and with Hannah close behind, entered the room. The man was awake and was lying in an elevated position on the bed. He looked at her strangely.

"I'm Leslie Sommers," Leslie introduced. She gestured toward her daughter, "And this in my daughter Hannah."

"Nice to meet you," He now smiled back. "Do I know you?"

"My mom saved your life!" Hannah blurted out as an eleven year old would do. Leslie blushed and was about to scold her daughter.

"Then I owe you a great deal," He smiled.

"I just wanted to make sure you were okay," Leslie walked up to the side of the bed. He had nice looking eyes. No wedding ring either.

She smiled and went on. "It was touch and go for a while there. I wasn't sure if you were going to make it."

"Thank you," He stretched out his hand. Leslie was hesitant at first, but then placed her hand in his. "Thank you Leslie." He looked past her and smiled at Hannah, "And you too, Hannah." Hannah grinned.

There was a light knock on the door. A willowy woman with black hair walked into the room. She appeared to be one of the staff with a white coat over a shiny blue blouse and black slacks. The only thing that seemed out of place was her black pumps and not more casual looking shoes.

"I'm Doctor Claudie Straussman," she introduced. "I'm the resident psychologist here on a consult from Doctor Granger." She looked at Leslie and Hannah. "May I have some private time with the patient?" Leslie and Hannah reluctantly left them alone. Once they were gone, Claudia walked over, pulled a chair up to the bed, and sat down.

"Could you tell me your name please," Claudia began. He thought for a minute with a perplexed expression on his face. "Do you know your name?" Claudia asked, noticing the look on the man's face. "No," he replied. Claudia read over his chart." Claudia was about to go on, when there was a knock at the door. She told him she would be right back and went to answer it.

Claudia saw a young woman professionally attired upon opening the door.

"I'm Detective Salerno," She announced showing her identification. "I'm here to interview the man Doctor Granger called us about."

"I'm in the process of doing just that," Claudia was a bit miffed at the intrusion. "Does it have to be now?"

"Yes," Lindsey insisted.

Claudia stepped aside and allowed Lindsey inside.

Lindsey moved the curtain aside and was shocked. "Mister Knight," Lindsey gasped.

"Who?" he answered.

"You're Andrew Knight," Lindsey insisted.

"I don't know you," He grew angry. "The last thing I remember is waking up in a horse barn. That's all!"

"They have been searching for your body in the lake at JFK Prep," Lindsey told him. "Everyone thinks you are dead. Detective Sergeant Roberts and Sheriff Delsmann went to see your wife earlier this morning."

"Wife?" He rebuked, and looked at his ring finger. He raised his hand for her to see, "I'm not married."

Claudia finally joined them after listening to their verbal exchange. Lindsey looked confused at her. "Why doesn't he remember?"

"As I earlier suspected, Mister Knight is suffering from trauma-induced amnesia," Claudia explained. "It is a direct result of the near drowning and subsequent heart attack that he suffered. His mind is trying to shield him from those traumatic events."

"How long will it last?" Lindsey asked.

"It could be days, months or even years," Claudia answered.

"Hello there!"

They turned around to face him.

"I am a real person," He chastised. "Not some stupid psychological test subject. If you're going to talk about me, at least do it to my face."

"I've got to tell Detective Sergeant Roberts about him," Lindsey announced. She immediately walked over to the room phone and placed the call to the Bayport Police Department. She waited and then spoke, "This is Detective Salerno. I need to speak to Detective Sergeant Roberts immediately. Yes, it's very important. She waited until Peter was on the other end, and blurted out, "Andrew Knight is alive!"

Talia was ready to leave for JFK Prep to continue the search for Andrew's body. Fortunately, the State Crime Lab had located another set of imagining equipment and it was being delivered to the lake in an hour. The phone rang and she stopped to answer it. Talia let the receiver slip from her trembling hand. Andrew Knight was alive! She quickly recovered.

She thanked the caller. Talia hung up; she knew exactly what had to be done.

Megan was sitting at the breakfast nook. Chloe was making pancakes on the griddle. The fresh brewed coffee added its own to the plethora of aromas wafting about the kitchen.

The front door bell rang. Chloe removed the pancakes and took off her apron. She was about to go answer the door, when Lisa rushed into the kitchen. She slid next to Megan and gave her a big squeeze. "He's alive," Lisa blurted out. "Andrew is alive!" Chloe slid in on the other side of the table.

"But how, when?" Megan stammered.

"Peter called me at the office this morning," Lisa told them. "Andrew turned up at a horse ranch near the JFK Prep grounds. The woman and her daughter found him in the barn. Peter told me that Andrew had to be revived from a heart attack."

"Dear Lord!" Megan cried out.

"It's okay Megan," Lisa hugged her again. "The woman is a nurse and she had a portable defibulator."

"We need to go," Chloe slid out and stood up.

"Wait," Lisa held up her hand. "There's more."

"What more?" Megan asked drying her eyes.

"Andrew is suffering from trauma-induced amnesia," Lisa informed them. "The resident psychologist at the hospital, Dr. Straussman, told Peter that, as a result of Andrew's near-drowning and heart attack, he has amnesia."

"I'm going to see my husband," Megan nudged Lisa to move. Lisa obliged and Megan slid out of the breakfast nook. "I'm getting dressed." Megan left to go upstairs.

"Okay." Chloe put away the food. "We're going."

Talia and her two deputies stepped off the elevator. Their very presence overwhelmed those at the third floor nurses' station.

"What room is Andrew Knight in?" Talia demanded.

"Room 322," one of the nurses answered checking the charts.

"Thanks," Talia said. They left to the nurses' relief.

It was just a short walk down the hallway to Andrew's hospital room. When they got closer, Talia saw a Bayport police officer standing guard at the door.

She briskly walked up and brushed past him. Talia reached for the door knob, the officer grabbed her by the wrist and pulled her hand away. Talia blasted him with a stern look.

"Sorry no one goes in," he informed her.

"Don't you know who I am?" Talia barked. "I am Sheriff Delsmann from the Bayport County Sheriff's department." She pointed to her two deputies, "We're here to arrest Mister Knight."

"Sorry," the officer said again. "I have my orders."

"Step aside," Talia commanded.

"Is there a problem here?"

Talia turned on her heels and saw Detective Sergeant Roberts along with two other detectives, who she did not recognize.

"I gave the order," Peter said.

"Why is that?" Talia balked.

"Mister Knight is in the protective custody of the Bayport Police Department," Peter informed her.

"It doesn't matter," Talia shot back. "He interfered with an ongoing investigation. And after being warned once more, he violated that order."

"Mister Knight was working for a client at the time," Peter returned the volley.

"Step aside," Talia growled.

"Mister Knight is well respected by the Bayport Police, the community, and will be treated accordingly," Peter now stood toe to toe with Talia. He glanced at the deputies and then back to Talia. "If you or your deputies take one step into that hospital room, all three of you will be placed under arrest."

"What about professional courtesy," Talia retorted.

"Like you did?" Peter said, with unmasked sarcasm.

"This isn't over." Talia pressed her index finger against Peter's chest.

"He has amnesia," Lindsey spoke up.

"What?" Talia looked at her. "He's faking it."

"You can't fake amnesia," a woman's voice came from behind.

Talia turned around to see a dark haired woman wearing a white lab coat. The other was a red-haired nurse.

"And you are?" Talia asked.

"Doctor Straussman," Claudia replied. "I'm the hospital's resident psychologist." She gestured towards the nurse with her. "And this is my nurse, Veronica"

"And your diagnosis is amnesia?" Talia scoffed.

"Yes," Claudia answered. She went on to say, "The amnesia he has is a direct result of the near-drowning and heart attack Mister Knight experienced. This is his mind's way of protecting him from the recent traumatic events that Mister Knight experienced."

"May I talk to him," Talia asked. She had calmed down now. Peter thought for a second, and said, "Okay, but we're going with you." The police officer stepped aside and allowed them all passage to the room.

When they walked into the room, the person all of them knew as Andrew Knight had his eyes closed. He opened them with the noise from their footsteps.

"What now?" He was perturbed at the intrusion.

"I'm Sheriff Talia Delsmann," Talia introduced herself to him.

"Am I in trouble?" he asked.

"No," Peter winked.

"Do you recall what happened at the Higgins home?" Talia went right into her questioning. She kept up the pressure. "At JFK Prep or at the lake?"

"No," he was a bit miffed at her barrage. "I only recall waking up in the emergency room, which was full of strangers. There was also Leslie Sommers and her daughter Hannah that came to see me. She told how she revived me in the horse barn." He muttered, "I don't know what JFK Prep is, who are the Higgins and nothing either about the lake. Don't you understand?"

"So you have no memory beyond that," Talia moved closer and stood at the side of his bed. She stared at his face and eyes. Talia was looking for any kind of recognition or reaction to her or her questions. She finally realized that it was like staring at a blank canvas, which was waiting for the painter to give it life. Talia stepped away and left the room.

"Like I asked," he said. "Do I need to worry?"

"No." Peter reassured him.

"Thanks," he said and closed his eyes again. All he wanted to do was get some rest. They walked out quietly so he could do just that.

As soon as Peter exited the room, Talia pulled him aside so the others could not hear their conversation.

"Listen," she spoke softly, and ardently, "If Knight ever does regain his memory or even comes near one of our ongoing investigations, and I will have him arrested. This I promise you."

"Now it's your turn to listen," Peter got up in her face. "You do not want to be on Andrew Knight's bad side, trust me." Peter walked away.

Talia waved her deputies over and then they left. As they walked along, Talia thought that this thing with Knight was far from over. One way or another she would have his head on a platter.

The car ride to the hospital couldn't have been any longer as far as Megan was concerned. She kept checking the speedometer to see how fast Lisa was driving.

Chloe was sitting in the back seat and was just as impatient. She just kept biting the nubs of her fingernail tips which were long since gone. She tried not to think about her dad at the moment because it would have just started her crying again.

Lisa kept thinking about Andrew as she drove them to the hospital. What would she say to him? She thanked God that Andrew was still with them, among the living. It truly was a miracle.

Bayport Memorial soon came into view as their car rounded the curve and over the bridge that spanned the river. Once they were over the railroad tracks, Lisa turned the car onto the street that ran in front of the hospital. Minutes later they were in the visitor parking lot. Once Lisa parked the car, they quickly exited and walked up to the hospital.

The circular door didn't move fast enough for them, nor did they bother to talk to the receptionist at the main desk. They just breezed past and to the elevators.

Chloe pressed the button and again, they had to wait. Megan felt the baby kick and she gently caressed her belly. The elevator finally arrived, the doors opened and they all stepped inside. Chloe pressed the button for the third floor, the doors closed, and they were finally on their way.

Megan was the first one off the elevator when the doors opened to the third floor. She took off quickly as she could with Lisa and Chloe not far behind. When they got to the room they saw the police officer on guard. He saw them coming, recognized Lisa, and stepped aside. Megan drew a deep breath, exhaled slowly and walked into the room with Lisa and Chloe.

The only sound in the room was the man's snoring as he slept. Megan walked over, bent down, and brushed his cheek with a kiss. He awoke somewhat startled. There were three women standing in the room.

Their faces were sad, yet unrecognized. This couldn't be good he thought.

The woman standing beside him with the black hair looked really pretty in her purple maternity blouse and black slacks. The others, the red head and brunette were dressed more casually in jeans and sweatshirts.

"And who are all of you?" He asked as he looked at each one in turn.

"Lisa Roberts," the red head was the first to start. "We went to high school together. Now we sometimes work together on cases."

"Right," he nodded. "I'm a private investigator."

"I'm Chloe," Chloe took her turn. "Chloe Hawkins, your daughter. I'm also a private investigator too."

"And that would make you..." Andrew looked at Megan.

"Your wife," Megan finished his sentence. "And we're going to have a baby."

"I see that," he said. He looked from one to another. "This is a bit overwhelming and I'm sorry, but I just don't recognize any of you."

"But D..," Chloe abruptly stopped, rethought her next words, and said, "We're here to help you, not here to force anything on you."

"Chloe is right," Lisa agreed. "We're here to help, because we love you very much."

"I can see that," he answered, his voice sounded sad. "It's just that I don't know you."

Megan touched his hand, he drew it back. "You feel nothing." Her eyes welled up with tears.

"I'm sorry," he turned away from her. Megan left the room bawling. Chloe left to go after her. Lisa remained behind.

Lisa approached and sat on the bed. He didn't move, which was a good sign.

"What would you like to know?"

"Who am I really?"

"You are Andrew Knight, a private investigator. You are adept in martial arts; know several languages, and your investigative skills are unrivaled. That is what you do, not who you are."

"Go on."

"You are a husband, father, friend, and are loved by all those around you. You are kind, loving, caring, and would do anything for anyone, at any time."

"Sounds like an obituary." He commented. "This is all good and such, but it still doesn't help me."

"The Andrew Knight we all know is in that head of yours. You just have to find him."

Lisa got up, smiled a little, and left him alone.

Chloe finally found Megan. She was in one of the family waiting rooms staring out the big picture window. Chloe joined her on the floral sofa. Megan grabbed another tissue.

"What we do for a living is not necessarily who we are," Megan shared her thoughts. "I believe they are our workself and our homeself."

"True, but sometimes they overlap, influence us, and guide us in what we do whether at work or at home," Chloe added. "My dad just can't stop being a detective one minute and a husband the next. That's who he is."

Megan stood up and walked back over to the window. Chloe stayed on the sofa and did not follow.

"Andrew is my husband, my lover, my best friend. But I don't know how much more I can take of what he does. It's too much of a strain for me to deal with right now."

"All I know is that the Andrew Knight we all love and care for is buried some where in the mind of the man in that room. We have to wait and see if that man rises from the ashes, or if it will be someone new."

Chloe finally joined Megan over by the window. The subdued colors of the winter sun stretched their way across the azure skies. The day was near an end; a new one was waiting to be born.

Chapter 6

Roxanne sang along with the music from the MP3 player as she rode to her bookstore. Riding her bike was Roxanne's way of going green and protesting the high gas prices, plus it was a beautiful scenic ride on the trail along the lake and through downtown Bayport. The song finished just as Roxanne turned into the lot behind her store. She parked and locked her bike in the bike rack and grabbed her backpack. Roxanne took her keys out and unlocked the door going inside. She closed the door behind her.

Roxanne set down her stuff behind the counter and went about turning on the lights and making some fresh coffee for her customers. She straightened the tables and chairs and then walked through the book racks. Roxanne straightened all of the books that were messed up or out of order. Roxanne would from time to time still bury her nose in a book, taking in a deep whiff of its pages.

Roxanne checked to see if the coffee was done; it was. She poured herself a cup. It was a special aromatic blend called 'Jamaica Me Happy' that she'd bought from the Red Bank Cafe. The coffee tasted good and warmed her up nicely. So Roxanne scooped up the morning paper one hand and with a cup of coffee in the other, she sat down on one of the comfortable sofas by the front windows. Roxanne started to read the newspaper when the door bell announced an interruption to her quiet time.

Chloe entered the quaint little book store. As she stood in the doorway, Chloe saw a woman, about her age. Her corn silk colored hair and dark brown eyes flattered a face that was well defined, with strong cheekbones and a slender, button-like nose. She wore a pair of chocolate slacks and a floral pheasant top.

Roxanne got up from the couch when she saw a woman about her age. Her coal colored hair was cut in a very flattering way, and her eyes were dark brown. She wore a burgundy pant suit.

"I'm not open yet," Roxanne announced.

"I need your help," Chloe announced back.

"You need my help?" Roxanne repeated.

"Andrew Knight is my dad," Chloe further explained. "I read about the case you worked."

"You're Andrew Knight's daughter?" Roxanne was puzzled. She walked over and asked, "May I hold your hands."

"Hold my hands?" Chloe made a strange face.

"I would just like to do a reading," Roxanne smiled.

"Um, sure," Chloe stretched out her hands.

Roxanne took Chloe's hands in hers. She closed her eyes and breathed deeply, and cleared her mind.

Roxanne saw a myriad of images flash before her mind's eye.

"I see a large building surrounded by woods. There is a woman giving birth, but she has her eyes closed," Roxanne said.

"I was born at Evergreen Sanitarium," Chloe answered. "My mom was in a coma."

"I also see a battle, a civil war battle," Roxanne continued.

"My dad's last case involved civil war reenactors that were being murdered," Chloe said. She was distracted by the wonderful smelling coffee.

"I see you and your father standing before a grave. He is tracing the name with his finger tip," Roxanne finally opened her eyes. "There was someone watching the both of you. I couldn't see them clearly. The anger they felt shrouded their identity from me."

"We will get back to that later," Chloe quickly shrugged it off. "I came here for your help on a case that my dad started working on."

"Please forgive my lack of manners," Roxanne apologized. "Would you like some coffee or perhaps tea?"

"That coffee smells wonderful," Chloe said.

"Would you like a cup?" Roxanne asked.

"Yes, please."

"I'll be right back," Roxanne said. "Please sit."

Chloe sat down on the sofa where Roxanne had just been. Just as she settled in, Roxanne returned with a cup of coffee for her. Roxanne sat down.

"A case he was working on?" Roxanne asked. "Did something happen?"

"A few days ago my dad fell through the ice on the lake of the JFK grounds," Chloe took a sip of the wonderful brew. She continued, "He survived and turned up at a horse ranch nearby. He had a heart attack," Chloe inhaled and exhaled quickly so as not to start crying again. She went on, "He survived, thank God. Because of the near drowning and heart attack, my dad has trauma-induced amnesia."

"Oh my God," Roxanne tearfully moaned.

"We as a family have to deal with," Chloe answered.

"So, um back to the case," Roxanne said. "Are you taking it over?"

"I was in my dad's office looking through the case file," Chloe said. She held up her cup for a refill. Roxanne laughed and took Chloe's cup. She went to fill it. Roxanne returned shortly and retook her seat.

"While on the computer, I read through the rest of his case files." Chloe took a sip. "When I got to the case he worked on with you, it came to me that your psychic abilities would be able to help find the missing teenagers, and possibly the person who attacked the Higgins Family."

"So did you talk to the client?" Roxanne asked.

"I set up a meeting for tomorrow," Chloe said. She finished off the coffee and put down the cup. She looked forlorn, "I was hoping that you would join me on the case." She brightened up a little, "Besides there was a note in the case folder stating that my dad was going to contact you anyway."

"You really are his daughter," Roxanne laughed.

"Will you help me?" Chloe asked.

"I will help you," Roxanne answered.

"Great!" Chloe exclaimed.

Chloe rose from the sofa. She thanked Roxanne again as they shook hands. Chloe said good bye and left. A frightening feeling washed over Roxanne as she looked at her hand. It was a sensation of death. But whose death was it?"

Chloe arrived early at her dad's office building earlier the next morning. His new assistant, Amanda, in business attire and with closely cropped blonde hair, was just unlocking the front door.

"I'm Chloe Hawkins," she said to Amanda.

"I know," Amanda answered. "Missus Knight phoned me at home last night. She explained that Andrew's daughter would be taking over the Collins case."

Chloe followed Amanda inside and closed the door behind them. Amanda put her stuff down on the desk and went to make coffee. Chloe went into her dad's office and pulled the Collins' case file. Roxanne should be arriving soon. Chloe put the file folder on the desk and walked out into the reception area. Amanda was now seated at her desk.

Chloe straightened her burgundy pant suit. The front door opened and two women, one older and one younger, walked into the main reception area. Chloe smiled at Roxanne, and the other woman, who she presumed was Nedra Collins. They walked over. Chloe turned in their direction when they came up to her.

"Hello Chloe," Roxanne said

"Nedra Collins," Nedra said. They shook hands. Nedra was now more somber and asked, "How is your dad doing?"

"He's still at Bayport Memorial," Chloe explained. "Doctor Straussman recommended him for observation. He is still suffering from amnesia."

"I hope he gets better," Nedra replied.

"Let's go into the office," Chloe said. She gestured towards Roxanne. "I've brought Miss Turner in as a consultant on the case."

"Okay," Nedra smiled.

The three women walked into Andrew's office and closed the door.

Chloe sat in her dad's leather chair while Roxanne and Nedra took their seats in front of the desk. Amanda walked in with coffee for all of them. They thanked her.

"Would you please share with me what has happened so far," Chloe looked at Nedra.

"My son, his girl friend, and four other teenagers went out to the abandoned prep school out by St. Nazianz," Nedra informed her. "There were no traces of them when the Sheriff's department investigated the scene. All they found was the Ouji board and melted candles."

"When your son didn't come home, that's when you called my dad," Chloe said. "Is that correct?"

"Yes," Nedra answered.

"JFK Prep is owned by a developer out of Chicago, right?" Chloe asked.

"Is that important?" Nedra answered.

"Possibly." Chloe said. "Why were they at the abandoned school?"

"I don't know," Nedra explained. "I thought they were going out to celebrate my son Chad's birthday."

"I presume they first played with the Ouji board," Chloe surmised.

"Yes," Nedra replied.

"And then went to make out?" Chloe added.

"I believe so," Nedra said.

"There was no trace of them," Chloe said, looking over the notes in the case file.

"Well, we need to get a look at where they were," Chloe said. "I'll have to contact the current owner of the school grounds to get permission to investigate the area. Once I've done that we can proceed from there."

"I'd like to come along," Roxanne said.

"Not a good idea," Chloe hesitated.

"But I could be of help," Roxanne insisted.

"I'm not sure." Chloe was still reluctant.

"What's it going to be?" Roxanne pressed further.

"You can come with me," Chloe finally agreed.

They thanked Chloe and…

The sunlight was nearly swept away and darkness poised ready to take its place. Chloe, along with Roxanne slowly drove up the gravel driveway. Both wore more appropriate clothing for their investigation.

Before them loomed a historic monument of faded brick and broken windows. Even in the daylight the main building of JFK Prep struck an eerie chord.

Roxanne couldn't help but stare at the front of building as they stopped in front of it. She hadn't even stepped inside as of yet, but felt a great forebodingness about it.

A woman in her late fifties emerged from the black BMW with Illinois plates. She was quite slender, dressed professionally, and her silver hair had nary a strand out of place. She strode with confidence towards Chloe's car.

Chloe and Roxanne got out and greeted her.

"Georgina Rowlands," she introduced herself to them. It was as if they should've been impressed just by the mere mention of her name. They were not.

"Chloe Hawkins, "Chloe replied. She gestured towards Roxanne, "And this is Roxanne Turner."

"A pleasure," Georgina answered.

"Let's go inside," Chloe insisted. Just before they were about to head off, Chloe went back in her car and grabbed a couple of flashlights.

As they walked in the direction of the side entrance, Georgian explained, "The investors I represent bought the property in order to fix it up and turn it into a seminary. That was a few years ago and unfortunately progress has been quite slow."

"Why is that?" Chloe inquired.

"I've gone through several contractors, because of," Georgina paused. She went on, "oh, how shall I put this. It was because of certain incidents happening on the property."

"What incidents?" Roxanne asked.

"Well," Georgina answered as they came up to the side door. "Certain unexplained things."

"Supernatural things?" Chloe surmised.

"So they claim," Georgina replied.

They stopped in front of the massive wooden door. Georgina used her key to unlock it and soon they were inside. The painting of the woman immediately caught Chloe's attention. She walked up to it. Chloe ran her fingers ever so gently across it and felt the brush strokes and imperfections of the wall that made up the beautiful painting.

"Do you know who painted it," Chloe turned and looked at Georgina.

"No," Georgina answered. "But we made several attempts to cover it up and it just reappears."

"What do you mean it reappears?" Roxanne asked.

"We've painted over it several times," Georgina was exasperated in her reply. "We even tried paint remover on the damned thing."

"Paint remover?" Chloe exclaimed. She examined the painting more closely. The brush strokes showed no signs of damage. "It looks untouched."

"So you wanted to see the dorm rooms," Georgina said, changing the subject.

"Yes," Chloe answered.

"They're this way up the stairs," Georgina gestured with her hand towards the stairs leading to the second floor. "Please follow me."

As they ascended the stairs, Roxanne had a strange feeling wash over her. She turned and looked back at the painting, but there was nothing unusual about it. Roxanne shook it off as nothing more than an overactive imagination. She joined the others whom were already at the top of the stairs. Georgina led them down the hallway past a rusted bed frame with a musty smelling mattress that still held the impressions of previous use.

"The kids make out on it," Georgina explained rather nonchalantly.

"Disgusting," Roxanne shuddered.

"Here we are," Georgina announced.

The room was plain looking. The walls were faded and the paint was chipping. There were several cracks in the ceiling that spread across it like spider webs. Only a single window provided very little light into the room. The majority of the panels were boarded up with plywood. A circle of melted candles on the floor reminded Roxanne of a bizarre-looking birthday cake.

"I have to be going," Georgina glanced at her watch. "I have a meeting this evening with another contractor." Georgina handed Chloe the keys. "Just lock up when you leave. I'll pick up the keys from your office tomorrow morning." She left the two of them alone.

Chloe put the keys in her pocket. Roxanne stood there as Chloe walked around the dorm room checking things out.

"Are you getting anything from the room," Chloe asked as she paused by the window.

"No," Roxanne answered. "Why?"

"Why don't you try in that circle of candles," Chloe suggested, but first she handed Roxanne a flashlight.

"Alright," Roxanne said. She walked over to the candles, stepped inside the circle, and sat down on the floor. She set down the flashlight beside her. Roxanne closed her eyes. Chloe shone the light in Roxanne's direction.

Roxanne breathed rhythmically with each beat of her heart focusing only on that and not anything or any other sounds in the room. At first, the images swirled about in a blur of light and shadows, but soon things came into focus.

Roxanne opened her eyes a few minutes later. Chloe was gone! Roxanne flipped on her flashlight and searched the room. Where could Chloe have gone?

"Just breathe Roxanne," she told herself. Roxanne drew in a deep breath; exhaling it slowly. As she did this, Roxanne heard voices coming from somewhere down the hallway. This surprised her, since Roxanne thought that they were the only ones in the building. Maybe while she was in her trance, someone else had entered the place and Chloe went to check things out. So Roxanne decided to check things out too. She headed off in the direction of the voices.

She had only gone a short distance down the hallway, when Roxanne stopped outside another of the dorm rooms. She could hear the voice more clearly now. Roxanne turned the door knob and opened the door. There was a boy and girl making out. Embarrassed, Roxanne closed the door. Roxanne suddenly felt chilled; like if someone had put their cold hands up her back. She spun around, casting her light in that direction, but saw nothing! Roxanne mustered up enough courage to continue down the hallway. Roxanne decided she's gone far enough and was about to turn back when a terrible scream pierced the stillness. She'd barely gotten out of the way when the door flew open and the boy and girl inside rushed out and headed off in the direction of the scream. Roxanne quickly followed. She stopped when they knocked on the door.

"Did you hear it," the frizzy haired boy asked the one with the earrings.

"Yeah," he replied. "It sounded like my sister."

"Come on," a dark haired girl said.

The four of them ran down the hallway in the direction of the scream. Roxanne turned off her flashlight and followed at a safe distance. When they got there, a girl with short cropped black hair was curled up in a fetal position murmuring incoherently.

"Where's Chad?" the boy with the earrings asked. She didn't answer.

Roxanne couldn't see because the rest of them blocked her view. She tried to push past them when they all heard it; an eerily moan.

"What's that, Jazz?" one of the girls asked with her eyes wide with fright.

"I don't know," Jazz answered sharply.

Roxanne, who for some reason hadn't been noticed by the group, left them and headed off in search of the source of the moaning. When she got to the staircase, Roxanne switched on her flashlight and followed the descending steps. The beam of light finally came to rest upon a hooded figure. The person simply stood there not moving at all. Why didn't he move? Surely the light was bright enough for them to see that someone was there.

"Who are you?" Roxanne called out. No reply.

"What are you doing here?" Roxanne demanded. The hooded figure made no sound.

Roxanne was about to step forward, when the hooded figure started towards her instead. She immediately bolted up the stairs and back down the hallway to warn the others.

Chloe had witnessed Roxanne go into her trance. She was in awe of such a gift. Feeling that it was perfectly safe, she decided to explore the dorm room a bit more. It was too bad that the candles had all burnt out, because they would've been a welcome addition to her flashlight. Chloe searched the dorm room floor with her flashlight. She walked about looking for some clues that would help find the missing teenagers. As Chloe approached the closet she noticed a few drops of dried blood. Chloe grasped hold of the sliding door handle with one hand and opened it, readying herself for anything that might've popped out! Unfortunately there was only the Ouji board on the floor of the closet. She bent down and picked it up. Chloe closed the closet door and walked back over to Roxanne. Roxanne was still in her trance, so Chloe sat down outside the circle of candles and opened the game. When she laid out the game board, a blood stained piece of material fell out. Now Chloe knew the source of the blood on the floor by the closet. She didn't have an evidence bag, so Chloe carefully placed the piece of cloth in her pocket. Why hadn't the authorities or her dad confiscated the game to begin with, Chloe wondered? Chloe considered that perhaps they were too concerned with searching for the missing teenagers, or had they just blown it off as them just running away from home or something like that. Either way, Chloe had her first real clue. She glanced back over at Roxanne. Chloe was starting to get worried about the length of time that Roxanne had been in her trance. She was equally afraid to just wake her from it too.

Roxanne was on her way, when the rest of the teenagers were rushing towards her! She instinctively jumped out of the way. Roxanne watched them bound down the stairs towards the hooded figure. She went after them and when she came to the top of the stairs, Roxanne saw the hooded figure being chased by them. Roxanne decided to follow and practically ran down the stairs to do so. As she got to the bottom of the stairs, Roxanne heard what sounded like a heavy wooden door slam shut. She bolted down the long hallway and soon came to a wooden door. Roxanne opened the door and stepped through. She appeared to be in a church. Roxanne looked around and saw teenagers had the hooded figure surrounded. She immediately headed in their direction, but came to a sudden stop when a second person, wearing all black, stepped forward from the shadows. The person's identity was hidden by a hooded mask. The teenagers were startled by the appearance of the masked person. Before they could recover, the person in black attacked in a martial arts fury. The boys tried to defend themselves and the girls, but it was in vain. Within minutes all of the teenagers were on the floor, unconscious.

Roxanne had to go back to the dorm room where she and Chloe had been to when they arrived. She had to wake from her trance and tell Chloe what she had seen.

Chloe rose to her feet when she heard moaning sounds coming from beyond the door to the dorm room. She withdrew her gun and stepped up to the door. Chloe grasped hold of the knob, gave it a twist, and quickly opened the door. She entered the hallway with her gun in the ready position. Chloe saw nothing, but the moaning continued. She went back and retrieved her flashlight. When Chloe exited the room, she closed the door and walked in the direction of the stairs. The moaning sound was getting louder as Chloe neared the stairway. She slowed her pace and readied both flashlight and gun for when the time came to look down the stairs. Chloe's heart was beating fast, and her breathing was labored. She took a minute to calm down and stepped forward.

Roxanne finally woke from her trance. She looked around the dorm room. Chloe was gone! Roxanne rose a bit unsteadily to her feet. It felt like a thousand needles were pricking her flesh. Roxanne fought off the feeling, grabbed her flashlight, and went to look for Chloe. She exited the dorm room and headed towards the stairs. So far there was no sign of Chloe. Where could she be?

Roxanne walked down the stairs and as soon as she reached the first floor, she heard moaning sounds. She turned and flashed her light down the hallway leading to the church. Roxanne saw nothing.

"Chloe!" Roxanne cried out. There was no reply.

Roxanne continued down the hallway and upon reaching the door to the church, she stumbled from something on the floor. She shone her light down to see what it was. Roxanne gasped and was taken aback. It was a gun and flashlight.

"Chloe!" Roxanne shouted after she opened the door to the church. The sound of her voice echoed across the vast, empty sanctuary. Roxanne knew what to do. She had to get help. Roxanne closed the door and was about to turn around. She felt a blow to the head and was immediately rendered unconscious.

Chapter 7

Even before he opened his eyes, the light from the morning sun already lit them up. He rolled over on his side and put the pillow over his head. It was too late. No matter how hard he tried, the blasted light had woken him up. He finally opened his eyes to see the sun just coming over the lake. He put the pillow back and pushed the button to raise the bed. After playing with it a few minutes, he finally found the right position. There was a knock at the door. He replied to come in.

"Good morning," a red haired nurse smiled. She walked in carrying his breakfast tray.

"Good morning," he hesitated, "Veronica, right?"

"Well at least your short-term memory is still working," Veronica smiled, her green eyes scrunched up at the corners. She walked over and put the tray on his lap.

"Thanks," he replied. He removed the cover to reveal a hearty breakfast of pancakes and sausages. His stomach was growling, so loud in fact that Veronica heard it. She smiled.

"You're scheduled for a session with Doctor Straussman this morning at eleven," Veronica announced, as she looked at the screen of her palm pilot. She glanced in his direction just in time to see him take the last bite of his food. "My, you really were hungry," Veronica laughed. He unexpectedly burped. They both laughed. "Hey," she suggested. "Since we have time I want to take you somewhere."

"Where is that?" he inquired.

"Get in," Veronica announced as she grabbed the wheel chair and moved it to the side of the bed.

The Sunroom was very warm, sunny, accentuated with palms and wicker furniture, and not one single modern electronic device. There were board games, magazines, and books waiting to be read scattered on the tables in the middle of the room. A little alcove on the north side offered sanctuary from the world.

That's where he wanted to be today; secluded from the world. At the request of Doctor Straussman, he was staying at the hospital a few more days for observation. Apparently he was her test subject since he was her only patient with trauma induced amnesia. The woman he knew as Megan Knight had protested the decision at first, but then conceded that it may help. Either way, eventually he would have to leave and face an unrecognizeable world. It frightened him. Last night he dreamt about this Andrew Knight, the man they claim to be him, but there was no face to recognize. It was blank. So the sunroom was the perfect place to be right now.

Veronica wheeled him over to the alcove. There was someone else already there. He thanked Veronica and she left.

He got up out of the wheel chair and walked over to one of the empty cushioned wicker chairs. He grabbed a magazine and began to page through; not really reading anything of real importance. He looked her over. She was a young girl with the same colored hair as his. She was staring out of the windows and down on the city. She looked very sad. Shadowy circles camouflaged her eyes. It was like someone had stolen the light not only from her eyes, but from her soul.

Her silence befuddled him. He wasn't really sure why, or how come. Why would, how she looked or the apparent misery she felt, concern him? He tried to go back to reading, but couldn't. Something unsettling about her was calling him ask her why. Where did this querying feeling come from?

He slid the magazine back on the table, rose and walked over by her. He asked if he could sit down. No reply. He asked again. She gave a slow nod. He presumed that meant it was okay and immediately sat beside her. For the first few minutes they gazed out the large window at the soundless sights in streets below. Pretty soon his thoughts began to drift back to why she could be so miserable. What happened to her? Was it some incurable illness the doctor told she had? Did it have to do with family? What was it? There were so many questions twirling around in his mind; each jockeying for position. Finally, he just sort of blurted out, "My name is, um, um, its." He hastily stopped. Damn it, he swore in his head. All he had to do was just say the damn name, but he couldn't. For some reason it didn't seem to fit. How weird was that he thought. Is it your name that defines who you are, or is it your actions, thoughts, and feelings? You can write your name down on paper, wear it on a name badge, or have some one call it out in the middle of the night. That's what bothered him the most; your name does define who you are to others. Without it you're just a vessel with emotions, witnessed by those around you, but no identity to go with it. So what is in a name; everything! He tried again, "My name is Andrew," he benignly said. "Andrew Knight."

"Storm," her voice finally came out of the shadows. "My name is Storm Higgins."

"I like your name," He said, observing her closely. It felt weird. Why would he do something like that? Why would he even care? And yet it seemed as if from his observation he could tell a lot about her. For example, when she talked, he noticed her teeth were well cared for, so it meant that her parents had good insurance. Yet her eye teeth were longer; looking more like fangs. Why would she do that? He quickly shook off the feeling and recovered, and smiled. "How did your parents come up with it?"

"My mom..." Storm sniffed back her tears. Her shoulders sunk and she became withdrawn, not so much as before. "My mom gave birth to me during a really bad snow storm. They couldn't get to the hospital, so I was born at home."

He saw that talking about her mom was very upsetting. Something terrible must have happened recently. What could it be? Was her mom in the hospital or something worse?

"Are you okay?" He picked up on Storm's reluctance when she talked about her mom. He pressed further, "Did something happen to your mom. I mean, well, you can tell me only if you want to."

"My parents," Storm paused and exhaled deeply. "My parents and brother were killed recently. I was the only one to live."

"Was it a car accident?"

"No, they were murdered." Storm bust out in tears. She covered her face with her hands. He didn't know what to do. Should he comfort her? Call a nurse?

"Dear Lord," was all he could say. He simply sat there listening to her cry. He closed his eyes, and a single tear streamed down his cheek. For some weird reason, her pain had now become his pain. Who would murder a mother, father and brother? What kind of person could do that? Was it for money, or revenge, or something else? Why were all of these damn questions flooding his mind? His eyes flashed open; the room seemed to be getting smaller. He couldn't breathe; it was like there was no air in the room. He suddenly felt very ill and had to get away.

He bolted from the sofa and ran out of the room. He had to find a way to shut up the deafening, swirling noise in his head. But where could he go? That's when he saw the door marked 'Roof Observation Room'. He gave the door a shove to open and bolted up the stairs. Once he reached the top of the stairwell, he saw a glass enclosed observation room. It was empty. He closed the door. He grabbed a hold of his head with both hands and roared at the top of his lungs. His screaming ricocheted off the glass and engulfed him like waves crashing on the beach. "Make the questions stop!" He fell to his knees. "Make them stop! What is happening to me?" Images of people he did not know, places he couldn't recognize and feelings that couldn't be explained, joined in the menagerie leading to a torturous crescendo. The battle inside of him was too much to bear; it felt like the thunder of a thousand cannons. All of the suppressed memories and feelings that his mind had built up walls to hold back came flooding out. His head was spinning. He felt sick to his stomach. He tried to get up on his feet, but he couldn't move. He tried to resist with his entire mind and might but he no longer could prevent it. He grabbed a trash can and vomited until his body finally succumbed and he just lay down. The battle was over, but who was the victor?

Only an hour had passed by; just a small click to the hands of the clock in his life. He opened his eyes. The world was different now. Where was he? He glanced around the glass room. Where was he, oh that's right, the observation room on the roof. He rose to his feet a bit unsteady yet. He walked over to one of the windows. He moved close enough to see his face reflected in the glass. He moved his head from side to side, each time gazing out of the corner of his eye. He was in need of a shave. He bent even closer to the glass. His eyes were still green, although they looked a bit tired. He made his face contort into an overdone grin. He laughed and his face relaxed again. Staring at the face in the glass, he asked, "Who are you?" With his eyes, he met the eyes of the person reflected in the glass. There was no hesitation. No longer did the specter of doubt rear its ugly head. Unlike the dream he had had a night ago, his face was not blank. His lips parted with a slight grin. "I am Andrew Knight."

Storm was still sitting on the sofa. She saw the man suddenly get up and rush out of the room. She didn't know why.

Storm was about to get up and go back to her room, when the man reappeared. He seemed different to her. Unlike before, he was smiling. He briskly walked toward her.

Andrew walked back into the sunroom, fortunately Storm was still there. He smiled at her. Andrew walked toward her.

Storm smiled slightly as he stopped in front of her. He sat down again.

"Tell me about your parents," Andrew started off.

"What do you want to know?" Storm asked. "Why do you want to know?"

"Listen Storm," Andrew paused and quickly checked to make sure they were alone. "I'm a private investigator and have been hired by Wyatt's mom to prove he didn't murder your family."

"Wyatt would never do that," Storm blasted back. She quickly calmed down, "Yeah he was excommunicated from the coven, but he wouldn't. I mean my father didn't like Wyatt's lust for blood or the fact that he didn't respect the laws by the coven." Storm's bottom lip began to tremble and she looked away, "But he would never hurt us or me."

"Did you see the person who attacked your family?" Andrew asked. He grabbed a tissue from the end table and handed it to Storm. She thanked him. Storm dried her eyes. She turned back towards him. "No, I was shot in the back." Storm said. "Want to see the scar?" She started to lift her pajama top." "No that's okay," Andrew motioned for her to stop. "When I finally woke," Storm said. "I dragged myself down stairs. That's when I saw my family...my family was..." Storm broke down. Andrew gingerly put his arms around her, offering comfort. He held onto her for quite some time and could feel her pain with each sob. He was even more determined to find the person who did this.

"Listen Storm," Andrew said softly. "Just tell me where I can find Wyatt. I know he didn't attack your family." Andrew paused for a second. "Wyatt is the key. He is the link to this Night Blade, whom I suspect murdered your family." Storm thanked Andrew again, and she sat up.

"Wyatt hangs out at a lot at JFK Prep," Storm informed him.

"Thanks, Storm," Andrew smiled. She smiled back. Their respective nurses returned and took them back to their rooms. Life had given him his memory back and in the process, he got one up on Sheriff Delsmann. Today was a great day!

The sounds of gentle, rolling waves and ocean breezes enveloped the room. Soft light from candles and their aromatic scents of lavender wafted about in a relaxing splendor. Megan lay in the soothing water with her eyes closed. She loving caressed her growing tummy; reassuring her unborn child that everything was alright. The hospital, more specifically Doctor Straussman, called to inform her that Andrew was being released this afternoon. So she decided to take a relaxing bath and then get dressed. Megan sat up and pulled the drain plug. She stood and reached for a towel. Megan wrapped it around her and she stepped out of the tub.

Megan walked into the bedroom and sat down at the table and mirror. She put on her makeup, touched up her eyelashes with mascara and her lips with dark blood red lipstick. Megan walked over to the bed and let the towel gently drop to the floor. She checked herself in the full length floor mirror. Megan turned around slowly admiring her nude form. She ran her hand up ever so delicately caressing her body along the way. Megan stopped and cupped her breast. Megan closed her eyes. She imagined it was Andrew touching her as she moaned deeply. Megan opened her eyes and grabbed a pair of black lace maternity panties. She bent down and put them on. Next Megan slipped on a seductive black maternity skirt and spaghetti strap camisole top. It accentuated her curvaceous bosom. One way or another Megan was determined to get her husband back. She took a pair of lace strap black shoes from the closet and slipped them on. Yeah, Megan knew she was way over dressed, but the situation called for drastic measures. She was determined to jolt back Andrew's memory, and the little black outfit she wore should do the trick.

Megan grabbed the matching purse and her keys. She left the house.

Andrew was really happy to actually put on some normal clothes. He was glad to finally be going home. He had just finished putting on his shoes, when there was a knock at the door.

"Hello Doctor Straussman," Andrew greeted her cheerfully.

"I still don't feel it's a good idea for you to go home so soon," she protested.

"And I feel that being there might jog my memory," Andrew shot back.

"Fine," Doctor Straussman flopped down in a chair. She looked up at him, "You do have my number, right?"

"Yes." Andrew patted his pants pocket.

"Are you ready?" Veronica entered.

"Do I really need that?" Andrew rolled his eyes when he saw the wheelchair.

"It's policy," Veronica insisted.

"Fine," Andrew took his place in the chair. Veronica wheeled him out of the room. As they moved down the hallway towards the elevator, Andrew would peek into the room with open doors. Some of the beds were empty, others with the sick or dying. He had to go home; he would be forever stuck in this place. The only problem was that he had to keep up the charade in public. It was the only way to keep Sheriff Delsmann off his back. Plus it was the only advantage Andrew had in order to carry out his investigation. If Andrew could convince Sheriff Delsmann he still suffered from memory loss, she would leave him alone. Of course, eventually he would have to regain his memory at some point, Andrew knew that. When the elevator doors opened, Veronica wheeled him inside. As soon as they were set, she pushed the button for the main floor.

Sheriff Delsmann waited in the main lobby of the hospital. In one hand she had a bouquet of balloons, and in the other a box of candy. People passing by smiled at her. Talia smiled back. They probably thought the gifts were for a loved one. In fact they were for Andrew. It wasn't that Talia cared about him or anything like that. The real reason she was here was to see if Andrew Knight had managed to regain his memory. Talia wanted to observe the reunion with his wife. She was hoping to catch some glimmer of recognition in Andrew's eyes when he saw his wife. That's all Talia would need. She couldn't wait to put Andrew Knight in the place he should be; not at home, but in jail! Talia straightened her taupe pant suit and brushed aside some loose strands of hair. Talia was almost giddy at the prospect of exacting her revenge on Andrew.

Megan parked the red AC Cobra and immediately got out. She walked somewhat briskly to the main entrance of Bayport Memorial Hospital. As soon as Megan entered the main lobby she saw Sheriff Delsmann standing there with balloons and chocolate. Megan was not happy to see her and the displeasure was quite evident on her face.

"Hello," Megan's voice oozed with displeasure.

"Hello Missus Knight," Talia replied in opposite.

"Why are you here?" Megan asked.

"I just wanted to express my happiness that Mister Knight is finally going home," Talia answered smiling. "I also wanted to apologize for my behavior."

"I see," Megan answered coldly.

When the elevator doors finally opened to the lobby, what Andrew saw caught him completely off guard. There was Sheriff Delsmann holding a bouquet of balloons in one hand and box of chocolates in the other. Presumably, there were for him, but why and what was she up to? The other was Megan. She was dressed to the nines in a black skirt and camisole. She had smoky eyes and blood red lips. Holy crap, Andrew lamented. How was he going to convince both of them that his memory still hadn't returned? Andrew closed his eyes and drew a deep breath to regain his composure. Veronica moved him forward as they headed towards the two women.

Megan and Talia turned at the same time and saw Andrew being escorted by a nurse pushing him in a wheel chair. Megan was jumping up and down inside, but on the outside she was very composed. Talia was the opposite, very bubbly and excited.

"Hello," Andrew greeted them.

Megan thought his eyes had an expressionless look to them. He still didn't recognize her. So dressing the way she did had no effect on him. Megan felt embarrassed.

Talia was also frustrated. When Andrew saw his wife there was no expression of recognition on his face at all.

Andrew was using every once of both his mental and physical abilities to convince both of them his memory hadn't returned. When Sheriff Delsmann looked away for a minute, Andrew stole a longing glance at Megan. She was beautiful. His arms were aching to hold her; to kiss her full, red lips. He just wanted to end the charade right now and tenderly caress and kiss her growing tummy. Andrew knew he couldn't and it was killing him on the inside.

When Sheriff Delsmann turned back, Andrew had already composed himself again and sat emotionless. Talia handed Andrew the balloons and box of chocolates.

"This is a peace offering," Talia smiled widely.

"Thank you," Andrew said. He put the box of chocolates on his lap and held onto the balloons. "I don't know what you're apologizing for, but hey the chocolates sound really good about now because I'm starving."

"Well, you're welcome," Talia laughed.

"We better get going," Megan insisted.

Talia stepped aside as Megan and Veronica escorted Andrew outside. She watched Megan go and get the car. Talia quickly left and went to her own car.

It was a quiet drive home. Megan glanced at Andrew from time to time as he slept. Soon they were home. Andrew woke and stared at the Victorian-style house. Megan got out of the car and walked around to his door. She opened it and Andrew emerged. She grabbed the candy and bouquet of balloons.

As Andrew opened the front door and walked inside the foyer, he gazed at everything around him. Megan thought it seemed like it was the first time he was ever there.

"Let's go into the family room," Megan suggested.

"Okay," Andrew answered.

Megan led him to the family room. She set the gifts from Talia on the coffee table. Andrew wondered around the room taking it all in before sitting down on the sofa. Megan sat in one of the chairs across from him. It seemed like a very long time until Megan broke the silence.

"So is any of this familiar?" Megan asked hopeful.

"Ta beauté fait mon coeur se remplir de l'amour."

"What are you saying?" Megan uttered.

"J'ai manqué la chaleur de tes lèvres, le confort de ton étreinte et l'amour dans ton coeur."

"Why are you speaking French?" Megan angrily asked. She thought Andrew had finally snapped. Megan stood and was about to walk out of the room.

"Ne t'en va pas, plait," Andrew pleaded with her not to go. He got up and went after her.

Megan was standing there crying. Andrew walked over to her.

"Tu parlez-vous français?" He asked if she spoke French.

"Oui," Megan answered yes. She wiped her eyes. "Tu m'as enseign" She was annoyed and him that he had taught her. She asked if he lost his mind, "Avez-vous perdu votre esprit?"

"T'es amusant," Andrew teased that she was being hilarious.

"Tu parles français? Pourquoi?" Megan demanded why Andrew was speaking in French.

"Il y a un dispositif d'écoute sur les ballons," Andrew told her there was an bug the balloons.

"Qui l'a fait?"Megan demanded who did it.

"A qui penses-tu?" Andrew asked who she thought.

"Évidemment, Shérif Delsmann," Megan replied. Suddenly she realized something else. "Ta mémoire est retournée!" Megan exclaimed estatically that Andrew had his memory back. The embrace they both were longing for finally happened! When they parted, Andrew led Megan into the kitchen. They slipped into the breakfast nook and sat down. Andrew told her it was safe to finally not speak in French any more.

"When did you get your memory back?" Megan asked, caressing his hand.

"Just yesterday at the hospital," Andrew answered.

"Today was just an act," Megan said. "For Sheriff Delsmann..."

"And for you," Andrew finished.

"Why is she so determined?" Megan asked.

"I don't know, but as long as she believes I still have amnesia, it will be fine." Andrew kissed her hands.

"There's something else," Megan turned more serious now. "Chloe and Roxanne are missing. Chloe took over the case for you and she asked for Roxanne to help her locate the missing teenagers. When the authorities arrived at JFK Prep, the only traces they found were Chloe's gun and nothing else."

"Damn it," Andrew cursed angrily. "Didn't the authorities find any other trace of them in all this time?"

"No, not according to Peter," Megan answered.

"This complicates things greatly. He sighed. "I need to find them all and time may be running out."

"What about Sheriff Delsmann?" Megan asked.

"Are you up to more French?" Andrew had a devious grin on his face.

"Oui," Megan smiled back.

Talia parked her car a few blocks down from the Victorian house. She turned the car off and reached for the briefcase on the back seat. Talia opened the briefcase and turned on the monitoring equipment. The judge had denied her request for wiretapping Knight's phone. Desperate times call for desperate measures, so Talia took matters into her own hands.

She keyed in the frequency and placed the headphones on. Talia listened. She heard Andrew and Megan enter the house. Talia heard Megan say 'Let's go into the family room.' She then heard Andrew respond 'okay'. At the moment, there were only footsteps and the sound of Megan putting the candy and balloons down. Talia listened more intently, but wasn't prepared for what she heard next.

"What the hell," Talia cursed. "He's speaking French!" Talia couldn't believe it. She berated herself that she never finished learning French. Either Knight had totally lost his mind, or he found the bug. But how, the device was a nearly invisible clear strip. It was the most advanced electronic listening device ever made. She surmised it was time for some old school tactics. Hopefully, Knight was still suffering from amnesia, and that way he wouldn't suspect being followed. Talia closed the briefcase and started the car. If he did have his memory back, well, it wouldn't be good.

Chapter 8

The room was black. A strong musty smell filled Chloe's nostrils. The walls felt cold and damp to the touch. Chloe didn't know what day or hour it was. She didn't even really know where she was. Chloe tried to move, but her hands felt like they had been glued together. She lifted them up and touched them with her lips. It wasn't glue but a thick rope. When Chloe tried to stand up, she couldn't do so. Her legs were bound in the same way. She heard soft moaning coming from somewhere in the dark.

Roxanne moaned softly when she opened her eyes. There was only blackness. Her hands and legs felt heavy, almost burdensome. She brought up her hands and touched the side of her face. She was right, they were bound with rope. A swirling of odors filled her nose and she didn't like it one bit. Roxanne heard some rustling around in the dark; she wasn't alone.

Chloe shifted her body to a more comfortable position. She decided to take a chance that the moaning was from someone familiar.

"Roxanne?" Chloe called out. She waited for an answer. 'I'm here Chloe' she heard.

"I'm glad you're alright." Chloe started to cry. She didn't exactly know why she was crying; maybe it was tears of elation.

"Me too," Roxanne replied. "So where are we exactly?"

"I think were in the catacombs beneath JFK Prep," Chloe answered, though not really sure. But what her instincts told her, it might be.

"How did we get here?" Roxanne asked.

"Someone knocked us out and carried us down here." Chloe replied.

"Who would do that?" Roxanne asked.

"Probably the same person who did it to those kids," Chloe said.

"So you think they're okay?" Roxanne asked.

"I hope so," Chloe replied.

"Do you think someone is looking for us?" Roxanne's tone was unsure, and Chloe picked up on it immediately.

"Um, they probably are," Chloe gauged her words carefully. "But they may have given up since there was no trace of us."

"Are we going to die?" Roxanne's voice trailed off. Chloe didn't answer. Roxanne pleaded, "Are we?"

"The one who can help us has no idea we're here." Chloe finally replied.

Father Michael stepped from the confessional to see Andrew kneeling in one of the pews. Father Michael walked over and sat down next to him.

"What brings you here my son?" Father Michael asked as he removed his stole. He put the Bible and the stole beside him.

"I need your help," Andrew answered with whisper and his eyes closed.

"What kind of help?" Father Michael asked.

"We need to talk somewhere private," Andrew continued in a whisper. "I'm being followed. The person is in the last pew to our left." Father Michael was about to turn and look, but Andrew told him not to. "He's from the Sheriff's department. Apparently Sheriff Delsmann feels I need a shadow." Father Michael nodded that he understood.

"The Confessional is always open my son," Father Michael said loudly, he picked up his stole, kissed and placed it on himself. He grabbed his Bible and headed to the confessional. Andrew made the sign of the cross, put the kneeling board back into place, and entered the confessional.

Andrew knelt in front of the screen.

"Bless me Father for I have sinned," Andrew said, making the sign of the cross.

"How long has it been since your last confession," Father Michael inquired.

"Too long," Andrew confessed.

"What are your sins," Father Michael asked.

"I did not do my job," Andrew first confessed.

"How is that?" Father Michael queried.

"I haven't found the missing teenagers yet, or Wyatt," Andrew explained. "And now my daughter has disappeared along with Roxanne Turner."

"How did this happen?" Father Michael further asked. "You are the best I know."

"Do you know about the catacombs out at JFK Prep?" Andrew asked.

"They were sealed off when it was still the seminary," Father Michael replied. He put his Bible beside him. "I was there when they did it. Why do you ask?"

"I believe that everyone that is missing, is locked away somewhere in the catacombs," Andrew answered. "That's why the authorities haven't found them yet."

"They were sealed!" Father Michael was resolute.

"There were no hidden doors, at all?" Andrew asked.

"How do you know about that?" Father Michael was caught off guard.

"I had a friend of mine at the Bayport Daily Herald, pulled all the information from the last fifty years about JFK Prep," Andrew explained. "In the story about the fire, the reporter mentioned the catacombs beneath the seminary. It also mentioned that there were several secret entrances built just in case of emergency." Andrew paused, and leaned closer to the screen, "I believe that whoever took the teenagers, along with Chloe and Roxanne, used one of those entrances to hide them all in the catacombs."

"There were more than just catacombs," Father Michael finally confessed. "There were also several rooms used for storage along with living quarters. A person could literally stay down there for months and be able to survive."

"So they could still be alive?" Andrew breathed a sigh of great relief. He was afraid that his mission would be one of 'recovery' and not 'rescue'. He pressed further, "I need to know where one of the entrances is?" Father Michael whispered the location to Andrew.

It was time to leave, so Andrew thanked Father Michael and left the confessional. When Andrew exited, he saw that his shadow was still there. Andrew walked past the man, pretending not to notice him and preceded out of the church. The man followed a few minutes later. When he emerged, Andrew's car was still there, but Andrew was nowhere to be seen. He had seemingly vanished into thin air! The man cursed and began a frantic search of the area.

As soon as his shadow took off, Andrew sat up in his car. How stupid for the man to not even check for such easy rouse. Andrew was sure that Sheriff Delsmann would have a long talk with her man. Andrew started the car and took off.

A crisp winter wind rustled through the bare branches of the trees. The full moon shone across the land creating patches of light and shadow. Among the shadows and light, a dark figure crept towards the empty church.

Andrew paused at the side door. He gave the handle a twist and pushed open the door and stepped inside.

The sanctuary of St. Ambrose reminded Andrew of the grand churches in Europe.

Andrew walked up to the altar. Andrew knelt down to examine it. As he ran his fingers underneath the edge, Andrew suddenly felt the recessed switch that Father Michael told him about. He pushed it and a secret panel opened in the middle of the back of the altar.

Andrew crawled through the opening and into the darkness. Using his hands and feet as a guide, Andrew descended the stairs which led him to a small chamber. Andrew felt his way around the room. On the wall, he found oil lanterns hanging on the wall. A little further, his hand found a light switch. Andrew wondered if it would work after all these years. He gave the switch a twist. There was a quick spark of electricity and the light bulb filaments began to glow with life! That's when Andrew noticed not only one, but three branches of passageways leading away from the room he was in. Andrew knelt down to examine the dirt floor. He was looking for any signs as to which passageway was used. Since the dirt was compacted, it yielded no signs. Andrew decided to take the one on the right first. He grabbed one of the lanterns just in case, lit it, and headed down the passageway.

The passageway was carved out of the surrounding dirt and was lined with bricks and cedar posts for support. The wood smelled musty and looked rotted. The mortar between the bricks was starting to crumble and chip away. A string of clear light bulbs ran along the wall.

Andrew walked cautiously down the passageway. He hadn't gone too far, when it came to a dead end. A brick wall had been built to block off the passage. Andrew turned around and headed back to the room he had just come from. As soon as Andrew got there, he took the passageway on the left.

Sheriff Delsmann arrived at JFK Prep with several deputies in tow. They blocked the entrance with their cars and immediately exited. The groundskeeper had phoned in a report of someone entering the St. Ambrose chapel. Talia was almost certain it was Andrew. She more than suspected that he in fact, had discovered the bug on the balloon bouquet. Why else would he have spoken in French? This time his rouse wouldn't work and also, he would not escape.

Talia and her deputies quietly approached St. Ambrose chapel. She motioned for all of them to take a knee. She laid out her plan. Talia explained that she wanted half of them to secure all exits from both the chapel and the dormitory. If they did see Knight trying to leave, they were to use maximum force to apprehend him. Talia instructed the remaining deputies to come with her and search the chapel. When she had found out that Andrew lost the deputy trailing him, she was extremely upset. She ripped the deputy up one side and down the other. Finally, after she had calmed down, Talia went to see Father Michael. She confronted him and threatened to put him in jail for obstruction and aiding and abiding Knight in his criminal activities. Talia had also threatened to inform the archdiocese with the news of his recent activities. Father Michael finally succumbed and told her what he had told Andrew about the secret entrance to the catacombs. Talia thanked him, and then issued a warning that he was never again to help Knight. Talia had all deputies did a weapons check. Once she was satisfied, she led her group into the chapel as the others went off to secure all the entrances. Talia smiled because at some point today, Andrew Knight would be wearing a pair of handcuffs.

Hidden among the shadows of the bushes and trees, Talia and her men were being watched. She watched with great intent as Talia and her men entered the chapel. She would have to be stopped. It was a risk, but one they were willing to take. No one was going to be allowed to discover the unholy ones that were locked away. With immense stealth, they moved along the safety of the shadows. She quickly stopped and withdrew behind the trees as they saw the deputy standing guard. In silent precision she withdrew the crossbow and notched the arrow. Taking aim, she fired! The arrow whizzed with deadly accuracy though the air, finally finding its mark. The deputy fell to the ground, an arrow protruding through his throat. There was no cry for help. From the shadows, she moved to the door and entered inaudibly into the chapel.

The passageway on the left also proved to be a dead end. Andrew was now on his way down the center one. All of the light bulbs had been removed about fifty feet down the passageway. Andrew had to use the lantern to see the rest of the way. He had tried several doors, all which were unlocked. Most of them were storage rooms with dust covered shelves and cans of vegetables. One of the rooms that Andrew found kind of interesting had several book shelves and a couple of desks. It was probably a library of some sort. He had examined some of the books. Most were of a religious nature.

Andrew left the room. He was about some hundred feet from the beginning of the passageway. That's when a faint moaning sound was heard. Andrew shone his lantern in that direction. There he saw a heavy wooden door. When he tried it, Andrew discovered it was locked! Andrew set the lantern down. Andrew removed the lock pick kit from his pocket and once he selected the proper tool, started on the lock. Andrew smiled when the lock finally 'clicked', indicating that he had succeeded in opening it. Andrew retrieved the lantern and after opening the door, shone it into a rather large room. That's when he saw several bodies lying on the floor.

Andrew stepped through the opening and knelt beside the first body. It was a boy with thick black hair and he had several earrings in his left ear with a beaded chain running to one in his nose. The boy wasn't moving, so Andrew checked for a pulse. He was alive. Andrew moved onto the next. He was a rather thin kid with frizzy black hair. His breathing was shallow. Andrew rose and strode over to the three girls lying huddled together more towards the back of the chamber. Andrew again knelt down putting the lantern next to him. All three girls, one whom was dressed gothic, and the others whom were dressed Victorian, but wore the black makeup and hair like the rest, were also breathing slowly. Andrew recalled the descriptions that were given to him by their families. The boy with the frizzy hair was Jazz and the one with the earrings was Seth. The two Victorian girls must be Melissa and Gabriel. The girl Andrew was next to was Amber, and lying beside her, was Chad. Andrew retrieved his lantern and relit it. Andrew took out his phone. He had no signal. He put his phone away and continued the search. Andrew walked down the passageway and hadn't gone very far when he saw another door.

Talia and her deputies spread out in standard formation as they approached the altar. They quietly and carefully made their way amongst the row of dust covered and rotting wood pews.

The choir balcony offered the perfect overview of the pew rows below. It was the perfect view for a hunter to have of their prey. She loaded the crossbow and took aim at the nearest deputy.

Talia and her deputies abruptly stopped at the end of the rows of pews. She turned to instruct them, when the deputy furthest to the rear lurched forward, gurgling. The next thing Talia knew, he crashed into the pews. She held up her hand for the others to stay in place and ran over to check on him. Talia shone her light on the man. There was blood dripping from his mouth, and an arrow protruding from his neck!

"He's been shot!" Talia screeched, and watched in horror as her other deputies were attacked. She dove for cover. Talia heard one of the deputies return fire. The bullets struck the wood of the balcony just above her. Talia peeked up in time to see him stand to take aim at whoever it was on the balcony. There was a soft whizzing sound. He flew backwards on the pew with a thunderous crash that echoed across the wall of the chapel. Talia rechecked her weapon. She shone her light towards the back of the chapel. There she saw a set of stairs leading to the balcony. Talia swallowed hard, she reached for her radio, and called for assistance. The other deputies acknowledged they were on the way. She warned them to take extreme caution when entering the chapel and that there was a shooter in the balcony.

Chloe awoke when she heard what sounded like footsteps coming from somewhere in the dark. She nudged Roxanne. Chloe heard Roxanne stir and finally she too was awake.

"What is it?" Roxanne asked groggily.

"I heard a noise," Chloe answered.

"Who is it?" Roxanne asked worriedly. "Is it the person who brought us in here?"

"I don't know," Chloe replied. They listened further.

Andrew put the lantern down and tried the door handle. It was not locked. He stepped back and with great force; kicked open the door. The sound of aged wood cracking filled the passageway. Andrew rushed into the room with lantern in hand. The smell of death immediately fell over him. Andrew took out a handkerchief and covered his mouth. As he shone his light across the room, Andrew saw several skeletons. There must have been over a dozen. Andrew stepped further into the room. Scrawled in blood on one of the walls were the words 'Tod für die Untoten!' Andrew translated it aloud, "Death for the Undead." He felt ill to his stomach. Andrew left the room and closed the door. He bowed his head in silent prayer for the souls of those who he had found in the room. Andrew continued on his way. He hoped to find Chloe and Roxanne soon.

The holy ground of St. Ambrose chapel was covered in blood. Talia and her men had stormed the balcony. They were not prepared for the blood lust unleashed upon them. As soon as they cleared the stairs, the killer attacked. With deadly accuracy and unyielding fury the blades of steel slashed through the frailty of flesh. Talia and her deputies didn't even have a chance to get off a shot. She watched her deputy's fall down one by one before her eyes. Talia somehow had managed to escape back down into the chapel, but dropped her service piece along the way. She was unarmed. Talia crawled on her belly beneath the pews. She found refuge behind the pulpit.

Andrew stopped at the final door. It also was unlocked. He opened it quickly and rushed inside.

Chloe and Roxanne ducked as they saw a darkened figure rush into the room.

"Who are you?" Chloe demanded.

"Chloe?" the figure asked. "Is that you?"

"Dad!" Chloe screeched with excitement. She burst out crying.

Andrew shone the light and found a light switch. He flipped the light on, blinding each of them momentarily. Andrew rushed over to his daughter and Roxanne. He loosened them from the ropes. Chloe threw her arms around her dad and smothered him with kisses. Roxanne hugged them both tightly for fear of letting go.

"Who did this to you?" Andrew demanded amongst the shower of affection.

"We never saw who it was," Roxanne said.

Andrew helped them to their feet. They were both a bit unsteady at first, but soon were ready to go. Andrew led the way to where the teenagers were.

"I need you to call the authorities," Andrew explained. "You never saw me, okay?"

"Why?" Chloe asked.

"Sheriff Delsmann must still believe I have amnesia," Andrew further explained. "It's the only way I have the freedom to work on the case. We'll head back to the chapel," Andrew ordered. "Once there, you can call for help." The three of them walked down the passageway. A few minutes later they were in the room beneath the altar.

"Stay here," Andrew ordered. "I'll make sure the coast is clear." He climbed up the steps to the altar.

Talia peered around the pulpit. The hooded figure stood there staring back at her.

"I told you the next time we met it would be the end for you," she said.

"You are responsible for the deaths of law enforcement officers!" Talia shouted.

"Your interference will not be tolerated," she answered drawing the swords from the sheaths. "It is time for you to die."

"You're Night Blade, aren't you?" Talia said.

"I am," Night Blade replied. Night Blade ascended the steps leading to the pulpit and altar. Talia heard Night Blade boot steps come closer. She had no where to run. Talia rose to her knees.

"They will come looking for us," Talia said, with a look of final defiance.

"No one will find you." Night Blade raised both swords.

Talia closed her eyes. But instead of feeling the steel blades strike her down, there was a loud crashing sound and Night Blade cried out in pain. Talia opened her eyes to see Night Blade sprawled face down on the steps. Andrew was standing over Night Blade. But before Talia could speak, Night Blade jumped up and attacked with a vicious spin kick. Andrew dropped down and spun his legs; hitting Night Blade's other leg. Night Blade crashed to the floor again. Night Blade recovered and stood. Andrew made a lunge attack with a flurry of kicks and punches, driving Night Blade down the steps and towards the pews. For every move there after from the Night Blade, Andrew responded with retribution. Night Blade was bent over, trying to recover. Night Blade now stood and faced Andrew.

"This is none of your concern."

"You've killed innocent people."

"They honor the unspeakable creatures of lore."

"They're not vampires!" Andrew shouted angrily. "And you're not a slayer."

"But I am!" Night Blade drew a long bladed knife.

Andrew heard a voice cry out from behind him. He turned to look. Seeing the advantage, Night Blade attacked!

Talia watched them fight and cheered inside for Andrew. The man she hated had now turned out to be her hero. She stood and watched as Andrew and Night Blade talked. Talia gasped as Night Blade pulled a knife. She rushed over and grabbed one of the swords.

"Andrew!" Talia shouted, throwing him the sword.

Andrew saw the sword fly through the air towards him. He managed to grab hold of the handle. Andrew turned in time to see Night Blade rush at him with the knife. He in turn charged at Night Blade. With each lunge of Night Blade's knife, Andrew blocked with a master's proficiency. The clashing of metal resounded through out the chapel.

Chloe and Roxanne emerged from behind the altar. They gasped at the sight of Andrew battling a hooded figure. Chloe was about to rush to her dad's defense, but Roxanne held her back. Instead, using Andrew's phone, they called for help.

Andrew could sense Night Blade's frustration at his ability to anticipate the next move. For with each thrust of Night Blade's knife, Andrew met it with his own. Night Blade turned and bounded in the air landing, with both feet balancing on the back of a pew. Andrew did the same, taking the pew to the right. Their battle continued as they balanced like tight rope walkers. Blades of sharp steel clanged each time they met. Andrew unexpectedly jumped up and with a roundhouse kick, sent Night Blade flying down between the pews with a loud crash. Andrew descended upon Night Blade with the point of the sword, narrowly missing as they rolled beneath the pews. Andrew followed along as Night Blade crawled toward the back of the chapel, safe beneath the sanctuary of the wooden pews. From the last pew, Night Blade emerged and made a dash for the door, but Andrew sprung from the last pew in a mid-air, somersault landing in front of the doorway. Andrew twirled about and blocked Night Blade's escape. Andrew could hear Night Blade's labor breaths. Andrew tossed the blade aside and took up his stance. Night Blade did the same.

"No more weapons," Andrew announced. "Just you and me this time, okay?"

"Agreed," Night Blade replied with a low bow.

Chloe and Roxanne came to Talia's aid. The strain must have finally gotten to her and she suddenly passed out.

Night Blade lunged at Andrew with a savage combination of kicks and punches. Andrew was ready and blocked each and every one, with his own. Night Blade dropped to all fours and immediately balancing on her hands, delivered a double roundhouse kick, but Andrew instead jumped up and with both feet slammed into Night Blade's back. Night Blade let out a loud cry as Andrew drove her to the floor. Andrew flipped over and without delay, delivered a spin and snap kick combo, hitting Night Blade in the side of the face. Night Blade's head snapped back as blood expelled from her mouth. Andrew stood back ready. Night Blade arms were weak and she struggled to stand. She looked at Andrew and spat blood on the floor. No one had been able to anticipate their every move. The man that stood before them was unlike anyone they had battled before. Night Blade bowed gracious at first and within a spilt second rushed forth to the stairs leading to the balcony. Andrew, momentarily caught off guard, followed. Just as Andrew got to the top of the stairs, he looked up to see Night Blade grab a choir chair and smash through the large stain glass window. It depicted Jesus being held in the arms of his mother right after he had been taken down from the cross. But now shards of that beautiful window flew out in all directions. Night Blade didn't make a sound and she jumped out the window! Andrew bolted up to the window and he looked down below. Night Blade had miraculous survived by safely landing in the unpacked snow below. When Night Blade saw Andrew looking down, she gave Andrew a quick salute and took off into the darkness. Andrew simply shook his head. He turned around and walked over to one of the cushioned choir chairs. Andrew sat down to catch his breath. His muscles ached and he stretched them out. Next time Night Blade wouldn't get away.

Andrew left the balcony and went back down the stairs. He walked along the main aisle and up to the pulpit area. Talia was awake now. All three women immediately swarmed over Andrew, and smothered him with hugs and kisses.

Talia left them and placed a call for help. She went to check on her fallen men.

Andrew watched as Talia checked on each of her deputies. By the expression on her face, he could tell that they were all dead.

Chloe was relieved that her dad was alive. She could not believe what had all just happened. It all seemed so surreal.

Talia rejoined them and sat down on the steps. The rest followed suit.

The sanctuary was silent now. The peacefulness wrapped around them like a comfortably, warm blanket. It felt good.

Chapter 9

Andrew woke early. It was still dark and the sun was not up yet. Andrew quietly slipped on his robe and tip toed out of the bedroom. Megan was sound asleep and didn't move at all. He crept downstairs and to the kitchen. Andrew made himself a cup of tea and sat down at the breakfast nook. As he sat there drinking his tea, Andrew mulled over all of the past events. First, he started with all of the things that were factual and based on reality. Wyatt was the prime suspect in the brutal murders of the Higgins family. Sheriff Delsmann was attacked that same night. The remaining families of the Ravenclaw coven have gone into hiding. Andrew himself was attacked a few nights later. He believed that it was a member of the Knights of VanHelsing; possible Night Blade or one of the others. Why he or she attacked him is still a mystery at this point. Recently, Sheriff Delsmann and her team of deputies were attacked. They all died at the scene. The teenagers that Andrew found in the catacombs were all recovering nicely, and so were Chloe and Roxanne. The teenagers were from two of the clans in the Ravenclaw coven; the Moore's and the Hancock's. They had snuck out without their parents knowing about it. Once the families realized that they were gone, Vlad Ravenclaw notified the authorities. Andrew, with the support of both the Sheriff's department and the Bayport police had setup to interview the teenagers and Vlad Ravenclaw at the safe house in a few days. In the mean time, Andrew needed to find an expert on vampire covens, and also the Knights of VanHelsing.

Andrew got up and refilled his cup with more Earl Grey tea. He sat back down at the breakfast nook table. Andrew took a sip of tea, drinking in its aroma and relaxing liquids. Andrew contacted his friend at the Bayport Herald. She told Andrew about a feature story that the paper had done last year on author, Kara Sadler. This Kara Sadler had presented information from her book at a conference sponsored by the police department, local churches, and the healthcare community. The book she had written was titled Vampire Chronicles. The book was about the subculture of vampirism and its affects on adults and teenagers. Andrew finished his tea. He got up and put the dishes in the sink. Andrew left the kitchen to go back up stairs.

Andrew walked down the hall. He stopped and opened the door to his office. Andrew slipped inside closing the door behind him. He sat down at his desk and turned on the computer. First, Andrew went on Google and did a search for Kara Sadler. He had over a thousand hits. Andrew thought for a second and went to the 'free people search'. He keyed in her name.

It came up with four Kara Sadler's. There were one in Tennessee, Oklahoma, Illinois and Ohio. His friend at the paper had mentioned Kara Sadler was from somewhere in Illinois. He wrote down the address and phone number. Andrew logged off there and went to the Chicago Police department home page. Andrew recalled that Talia was a detective in the Chicago police department prior to becoming Sheriff. He copied down the phone number. Andrew picked up the phone and pressed the number. He waited for a minute or two and when the operator answered, Andrew said, "Detective Flannery, please." Andrew listened further, and repeated, "He gets off at 12 a.m." Andrew was about to hang up when the operator asked him a question. "Andrew Knight," Andrew replied. "We go back a ways." Andrew listened further, and said, "Yeah I know about Riley's. Just tell him that Andrew will meet him there at midnight, tonight." Andrew hung up the phone. He shut down the computer and went back to bed.

Father Michael rose when his alarm went off. He got out of bed and dressed for his usual early morning walk. Father Michael went downstairs of the rectory and grabbed the keys. He was out the door in a matter of minutes and on his way down Marshall Street.

Father Michael loved the early morning sounds and sweet smells wafting through the air. As he walked along, the aroma from Hartman's Bakery filled his nostrils. It made his mouth water. He could smell fresh coffee being brewed for another day at the Chat Room Café.

As he was passing by Washington Park, Father Michael stopped abruptly as a hooded figure sprung from the bushes.

"Hello Father Michael." Night Blade greeted him with a bow.

"What do you want?" Father Michael asked.

"We want you to stop looking for Wyatt," a second voice came from behind. Father Michael spun around to face them. "He didn't kill the Higgins'," Star Blade said.

"We need to talk to him," Father Michael answered.

"We already have," a third voice announced.

"And you must be Moon Blade," Father Michael turned to his right. He saw the third hooded figure. Moon Blade bowed with arms extended.

"His mother has hired a private investigator to find him," Father Michael answered.

"We know," Moon Blade answered. "It's Andrew Knight."

"Then you know that he will find him," Father Michael said, proudly.

"We want you to call him off." Moon Blade took a few steps closer. "Before someone gets hurt, or before Knight gets hurt."

"Why did you hurt those teenagers?" Father Michael changed subjects.

"They and the others do unspeakable things. Just like those centuries before them, so they have to be punished," Star Blade spoke first. "They drink human blood and practice unholy rituals."

"So we have fought against this plague for centuries," Moon Blade spoke next. "And will continue to do so."

"Its murder," Father Michael rebuked. "And that's a sin against God."

"We do God's work," Night Blade shot back. "And by His will, we punish those who are vampires." Night Blade moved closer and so did the others. Night Blade drew her swords first. Moon Blade and Star Blade did the same. They raised their swords, crossing them above Father Michael's head.

"Tell Knight to back off," Star Blade commanded.

"Or he will get hurt," Moon Blade added.

"Andrew handled Night Blade quite well," Father Michael smirked.

"He may have defeated me," Night Blade got up in Father Michaels face. "But he is no match for the three of us, nor any of our fellow knights. If he pursues this further, Andrew Knight will die!" All sheathed their blades and instantly disappeared.

Father Michael finally breathed a sigh of relief. He was too shaken and immediately returned to the rectory. As soon as Father Michael got inside, he made a call.

Nick walked into Riley's Blues Club. The place was packed. Nick strode up to the bar, took off his leather jacket and lay in across the stool. He nodded at the pretty girl behind the bar and she nodded back. Nick took out a pack of smokes and lit one up. A few minutes later the girl brought him his drink, a double whiskey on the rocks. It had been a real bad day at work. Most of the morning was spent testifying in court and he had mounds of reports to fill out.

Nick slammed down his drink and ordered another. He lit up another smoke. Nick spun around and scanned the crowd. He liked Riley's, a blues club, because it was a great place to hang out after work.

Nick finished his second drink and was about to order another when someone tapped him on the shoulder. He spun a round on the stool to see Andrew standing there.

"Hey Nick," Andrew smiled.

"Knight, you son of a b---" Nick hopped off his stool and gave Andrew a bear hug. "How the hell are you?"

"I'm fine," Andrew grinned. His mood suddenly changed, "We need to talk."

"What's up?" Nick ordered them each a drink. "Why are you really here?"

"I'll explain," Andrew answered as Nick handed him the glass of scotch.

"Follow me." Nick led the way. They walked through the main area and finally found a secluded booth near the back.

They slid into the seats across from each other. Nick offered Andrew a smoke, which he took. Nick lit his, then Andrew's.

"So, why all the mystery s---?" Nick asked as he sipped his drink.

"Do you know a Talia Delsmann?" Andrew took a drink from his glass.

"Yeah, I know her," Nick answered. "We worked together on the south side. Why?"

"She's the Sheriff for Bayport County now," Andrew explained. He quickly finished his drink, but it was Nick that finished his thought.

"What about her?" Nick pressed further.

"Were there any cases that stick out in your mind," Andrew asked. "You know, anything involving vampires?"

"What the hell?" Nick choked on his drink. "Vampires? Are you kidding me?"

"Just answer the question," Andrew insisted.

"Yeah, there was one case," Nick recalled. "The department had received a great deal of missing person reports for several months. There were no solid leads. All of them had disappeared under mysterious circumstances. During that time, we were asked to investigate an abandoned house on South Lake Park Avenue in Oakland. The neighbors had been complaining about noises coming from the house." He paused and flagged down a waitress to order more drinks. She took their order and left. "When we first got to …" Nick stopped when the waitress returned. "We never found those responsible. It was like they were f--- ghost, shadows. There were other reports all over Chicago. They even set up a task force, but nothing came out of it. We never found those responsible."

"Is there more?" Andrew pressed.

"Yeah," Nick answered. "There's more to it. You see, one night after work we came to Riley's for some drinks. It had been a really rough day for us and we needed to unwind." Nick paused and took a drink. He cleared his throat and continued, "Anyway we got really wasted and that's when Talia told me her secret."

"What secret?" Andrew curiously inquired.

"She told me that at one time she was a, s--- I can't even say it now," Nick cursed. "She told me that she had been a slayer in her past. She told me she was a vampire slayer and member of this secret society. Talia confessed the horrible things they had done. Well, let me tell you I was f--- blown away." Nick swallowed down the last of his drink. He lit a cigarette and inhaled deeply before continuing. "I told her that partners don't hold s--- like that back. I mean we depend on each other and when you find out something like this, well it f--- blows you away. Know what I mean?"

"I know," Andrew swallowed hard this time.

"Talia even told me that she still had all the stuff," Nick continued. "You know, the outfit, body armor, weapons and s---.like that."

"I see," Andrew said, in shock. He realized that it was Talia that attacked him while at the Higgins home that night, and not the others.

"So what do we do now?" Nick asked, as he extinguished his cigarette.

"I want you to take me to the house on Lake Avenue," Andrew finally answered.

"It's been a year since." Nick was visibly shaking.

"Take me there." Andrew insisted.

The two men finished their drinks and they left.

The abandoned two-story mansion with white columns had been boarded up poorly on the first floor. There were uncovered broken windows on the second floor. The black iron fence was standing tall, but was spattered with patches of rust.

Nick parked the car. They both got out. Andrew glanced up and down the street. It appeared that they were alone, but he couldn't shake the feeling that someone was watching them.

Nick led the way up the steps and to the front door. He stopped to look at Andrew, whom nodded that they proceed. Nick opened the screen door and gave the main door a shove with his shoulder. The simple lock on the door easily gave way. The two men stepped inside.

It appeared that some squatters had been living in the house for quite some time. Andrew surmised that they left in a hurry as they left blankets and personal items behind. Andrew surveyed the room with his eyes. Paint was peeling off the walls and cracks spread out across the ceiling.

"What did you find then?" Andrew looked at Nick.

"Things seemed pretty normal on the outside when we got here," Nick began. He nervously scanned the room. Andrew thought it was as if some ghost from the past was still haunting Nick.

"What did Talia do?"

"She freaked out, man and took off on me," Nick answered. "We immediately called for back-up and got out the house."

"What was it?" Andrew pressed further.

"There were dead bodies everywhere." Nick pointed at the floor. He looked at Andrew with tear-filled eyes. "There were more in the basement."

"Take me there," Andrew asked.

"No way man," Nick stood frozen.

"Then I'll go," Andrew left as Nick stayed behind.

Andrew walked down a short hallway before finally coming to the door that led to the basement. He flipped on the flashlight, grabbed the handle and pulled the door open. A wall of foul air hit Andrew making him gag for a few minutes. Andrew took out a handkerchief from his pants pocket and covered his nose and mouth. He immediately started to descend into the abyss.

Nick dried his eyes.

"Get a grip man," he scolded himself. "You're a f---cop for God sake."

Nick took his flashlight and shone it around the room. He was about to turn when he felt a blow to the back of the head.

Andrew cautiously made his way across the dark basement area. He shone his light down on the floor. There were still blood stains on the concrete. Andrew scanned the wall with the light and suddenly froze. The hairs on the back of his neck stood up and an icy chill washed over him. In the light he saw the words 'Tod zu den unheiligen' *Death to the unholy*, scrawled in blood on the wall. Everyone in the house had been victims of the Knights of VanHelsing. Andrew hurried back up stairs.

When he got to the living room, Nick was lying on the floor unconscious. Andrew whirled around just in time to block the blow meant for his head. He followed with a fore fist punch to the hooded figure's chest, but it had no affect. Instead they struck Andrew squarely on the jaw which sent him reeling backwards, crashing into the wall.

"You're not Night Blade," Andrew stood wiping the blood from his mouth. His punch had no affect because the body armor they wore. "Who are you?"

"I'm Trinity Blade," he said. "And I'm a Knight of VanHelsing."

"How many are there of you here?" Andrew asked.

"You mean in Chicago," Trinity Blade answered.

"Yeah," Andrew spat out blood.

"There are only three of us, no more," Trinity Blade explained. "No less."

"So where are the others?" Andrew asked.

"Even if I tell you, it won't do you any good," he voiced a smirk.

"Just tell me." Andrew shrugged his shoulders.

"They're out hunting." Trinity Blade was proud.

"Where?" Andrew continued.

"Jackson Park," Trinity Blade replied.

"Thanks," Andrew smirked this time.

"Why are you smiling?" Trinity Blade started to say. Nick smashed him across the back of the head and Trinity Blade slumped to the floor.

"Take that you a---," Nick cursed.

"You call in the troops," Andrew bolted towards the door, "I'm going hunting."

"Wait!" Nick called out, but it was too late. Andrew was already gone.

Nick knelt down and placed a pair of handcuffs on Trinity Blade. "We finally got you mother---," Nick said as he leaned closer to the unconscious man's masked head.

The cab pulled into the parking lot of Jackson Park, just off of East Hayes Drive. The lone occupant paid the cabbie and thanked him. As soon as the cab took off, Andrew headed towards Wooded Island.

A small crowd was gathered in a picnic area a few yards from the west lagoon. A few were standing and talking; others were seated on the picnic tables. Shortly, three young girls joined the crowd. One by one, each girl extended their uncovered arms, which bore scars from before. One of the crowd, a tall, and lanky youth drew a knife and made a fresh cut. One by one the others gathered for the feast and drank of the warm blood. The blood dolls arched their heads back almost as if in ecstasy.

Suddenly, a scream from the group raised the alarm. Everyone else turned to see two hooded figures rushing towards them. "Run!" the lanky youth bellowed out his warning. The three girls took off screaming, as the rest bolted to get away. The boy turned to face the hooded figures, and brandished his knife. One of the hooded figures drew a sword and jumped in the air with a somersault, landing behind the youth. With one swift thrust of the blade, the boy crumbled to the snowy ground in a puddle of his own blood.

"After them!" Alpha Blade shouted, before heading after three teenagers running towards the west lagoon.

"I am," Omega Blade shot back, and took off after the rest heading east.

Three girls were huddled together beneath a large evergreen tree. The branches were low to the ground and offered protection, or so they thought. One of them turned around to see Alpha Blade sprinting towards them. The girls left the safety of the tree and made a dash towards the path. For some unexplained reason, they suddenly stopped and turned around. Alpha Blade was sprawled face down on the ground. A dark haired stranger they had never seen before was standing over Alpha Blade. He had tossed the swords a safe distance away. The girls walked up to the man. He smiled at them.

"My name is Andrew," Andrew calmly said to the girls. "You're no longer in danger. You can go home now."

"Thank you," the girls said, and took off running.

When the rest of the group got to the west lagoon, there were areas open of water. They had no where to go and were trapped. Each one turned around to see Omega Blade standing a few feet away.

"Stop hunting us!" the pretty brunette screamed.

"We haven't done anything wrong!" a boy with curly golden blonde hair added.

"Leave us alone!" a slender red haired girl's voice joined them.

"Ihr seid die unheilige, die Söhne u Töchter Draculas," Omega Blade recited his matra, calling them sons and daughters of Dracula. He drew his swords. "Sie haben gegen Gott und Menschen gesündigt." He accused them of sins against our God and man.

"You're insane," the red head said. She shouted, "Speak in English!"

"Es ist zeit zu sterben!" Omega Blade raised his swords and said it was time to die.

"Hände weg von den kindern," a voice came from the dark.

Omega Blade spun around to see a dark haired stranger. Each of the teenagers watched as he strode towards all of them.

"Mit mir sie kämpfen, nicht mit den Kindern," Andrew announced that Omega blade leave the teenagers alone and the fight was with Andrew. He continued the sins against God and humanity was with Omega Blade, "Die Sünden gegen den Gott und Menschheit sind deine, nicht der anderen."

"The sins are theirs," Omega Blade quoted back. "I have no quarrels with you..."

"Knight, Andrew Knight," Andrew bowed respectively.

"My fight is with them," Omega Blade gestured towards the teenagers.

"You kill innocent, unarmed men, women and children," Andrew stepped closer. "You have a choice, either surrender now, or face the consequences."

"My brothers will be here soon," Omega proudly announced.

"I don't think so," Andrew said as he produced the swords he had taken, and that were hidden behind his back.

"You die!" Omega Blade screeched and rushed towards Andrew.

Andrew jumped in the air. He landed and smashed into Omega Blade with a spin kick. Omega Blade stumbled a bit. He recovered and swung his swords at Andrew, who blocked the attack. The teenagers watched as the two men parlayed and thrusted their blades of steely death, each trying to gain the upper hand. Finally, in one finishing move, Andrew did a backwards flip over Omega Blade's head, landing behind him. Andrew knew that Omega Blade was wearing body armor, so he slashed the back of the man's legs. Omega Blade screamed out in pain and stumbled to the ground and let go of his swords. He rolled around in agony as blood stained the snow. Andrew tossed the swords aside and drew his Beretta. He walked over and with his foot, rolled Omega Blade on his back. Andrew pointed his Beretta at Omega Blade.

"You can't kill me like this," Omega Blade shouted at Andrew. "I have my rights!"

"It ends now," Andrew said calmly and pulled the trigger. The sound of the shot broke the stillness.

Jackson Park was swarming with police by now. They had discovered the body of the lanky boy by the picnic area. About fifty yards from there, Nick found a hooded figure lying unconscious on the ground. They woke him and placed the man in custody. As they were about to leave, Nick heard a gun shot. He ran down the path towards the west lagoon. Several officers followed him.

When Nick came to a clearing by the lagoon, he saw Andrew standing over a hooded figure lying on the ground. There were two girls and a guy huddled together crying. Nick drew his gun and ran up.

"Put the f--- gun down," Nick cursed at Andrew. "Step away!"

Andrew put his gun down and stepped back.

"Yeah, he stopped that man from killing us," the curly blonde haired boy added.

"Thank you, Mister Knight," The red haired girl smiled at Andrew. She walked over and hugged him tightly. Andrew slipped his arms around her and told her that everything would okay now.

Nick kneeled down and exaimed the man. He was relieved that Andrew hadn't shot him. Nick rolled the man over and put handcuffs on him. He hoped that the arrest of these three so called 'Knights' would finally put all of this to an end.

Nick walked up to Andrew and offered him a cigarette. Andrew graciously accepted. He really needed one after his fight.

Neither one said a word, and just stood their and smoked their cigarettes. It would be dawn soon and with it the promise of a new day. Andrew hoped it would be a good one. So did Nick.

Chapter 10

The bright sun rose from the eastern sky dressed in hues of red, orange and yellow. Its light and warmth filtered into the room. Andrew woke, stretching every aching bone in his body. He got out of bed and strode into the bathroom. Andrew stopped to look; his upper torso was covered with bruises. He continued on and got in the shower. The soothing waters felt good. Andrew thought about his upcoming meeting today with author, Kara Sadler. He had done some further research on her last night. Andrew also had read her book <u>Vampire Chronicles</u>. She had gone into seclusion once her book was published, and that was one year ago. Andrew also found out that Kara lived in German castle that was transported stone by stone to somewhere in the outskirts of Woodstock. He further read that the castle was impenetrable and had the most up-to-date security systems in place. The question foremost on Andrew's mind was, why did she need it? What was she afraid of?

Andrew finished his shower and grabbed a towel after turning the water off. He left and went back into the room. Andrew let the towel slip to the floor and strode to the closet. He picked out his favorite navy blue suit and laid it on the bed. Andrew opened the package of a brand new, white, dress shirt. Once dressed, Andrew put on a pair of black dress shoes. The room phone rang. Andrew picked it up and asked who it was. They told him that there was a car waiting for him in front of the hotel. Andrew thanked the desk clerk and hung up the phone. Once he was off the phone, Andrew left to go and meet his ride.

When Andrew exited the hotel, there was a black limo with tinted windows waiting for him. As Andrew approached the car, the rear door opened unassisted. As soon as he was seated, the door closed. The driver of the limo took off effortlessly into the early morning traffic.

The interior of the limo was decorated with black leather and silver fixtures. There was a bottle of champagne chilling and a single glass. There was a note attached to the bottle. Andrew removed the note and read 'With my compliments, Kara'. Andrew tossed the note aside and opened the bottle. He poured himself a glass. Andrew knew it was early, but why should he waste a perfectly good bottle of champagne. Besides, he did not want to disappoint his hostess. Andrew downed the glass of champagne. Suddenly, he felt ill and things began to look blurry. He tossed aside the glass. It was laced with some kind of drug. Before Andrew could call out, he passed out cold.

Things still were a bit blurry when Andrew opened his eyes. He closed them again, trying to focus and to shake off the affects of the drug. When Andrew opened his eyes again, the room was much clearer now.

The room looked like something directly out of Camelot. Intricate tapestries were draped on each of the four walls, the furniture dark and heavy. A fire was roaring in the large stone hearth. And there amongst it all was Kara Sadler, seated in a high back leather and wood chair. She did not look the same as the photo on the book jacket. Gone was the golden hair and bright blue eyes; instead her eyes were dark brown and hair the color of night with streaks of red. Andrew further remembered Kara had worn a more conservative taupe skirt with white blouse and matching jacket in that photo. All of that had given way to a wardrobe of black.

Kara smiled at Andrew through sumptuous blood red colored lips, and twirled her hair with a slender finger and nail polish of the same color. A white blouse seductively opened revealed Kara's ample bosom. A black leather vest was loosely tied; knee high leather boots and pants completed the look. Andrew knew he was in trouble.

"How are you?" Kara's voice sang to him.

"I'm fine," Andrew replied, sharply. "What was in the champagne?"

"I had to keep the location of my home a secret," Kara touched her bottom lip.

"Why?" Andrew asked curiously.

"Since my book came out, well as you might imagine there are people who are quite upset with me," Kara gestured with her hands. "I've made some powerful enemies."

"It that the reason for all of the security?" Andrew asked the obvious.

"Yes," Kara gazed at Andrew intently.

"In your book you talked about several things." Andrew changed the subject. "One of them was about the Ravenclaw coven, specifically the Higgins. The other was the Knights of VanHelsing." Andrew went further. "Isn't it a strange coincidence that the Higgins family was murdered and that the Knights of VanHelsing are after you?"

"What makes you say that?" Kara scoffed with the wave of her slender hand.

"In your book you talked about the centuries old feud between those practicing vampirism and the Knights of VanHelsing," Andrew explained. He looked at her intensely, "You interviewed the Higgins family along with the others from the clan. You even interviewed Ravenclaw himself. In the book you describe him as a 'brooding monster ready to feed his blood lust at any moment', is that not true?"

"It is true," Kara answered coolly. "I even took part of a blood ritual. It was the only way I could truly understand why they do it."

"You also interviewed one of the Knights of VanHelsing, right?" Andrew continued.

"Yes," Kara voice turned somber, almost to a whisper. Andrew wondered if it were out of respect or out of fear. "I interviewed the one called Moon Blade.

She explained to me, the history of the Knights of VanHelsing. The order had its origins in the Ore Mountains of Germany. There is a secluded castle nestled high in the mountains called Gothica. All of the Knights trained there and then assigned specific areas in a country."

"And there are only three, no more, or less," Andrew added.

"How do you know that?" Kara was shocked.

"I fought two of them in a Chicago park last night," Andrew answered. "One of them recited the mantra for to me."

"And you survived?" Kara was still shocked.

"I survived." Andrew forced a grin.

Kara stood up. She glided towards him as if skating on ice. Kara stretched out her hand towards Andrew. "Please come with me." Kara said. Andrew took her hand and stood up from the chair. Kara's hand felt warm, almost hot. She smiled, and revealed teeth white as snow. Andrew saw her fangs.

Kara led Andrew out of the great room and into an open air foyer. From there, they took one of the two stair cases which led to the upper rooms. All the while they walked; Kara kept a firm, but gentle hold of Andrew's hand. Soon she stopped them in front of a heavy-looking wooden door. Kara turned the ornate door knob and pushed the door open. The large bedroom was decorated similarly to the rest of the furnishings in the castle.

Kara continued on with Andrew in tow towards the bed. Andrew saw some men's clothing. Black pants and a white shirt, which were laid out on top of the bed. At the foot of the bed was a pair of black boots.

"I want you to dress for dinner," was all Kara said. She left Andrew standing there and walked out of the room, and closed the door behind her. Andrew heard the sound of a key turning. He was locked in!

"Watch it," Andrew scolded and also reminded himself. "She's up to something."

Andrew walked over to the dark maroon, heavily curtained, window. He drew aside the curtain. The window in the room faced toward the west. The sun was low in the sky, painted with shades of fire. It would be dark soon. Andrew wondered what the night had in store for him. He let the curtain loose and it swooned back in place. Andrew reached inside his suit coat and took out his phone. He was surprised that Kara let him keep it. Andrew slid the cover open and was immediately disappointed. There was no signal. He walked around the room, but it did not change. Andrew put the phone away, he would try later. Andrew returned to the bed and removed his clothing. He put on the clothing that Kara had laid out for him. He finished it off with the boots. Andrew walked over to the full length mirror. He looked like someone out of a vampire movie. Andrew left and sat down in the leather chair by the bed. The only thing he could do was to wait for Kara to release him from the room. He was not happy about it.

The banquet room was aglow with candle-filled crystal chandeliers. The long, wooden table was dressed like a bride on her wedding day with white linen and accents of silver. White roses, seemingly dipped in the color of blood, were arranged in several bouquets on the table. Place setting of fine china and crystal long-stemmed wine glasses were set across from each other at one end of the table of an intimate dinner for two.

Andrew entered the banquet room and took his place at the table. Kara had not arrived as of yet. An older woman, dressed as a servant and with gray hair tied up in a bun, brought in a bottle of wine. Andrew thanked her. She said nothing, not even a smile. Andrew opened the bottle with the cork screw and let it breathe for a couple of minutes. He was about to pour, when Kara made her appearance.

Kara had on a strapless black, flowing gown. Her fair skin was accentuated with a black onyx layered necklace. Kara's lips matched her fingernails which were a shade of dark green with diamond accents. Her long hair was neatly swept up and held in place with a diamond encrusted hair comb.

Andrew swallowed hard and stood up to help Kara to her chair. The scent of her intoxicating perfume filled his senses. Andrew did his best to shake off the affects as he seated Kara and afterward re-took his own seat. He poured each of them a glass of wine. Andrew handed Kara hers and was about to take a drink. He paused and Kara noticed.

"Trust me," Kara smirked slyly and raised the glass to her lips.

"Of course," Andrew raised his glass as well.

"To unexpectedness," Kara toasted and immediately took a sip.

"Salute," Andrew said as he also took a sip.

The older woman returned with the first course. She set before each one a bowl of soup and a basket of dark rye bread. Kara offered up the basket to Andrew and he took a piece of bread. Kara took one and set the basket aside. Andrew tasted the soup. It was delicious beef soup. Kara tore off some bread and paused for a moment. Andrew stared as Kara opened her lips and seductively slipped the bread in her mouth. He quickly focused on his own, but Kara smiled devilishly.

"You're a private investigator?"

"Yes," Andrew answered.

"Do you like it?" Kara asked. "I mean is it what you've always wanted to do?"

"Yes," Andrew answered again.

"Not much for conversation this evening," Kara teased with a seductiveness look in her eyes. She found Andrew extremely handsome and was attracted to him. It had been a long time since she was intimate with someone. Kara had noticed the wedding band on Andrew's finger, but it didn't matter. He was hers for at least this night.

"What made you want to write about vampires?" Andrew asked, pushing his empty bowl aside. "Why is there this fascination with it?"

"I think it is the idea of eternal romance; to live forever," Kara answered. She drank some wine. "I wrote the book to let people know that this whole culture exists and has done so for centuries. It is a fascinating world of loyalty, romance, and a respect for life."

"And now you are part of that world." Andrew drank some more wine.

"As they say, my transformation is complete." Kara lips spread into a sly grin.

"And the Knights of VanHelsing are after you because you revealed them to the world and they no longer can act in secret," Andrew said. He poured some more wine. He was about to go one, when Kara's servant came in and removed the empty bowls. She returned a short time later with the main course of roasted lamb, braised red potatoes and glazed medallion carrots. Andrew could have dined on the aroma alone. But he was starving and immedatedly dove in. Kara ate a fork full of potatoes as she watched Andrew eat his fill. She was aroused by the way he moved. Kara dipped her fingers in the glass of wine and ran them over her lips. She was no longer hungry for dinner, but instead wanted to feast upon Andrew.

Kara and Andrew had retired from the banquet room to the more intimate surroundings of her bedroom chamber. The flames from the fire danced across the logs burning in the hearth. A small round table with two linen cloths and a knife was surrounded by two chairs with Andrew in one and Kara in the other.

Kara had let her hair down and was tousled about her shoulders. She was completely entranced with Andrew and hoped he felt the same about her. If it was his desire to have her, Kara was willing to give in with all her heart and soul.

Andrew watched as Kara effortlessly rose from her chair. She walked over and stood in front of him. Kara undid the back of her dress and let it cascade to the floor. Her body glistened in the firelight. Kara stepped out of her dress and approached the table. She picked up the knife. Andrew quickly stood and took his place behind Kara. Her chest heaved with anticipation. Andrew slipped his one arm around her waist and drew her closer to him. Kara could feel his warm breath as it drifted down her neck. Andrew leaned closer and kissed Kara's shoulder. Her body tensed with anticipation and it was consuming her. Kara tingled as Andrew's other hand massaged her shoulder blade. She finally heard him murmur, "There it is." Kara felt a slight twinge of pressure. She looked at Andrew and seconds later closed her eyes. Kara went limp in Andrew's arms. Andrew lifted her up and laid Kara on top of the bed. Andrew drew back the covers and put Kara underneath. He recovered her. Andrew leaned down and kissed Kara on the forehead. She would be unconscious for several hours. Years ago he had traveled to China to learn kyusho jitsu. He studied under a kyusho jitsu master. The old master had taught him the pressure points to use for both defense and attack. Kara was comsumed with seducing him, and she never suspected that he was on to his game from the moment he arrived. Andrew felt bad, but it was the only way he could explore the rest of the castle. As far as he knew there was only the one servant. Now she could possibly also be the chauffer, but if not, he would have to be extra careful. Andrew gently caressed Kara's soft check and took off.

Andrew cautiously walked down the hallway. There were three more rooms beside Kara's on the second floor of the castle. He tried the second door on the left. It was not locked. Andrew opened the door and slipped inside. He was in the library. There were floor to ceiling book shelves on three of the walls. On the other was a massive window with no curtains. In the middle of the room were a retangular wooden table and four chairs.

Andrew ran his hand over the leather bound books as he walked along the premeter of the room. It appeared there was nothing worth looking for, and he was about to leave when the title on the binding of one book in particular caught his attention, <u>The Legend of Abraham VanHelsing</u>. Andrew took the book and sat down at the table. He lit one of the reading lamps and opened the book. According to the author of the book, VanHelsing was a real person and that he did in fact, hunt those who were 'vampires'. It further claimed that Bram Stoker base his book on the true adventures of VanHelsing. From what Andrew read, Vlad the Impaler's Grandson was the first of many 'vampires' and that VanHelsing killed him. Years later, as VanHelsing grew older; he could no longer carry on the fight by himself. So VanHelsing and his son Joseph formed the Knights of VanHelsing. Since his homeland of Holland opposed violence, the VanHelsings purchased a remote castle in the highlands of Germany. There they brought in teachers of all the ancient arts of combat. In fact the book stated that VanHelsing's daughter, Mary, was one of the first Knights. Once trained, a threesome of knights was assigned a territory to protect. For centuries, the Knight of VanHelsing hunted down and killed those who practiced vampirism.

There was a period of time from 1860-1960 were both the Knights and those practicing vampirism, disappeared. According to the book, vampirism experienced a rebirth in the seventies with a man by the name of Vlad Ravenclaw, a direct descendent of Vlad the Impaler. With this resurgence, the Knights of VanHelsing was also reborn. Andrew read further that once you joined the order, you could never leave, and if you did, you were marked for death if your identity was ever discovered. How could such hatred consume someone like this for centuries? The more Andrew learned about all of this, the more surreal it became. Andrew was about to close the book when he noticed the inside of the cover had previously been slit open. Someone had re-taped it to look like the original binding. Andrew used the knife he had removed from Kara's room and carefully split the tape. He found a folded piece of parchment paper. Andrew took paper and opened it up. It was a map of the location of the Knights of VanHelsing castle. The map contained a detailed description of where the castle was located, along with a mark where one could enter the castle undetected. Andrew refolded the map and tucked it in his shirt. He closed the book and quickly put it back in the shelves. Andrew quietly left the library and returned to Kara's room.

Andrew found Kara still unconscious. He walked swiftly and silently over to the bed. Andrew removed his shirt and then his boots. He folded the map and slid it into the toe of one of the boots. Andrew quietly slipped beneath the covers. He thought Kara looked beautiful and peaceful as she lay there. Her full lips were inviting to kiss, but Andrew abstained. Andrew drifted off into sweet slumber.

The next morning Kara woke to find Andrew in her bed. She smiled, remembering Andrew's arms around her. After that it was not so clear. Kara shrugged it off and got out of bed. She walked over to her large walk-in closet. Kara flung open the doors and went inside. She selected a sheer, full length black night gown. Kara slipped in on and left the closet. She saw that Andrew was still asleep. Kara smiled again and left to make them breakfast.

Andrew was aware of Kara's movement even with his eyes closed. He pretended to be asleep. As soon as Kara left the bedroom, Andrew bounded out of bed and over to the phone. He picked up the receiver, and upon hearing a dial tone, Andrew made a call. "Hi Nick, this is Andrew," he said. "I'm with Kara Sadler right now, but will meet you later today." Andrew hung up. He quickly got back in bed.

Kara returned some time later carrying a tray with a plethora of breakfast delights. She put the tray down at the foot of the bed. Kara walked over to Andrew, leaned down and kissed his forehead.

Andrew awoke, yawning and stretching. He smiled at Kara. "Good morning."

"Good morning indeed," Kara smiled back. "Are you hungry?"

"Starved," Andrew said, and sat up.

Kara retrieved the tray and brought it over to him. Andrew took hold of it as Kara came around and joined him in bed. Once she was settled, Andrew set the tray between them. Kara uncovered the first plate. A flavor-filled steam rose to reveal steak and eggs benedict for two. Andrew handed Kara a fork and knife as he took his own. He sliced off a sliver of the tender meat and put it in his mouth. It just melted in a taste explosion.

"Delicious," Andre leaned over and thanked Kara with a kiss on the cheek.

"Thank you," Kara said, blushing.

"Listen Kara," Andrew turned more serious now. "I have come up with a plan."

"What?" Kara asked putting down her own silverware. She had a forlorn look in her eyes as she focused on Andrew. "What kind of plan?"

"I am going to strike at the home base of The Knights of VanHelsing," Andrew put his utensils down.

"You can't do that," Kara's voice strained. "They're too powerful; too many to stop."

"Not if they don't know we are coming," Andrew took hold of Kara's hand and looked deeply into her soulful eyes. "Their blood lust of the destruction of the innocent has to be put to an end." Andrew moved closer. Kara sought his embrace with welcomed desire. "People like you, the Higgins and other who practice vampirism, just want to be left alone to your beliefs; way of life. We all celebrate life in different ways. We all want to live in peace and not fear." Kara rested her head on his chest. She felt the beating of his heart. It was soothing to her. It, for some strange reason, gave her a sense of peace, hope. Something she did not have. Andrew continued. "The Knights of VanHelsing have out lived their usefulness. I'm going to stop them."

"How are you going to do that?' Kara asked lifting her head to look at Andrew.

"I have something to show you," Andrew let go of Kara and got out of bed. She watched him retrieve one of his boots. Kara saw Andrew pull a folded piece of parchment paper out. He climbed back in bed. Andrew unfolded the paper to reveal a map.

"Where did you find this?" Kara asked as she pointed to it.

"I found it in the book The Legend of VanHelsing," Andrew replied.

"I never knew it was there," Kara's face showed her surprise.

"We can use it to find the castle and it all to an end," Andrew refolded it.

"What do you want from me?" Kara asked.

"I have set up a meeting with Detective Nick Flannery, from the Chicago police" Andrew replied.

"What can he do?" Kara further asked.

"Let's just go see him and I'll explain later," Andrew said as he picked up his fork and knife. He sliced off some more of the steak. He put it in his mouth with a moaning sound. Kara laughed and punched him in the arm. Andrew faked a cry of pain and went back to eating. Kara took up her own fork and knife and began to eat her food. She looked at Andrew and thought, today, after all, may just turn out to be a good day.

Nick got up off the sofa when he heard a knock at the door. It was already late in the afternoon.

He peered through the peephole and saw Andrew. But there was someone else with him. All he could see of her was streaked hair and a leather jacket. She looked very pretty.

Nick opened the door.

"How's it going?" he shook Andrew's hand.

"Nick this is Kara Sadler," Andrew introduced her.

"A pleasure." Nick shook hands with Kara. She was more than pretty; she was smoking hot. Andrew and Kara entered Nick's apartment and sat down on the couch.

Nick closed and locked the door. He joined them and sat in the recliner.

"So what's up?" Nick asked.

"You know those guys arrested in the park that night?" Andrew began.

"Yeah," Nick replied. "They're still in custody, waiting for a preliminary hearing."

"They are part of a secret society called the Knights of VanHelsing," Kara spoke up. She unzipped and took of her coat off. Nick's eyes were instantly drawn to her revealing peasant blouse. Kara noticed Nick looking her over. She thought he was striking with his brooding looks. She felt an instant attraction. Kara went on, "They are responsible for countless deaths, but have never been exposed to the light of justice."

"Well, those three in the Cook County jail will be facing justice," Nick announced. He stood up unexpectedly. "I'm sorry," Nick apologized. "Did you want something to drink?" Nick excused himself and went in the kitchen.

"Is he single?" Kara inquired to Andrew.

"He is," Andrew replied.

"Thanks," Kara leaned over and gave Andrew a peck on the cheek.

"Thanks for what," Andrew faked innocence.

"You know," Kara nudged him as Nick returned.

"Here you go." Nick handed them their drinks.

"So what are you planning on doing?" Nick asked settling down. He took a drink from his bottle of beer.

"We have a map of the location of Gothica Castle," Kara said. "Andrew has already contacted the German police. We leave for Berlin in two days. From there we go by train to Zwickau. Gothica Castle is located in the Ore Mountains."

"You're freakin' insane," Nick scoffed.

"I also telephoned Peter at the Bayport police department before coming here to see you," Andrew explained. "Peter told me that a person matching Wyatt's description boarded a plane to O'Hare"

"What do you want from me?" Nick asked pointedly.

"We want you to join us," Kara looked at Nick.

"But they know karate and s--- like that," Nick protested.

"I....we, can teach you some basic moves," Kara stuttered.

"Well, I need to finalize all the arrangements." Andrew rose. He finished his beer and put the empty bottle down. "I'll be back later." Andrew thanked Nick and flashed Kara a quick smile. Nick didn't notice. "See you two later." Andrew left, and closed the door behind him.

"So what now?" Nick was a bit nervous.

"What do you want to do?" Kara flashed Nick a full smile. He saw her fangs.

"We'll think of something," Nick joined Kara on the sofa. He moved closer to her. Nick took a chance and leaned in for kiss. Kara gladly accepted as their lips coupled in a long, breath-taking kiss.

Chapter 11

Talia was watching TV. She was in her comfortable sweats and hair unkept. Talia was munching on a bag of tortilla chips and sipping from a can of diet soda. The door bell rang.

"Are you kidding me?" Talia moaned. She put the chip bag and soda can down on the coffee table. Talia pried herself from the sofa and went to answer the door. She looked through the peep hole. It was Andrew. He looked very nice in his jeans and leather jacket. More importantly, he had food; real food. Andrew had a bag from Cranky Bill's in one hand and a six pack of beer in the other.

"Just a minute," Talia shouted and ran to her bed room. A few minutes later she returned with her hair brushed, wearing jeans and a black four button blouse. Talia opened the door.

"Did I catch you at a bad time?" Andrew asked.

"No, no," Talia stepped back to let him inside. She could smell the cheeseburger and fries. It made her mouth water. Andrew came inside and Talia closed the door behind him.

Andrew sat down on the sofa and Talia sat in the chair across from him. He had a wide grin on his face. He opened the bag and handed her a nice big...napkin.

"Hey!" Talia lowered her bottom lip. "Is this it?"

"Here." Andrew handed her a cheeseburger and bag of fries.

Talia opened the wrapping on the burger and took a big bite. Ketchup and mustard oozed from her mouth.

"Th...bur...really...good," Talia mumbled. Andrew snorted a laugh as he started in on his own burger.

"You're welcome," Andrew said. He put his burger down and cracked open a bottle of cold brew for each of them. Andrew handed Talia her beer. She took a big drink.

"So what do I owe the pleasure of your visit?" Talia stuffed some fries in her mouth.

"Can't I just stop over with beer and food?" Andrew looked wounded. "Or do I always have a motive?"

"Yes," Talia giggled.

"It's true," Andrew laughed.

"So all of this is some sort of bribe?" Talia gestured to her food.

"Not a bribe," Andrew said in his defense. "More like softening the mood."

"What is it?" Talia was now more serious.

"Recently I was in Chicago to see Detective Nick Flannery," Andrew began.

"Nick Flannery," Talia's face turned white.

"Yes," Andrew went on. "Anyway to make a long story short we ran into three members of the Knights of

VanHelsing. They attacked a group of teenagers in Jackson Park."

"Knights of VanHelsing?" Talia repeated.

"I know you were one of them in your past," Andrew calmly said. He looked at Talia, who turned away. "I also know you were the one who attacked me that night at the Higgins home."

"What do you mean?" Talia answered innocently.

"You were the only that suspected I was there that night at the Higgin's home," Andrew said. "Logic dictates that it was you."

"Yes, it was me," Talia broke down sobbing. "I…I never meant to harm you. It was like I was outside my body watching me attack you!"

Andrew rose and walked over by her. He knelt in front of Talia. "How did you get involved in the Knights of VanHelsing?"

"I was recruited while in college," Talia told Andrew. She stopped to collect her thoughts, and then went on. "I was flown to Berlin, Germany on a private jet. From there we took the train to a city by the Ore Mountains." Talia took a drink from her beer. She continued, "We traveled for two days until we got to this castle. Once there, my training began. I spent two years learning various forms of marital arts; how to shoot a cross bow and other weapons. I also learned German and a couple other languages. When my training was complete, I was given my Knights of VanHelsing name."

"So what happened next?" Andrew asked.

"I became the third member of my team," Talia further explained. "We were assigned to South Chicago.

From our training we were told to assume a normal identity during the day, and carry out our quests against the evil ones at night."

"You became a police officer, why?" Andrew asked. He opened another beer for both of them. He figured they needed it.

"I joined the force to help people both by day and night," Talia answered. "There was no conflict in my mind, until that night I told Nick who I was. He told me that I was breaking the law. He told me that I was killing innocent people. I just lost it and was sent to Whispering Pines, it was a mental facility in Glendale. I was there for over a year. During that time I learned about the Sheriffs job opening in Bayport County. I was given a clean psychological bill of health. I left Whispering Pines, but I also left the Knights of VanHelsing. I kept all of my gear and just put in away." Talia eyes were sad and filled with remorse as she looked at Andrew. "That night at the Higgins something, just snapped inside of me and suddenly all of my former life came rushing back." She put her beer down. Andrew put his down and Talia took hold of his hands. Talia's bottom lip trembled as she spoke, "I never meant to hurt you. It was like I was watching someone in my body making me do those things"

"I forgive you." Andrew let go of Talia's hands and put his arms around her. Talia rested her head on Andrew's shoulder. Andrew quietly said, "I know you have been through so much, but I have a favor to ask."

"What is it?" Talia lifted her head.

"We are going after the Knights of VanHelsing," Andrew announced.

"Are you insane?" Talia shouted. "They are too strong!"

"Everything is in place," Andrew said calmly. "The German authorities are on board with us. The only thing we still need is a diversion."

"Me," Talia added reluctantly. "You want me to be the diversion."

"Yes," Andrew said. "You would be the prodigal whom returns home. It is the perfect cover story in order to make this plan work. With you returning to the fold, they would never suspect we were there."

"I don't know if I could?" Talia turned away.

Andrew gently took hold of her chin and turned her to look at him.

"At the first sign of trouble, the police would storm the castle," Andrew told her. "I would never let any harm come to you." Talia took Andrew's hand in hers.

"I want to show you something," Talia said. They both stood and walked to Talia's bedroom. She opened the door and they went inside. Talia closed the door behind them.

Andrew sat on the bed as Talia walked over to the closet. She opened the door and stepped inside. Minutes later, Talia stepped out again carrying a large, leather case. She carried it over by Andrew and set it next to him on the bed. Talia proceeded to open the case as Andrew stood up to watch.

Inside the case was Talia's Knights of VanHelsing outfit: two swords with sheaths, crossbow and arrows, body armor, pants, shirt, full-length black leather overcoat, and boots.

"Just watch," Talia said. She stripped down to her bra and panties. Andrew blushed at seeing Talia's alluring, well-toned body. He watched as Talia first strapped on the body armor making sure it was snug. Next, she put on the pants, black shirt and boots. Once done, Talia strapped on the leather belt with the crossbow, and then the long, black leather overcoat. Finally, Talia put on the swords and sheaths. It was when Talia put on the hood, her transformation was finished. She drew both swords and had them at Andrew's throat before he even had a chance to react. Andrew saw the cold look reflected in Talia's eyes.

"I will do it," Talia said as she withdrew the twin blades and put them away. She removed her hood and tossed it on the bed. Talia removed all of her gear and let it drop to the floor. She undid her pants and shirt and let them drop to the floor also. Talia came up to Andrew and slowly undid her body armor. She stared intently into his eyes as she loosened each strap. "I never did thank you for saving my life that day." Talia finally removed her body armor and tossed it away. She stripped down to only her natural, striking self. She drew closer to Andrew. "How can I thank you?"

Andrew quickly brought Talia into an embrace. He held her tight. "You don't need to thank me," Andrew said. "You need to get dressed. We have to meet the others in Chicago later today." Andrew let go and left Talia standing alone in her bedroom. She simply gathered up her gear and one by one, put it back in the case. Talia returned to the closet and took out some clothes to wear. She was not sure about going back to Gothica. The thought of it scared her.

Chloe, along with Roxanne, followed the winding river of asphalt as they drove through the foreboding forest of shades of gray

After what seemed like an eternity, a gothic-looking mansion final came into view. Her dad had called Chloe and asked her to take over the interviews of Vlad Ravenclaw, Storm and the others. She agreed to help, but after asking what he was doing. Andrew informed her that he was traveling to Germany to find Wyatt, whom had fled there to avoid the authorities. So Chloe asked Roxanne to join her, hoping that her special talents would see through any shroud of deceit that Ravenclaw might throw at them.

Chloe parked her car next to the portico of the main entrance. Both women exited and walked up to the impressive door built of wood and metal. Roxanne grasped hold of one of the metal rings and announced their arrival. Soon the door creaked open and an older gentleman, attired in a black suit and tie greeted them.

"May I ask who is calling?" He looked at them with stern-looking eyes. It was as if he were scolding them for interrupting the household.

"Chloe Hawkins," Chloe gestured towards herself, and then Roxanne. "Roxanne Turner, my assistant."

"I will announce you to the master," the man said closing the door.

"Creepy," Roxanne commented.

"Yeah," Chloe added.

The door opened again. A bony, thin hand appeared gesturing for them to enter.

The two girls stepped through the open doorway and it seemed into the past. The grand foyer resembled the architecture of medieval times.

"Follow me please," the man said. He led them from the foyer down the hallway to the right. Portraits were hung on the wall, presumably ancestors of Vlad Ravenclaw. The one thing that struck both women, were the golden hues of the eyes in each painting. It made the men look surreal.

"Here we are," the man gestured towards an already open door. He left them.

Both of them entered.

The grand hall was overwhelming with its stone and mortar fireplace. And in spite of the warmth of the fire, the room seemed cold. Dark wood and heavy-looking leather furniture were arranged to face the hearth.

Chloe made note of where everyone was in the room. All of the youth were seated quite properly on the furniture. All were presentably attired in suits and dresses, respectively. It was as if the room itself had commanded their respect. Next to the hearth was Vlad Ravenclaw. Chloe didn't know what to make of the man standing there with long, straight black hair, well defined features and eyes which were dark and not a golden hue. His suit appeared to be of the finest material, tailored to show off his physically fit form. It wasn't the room that demanded the respect of those youths; it was him.

Chloe briskly walked over to Vlad and presented herself to him; Roxanne followed.

"Chloe Hawkins," Chloe extended her hand.

"A pleasure," Vlad took her hand and bowed. "Vlad Ravenclaw."

"Roxanne Turner," Roxanne said.

"A pleasure Miss Turner," Vlad now took hold of her hand. Roxanne shuddered.

"We would like to ask all of you some questions," Chloe announced taking out her tape recorder. "Would that be alright?"

"Direct, aren't you?" Vlad smiled, with stained fangs revealed. "I like that."

"May we begin?" Chloe took charge.

"By all means." Vlad gestured to two empty chairs in front of the hearth that faced towards the others. It was as if they had already been arranged that way on purpose.

Chloe and Roxanne were seated. Chloe loosened the buttons of her dark blue suit jacket. Roxanne did the same with her own dark brown one. Thus far she was disappointed at being unable to read the feelings of the others in the room. It was as if someone put up a psychic energy field to block her.

"I would like to start with Storm," Chloe announced, as she reviewed her case notes. She looked up and at Storm, whom was seated right in front of her on the long sofa. Storm drew her eyes up from the floor and on Chloe. She was ready.

"Is there anything out of the ordinary that you recall on the night your family was attacked?" Chloe asked.

"You mean callously murdered," Vlad interrupted.

"I'm asking the question here sir, not you," Chloe chastised him. "You will not interrupt me again."

"How dare you speak to me like this in my own home," Vlad eyes narrowed and his lips curled, fangs revealed.

"I'm here to find out why Storm's family was attacked," Chloe stood her ground. She continued, "My father and I were hired by Wyatt's' mother to find him and prove he had no involvement in the events of that night. That's what I am here to do sir. Are you going to let me conduct my investigation, or shall I go right now and turn this entire questioning over to the authorities? The choice is yours!"

"As you wish," Vlad sat back down. He was unaccustomed to being told what to do.

"Now," Chloe said as she pressed the record button again. "Please continue."

"Things were pretty normal that day," Storm said. "My parents were getting things ready for the winter solstice party. Since I was grounded, I spent most of the day in my room working on my missing assignments for school. My brother was helping my parents out."

"So nothing was out of the ordinary?" Chloe asked.

"No," Storm answered.

Chloe next turned her attention to the others. She decided to start with the boy with the thick and black hair. He had several earrings in his left ear with a beaded chain running to one in his nose.

"What's your name?" Chloe asked.

"Seth," he answered respectfully.

"Tell me what happened that night at JFK Prep?" Chloe asked.

"We all snuck out that night," Seth glanced at his uncle, Ravenclaw, who gave a look of disapproval.

Seth continued, "We decided to take my sister Amber's boyfriend with us. When we got there, we all headed to the upstairs of the old dormitory. There we played with the Ouji board game. Afterwards we all went to make out." Seth stopped and looked at the others. He saw by the look in their eyes that they were still as much afraid as he was. If it hadn't been for Mister Knight finding them, they would all have died. He never had a chance to thank Mister Knight. Seth continued, "Gabriel and I were making out, when there was a knock at the door. I was pissed off at the interruption and got up to see who it was. As soon as I opened the door, this person in a mask, punched me in the face. I fell to the floor as they went after Gabriel. I jumped up and was about to go after them, when two more dressed the same, grabbed me. One of them was touching my shoulder blades, almost like they were giving me a massage. Well, all of a sudden I felt this weird tingling and then I blacked out. The next thing I knew, I was in this dark, stinking room."

"That's what happened to us," added the boy with frizzy black hair.

"And you are?" Chloe asked.

"Jazz," he answered.

"Jazz is right. We were attacked the same way," the other girl answered. She had a Victorian look but still wore the black makeup and hair like the rest.

"And you are?" Chloe asked her.

"Melissa," she replied.

Chloe looked at Roxanne. She was hoping that Roxanne would use her special gift to pick up on the vibes in the room. Roxanne sensed what Chloe wanted.

"May I use your bathroom?" Roxanne asked Vlad.

"You may," Vlad replied. He pointed in the direction of the bathroom. "There is one just down the hallway on the right."

"Thank you," Roxanne said. She left the room.

"Please explain to me about who you are," Chloe turned her attention to Vlad.

"What do you mean?" he asked for clarification.

"Explain what kind of vampires you are."

"Is it important to the investigation?"

"It so that I have a better understanding, that's all."

"Very well," Vlad agreed. He began, "There are two types of vampires. There is Sanguine, which need to feed off of the blood of others, and cannot achieve satisfaction through any other feeding methods." Chloe shivered at the thought of it. Vlad continued, "Psychic are vampires that feeds directly upon the vital energy of a being, and cannot achieve satisfaction through the intake of blood." Vlad moved closer to Chloe. He went on, "Psi feeding methods can be long ranged or up close. The families in the clan are a mix of both." He smirked, "We are known as hybrid and require both blood and vital energy to satisfy our needs." Vlad glanced in the direction where Roxanne had gone. His lips spread into a thin smile and with narrowed eyes said, "You're assistant's psychic energy is strong. We could feed off of her forever."

Roxanne did have to use the restroom. Once she was done though, Roxanne stood in the hallway and closed her eyes. She slowed her breathing and concentrated on the energy all around her. At first, there was nothing but blackness. Roxanne cleared her mind to open it up to reach a higher plain of physic energy. It worked and a swirling of images filled Roxanne's mind. She saw a castle high in the mountains. There was a feeling of danger associated with it. Roxanne saw Andrew and some others she did not know sitting in a forest. The same feeling of danger filled Roxanne. She snapped open her eyes. Roxanne knew she had visions of the future. She immediately returned to the room were the others were.

Chloe was relieved to see Roxanne return. Roxanne retook her seat. Chloe sensed something was bothering Roxanne, but didn't know what it was. Vlad moved back over by the fireplace.

"Where is Chad?" Chloe asked as she again reviewed her case notes.

"He chose not to accept our protection," Vlad informed her. "He is with his mother."

"Well," Chloe said, putting her things away. "I think we are done for now."

"Do you know where Wyatt is?" Vlad suddenly asked. Chloe found it rather weird that he waited until now to ask.

"My father knows," Chloe answered. "And he is going after him."

"Where?" Vlad pressed further.

"That information is confidential," Chloe countered. "And you don't need to know."

"Rebellious, aren't you?" Vlad added.

"Professional," Chloe shot back. She grabbed her briefcase and walked out. Roxanne followed right behind her.

Andrew couldn't sleep. It was still dark outside and hours before the dawn. He decided to get up and make some coffee. Andrew had just sat down at the breakfast nook and was about to take the first sip, when Megan came shuffling in the kitchen. She went to the cupboard and took a glass. Then she walked over to the refrigerator and took out the milk. Megan poured herself some and put the container back. She looked all warm and cozy in her pink fuzzy robe. She sat across from her husband.

"Couldn't sleep?" Megan asked.

"No." Andrew took the first sip.

"Why?" Megan asked.

"Stuff." Andrew was withdrawn.

"I don't like the fact that you are going after this Wyatt!" Megan just sort of blurted out. "Why does it always have to be you?"

"We've had this discussion," Andrew grumbled.

"I know we talked about it eariler," Megan snipped. "We've never been able to finish it, because you always make up some excuse."

"You knew what I did when we first met," Andrew shot back. "You knew the risks involved. Why are you bringing this up now? I don't get it."

"I'm bringing it up because we're having a baby," Megan reminded. "And that changes things for me; us. I want you to be around to raise your son or daughter." Megan pushed aside her glass and reached out for

Andrew's hands. He moved his cup to the side and accepted her hands into his. "I don't argue with that fact, because most of your cases are pretty normal stuff, you know." Megan bit her lower lip and then went on, "It's just that you're going after these Knights of VanHelsing, and well, they're trained killers. From what you told me, they wouldn't hesitate to kill anyone, and that's including you. That's what I don't like."

"It not just me, you know," Andrew answered. "There is a team of us going to Germany. We're meeting with the authorities and are going to develop a plan of attack." Andrew looked at her and squeezed her hands. "Yes, I won't lie to you that there is some risk involved, but I can handle it."

"I...I don't want to lose you," Megan broke free of his grasp. Tears streamed down her cheeks. Andrew got up and rushed to her side. He laid his head on her ever expanding tummy. Andrew felt the baby move.

"What do you want me to do?" Andrew spoke more calmly now. "Work retail security? Retire for good?"

"No I don't want that," Megan gently caressed his hair. "I just don't want you to do something stupid and it ends up costing you your life. Besides, retail security would be too boring for you." Megan teased. "You'd probably end up getting fired for taking out a shoplifter with your martial arts moves." She laughed; Andrew joined her. He pictured bagging some middle aged shoplifter with a roundhouse kick combination. It made him laugh harder. Megan was laughing so hard it made her feel like she had to go to the bathroom.

"My mom called today." Megan sobered up and changed the subject. She needed to so as not to think about the other stuff. "She wants me to come for a visit. Is that okay?"

"I think it would be a great idea," Andrew agreed. Andrew opened up his arms and drew her into his loving embrace

"Ready for bed?" Andrew asked tenderly.

"Yes," Megan answered him in the same way.

Chapter 12

The Berlin airport was always a flurry of activity, with hundreds of passengers passing through. Lieutenant Otto Gunderson nervously paced back and forth as he watched the steady stream of passengers. He was interested only in the group disembarking from the United States flight. Would he recognize Andrew among the mob of faces?

"Lieutenant, you're wearing a hole in the floor." Detective Fredrick Schindler scolded.

"I'm just nervous," Lieutenant Otto Gunderson answered his junior partner.

Otto stopped pacing for now. He recalled working with Andrew on the Jensen kidnapping case about ten years ago. It was the only time they worked together. So as you can imagine, Otto was quite shocked to receive Andrew's call a few days ago.

"Lieutenant," Fredrick broke the silence between them. "I think I can see him." Each of them focused on the passengers getting off the plane. Otto spotted Andrew walking toward them, as well as another man and two women. All four were dressed alike in black clothing and long black trench coats.

Andrew saw his old friend Lieutenant Gunderson along with a younger man waiting for them at the departure gate. He was surprised at how much older Otto looked now. His hair was grayer and he had a lot more of it back then. Even Otto's clothes seemed to fit more tightly now than before. The other man with Otto had peppered blonde hair with a trimmed beard that followed his jaw line.

He was dressed stylishly in a dark blue suit and tan full length trench coat.

Andrew and the others walked up to the two men.

"Guten Morgen," Otto greeted Andrew.

"Guten Morgen," Andrew greeted back. He asked who was with him, "Wer ist dieser mit Ihnen?" Otto switched to English.

"This is Sergeant Schindler" Otto introduced him.

"Hello," Andrew shook hands with him.

"Fredrick." He smiled. "But call me Fred."

"Detective Nick Flannery," Andrew introduced those with him. "And this is Kara Sadler and Sheriff Talia Delsmann."

"Hello," Fred answered.

"Hello," Otto greeted them. He was caught off guard by Kara's black hair with red streaks. She was very striking. The other woman looked too young to have such authority.

"Welcome to Berlin," Otto spread his arms.

"We've booked you at the Hotel Augusta," Fred informed them.

"We have to report at the station first," Otto added. "We will rejoin you at the hotel."

"Sounds good," Andrew answered for the rest. The four of them went to retrieve their luggage as Otto and Fred waited. Soon the four returned, and with Otto and Fred, left the airport terminal. As soon as the entire luggage was squared away, they all departed for their separate ways.

Andrew and the others arrived at the Hotel Augusta. They exited the car as hotel staff greeted them and retrieved everyone's luggage.

Once in the main lobby, they all walked up to the desk. The front desk clerk, a young looking woman with coal black hair and attired in a crisp, clean hotel uniform, greeted them with a wide smile, "Guten Tag."

"Guten Tag," Andrew smiled back. He asked if she spoke English. "Sprechen sie Englisch."

"Ja, ich spreche Englisch," she answered 'yes'.

"Reservations for Knight," Andrew continued.

"Just staying for tonight?" she said looking at the computer screen.

"Yes," Andrew answered.

"The Hotel Augusta located in Berlin's elegant Charlottenburg district, offers individual rooms and suites. All rooms include a safe, minibar and TV. Some also had a balcony or terrace. This family-run hotel offers free Wi-Fi access and free parking. It stands beside Uhlandstrabe underground station, just a few steps from the famous Kurfürstendamm shopping street," she recited for all of them. She took a breath and continued, "Breakfast is served in the Augusta's bright breakfast room each morning. Many restaurants, bars, cafés and shops can be reached on foot. The ICC (congress centre) and the exhibition grounds are a 10-minute bus ride from Hotel Augusta." When she was finished, Andrew and the others chuckled.

"Thanks," Andrew said as she handed them their room key cards. They left the lobby and took the waiting elevator to their floor.

The day was near an end, when Otto and Fred were finally able to make it to the hotel.

Kara greeted Otto and Fred when she opened the door. From there they saw a table filled with a variety of food and beverages. A little further in the room was a laptop and projector screen set up in the seating area. Andrew, Talia and Nick were chatting by the fireplace. They were snacking on some of the food.

"We're set up in the sitting area." Kara stepped aside to let them in.

They entered and Kara closed the door.

Andrew and the others greeted Otto and Fred. Andrew put his drink and plate of food down. He went over to the laptop and called up the PowerPoint presentation. Soon the first slide was on the screen for all to see. First, Otto and Fred grabbed some food and a beverage. They sat down with Kara, Talia, and Nick. Andrew remained at the laptop to run the PowerPoint presentation.

"What you see is a digital copy of the map I found in the book at Kara's home," Andrew explained the first slide. "It was in a book about the Knight's of VanHelsing." He took a drink. Andrew pressed the button and the next slide appeared on the screen. The map from the book was super imposed over a map of Germany with a red star on it. "What I've done is superimpose the map from the book over a map of Germany," Andrew said. "The red star indicates the location of the Gothica castle." He changed it to the next slide that had zoomed in closer. "Gothica is located in the Ore mountain range. There are very few roads in the area. Gothica is only accessible by air."

"They would see anyone coming," Kara added.

"Exactly," Andrew put up the next slide. It was a detailed itinerary.

"Tomorrow morning we take the train to Zwickau," Andrew explained. "I've booked two compartments." His throat was parched and he took a drink. Andrew continued, "Once in Zwickau we will meet with the local authorities."

"All arrangements have been made with Captain Brewster," Otto spoke up this time. "We are to meet him at the local police station."

"So how do we get to Gothica?" Fred asked.

"From Zwickau we go by helicopter to here," Andrew pointed to a place on the map about twenty kilometers from the castle. "They will drop us here and we go the rest of the way on foot." Andrew called up another slide. It was a satellite photo of the Gothica castle.

"How did you get that?" Otto asked, nearly spitting out his drink.

"A friend of mine works at the CIA," Andrew answered. "He owed me a favor."

"How do we get inside?" Fred asked. He got up to get more refreshments.

"This is the plan," Andrew finally said. "Talia will be the diversion. She will be in her Knights of VanHelsing clothing and gear." Andrew stopped to wait until Fred returned with his food and drink. Andrew continued, "The rest of us will be entering the castle through the secret entrance here." Andrew pointed to a section of the castle wall.

"Where will Talia be?" Otto asked.

"They will take me to the main hall," Talia answered. "There I will meet with our leader. From there I will be taken to the debriefing room."

"Talia will neutralize anyone in the room," Andrew shot her a stern look, "And no one is to be killed." He went on, "Talia will activate her locater beacon. And we will join her in the briefing room."

"From there Kara and Nick are to open the main doors so the authorities can storm the castle," Talia added. She recalled and went on, "Once the facility is neutralized everything will be fine."

"And that's where we come in," Otto said.

"What about the rest of those Knights of VanHelsing?" Fred asked worriedly.

"If there are any there," Talia smirked. "Andrew and I will take care of them."

"What about tonight, here?" Otto asked all of them. "What are your plans?"

"We're going out to dinner," Andrew closed out the program and the screen went blank. "Our train leaves tomorrow at around noon. I think we need to have some much needed fun and relaxation."

"We'll take our leave of you then," Otto stood up, and so did Fred. They put their empty plates and cups on the table. They said their good byes and left.

"So where are we going for dinner?" Talia asked. She gestured towards Kara and herself. "And what should we wear?"

"I had some dresses delivered to your room," Andrew smiled. "So you can decide."

"What about us?" Nick asked.

"I had several tuxes delivered for us as well," Andrew answered. "I think we should get dressed for dinner."

Kara and Talia immediately left to go and try on the dresses. Andrew laughed at how giddy they were. He and Nick also went to get dressed.

When Talia and Kara exited their hotel suite, Andrew and Nick were waiting for them. They smiled and each thought, Andrew and Nick looked very dashing, in their chalk stripe two button notch tuxedos, with snow white shirts and matching ties. The look was completed with square-tow, lace-up black shoes.

Andrew and Nick were waiting out in the hallway when Talia and Kara came out of their hotel suite. Both were just blown away at how stunning the two women looked. Andrew smiled at the choice of dresses each wore. Kara had chosen the red satin banded strapless cocktail dress. Its sweetheart neckline with a folded bow highlighted her features. Her hair was swept up and held in place with a matching hair comb. Andrew glanced at Nick, who couldn't take his eyes off of Kara. She walked up to Nick and slipped her arm in his.

Talia stood there as if waiting for Andrew's approval. She had chosen a ruche black off-the-shoulder cocktail dress with cap sleeves, and a hemline that fell above the knee. The black ruche material flattered the curves of her shapely figure and the sparkling jewels created a stunning focal point on the neckline. Talia walked up to Andrew and he offered his arm to escort her.

"So where are we going?" Talia asked.

"The Vox," Andrew answered.

The four of them got on the elevator and took it to the lobby. Andrew had arranged a limo for the evening. He thought they all needed a night to just have some fun and enjoy each other's company before things turned serious. They thanked Andrew and got inside. Andrew instinctively looked around first. He didn't know why he had done it. He thought it was probably from all those years of being an investigator, either way, nothing looked suspicious, so he climbed inside. The limo took off and easily glided into traffic. They were on their way to the Vox.

The Vox, located inside the exquisitely detailed Hyatt hotel, was the height of German fine dining. The tables were dressed in their finest whites and complimented with black lacquered chairs and soft table candle lighting. Patrons gathered to enjoy a grand meal and visit with each other. They were treated to the superior service by the wait staff. Each one of them was attired in crisp-looking white shirts adorned with black bow ties, along with neatly pressed black trousers and shiny flat black shoes. The waiters and waitress glided effortlessly through the room like swans on a smooth lake, all the time smiling and making sure everyone was taken care of.

Andrew and the others approached the hostess podium. She smiled and asked for the name of the registration.

"Name bitte," Name please, she asked.

"Knight," Andrew replied.

"Der Tisch ist fertig." She told him the table he had reserved was ready for them. She motioned for their waitress, who walked up, ready to escort them.

"Kommen sie bitte, mit mir." She told them to come with her.

They followed her to a table by the window, which gave them a grand view of the city of Berlin. Andrew and Nick seated Kara and Talia first and then took their own.

"Ich möchte die Weinkarte sehnen?" Andrew asked if he could see the wine list. She handed it to him. Andrew looked it over and soon selected his choice.

"Zwei Flaschen Hausweins bitte, abgekühlt." He ordered two bottles of the house wine chilled. "Danke," he said. She smiled and left to fill the order.

"Where did you learn to speak German?" Talia asked amazed at how fluent he was.

"I studied with a friend of mine," Andrew answered.

"So what are we going to eat?" Kara glanced over the menu. Luckily the lists were in both English and German.

"They serve French and German food," Andrew answered. "What would you like?"

"I've never tried authentic German food," Kara spoke up.

"Me too," Nick agreed.

"How about we all try it," Andrew suggested.

"Okay," they all agreed.

The waitress returned with their wine and glasses. She opened the first bottle and poured a small amount in a glass and handed it to Andrew. He took the glass and sipped from the contents of the glass. Andrew held the wine in his mouth. It was a Bloom Riesling with aromas of peach and honeysuckle giving way to a pleasing palate full of sweetness and acidity.

"Sehr gut." Andrew said it was good.

"English please." Talia pleaded with a pouty look.

"Alright," Andrew smirked. He looked up at the waitress, "Englisch bitte."

"What would you like to start with?" she asked.

"May I order for us?" Andrew offered.

"Sure," the others answered looking a bit overwhelmed with all the choices.

"One minute please," Andrew said. He studied the menu and ordered an appetizer of Koeniginpastetchen (flaky pastry shell filled with veal ragout in Riesling sauce with mushrooms). As well, he ordered a Gurken Salat (cold cumber salad). And for the main course it was Jägerschnitzel (tender milk-fed Veal Cutlet, floured and sautéed in butter, topped with a Mushroom-Creme Sauce, served with Potato Pancakes and Red Cabbage).

"Very good," their waitress smiled. She took their menus and went to fill their order.

Andrew poured the wine and passed a glass to each of them. He raised his glass and proposed a toast, "To friendship." Each repeated his toast and drank from their glass.

"So will everything be ready when we get to Zwickau?" Nick asked.

"Everything we need will be there," Andrew replied.

"Let's change the subject," Talia suggested. She just wanted to concentrate on the evening and not what they were going to face in the not too distant future.

The waitress returned with their salads and appetizers. Everyone was famished and quickly dug in when she left.

"This is delicious," Talia said, taking a bite of her Koeniginpastetchen.

"Mmmm," Kara murmured while sampling the Gurken Salat.

"So what are plans after dinner?" Nick inquired.

"Back to the hotel," Andrew replied.

"Can't we go dancing?" Kara and Talia flashed seductively looking eyes. Andrew moaned. He gave in, "Fine, we'll go dancing, but after that it's off to bed."

"Yeah," Talia and Kara happily clapped their hands.

The main entrée arrived at the table just as they all finished their first course. The tender milk-fed Veal Cutlet, floured and sautéed in butter, topped with a Mushroom-Creme Sauce, served with Potato Pancakes and Red Cabbage, looked absolutely mouth-watering.

With more than 240 different sorts of whisky, the Vox Bar had one of the largest selections of whisky in Germany. The dark parquet flooring and the elegant lounge seating of Vox Bar created a warm atmosphere and one in which Andrew and the others were sure to enjoy. As they sat at the booth, Kara and Talia couldn't help but notice the collage of oversize black-and-white photos of famous Jazz legends which provided an atmospheric background. When they first entered the Vox Bar, a floor sign noted that the top international jazz and blues performers, played live in the bar Monday to Saturday, from 10 p.m. onwards.

Andrew noticed the newly added smoker's lounge. A glass wall with an intricately etched glass door and windows allows guests to not only see the bar at all times but also to enter it directly. Another entrance led into the lobby.

Kara grabbed Talia by the hand and practically dragged her to the dance floor. The band, Maxx12, had just started playing.

Andrew undid the buttons for his tux coat and sat down. A waiter stopped at their booth. Andrew placed the first round order for drinks. A short time later he returned and delivered a tray full of drinks. Andrew tipped him before grabbing his own glass of scotch. Nick grabbed his whiskey and coke.

"Do you ever get nervous?" Nick asked.

"Sometimes," Andrew answered. "Why?"

"It just hit me that we're taking on some serious s--- with these Knights," Nick slammed down the rest of his drink. "And well it scares the s--- out of me."

"We have a plan and everything is in place," Andrew tried to reassure Nick. "They have no clue that we are coming. So we have the advantage here Nick."

"So you're that sure?" Nick asked again. "I wish I had your confidence."

"Talia has the tough part" Andrew answered, as he finished off his first drink. "She has to convince them she is still a member of the order. That, is the scary part, because I think Talia isn't sure who she is sometimes. Her psychological condition is very delicate and she could snap at any time. There is even a distinct possibility that Talia may betray us all."

"What about Kara?" Nick grabbed his second glass.

"Kara?" Andrew paused. He thought back to time he spent with her. She was amazing, powerful and very beautiful. He was drawn to her, and had almost given into her intoxicating charms. Andrew finally replied, "She's amazing. I hope things work out for the both of you. I think you both need each other."

"She is amazing," Nick had a wide grin on his face. "I've never met any like her before." He turned towards the dance floor and watched her dancing with Talia. Kara moved with such seductiveness, free-spiritedness, it made him want her even more. Nick turned back to Andrew. He raised his glass, "Thanks man, for bringing us together."

"Your welcome," Andrew raised his own glass.

Talia left Kara on the dance floor and walked back to the table. She sat down next to Andrew. Kara was now dancing with a tall, blonde stranger, dressed in a white shirt and black trousers. Everyone just stared at the provocative way they were dancing. Nick slammed down his glass and tore off for the dance floor. The two men started screaming at each other. Andrew bolted from the booth and stepped in between. Very shortly, he had defused the situation. Nick grabbed Kara by the hand and led her out of the room.

Andrew rejoined Talia back at the booth.

"I think we should go back to the hotel," Andrew announced.

"Could we go for a walk?" Talia suggested.

"Okay," Andrew replied.

He stood up. Talia rose up and walked over to him. She stopped for a minute. Her eyes met Andrew's. Talia reached out with her hand. Would Andrew take it? It seemed like an eternity, but then it happened; Andrew took her hand. They walked out of the bar.

Kara and Nick walked closely arm in arm. Kara had apologized to Nick for the way she acted earlier in the Vox bar. He forgave her and they decided to make it up with a romantic walk.

The night air was crisp; the moon bright and full lay still in the velvet sky. Kara and Nick had discovered a small, wooded park not far from the Grand Hyatt. They decided to take a stroll and soon found a secluded bench to sit on. When they sat down, Kara pressed up against Nick and leaned in, waiting for him to kiss her. Nick did not disappoint her and filled Kara's desire. As their lips drew apart, Kara looked intently at Nick and him at her.

"We should go back..." Kara started to say, but froze.

"What is it?" Nick asked seeing the horrified expression on her face.

"Nick!" Kara screamed.

From the dense bushes, three Knights of VanHelsing attacked. One of them took off after Kara. She tried to run but they quickly grabbed hold and restrained Kara. They covered her mouth so no one could hear her scream.

Nick tried to fight the other two off, but was no match for the deadly pair. With only a few moves, Nick was out cold on the ground. The last thing Kara saw was one had drawn a sword; then all went black.

"Nein, nein! Tötet ihn nicht," the other warned not to kill him. They pushed the blade away from Nick's body.

"Sie werden uns verfolgen," the second one cursed back. "Sie werden zu Gothica kommen." They asked if they will come to Gothica. They put away their blade and asked about Andrew and that he must be stopped. "Was machen wir mit Andrew Knight? Er muss angehalten werden!"

"Wir werden uns mit Andrew Knight befassen, sorgen Sie sich darüber nicht," the first one replied not to worry about Andrew and they would deal with him.

They joined the third one and then two of them carried Kara off. The third watched to make sure no one followed.

Andrew and Talia strolled along hand in hand. It was a perfect evening with the stars twinkling in the ebony sky above. The sights and sounds of Berlin were something Talia would not soon forget.

Talia wondered as they walked along, why she had hated Andrew so much in the beginning. She was glad they were closer, and that they now were actually friends. But Talia also found herself feeling more than that sometimes, especially recently. Andrew was very handsome, intelligent, and he had a certain air of assuredness about him. Was she falling for him? That was not possible; Andrew was married and his wife was going to have a baby. Yet she was falling for him; right or wrong. Did he feel the same?

"Look, there's a park over there," Talia said. "Let's check it out."

"Alright," Andrew answered. Talia squeezed his hand tighter. He wondered why.

They quickly crossed the street and entered the park. Talia and Andrew took one of the paths and had just come around the corner when they saw a dark heap on the ground.

"Stay here," Andrew let go of Talia's hand. "I'll check it out."

Andrew walked over but suddenly froze. He realized that the heap in fact was Nick, all bloody and bruised and lying on his side. Andrew rushed over to him and knelt down. Talia had joined him now. She looked worried upon seeing the way Nick looked.

"What happened?" Talia worriedly asked.

"He's coming around," Andrew answered as he cradled Nick in his arms.

Nick opened his eyes, trying to gain his bearings. Things were still a bit hazy, but he could make out the shapes of two; one cradling him and the other towering over him. Nick closed his eyes to refocus. Now he saw Andrew and Talia.

"What happened here Nick?" Andrew demanded. He stopped as a horrible chill filled his very being. Andrew urgently scanned the area. Kara was missing! "Kara's gone!" Andrew shouted. "Call for help."

Talia took out her cell phone from her purse and called the police.

Andrew turned his attention back to Nick. "What happened?" he asked again.

"There were three of them," was all Nick had to say. Andrew knew who it was. His whole body sunk at the realization that the Knight's of VanHelsing knew they were in Berlin. Andrew couldn't worry about that. Right now he had to find Kara. Andrew ordered Talia to wait here until the authorities arrived. He knelt down and surveyed the area. Suddenly Andrew bolted off deeper into the park.

"Andrew, don't!" Talia screeched after him. She saw him fade into the darkness. Talia was trembling so badly, Nick had to soothe her.

Andrew had tracked Kara and her kidnappers through the wooded park and to the river. He watched from cover as the three Knights of VanHelsing stopped beside a black van. They laid her down on the grass and proceeded to unlock the van. Andrew tossed aside his overcoat and made his move.

Silver Blade was unlocking the driver's side door when he felt a tap on the shoulder. Thinking it was either Bronze Blade or Gold Blade, he turned around. Instead, it was Andrew who simply said good night. 'Gute Nacht.' He grabbed Silver Blade by the neck and delivered a knockout blow to his head. Silver Blade slipped to the ground, unconscious. Andrew moved to the side of the van and inched his way along. Fortunately for him, the open back doors of the van provided him cover.

Andrew heard the two of them talking. They were saying that they still needed to capture Talia. But they weren't sure how to get to her since she was already at the hotel. One of them stopped suddenly. Perhaps they realized that Silver Blade hadn't joined them yet. Andrew pressed up against the side of the van as Bronze Blade came around the side of the door. Andrew hit him quickly with a snap kick to the head and Bronze Blade was out cold on the ground. Andrew bolted around the door and came face to face with Gold Blade.

"Wie fanden Sie uns hier?" Gold Blade surprised, asked how Andrew found them.

"Ich folgte jemanden durch den park," Andrew replied, he tracked them through the park.

Golden blade said nothing further but instead reached for his swords. Andrew had anticipated the move and with a front snap kick hit Gold Blade in the chest which sent him skidding backwards and to the ground. Andrew didn't give Gold Blade a chance to react and rushed him and grabbed the two swords. He flung them some distance away. Gold Blade stood and was about to grab the crossbow from his belt. But again, Andrew anticipated the move and with a devastating double spin kick, hit Gold Blade first in the chest and then the head. Gold Blade crumbled to the ground.

Chapter 13

Nick checked the door locks for the third time now. In all his life he was never more terrified then right now at this very moment. Even all the dangers he faced as a detective in Chicago, didn't compare with the Knights of VanHelsing. They frightened him and he didn't like it at all.

Nick rechecked the door locks and went to sit down on the sofa in the sitting area. Talia was asleep in one of the beds. After they had squared things away with the authorities, he and Talia returned to the hotel. The hotel doctor gave Talia a sedative so that she could get some rest. Nick grabbed a bottle of whiskey and glass from the table. His hands were shaking as he poured himself a drink. He drank it quickly and poured another. Andrew was still missing and that really concerned him. Where the hell was Andrew? Why did he go after those who kidnapped Kara, especially since he was unarmed? Nick drank another glass full of whiskey. Suddenly he felt very sleepy. The glass slipped from Nick's hand, onto the floor and he passed out.

Talia wasn't asleep at all. With Nick was distracted while talking to the doctor, she had slipped the sedative in the bottle of whiskey. Talia wasn't going to let Andrew face those whom kidnapped Kara, alone. She had to help. Talia pretended to fall asleep and had waited for Nick to pass out. And now he was out cold. She bounded out of bed and quickly over to the closet. Talia flung open the door and reached inside for a large leather case that was on the floor. Talia brought the case over by the bed and opened it. She put on her Knight's of VanHelsing outfit, except for the hood. Talia strapped on the belt with the crossbow and scabbard full of arrows. She closed the case and put in back in the closet. Talia left the room and closed the door behind her. She briskly walked to the elevators. As soon as the door opened, Talia stepped inside. The only thing Talia worried about was that it might be too late.

Andrew turned around to see Silver Blade take aim with a crossbow. He had no where to go. It was over.
Talia had just cleared the park when she saw Andrew knockout one of the Knights of VanHelsing. She started towards him when she saw one of them rise up from the driver's side. Talia froze when she saw them load up their crossbow.
Silver Blade let out an unexpected yelp and fell face down. An arrow was protruding from the back of his neck. Andrew first looked at Silver Blade in disbelief and then looked up to see Talia. She saved his life.
"Andrew!" Talia called out. She tossed aside the crossbow and ran towards him.

Andrew swept Talia up in his arm and twirled her around for a few seconds and put her back down. The overpowering stress of that moment finally hit them and for one brief moment they forgot themselves. Talia and Andrew's lips locked together in a long, hot blooded kiss. And as suddenly as it happened, they parted. Talia touched her lips. She had never been kissed like that in her entire lifetime. Andrew walked away. He was embarrassed at what just happened between them. Talia stretched out her hand towards him and was about to say something, but never had the chance. She felt a blow to the head and everything instantly went black.

Andrew awoke. Every bone and muscle in his body hurt. The last thing he remembered was that kiss between he and Talia and how he had walked away. That was it; no memory of what happened after that.

Andrew, more focused now, looked beside him. His blood ran cold and a sickening feeling came over him. Next to Andrew was the body of Sergeant Fredrick Schindler. The realization of the circumstances finally hit him; Sergeant Schindler was a Knight of VanHelsing! Andrew saw that Fredrick was in street clothes and not his Knight's outfit. Andrew took a quick look down at his own clothing and froze. He was dressed in Fredrick's outfit! Andrew rose unsteadily to his feet. He surveyed the area. The van was gone, but more importantly, Talia was also gone. He had failed to protect both her and Kara. The plans he had made were now compromised. The Knights of VanHelsing had found they were in Berlin through Fredrick's deception. Andrew recalled that Talia had told him that the

Knights would assume a secret identity and blend in during the day. Fredrick had them all fooled. The Knights of VanHelsing were setting him up for the death of Fredrick; the death of a police officer. Andrew started to leave, when he heard the sirens of the approaching authorities. If he were caught, it wouldn't be good. Andrew tore off back towards the hotel. He hadn't gotten very far, when three officers appeared. They drew their weapons.

"Die hände halten, wo wir sie sehen können." They ordered him to put up his hands.

Andrew did as requested and put up his hands. Two of the officers put their weapons away as they approached Andrew. The third kept his gun pointed at Andrew. There wasn't time for this and he couldn't afford to be arrested. So Andrew did what he had to do. Andrew grabbed the two officers and slammed them into each other and while they were disoriented, he jumped in the air and with a double spin kick, removed the gun out of the officer's hand and delivered a knock out blow to the head. Andrew landed and turned around to face the first two officers. They rushed him, but Andrew had them on the ground and out cold in seconds. Andrew took off when he heard more sirens approaching his way.

Lieutenant Gunderson got out of his car just in time to see Andrew, wearing strange garb and leaving the park. Just as Andrew crossed the street, one of the officers that he had assaulted, came rushing up to Lieutenant Gunderson. He explained through gasping breaths what had happened. Lieutenant Gunderson's face turned white and he immediately got on his radio. He issued an arrest order for Andrew.

"We need to get to the Hotel Augusta immediately!" he shouted.

Andrew thought about it as he walked along back to the hotel. He could not believe that the mission had been comprimised. Andrew knew he had to finish no matter what though, and quickened his pace with a great deal of urgency.

Nick woke up with a throbbing headache. That wasn't the worst part though. Talia was gone! Nick rose to his feet and immediately felt nauseas. He ran to the bathroom and made it just in time to the toilet. Nick hung onto the bowl for dear life. It felt like his insides were trying to come out. Soon the nausea passed and Nick walked unsteadily to the bed. He finally noticed the pile of black clothing on the bed along with an open suitcase and its contents strewn about. It looked like someone had been in a great hurry.

Nick looked around the room for other signs. He had a hunch it was Andrew, but wondered several things; why Andrew was in such a hurry; why he didn't wake Nick, and where did Andrew go?

Nick decided to search the room further for some clues as to what happened with Andrew. He started in the bathroom first. Nothing was out of the ordinary. Nick went next to the sitting area, but again nothing was out of order. He returned to the sleeping area and examined the pile of black clothing and that's when

Nick found a folded piece of paper. Nick unfolded it and discovered it was a note from Andrew that read:

Nick,

I had to leave in a hurry and will explain later. You will get a visit from the police. Tell them only what you know and that you never saw me or know what happened. They will want to search the room, let them. They will not find any trace of me. After they have gone, meet me at the Berlin Train station.

You will be followed, so let me come to you. Once you have read this note, destroy it.

Andrew

Nick had just refolded the note when the door flung open with a loud crash and police officers stormed the hotel room. They shouted out a warning with weapons drawn. Nick quickly jammed the note down the front of his shirt. He raised his hands in the air and the police swarmed over him. Two officers roughly grabbed Nick and pushed him face down on the bed while the third handcuffed him. Once Nick was secure, Lieutenant Gunderson entered the room. He strode briskly over by Nick.

"Sit him up," Otto ordered. The officers immediately complied.

"Where is he?" Otto demanded of Nick.

"Who?" Nick answered back.

"Who do you think?" Otto was upset with Nick's apparent indigence. "Andrew, where is he, Nick?"

"I haven't seen him since earlier this evening," Nick was more cooperative now.

"He was here," Otto pointed out the open suitcase, strewn about clothing, and the pile of black clothes on the bed. "You never saw him. You are lying."

"I was passed out on the sofa over there," Nick nodded in the direction of the sitting area with his head. "I only woke just minutes ago, I swear."

Otto looked Nick over from head to toe. He finally nodded that he agreed that Nick was telling the truth.

"Why are you looking for Andrew?" Nick asked, after being allowed to sit down.

"Andrew is suspected of the death of Sergeant Schindler," Otto explained. He sat down next to Nick. He motioned for the officers to take off the cuffs. Otto looked sad as he continued, "Andrew fooled us all I'm afraid." He turned towards Nick and went on, "All this time Andrew was a Knight of VanHelsing and we never knew it. I suspect that with the plans to attack this Gothica castle, Andrew was setting us all up to be captured."

"That's in…" Nick began, but remembered Andrew's note. He switched to, "That's incredible. I mean I never suspected."

"Ya, ya," Otto agreed nodding his head in agreement.

"Like I said," Nick added. "I never saw him."

"I believe you," Otto said. He rose to his feet and motioned for the other officers to follow him. Otto turned to look back at Nick, "Let us know."

"I will," Nick answered.

"Good." Otto smiled and closed the door.

Once he was out of the room, Otto turned to the officers that were with him. "Keep a watch on him," Otto ordered. "I am certain that Andrew will try and contact Nick." They nodded that they understood.

Nick was relieved when Otto and his officers left the room. He went to the bathroom and took some peptol bismol. His stomach was still rumbling a bit, but he felt a little better. He left the bathroom and went back to the bedroom. Nick grabbed his passport and coat. He glanced around the hotel suite once more, and walked out the door and closed it behind him.

The Berlin Central Train station was a monument that offered state-of-the-art conveniences for travelers and considered the biggest train station in Europe.

Nick stood on a row of seats to get a vantage point over the menagerie of travelers mulling about. Out of all the hundreds of people in the station that day, a few really stuck out to him. He saw a mother with pink streaked blonde hair talking on her phone while walking ahead of a screaming child. Nick turned in another direction and saw a group of Chinese businessmen in a rush to catch their train. He turned for the third time and saw a couple with black hair wearing jeans and navy blue pea coats. They were walking with their arms around each other and carrying duffle bags. Nick felt a tap on his leg. He looked down and saw a police officer.

"Komm, bitte, nach unten," he asked Nick to get down. Nick shrugged his shoulders that he did not understand. "Komm, bitte, nach unten," the officer repeated, this time motioning for Nick to come down from the chairs. Nick finally understood and did as the officer asked. Once he was down, the officer left. Nick felt sick again and made a dash for the restrooms.

Otto peered down from the second floor balcony. He was using the glass elevator for cover. He had received a call that Nick had gone to the train station. Otto suspected that Andrew had made arrangements to meet Nick and proceed with their plans to go to the castle Gothic. But so far Andrew was a no show. Otto moved a little further over when he saw Nick go into the rest room. A few minutes later, a dark haired couple stopped in front of the restrooms. The man kissed the woman and walked in the men's room. She stayed outside and waited.

Nick was washing his face in the sink when the guy he had seen earlier walked in. He smiled at Nick. "Bonjour," he said before going into an available stall. Nick simply nodded and continued splashing cold water on his face. He heard the toilet flush and saw the man come out and walk over to the sink next to him.

"Je vois que vous ont été suivies. Vous n'avez pas idée de qui je suis," the man said.

"I have no idea what you just said." Nick shrugged.

"Vous ne parlent pas français," the man said.

"French," Nick recognized the word 'français'. "No I do not speak French."

"Too bad," he said. "You really should learn another language Nick," the man replied.

"How do you know my name?" Nick was shocked.

"Kara and Talia are counting on us," he continued.

"Andrew?" Nick took a closer look at the man with the black hair and full, trimmed beard. "Holy s---" Nick gasped when he finally knew it was Andrew beneath the disguise. "What the hell are you doing? The cops think you killed Fred. Did you?"

"Fred was a Knight of VanHelsing," Andrew said. "Talia killed him to save me. I was knocked out and they set me up to make it look like I was a Knight of VanHelsing." Andrew moved closer to Nick. "When you leave the restroom, I want you to get out of the station and take a cab. Have the driver take you around for a few minutes and return. By that time, the police will have left the station to follow you." Andrew reached inside his coat and took out an envelope. "Here is your ticket. Don't be late." Nick took the ticket and put it in his coat pocket.

"Who is the girl?" Nick finally asked.

"Emma Strauss," Andrew answered. "I met her when I came to the station early this morning. We sat down and started talking. Emma told me she attends the University of Berlin. She was on her way home to Zwickau. I asked if she would do me a favor. I offered her five hundred euros to help me out. She needed the money."

"You are something else." Nick shook his head.

"Now you're going to leave first," Andrew instructed Nick. "I will follow in a few minutes. Just meet us on the train."

"Okay," Nick agreed. Nick left the bathroom. Andrew followed a few minutes later.

Otto saw Nick come out of the restroom. A few minutes later the other man came out. He walked up to the girl and gave her a kiss and then they walked in the direction of the train platforms. Otto was disappointed. Andrew had never showed up to meet with Nick. Otto called on his radio to follow Nick and to keep an eye on him. The officers radioed back that Nick had gotten into a cab. Otto radioed back that they should follow him. Satisfied, Otto took the glass elevator to the first floor. He was headed towards the exit, but suddenly stopped. Otto thought back to the case he had worked on with Andrew. He recalled that Andrew always traveled with a suitcase with a variety of disguises, clothing, and identifications. Otto even witnessed Andrew's transformation into a disguise on that case long ago. Andrew could blend in anywhere, anytime. Otto slapped his forehead. "Dummkopf! Andrew war der andere Mann im Badezimmer," Otto realized that Andrew was the other man in the restroom with Nick." Otto shouted in his radio to stop the cab Nick was riding in. He also told them he was going after Andrew. When the elevator doors opened, Otto took off in a full run towards the train platforms.

As planned Nick had managed to lose the police that were following him. He had just entered the station when he saw Otto running towards the train platforms. Nick also saw that Andrew and Emma had just boarded the "Red Train" Thalys for Zwickau

Andrew hustled Emma onto the train when he saw Otto rushing towards them. Andrew also saw Nick. The voice on the speaker announced that the train was now departing.

Otto saw Andrew and the woman board the train. He sped up his pace to get on the train and stop Andrew before he got away. He had just reached the steps when the train began pulling out of the station.

Nick was almost to the train when he was pounced on by several uniformed police officers. They pushed Nick to the floor to restrain him. He looked up to see Andrew moving towards the back of the train. Otto was closing the gap between them.

Andrew was practically at a full run. He glanced back for a second to see Otto getting even closer. The train was picking up speed and the scenery began to move past still faster as it headed on the way. Andrew had just reached the door of the last passenger car and was about to enter the sleeping compartments sections.

Nick's heart sunk when he saw the train leave the station. Andrew was certain to be captured by Otto. There was no way he could escape. The uniformed officers shoved Nick along as they approached the exit. If Andrew did manage to escape Otto, he would have to face the Knights of VanHelsing alone. That prospect worried Nick greatly.

Andrew rushed past the sleeping compartments and paused briefly at the exit door. He looked back to see if Otto had caught up with him, but he hadn't. Andrew exited the sleeping car, crossed the platform and forced open the door to the baggage car. He quickly closed it behind him. He threw down the duffle bag and began to strip off the beard and wig.

Andrew knew he only had a few minutes before Otto arrived.

Otto exited the last sleeping car. The rush of the wind from the speeding train almost sucked him out. He had to hold on tightly to the railing of the steps. Otto pushed open the door to the baggage car and jumped inside.

Andrew had managed to change his clothes and identity, but it was too late. When he turned around, Andrew saw Otto standing there.

Otto pointed his gun at Andrew. It was the end of the chase and he was glad. Otto moved away from the door, all the time keeping his distance but gun trained on Andrew. He was well aware of Andrew's martial arts skills and wanted to keep as far away as possible.

"I have you now," Otto spat out his disgust for Andrew. "How could you do that to Fredrick? How could you shoot him from behind like that? You are a coward!"

"I didn't do it," Andrew answered in his own defense. "Talia shot him to protect me." Andrew moved closer, but Otto threatened him with the gun. Andrew retreated. "Fred was a Knight of VanHelsing. He and the two others with him were kidnapping Kara. I had trailed them to the place by the river."

"Liar!" Otto cursed. "I knew Fredrick since he was a young boy. I would have known if he were one."

"Was Fredrick ever gone for at least a year or more?" Andrew asked.

"Ya," Otto answered. "But he told me it was for school."

"That's when he had his training," Andrew said.

"Just shut up," Otto threatened with his gun. He reached for a pair of handcuffs on his belt and tossed them at Andrew. "Put them on," Otto ordered.

"I will not." Andrew threw them to the floor.

"Pick them up," Otto stared wild-eyed at Andrew.

The door opened unexpectedly, causing both of them to look. Before Otto or Andrew could react, they were attacked. Otto tried to fire his gun, but one sword blade tore it from his grasp and the other slashed him across the chest. Otto stumbled as blood began to seep through his once white shirt. Andrew had just managed to grab his duffle bag as a shield only seconds before the Knight of VanHelsing swung at him with both razor-sharp blades. Instead of Andrew being ripped to shreds, it was the duffle bag that was ripped to shreds instead. Andrew instantaneously tossed aside the bag and followed it with a round house kick. He caught their attacker in the back and the force of the blow sent them reeling towards the door. They hit the door with a loud thud and stumbled to their knees. Otto's shirt front was drenched with blood as he rushed to get his gun. The Knight recovered quickly and with one final attack, ran Otto through with the blade. Andrew screamed out his anguish as Otto lurched forward when the blade was withdrawn. Otto stared expressionlessly at Andrew as he coughed up blood. The Knight of VanHelsing pushed Otto down to the floor with their boot. Andrew now faced them alone.

"Let's make it fair," Andrew bowed respectfully.

"Agreed," she said. She tossed Andrew the sword.

Andrew looked over the blade he held in his hand. "I've never had much use for one of these," Andrew lowered the blade.

"Then it will be over with soon," she answered back.

Andrew immediately raised his blade to counter her first strike. She parlayed the blade to the right, but Andrew blocked it again. With each strike Andrew countered with his own move. They circled each other as the sound of clashing metal resounded throughout the baggage car. Andrew went on the attack with blade strikes and kick combinations driving her up against the luggage netting. She tried to counter, but with every thrust of her sword Andrew blocked, with his own moves. In desperation, she brought her knee up and caught Andrew unexpectedly in the groin. He tumbled to the floor, writhing in agony. Seizing the opportunity, she raised her blade and rushed forward. She drove her sword downwards towards Andrew's unprotected chest. At the same moment Andrew drove his sword upward driving it into her, just inches below the body armor she wore. The sword slipped out of her hand and to the floor. She stared in utter disbelief at the sword protruding from her belly.

"I never said I didn't know how to use one," Andrew said withdrawing the blade. She crumbled to the floor mortally wounded. Andrew rose to his feet and tossed the sword away. He grasped hold of her mask and tore it off. Andrew recognized her. She was the hotel desk clerk that had checked them into the hotel.

"They…they know you are coming," She choked up blood and it ran down the corners of her mouth.

"It doesn't matter," Andrew replied unemotionally. "Now it's personal." Andrew bent down on one knee in front of her. "All I wanted to do was to bring Wyatt back to Bayport. The Knights of VanHelsing made it worse by bringing him to Germany."

"You...you will surely die," She shivered violently.

"What's your name?" Andrew asked.

"Hannah," she gasped with a whimper.

"It didn't have to come to this Hannah," Andrew grasped her by the shoulders. "I'm..." Andrew didn't even have a chance to say he was sorry. Hannah's face lost all expression and she went limp, and gently slipped from his grasp to the floor. She was dead. Andrew rose to his feet again. He knew that Hannah already had to be on the train waiting for them to arrive. She couldn't have been in the passenger cars, because he would have seen her. So that meant that Hannah had booked a sleeping compartment. It was the only possible way for Hannah to change unnoticed. So Hannah's sleeping compartment had to be close to the baggage car. Andrew retrieved Otto's gun and extra clips. He rummaged through his shredded duffle bag for his passport and a few other things he needed. Andrew paused at the door and took one last look around. There was no sign of him being in the baggage car. Andrew opened the door and slipped out. He went to find Hannah's compartment.

Andrew entered the sleeping car again. As he walked along, Andrew would pause at each door to listen. After several unsuccessful attempts, and when he was at the last door, Andrew heard someone about to exit the compartment.

The train was nearing the station in Zwickau and it was one of Günter's duties as a porter to check the baggage car. It wasn't one of his most important or favorite duties, but nonetheless important.

Günter had just exited the last sleeping car when he noticed that the lock on the door to the baggage car was damaged. He first called on his walkie talkie for assistance, opened the door and stepped inside.

The horrific site that greeted him caused Günter to immediately exit for some fresh air.

"Hilfe!! Hilfe!" Günter screamed into his walkie talkie. "Helfen Sie mir gleich jetzt!" Günter felt sick and dropped to his knees. He vomited. Never had he seen, in all his years as Porter, such a terrible sight.

Unexpectedly, the train came to a metal grinding stop and it nearly caused Günter to fall from the platform. Fortunately, he was able to grasp hold of the railing in time.

Günter heard the sirens of the approaching police cars. He was greatly relieved, and knew that now everything would be alright.

Captain Brewster of the Zwickau police department boarded the train. His officers had already secured the passengers and crew. Minutes earlier, they had received an emergency call from the Conductor that one of his Porters had discovered the bloody bodies of a man and woman in the baggage car. Captain Brewster disliked the thought of those suspicious deaths occurring within his jurisdiction. There hadn't been anything like this in Zwickau for quite some time.

Some of the passengers wore angry faces at being inconvenienced by the whole mess. Captain Brewster strode with an air of authority through the passenger cars. Others looked concerned or frightened from not knowing exactly what was going on. One woman in particular struck an odd chord with him by her nervous behavior. She was seated alone and kept staring back in the direction of the baggage car. Did she know something? Was she still waiting for someone? Captain Brewster signaled one of his officers to stand guard over her. He continued towards the baggage car.

A young man with short cropped blonde hair was sitting down on the platform drinking some water. Captain Brewster wasn't much for small talk or pleasantries.

"Captain Yuri Brewster" Captain Brewster announced. "What happened here?"

"I was supposed to check the baggage car before arriving in Zwickau," Günter explained. "I saw that the lock was broken and went to investigate. And that's when I saw the two people dead in the baggage car."

"I'll be right back," Yuri informed him. He opened the door to the baggage car and stepped boldly inside.

Chapter 14

There were indeed two people dead on the floor of the baggage car. One was an older man, the other a young woman. There were two blood stained swords along with a shredded duffle bag.

Yuri knelt beside the woman first. She was dressed entirely in black from head to toe. Yuri opened the long black leather coat to reveal a leather belt with a crossbow clipped to it along with a scabbard full of arrows. There was also a leather sheath with a dagger still in it. Yuri patted her down and felt something underneath her blouse. He opened a few buttons to discover that she was wearing body armor, and had been stabbed just below where it ended. Yuri took his walkie talkie and ordered to have a crime scene team come to the baggage car. He rose to his feet and walked over to the man.

The man was dressed professionally in a suit and overcoat. Yuri knelt down and rolled the man to his side. He patted the man down and removed what appeared to be a leather wallet from the man's overcoat pocket. But instead, when Captain Brewster opened it and inside there was a police badge. It identified him as Lieutenant Gunderson of the Berlin police department. This was the same Lieutenant Gunderson that had contacted him about the operation to go to Gothica and the Knights of VanHelsing. Captain Brewster glanced back at the woman. He realized now, that the way she was dressed, matched the description Lieutenant Gunderson had given him of a Knight of VanHelsing. Yuri also noticed that Lieutenant Gunderson's service piece was missing. So he instantly surmised that a third person was involved in this whole mess. Captain Brewster spoke again into his walkie to secure all passengers, including the ones in the sleeping cars. Captain Brewster jumped up and exited the baggage car. He ordered Günter to come with him.

Yuri and Günter entered the sleeping car and had just started down the hallway when a man burst out of one of the sleeping compartments.

"That man tried to attack me!" he blurted out with the door open.

"Step aside," Yuri ordered. He entered the sleeping compartment.

The man on the floor was unconscious and beside him was Lieutenant Gunderson's missing gun. Yuri knelt down and retrieved the man's passport. The photo and information identified him as Andrew Knight. This was the man being sought in the death of the police sergeant from the Berlin police.

"May I see your papers please?" Yuri rose and walked over to the man. He gave up the passport. Yuri opened it.

"Exactly what happened here Mister Schultz," Yuri asked referring to the passport. "Mister Eric Schultz."

"There was a knock at the door," he explained. "When I opened it, that man there forced me back inside."

"How did you subdue him?" Yuri curiously asked.

"He was watching out the window and I hit him over the head," Eric replied. "I had taken some self-defense classes and, well, used it to knock him out.

"Well," Yuri said handing him back his passport. "This man is suspected of killing a police officer in Berlin. It was very brave of you, but stupid to take this man on."

"I never realized that," Eric answered, wide-eyed.

"We will take him into custody," Yuri further said. "You are to remain on the train until after everyone is questioned."

"What happened?" Eric asked.

"Two people were found dead in the baggage car by a Porter," Yuri explained. He looked down at Andrew. "I suspect that this man was also involved somehow."

"I need to let my boss know that I will be delayed," Eric said. "May I text her?"

"By all means," Yuri answered. "Then I would ask you to move to the passenger cars so that we may question you and the others further."

"Alright," Eric replied. He took out his phone as Yuri radioed for assistance.

Blackness. There was nothing but the sound of her breathing. Was there anyone there beyond the dark? Was she all alone? No way to measure time.

Darkness. There was nothing but the sound of her gentle breathing. The last images burned in her mind were of Andrew lying on the ground. Was he still alive?

Abyss. The sound of her breathing grew more labored. Panic had taken over and she felt wetness in the corner of her eyes. Where was she?

Nightshade. Her breathing was grew faster and faster. She couldn't catch her breath. Her arms and legs were bound with rope. Was any one there?

Ebony. This time there were new sounds. A key being turned in a lock and a heavy sounding door opening. Footsteps drew near with an air of purpose. The door closed. The footsteps stopped. She was not alone.

Nothingness. Her breathing had slowed down. She listened to see what the other person was doing. They were not moving. Were they looking her over? Were they toying with her by remaining silent? She tried to speak but her mouth was bound with tape. Why were they not speaking?

Bleakness. Her breathing was calmer now. She strained to hear what was going on.

"Welcome home, Raven Blade," an all too familiar woman's voice spoke from the dark. Suddenly, the darkness had withdrawn and firelight strained her eyes. The tape was stripped from her mouth and the tingling felt like a thousand needles striking at once.

"I no longer go by that name," Talia replied.

"To me you will always be Raven Blade," the woman answered. Her hair was black and streaked with stokes of silver gray. The black dress she wore was long and flowing. Flesh, the color of alabaster, peaked out from beneath the accentuated v-neck. "But you have betrayed us to the outsiders."

"What I did in the name of good was wrong, Anastasia," Talia answered.

"We purge the world of evil," Anastasia calmly replied. "As you recall it all started with my great-great grandfather, Abraham VanHelsing."

"Andrew will come," Talia suddenly announced defiantly.

"We know," Anastasia replied. "He won't last much longer. He is no match for us."

"He will come," Talia repeated.

"He will die!" Anastasia answered bluntly.

"Where is Kara?" Talia demanded.

"She is safe," Anastasia replied. Her phone buzzed. She took it out of her pocket and saw that there was a text message. She smiled and glanced in Talia's direction. "I just received a text message from Gold Blade."

"What is it?" Talia asked.

"He just texted me that Andrew Knight has been arrested by the Zwickau police." Anastasia had a wide grin of satisfaction on her face. "It looks like your so called hero is out of action and won't be coming to rescue you or Kara." She texted Gold Blade that she would send a helicopter to pick him up and that she needed his location. Anastasia waited for a reply. He texted his location and that he would be ready. She walked over to the door and opened it. Two knights entered the room and loosened Talia from the chair. They each grabbed her by the arm and escorted Talia out of the room.

Kara bolted straight up. She scanned the room with wild-eyed confusion. Where was she? The room had one single window, no furniture save for a simple desk and chair, along with the bed she was lying on.

The last thing Kara saw was Nick being attacked. She didn't even know if he were still alive. Kara started to cry, but she quickly scolded herself for being a wimp and stopped. She also realized she was no longer wearing her dress. Someone had changed her into a black jumpsuit and shoes. Kara bounded off the bed and over to the door. She tried the handle, it was locked. She went over to the window. It was tall and narrow without any way to open it. Kara was trapped.

Eric had changed into his knight's garb and was just strapping on his weaponry. Andrew was still unconscious and had been moved to the bed. Eric heard the helicopter in the distance. He pulled the door open quickly and knocked out the solitary officer standing guard over him and Andrew. He grabbed both suitcases and headed for the exit. He never intended to go to the passenger's cars as ordered. Eric had to get to Gothica at all costs. He set one case down and opened the door. Eric propped the door open and retrieved the case. He quickly descended the steps and ran towards the open field not far from the train.

Captain Brewster was interviewing a male passenger on the train when he heard what sounded like a helicopter. He stopped to peer out one of the windows. There in the distance was a black helicopter preparing for a landing in the field not far from the train. Yuri was about to turn his attention back to the investigation, but something else caught his eye. There, not far from the train, he saw someone in a Knight's of VanHelsing uniform running while carrying a suitcase in both hands. Yuri grabbed his walkie and called for the officer standing guard at that location. There was no reply. Yuri immediately started screaming in it for some of his men to stop the person.

Eric felt the rush of the wind from the helicopter blades as he approached it. The door slid open and one of his compatriots in full gear, reached out to give him a hand. Eric tossed up one of the suitcases.

Yuri and several of his men took off in pursuit of Eric. They bounded over the rails and quickly rushed towards the helicopter. Yuri saw the door slide open and someone reach out towards Eric. Yuri drew his gun and fired off several shots.

Eric froze as the dinging of bullets struck the helicopter. They were shooting at him! He tossed in the last suitcase inside and reached for the crossbow. Eric loaded an arrow and fired!

Yuri felt a pressure in his thigh and he tumbled down in the grassy mud. He rolled over and saw the arrow shaft buried in the flesh of his leg. He managed to pull himself up on one foot and fired until his gun was empty.

Eric jumped inside as another volley of shots struck frighteningly close; too close as far as he was concerned.

"Take off now!" Eric barked as he loaded another arrow. He fired again.

Yuri was knocked to the ground from the forced of the arrow as it slammed him in the right shoulder.

His gun flew out of his hand and seconds later, landed some distance away from him. He screamed at his men to keep firing, but it had no affect. Yuri watched helplessly as the helicopter disappeared from sight. His men helped Yuri to his feet and helped him back to the train. Yuri grimaced in pain as he hobbled along back to the train.

The glowing red sun was slowly disappearing on the distant horizon as the sound of metal whirling blades filled the still air of the valley. It would be dark soon, and time for Gold Blade to finally come home again.

Gothica castle had been forged out of the very mountains of the Ore Mountain range. With its towering, impenetrable walls, no one dared attempt to challenge it. It stood solitary, forbidding to all who dared enter the valley long forgotten by both man and time.

Kara watched from the window as the helicopter touched down. The door slid open and a solitary figure jumped out. Whoever they were, the person was in full knight's garb right down to the weapons. The person strode with an air of confidence towards the woman that was waiting for them. Her hair was black and streaked with stokes of silver gray. The black dress she wore was long and flowing. Kara thought for a second and snapped her fingers as she remembered. Of course, the woman was Anastasia VanHelsing, the leader of the Knights of VanHelsing. Kara watched them embrace and soon after, walked together arm in arm inside the castle.

Talia had been staring out the narrow window of her room ever since she was taken there after her interrogation by Anastasia. She was reflecting on the cards life had dealt her. Some were good cards worth holding onto. Others were not so good and Talia wished she could have traded them in for better ones. Talia grew tried and was about to step away from the window, when she saw a helicopter approach the castle. She watched the helicopter land. The side door of the helicopter slid. Talia's blood ran cold at the sight of a Knight of VanHelsing. Talia also saw Anastasia waiting to greet them.

Gold Blade and Anastasia walked down the long stone hallway and finally stopped at a large metal and wooden door. Anastasia twisted the knob and gave the door a gentle push to open it. She led the way inside and Gold Blade followed. Anastasia closed the door behind them. She locked it.

Anastasia walked over and sat down on the canopy bed. She stretched out her arms invitingly for Gold Blade to join her. He walked over but stopped just short of her reach.

"Please remove your hood," Anastasia asked.

"Both Silver Blade and Bronze Blade are dead," Gold Blade sadly informed her.

"How?" Anastasia demanded.

"Silver Blade was killed in the park and Bronze Blade was in a fight with Andrew Knight and some policeman from Berlin," Eric answered.

"You removed all of their identification, right?" Anastasia asked.

"I know the drill," Eric shot back.

"At least we have the others," Anastasia answered instead. "And Knight is out of the picture. He will be in a German prison for quite some time." Anastasia laughed.

"Where are the women?" Gold Blade inquired.

"Safe on the third floor in two of the empty guest rooms," Anastasia answered.

"Now forget about all that and take off your hood," Anastasia ordered.

"We both know the rules," Gold Blade reminded. "Our identity is to remain a secret." He gestured around the room. "Even within the walls of Gothica, a knight's face is never to be revealed."

"I know the laws." Anastasia was getting upset.

"I will not remove it." Gold Blade was defiant.

"But we were lovers once and you showed me your face." Anastasia pouted. "Why not again?" She rose from the bed and walked over to Gold Blade. She slipped her arms around his waist and laid her head on his chest. "Perhaps we could rekindle the passion we once had." Anastasia drew her glance upon his hooded face. "What happened that night is in the past."

"Not that far in the past," Gold Blade grabbed her arms and slipped from her embrace.

"He meant nothing to me," Anastasia eyes swelled with tears.

"Nothing?" Gold Blade scoffed.

"Do not get upset, Eric," Anastasia finally said his name. "Please remove your weapons and place them on the table." Anastasia gestured towards the table not far from the bed. Eric went over and removed his belt.

He laid it on the table. Next, he took off the scabbards that held his swords. He laid them also on the table. Then he took off his long leather coat and gently draped it across his things. Eric walked back over to Anastasia.

"Listen Ana." Eric took hold of her hands.

"You haven't called me that name in years." Ana started to cry again. Eric took her in his arms. It was a rhapsody for Ana to final feel Eric's embrace. "Why now?" Eric lifted the hood just a little. Ana exhaled deeply and her bossom quivered as Eric brushed his lips against the flesh of her neck.

"I'm not the same man as I was before," Eric whispered. Ana felt a chill from the warmth of his breath.

"What do you mean?" Ana broke free to face him.

Gold Blade finally removed his hood for Ana.

"You!" shrieked Ana. She gave Andrew a shove and ran for the door.

Andrew took off after Ana and reached her as she was about to unlock the door. Andrew grabbed Ana and tossed her aside. Ana rebounded and slammed Andrew with a kick to the chest, but it had no affect because of the body armor he wore. Andrew countered with a spin kick that struck Ana in the midriff. She doubled over and Andrew finished her off with another blow to the head. Ana crumpled to the floor and was out cold. Andrew walked over to the door to make sure it was still locked; it was. Andrew walked over and scooped Ana up into his arms and he carried her over to the bed. He gently laid her down.

Andrew sat next to her and reflected on recent events. Andrew knew that Hannah was not alone on the train. She had to have a backup. So when Andrew left the baggage car he searched for her partner. It was either by luck or whatever, but Andrew located him in the first sleeping cabin he tried. Andrew chuckled as he remembered the shocked look on Eric's face when he opened the door of the compartment to see Andrew standing there and not Hannah. Even before Eric could react, Andrew knocked him out and pushed him back inside. The idea to switch identities just came to Andrew as he was searching the compartment. Andrew had taken both their passports and with his pocket knife carefully slit open the lamination. Once he had switched their photos, Andrew used a bit of superglue he had found in a drawer in the compartment. When the police arrived, Andrew waited for the right moment to step out of the compartment and put on his act. He knew at first that Captain Brewster was suspicious of him, but when he saw the passports all of that disappeared. In order to convince those at Gothica, Andrew sent the text message. He knew it would be the only way to convince them that he, Andrew, was out of the picture even if only for a little while. Hopefully, and it was, long enough to get inside the castle. Also, Andrew had to conceal his identity, and betting on the fact that none of the other knight's had seen each others faces, Andrew dressed in the knight's garb. Andrew felt bad that he had to shoot Captain Brewster, but it was necessary to convince the ones in the helicopter that he was in fact Gold Blade.

Andrew bounded off the bed and over to the dresser. He opened the drawers and searched for something to tie Ana up with. Andrew found a bunch of silk scarves.

He tied several together to make them a bit longer. Andrew returned to the bed and secured Ana's hands and feet together. He further secured Ana to the bed posts. And as a finishing touch Andrew tied a scarf in Ana's mouth to keep her from calling for help. Once he was satisfied that Ana would be unable to escape, Andrew retrieved the coat and weapons. He strapped the belt back on, put on the leather coat and finished securing both sword scabbards on his back. Andrew slid the hood back on and took one last look at Ana. She was still out. Andrew walked to the door and unlocked it. He opened the door and peered out to see if the coast was clear. Andrew stepped into the hallway, relocked the door and closed it behind him. The sound of the heavy door, closing signaled the beginning of his search for Kara, Talia, and Wyatt.

Andrew crept along the dimly lit hallway of the third floor. Not a soul was in sight and he hoped that was a good thing. Andrew had tried several doors and found them to be unlocked. There were only four doors left to try. Andrew grasped hold of the door knob of the first one and gave it a twist. It was not locked. He tried the next one and it was also unlocked. Andrew quietly crossed over to the other side of the hallway. A sense of disappointed and doubt set in for a second as Andrew reached for the door handle. He gripped it firmly for fear of letting go and gave it a turn. It was locked! Andrew knelt down and reached inside the long coat. Andrew retrieved his lucky lock pick set that he had remembered to take from his duffle bag on the train. Andrew inspected the lock and removed the necessary picks.

Talia was lying in the bed when she heard some sounds coming from the door. She quietly slipped off the bed and over to the door. Someone was about to come inside, so Talia readied herself for an attack. Whoever it was; was going to get the surprise of their life. Talia heard the click in the lock and she poised for her attack.

Andrew slowly opened the door and stepped inside. Out of the corner of his eye, he caught some movement. Andrew immediately dropped to the floor as a fist swung to hit him. Andrew kicked out his foot and knocked the person to the floor. He jumped on them and pinned the person down.

Talia saw the door open. With all her might she swung her fist at the person, but instead, struck only air. The next thing Talia knew she was on the ground and the person had managed to pin her down.

Andrew took off his hood when he saw it was Talia.

"Andrew!" Talia squealed with joy.

Andrew offered Talia his hand. She took it.

Talia threw her arms around Andrew and squeezed him tightly.

"Okay," Andrew announced that it was enough.

"What? Talia babbled. "How did you get here?"

"I will fill you in later," Andrew said putting the hood back on. "We need to get Kara."

They left the room.

Ana woke to find herself bound to her bed. She was pissed. How could a private investigator from Bayport,

Wisconsin manage to out wit, out smart and out fight her knights? Apparently she had underestimated Andrew Knight as an adversary. Years ago during a training session Ana had dislocated her right wrist. Now any time she wanted to, Ana could dislocate it. Though it was painful, it was the only way to get out of her bonds. Ana closed her eyes and gave her wrist a sharp twist. She grimaced at the sound of her bones slipping out of place. With her wrist limp, Ana slipped out of her bonds easily and sat up. Now came the part she dreaded, putting her wrist back in place. Ana howled when she snapped her wrist back.

Ana quickly untied her feet and jumped off the bed and over to her walk-in closet. She undressed and immediately put on her knight's garb. Ana slipped on her long coat and strapped on the scabbards that held her custom made, pearl handled, swords. They were a gift from her father when she took over as leader of the Knights of VanHelsing. Ana strapped on the belt with crossbow and arrows around her waist. Andrew Knight and the others were not going to get away. Ana walked out of the closet and closed the door behind her. She immediately unlocked the door and left her room.

Ana took off in the direction of the third floor to stop Andrew from setting Talia and Kara free.

Kara was lying on the bed when she heard the door open. She didn't even bother to get up at first.

Finally, Kara sat up. She saw Talia being escorted in the room by one of the Knights.

"What do you want from me now?" Kara demanded.

"For all of us to go home," Talia answered.

"We're prisoners," Kara retorted.

"Do you want to or not?" He removed his hood.

"Andrew!" Kara couldn't get off the bed fast enough. She jumped on him and they both fell to the floor. Kara smothered Andrew with kisses.

"Okay," Andrew pushed Kara off. They stood up.

"How?" Kara asked with curious eyes. She looked around. "Where is Nick?"

"We need to find Wyatt and get the hell out of here," Andrew said. He put the hood back on, "I will explain it all once we get out of here."

The three companions walked out of the room and went off in search of Wyatt.

The lower floors were quite opposite of the third. There were several Knights about and it made Kara and Talia very nervous. Andrew had come up with the cover story that he was taking them to be interrogated. They must have believed him, for the others left them alone.

As they walked along, one of the Knights followed a few paces behind. Either they did not believe the cover story or it was for another reason. Perhaps they wanted to make sure that Andrew did, in fact, take them to the interrogation room.

Andrew was aware of them being followed. He whispered for the girls to remain calm and just keep on walking. They did as Andrew instructed and remained silent as they walked along. When they reached a side passageway, Andrew told them to head in that direction. Andrew had them press up against the wall when they had gotten to a bend in the passageway. When the Knight that was following them reached the bend,

Andrew struck! Within seconds he knocked out the person and had them on the floor. Andrew removed the person's hood to reveal it was a young man who looked to be no more than seventeen or eighteen.

"That's Wyatt," Talia blurted out, but immediately covered her mouth.

"Holy crap," Kara added. "Now what?"

"He must have recognized Talia and decided to follow us," Andrew surmised. "Otherwise he had no reason not to believe our cover story." Andrew said disappointedly. "Unfortuantely the only way out of here is by helicopter, and none of us know how to fly."

"I know how to fly," Kara announced. "I have my pilot's license."

"You do?" Andrew and Talia said at the same time.

"Like yeah," Kara repeated with a head bob.

"So how do we get Wyatt and us out of here?" Talia looked to Andrew.

"We make a break for it," Andrew answered. "Andrew knelt down and lifted Wyatt over his shoulder. "Let's go." Talia led the way to the to the helicopter area as the others followed.

The full moon was just peering over the majestic mountains. Ana was getting angrier by the minute. When she got to the third floor, she discovered that Andrew had already freed Talia and Kara. The next person he would search for was Wyatt. Ana smiled that there was no way out of all the knights at Gothica Andrew would be able to locate Wyatt. Ana walked over to the window and cast her gaze upon the moon. She could almost feel the light as it fell upon her.

Ana closed her eyes for a moment to draw it in as if it was an elixir for her soul. She opened her eyes again and that's when Ana saw Andrew and the others on the helicopter pad. Ana cursed and departed the room at a full run. There was no way she was going to let them escape.

Kara opened the door and climbed in the pilot's seat. She began the preflight sequence. The whine of the rotors coming to life filled the night air. Andrew slid the side door open and put a still unconscious Wyatt inside. Talia stood beside Andrew, keeping watch and soon her fears were realized. A small army of knights were approaching their position with Ana in the lead. Talia shouted at Andrew, but the wind and the noise from the rotors drowned her out. She watched in terror as Ana and the knights loaded their crossbows. Talia gave Andrew a shove and when he turned, Andrew saw the army of knights.

"Get inside!" Andrew tried to push Talia to the open door. She instead spun around and faced Andrew to shield him. As each arrow struck, Talia moaned as her body jerked. When it was over, she lunged forward and Andrew caught her in his arms. Her eyes looked hollow as she stared up at Andrew.

Talia brought up her hands and gently, lovingly and cupped Andrew's face. She drank in the sadness it showed.

"Do you know what true love is Andrew?"

"No," Andrew's answered, tears clouded his eyes.

Talia strained as she rose up. She drew closer. Andrew and Talia's lips came together in one last, tender, loving kiss.

"Sacrifice," Talia whispered as their lips drew apart. Talia was gone.

"Andrew!" Kara screamed. "We have to go!"

Andrew ignored her and gently laid Talia down. He finally turned to look at Kara. "Get out of here." Andrew closed the door as Kara was still screaming at him to get in.

Kara saw Andrew gingerly lay Talia down and let loose the belt and drop it to the ground. Her eyes widened in further disbelief as Kara saw Andrew withdraw the twin swords from their scabbards. Kara kept shouting at Andrew. She couldn't believe that he was going to take on Ana and her army of knights. They were trained killers! Kara was crying so hard she could barely see the instrument panel. She wiped her eyes and grasp hold of the throttle and the engines roared to full power. She would take off and then circle back to pick up Andrew.

The helicopter started to rise to the heavens. Kara turned the helicopter about and she saw Andrew, who was just about to attack. That's when Kara also noticed the knights on the parapet above. They were loading wall mounted ballistas! Just as she turned the helicopter, they fired the first volley. Six highly deadly bolts rushed towards the helicopter. Kara forced the helicopter lower and they harmlessly flew by. Kara saw them make adjustments and reload for another volley, so she headed towards the valley and trees below. A second wave screamed towards the defenseless helicopter. Kara felt a sudden violent shudder, pieces of metal and black smoke shot past the side windows. They had hit the rear rotor! The controls went heavy in

Kara's hands. The helicopter was spinning as Kara tried to gain control. The trees and snowy ground drew closer and closer!

Ana couldn't believe that Andrew was going to charge their position. She ordered her knights to remove their belts and make ready for Andrew's attack. He was truly a fool to take them on. These were the best of all her knights; her elite guard. Ana let her belt drop as well and drew her own blades.

Andrew gave his battle cry and jumped up into the air. As he came back down, Andrew hit the first two with devastating kicks. Their heads snapped back with a sickening sound and they flew to the ground dead. Andrew landed and with his swords struck two more even before they could raise their own swords in defense. Andrew was in a fight to the death. The anger raging inside Andrew made him strong and unstoppable. The clashing of steel and the sounds of cracking bones echoed across the walls of Gothica. Two more knights charged into the mêlée. Andrew twirled about and drove his blades into their chests. Blood flowed and covered the grayish stone of Gothica. Andrew smashed and kicked his way amongst Ana's elite. Finally, the last knight tumbled down and joined the rest of his fallen comrades. Andrew stood tall amongst the bloody and broken heap. He looked up in the sky just in time to see a barrage of steel tipped bolts fly towards the helicopter. Andrew recoiled when one of the bolts slammed into the rear rotor. It exploded, sending pieces of metal flying amongst streams of black smoke. Andrew saw the helicopter plunge towards the forest below.

Ana stood still. She was in shock. Andrew had defeated her knights; her very best! There Andrew stood victorious amongst the bloody heap he had created. Andrew Knight had to die!

Ana readied her pearl handled swords and charged at him. Andrew was distracted and it gave Ana the advantage. She was nearly upon Andrew and flew in the air and smashed into his back. Andrew sprawled to the ground. Ana brought both blades down but Andrew rolled over and blocked with his own. He jumped to his feet and swung at Ana, who blocked and twirled with a spin kick. Andrew blocked and drove his blades at Ana. She blocked with one and attacked with the other. Andrew met each with his own. Ana spun and hit Andrew with a powerful kick to the back. He fell forward, dropped, and rolled to his feet. Ana, with her blades ready to strike, rushed towards him. Andrew was ready. With one sword he slashed through the flesh of Ana's leg and with the other, thrust it into her shoulder. Ana stumbled and let loose her swords which clattered to the stone ground. She rolled over to see Andrew towering above her.

"The Knights of VanHelsing will live on," Ana was defiant. She closed her eyes and waited for Andrew to strike her down. Andrew rendered Ana unconscious instead with a blow to the head.

Hours later, after the battle with Ana and her knights, Andrew finally had the courage, and took Talia's body into his arms. He looked up and searched the parapets. There was no sign of any knights. Andrew carried Talia inside the castle. He ascended the stairs to the third floor of Gothica and looked for a place to lay Talia's body.

Andrew soon found an unoccupied bedroom chamber. He opened the door and stepped inside the room. There was a beautifully adorned canopy bed. Andrew walked over to the bed and laid Talia on her side. He swallowed hard and grasped hold of the first arrow. Andrew breathed deeply, emotionally for several seconds. His hand trembled, and Andrew closed his eyes as he removed the first arrow. For each arrow Andrew took out of Talia, the anguish and tears built to an emotional crescendo. And as the last arrow was withdrawn, Andrew slumped to the cold, harsh floor. He stared at the bloody object in his hand for a moment, and tossed it away. Andrew pulled himself up and pulled back the covers. He gingerly rolled Talia on her back. Andrew drew up the covers to her waist and folded Talia's arms across her chest. It looked as if she were only sleeping.

Andrew tenderly kissed Talia's lips. He would come back for Talia's body and bring her home. Andrew knew that her knights would search for Kara and Wyatt. Andrew hoped he wasn't too late.

The passageways of the Gothica were empty. Andrew walked alone, a shadow of his former self.

Chapter 15

Andrew drew into the clearing among the forest and was met with a strange and unexpected sight. It was a graveyard of rusted heaps of war birds from the past. And there among those deteriorating carcasses was the newest addition, the black helicopter. It was still relatively intact and rested on top of a cargo plane. He was amazed that somehow Kara had managed to land the helicopter.

Andrew scanned the snowy ground. There were several boot prints that came in from the north, the direction of Gothica castle. Andrew followed them until he was at the cargo plane. It was at the plane that Andrew saw two more sets of boot prints. He crouched down to examine them more closely. One set was not as deep as the other. That must be Kara's. The others must be Wyatt's, for they were deeper. Andrew deduced that Wyatt was injured by the way his left boot dragged as he walked. Also, Andrew saw a perfectly round hole next to the boot print. Wyatt had to use something to support his injured foot or leg.

Andrew rose and began to follow their tracks. When he was some distance from the cargo plane, Andrew saw that the knights picked up the trail and were following Wyatt and Kara. Andrew continued on until all but the knights' tracks disappeared. He could see that the knights continued their search in the surrounding woods. Andrew stopped. He deduced that the knights' thinking was only one dimensional. They would assume that Kara and Wyatt would continue on through the rough terrain in order to escape. So therefore, the knights' would simply search for them until they finally would just give up. However, Andrew thought that if Wyatt was injured, there would be no way for him or Kara to do that. Kara and Wyatt would have to find some place to hide and wait out the knights. It would have to be some place close by. Andrew turned and ran back to the war bird graveyard.

Andrew stopped at the set of tracks by the cargo plane. This time he knelt down and examined the boot prints more closely. A slight smile spread across Andrew's lips as he came to a realization. Both sets of prints were made by the same person. Andrew further deduced that first one set of booth prints were made up until they disappeared. Then Kara grabbed a stick and used it to support her as she walked backwards. That was why the other set was deeper and the stick mark was next to them. Andrew stood up and walked over to the side door of the cargo plane. The door was slightly open. Andrew leaned closer and peered through the crack. He saw a taught string rigged to the door. Andrew stepped aside and flung the door open. An arrow flew safely past him and buried itself in the snow.

Andrew jumped inside the plane and tucked and rolled as another arrow zoomed overhead. Andrew sprung to his feet and blocked a kick meant for his face. He grabbed the person's leg and pushed them down.

"Kara!" Andrew called out. The attack ended.

Kara jumped up and threw her arms around Andrew. She gave him a full, on mouth, fervent kiss. Andrew gently pushed her away.

"Sorry," Kara apologized. "It's just that I thought they had killed you, and with the crash and all, well, I just got carried away."

"It's okay," Andrew reassured her. He came up to her and put his arms around her. Kara rested her head on Andrew's chest. "I thought you were dead too. But we're okay now." Kara looked up at Andrew, "How did you know we were in here?"

"I followed your tracks," Andrew answered.

"If you did, then…" Kara started to say.

"Don't worry your rouse worked on the Knights," Andrew reassured. "They believe that you two are somewhere in the forest." Andrew glanced down at Kara, "By the way that was pretty ingenious of you to make both sets of tracks." Andrew now looked around the interior of the cargo plane. There among the deteriorating wooden crates, was a sleeping area made up of old parachutes and canvas tarps. That's where Andrew saw Wyatt, who hadn't woken up during all the commotion."

"What's wrong with Wyatt?" Andrew asked.

"He was knocked cold," Kara answered.

"Let's sit down and then you can explain it all to me," Andrew suggested. Kara gave him a squeeze and took hold of Andrew's hand. She led them over to Wyatt. She and Andrew sat down on the cushioned floor.

"The last thing I saw was the helicopter out of control," Andrew said. "How did you manage to gain control?"

"It was part of my training," Kara explained. "We used a simulator to learn how bring a helicopter out of crash situations just like that."

"What happened after you landed?" Andrew asked.

"During the landing, which was still quite rough, Wyatt was knocked out," Kara answered. "Fortunately there was a hole in the top of the cargo plane, so I lowered the both of us inside. After I got Wyatt secured away, I climbed back up to the helicopter. I grabbed the medical supplies and that's when I noticed a weapons storage box. When I opened it, I found several crossbows along with arrows inside." Kara paused to catch her breath as she was speaking so quickly to get all the information out for Andrew. Kara went on, "So I took the medical supplies down first and then went back for the weapons. I knew we had to lead the knights away from the plane. But with Wyatt still out cold, I had to make both sets of tracks. When I got to the edge of the clearing, I found a stick and used it, as a support. When I was done, it looked like Wyatt was injured. When I got back to the plane, I found some twine and rigged up the cross bow traps. It was just in case we had any unwanted guests."

"Like me?" Andrew interjected.

"No," Kara laughed. She turned more serious again, "After that I needed to get some rest. I had lain down beside Wyatt and fell asleep."

"Well, you're not going to like this," Andrew started to say.

"No, no, no way..." Kara protested.

"We need to go back and get the other helicopter," Andrew insisted. "It's the only way out of here."

"What about Ana and her knights?" Kara was afraid.

"We'll use the secret entrance to get inside," Andrew reassured Kara with an embrace. "I will take care of Ana and the rest." Andrew answered. He took a deep breath. "There is one more thing."

"What's that?" Kara asked.

"We need to find out where Ana has the list of all the Knights of VanHelsing," Andrew answered. Kara saw the serious expression on his face. "It's the only way we can put a stop to the Knight's forever."

"It too dangerous of a thing to do," Kara warned. "If they know you have it, you're a dead man."

"Once I have the list," Andrew came back. "They are finished."

"What about Wyatt?" Kara nodded in his direction.

"He should be fine here until he wakes up," Andrew stood up. "We'll just reset your traps and settle in for a bit. The sleeping area you built, should keep us warm. We'll need to stay inside the plane until tonight. That's when we make our move." Andrew walked over to the crossbows Kara had rigged up. He reset the twine and loaded the crossbows. Andrew joined Kara, who was already lying down, and lay behind her. Kara was shivering. Andrew spooned Kara, sharing his warmth with her. Kara reached back and brought Andrew's arm over her. She took hold of his hand and gave it a squeeze.

"When I saw you charge Ana and her knights," Kara spoke softly. "I thought you were going to die." She started to cry. Andrew bent down and kissed Kara's cheek and gave her a reassuring squeeze. "We're okay now. Soon we'll be on our way home."

"It's not okay for Talia," Kara was still crying. "She sacrificed herself for us; for you." Kara turned over and faced Andrew. "Why did she do that?"

"For love," Andrew sniffed. He finally broke down. Kara drew Andrew to her and let him rest his head on her bossom. She held onto Andrew tightly with tears in her own eyes. Kara didn't know if they would even make it back home. Kara dried her tears and that's when she realized Andrew had fallen asleep. Kara closed her eyes and was soon asleep too.

Wyatt jolted awake. He looked around. The surroundings were unfamiliar. Wyatt had a hunch he was inside an old cargo plane with all the wooden crates and things. He looked closer and saw a man and a woman asleep. They were the same ones that had kidnapped him from the castle. Wyatt had to get away and back to Gothica. He moved ever so slowly so as not to wake them. Wyatt finally slid off the bed of old parachutes. He looked at the door and saw the rigged crossbows. There was no way he could use that door. Wyatt looked around and saw the hole in the ceiling of the plane. He crept quietly over to it and used the crates as his escape staircase. Wyatt pulled himself up and was just about out when he cut his hand on the jagged metal of the hole. Blood seeped from his wound. Wyatt licked his lips at the sight of the blood. Forgotten urges consumed Wyatt as he brought his hand up to his lips. Wyatt lapped up the crimson from his hand. Now was not the time for this. Wyatt pulled his hand away and finished the climb. He looked at his surroundings. Wyatt saw Gothica off in the distance. He smiled broadly. Wyatt slid down and tucked and rolled when he hit the snowy ground. He glanced back at the cargo plane one last time, smiled at the success of his escape, and immediately took off for Gothic. Wyatt ran as fast as he could go. He had to tell Ana and his fellow knights where the man and woman were hiding. His courage would surely impress Ana and she would make him one of her elite squad.

Andrew was the first to wake up. He looked up at the hole. It was still daylight. They would have to wait until dark to slip back into Gothica. Andrew glanced down at Kara. She was sleeping so peacefully, that he did not want to wake her. Andrew turned to check on Wyatt, but he was not there! Andrew jumped up and searched the plane with his eyes. The rigged crossbows were still in tack. That meant Wyatt had to have climbed out the hole in the ceiling. Andrew hopped up on the crates and was about to climb out of the hole when he noticed blood on some of the metal. Wyatt must have injured himself when he climbed out. Andrew finished his climb and sat down on the top of the cargo plane. He could see a trail of blood droplets on the plane and in the snow down below. Andrew already knew where Wyatt was headed; straight to Gothica. He also knew that Wyatt would tell Ana and her knights exactly where they were. Andrew went back to the hole and dropped down inside.

Kara woke up to see Andrew drop back down inside the plane. Why had he gone outside in the first place? Kara glanced around and saw that Wyatt was gone. She jumped up in a panic.

Andrew hopped down from the last crate and walked over to Kara, who was awake now.

"Wyatt is gone and he has headed back to Gothica," Andrew said. He looked worried.

"What do we do now?" Kara was scared.

"We have to get out of here before they come for us," Andrew answered. He left and went over to the rigged crossbows. Andrew released the triggers and removed the strings. "We need to take these with us."

"They will know we are coming," Kara wailed. "How do we get back inside Gothica?"

"We have to use the secret entrance," Andrew informed her again.

"It will be guarded," Kara answered back sharply.

"We will have to be smart and careful," Andrew reassured her. "Once inside we need to find all the information we can about the Knights of VanHelsing."

"When I interviewed Ana for my book, she mentioned a journal with all the names, real names, of the knights," Kara recalled. She paused briefly as another thought filled her head. "That book also contains the names of all the 'vampires' that were killed by the knights over the years." Kara was more worried than ever. She warned Andrew, "With that book you could put and end to centuries of innocent deaths at the hands of Ana and her knights. It would be too dangerous for it to be in your possession. They would never let you use it or keep it."

"It is the only way to finally put an end to their reign of death," Andrew shot back. He took one last look around. "We need to get going."

"Okay," Kara agreed.

Andrew climbed up the crates with Kara right behind him. He handed her his crossbow. Andrew pulled himself up and out on top of the cargo plane. He looked around and was relieved that the coast was clear. Andrew told Kara that it was clear. She handed him up the crossbows and arrow scabbards. Kara boosted herself up and climbed out of the plane. She joined Andrew. They slid down together and headed off towards the forest. They would have to find a place to hide until dark.

Ana dropped down on one knee just at the crest of the meadow and surveyed it through her spy glass. She saw the helicopter that rested on top of the cargo plane. There was no movement. Either Andrew or Kara were still inside, or already gone. Ana hoped that they were still inside the plane. It would make things much easier. When Wyatt showed up at Gothica, Ana knew that Kara was still alive. When her knights had searched the surrounding forest and had not found any trace of them, Ana was furious. She wondered how they could have escaped. The surrounding forest and mountains were virtually impossible to traverse on foot. Ana knew they had to be somewhere close by, but never suspected the old airplane graveyard. Andrew had become a liability and needed to be eliminated. Ana suspected that

Andrew might be after journal. Ana smirked that Andrew would never find it, but if he ever did, he would never have a chance to use it.

Ana looked one more time through the spyglass. There was still no movement. Ana signaled her knights to advance on the plane. They loaded their crossbows and crept forward. Ana loaded her own weapon and advanced onto the cargo plane.

The knights took up positions at the door and on top of the plane. Ana immediately signaled for the attack on the cargo plane to begin. The two knights who were next to the side door, pulled it open and ducked, but nothing came out at them. They slipped inside as the ones on top of the plane dropped down to join them. Ana entered the plane once her knights had it secured. Andrew and Kara were gone. That meant they were on their way to Gothica. But it was too risky to try and enter during the light of day. Ana suspected that Andrew would attempt it only when it was dark. Either way, she and her knights would be ready for them. Ana promised herself that she would repay Andrew for the defeat he had brought upon them. Ana would make certain that Andrew and Kara would die before the dawn tomorrow. Ana instructed her knights to follow and they left the cargo plane.

Ana surveyed the surrounding landscape. She knew that somewhere out there, Andrew was watching at this very moment. Ana narrowed her eyes and clenched her jaw. She needed to anticipate Andrew's next move. What would it be? Ana motioned for her knights to follow and they began their trek back to Gothica.

The secret entrance appeared to be unguarded. Andrew and Kara watched from the safety of some bushes a short distance away. The sun was starting to set and the light was fading fast. Andrew knew that there were some of Ana's knights around, but wasn't sure where.

"Tell me more about your interview with Ana for your book," Andrew asked as he settled down. Kara sat down beside him.

"What do you want to know?" Kara answered.

"Where did you interview her?" Andrew asked.

"We were in the library, why?" Kara inquired.

"Where did you sit?" Andrew continued.

"Why is that important?" Kara pressed.

"Where did you sit?" Andrew repeated the question.

"Is that important?" Kara was still confused.

"Yes," Andrew finally answered. "Ana doesn't do anything without reason. Everything she does has a reason or purpose." Andrew paused to check the secret entrance area, there was no change. He turned back to Kara, "Ana believes that she is the one who decides who lives and who dies and so on. I believe that it was a power trip that led her to have you conduct the interview in the library. Ana was probably gloating with superiority by having you seated near the Knights of VanHelsing book and not even have known it."

"Why wouldn't she hide it in her room," Kara asked, "Where it would be safer?"

"That would be the first place someone would look," Andrew answered. He stopped again to check the area by the secret entrance. There was no movement.

Andrew continued, "They say the best way to hide something is right in plain sight."

What would it be?" Kara asked. This time she checked the area. Kara thought she saw a shadow move across the castle wall. She rubbed her eyes and looked again. There was movement. "Look," Kara whispered and pointed to the shadow. Andrew looked and watched. A few minutes later, two knights walked past the secret entrance and into the shrubbery next to it.

"So how are we going to get inside and to the library?" Kara bit her lip.

"I want you to stay here," Andrew ordered. "I will be right back."

Kara watched as Andrew left the safety of their hiding place.

It was dark now, and the moon's light was cast upon the stone block castle walls. A cool night air rustled throughout the forest of trees.

Two knights kept their vigil. A very important task they were given to fulfill; to keep out their most dangerous adversary. He wasn't the blood thirsty enemy of ancient past. No this one was more deadly. This one had knowledge of their centuries old quest. This enemy sought to destroy them once and for all.

The forest's darkness was still now. The two knights listened with strained ears. With tired eyes they searched the darkness in vain. They knew this enemy was out there somewhere, watching and waiting to strike. Instead, a voice unexpectedly broke the silence; 'Hello, how are you?' The two knights turned to see, and when their eyes set upon him; they froze for a moment in fear. They recovered and instinctively reached for the cross bows that were clipped on their belts. It was too late for them; the enemy had the upper hand. He struck them down unforgivingly and the two brave knights fell where they stood.

The enemy knelt down and in turn searched each one. What was he looking for? Minutes later he found what he was looking for; the key to unlock the secret panel. He stopped for a moment and cast down his eyes on the knights. He wondered what their fate might be. What would their master do since they allowed the enemy to enter the gate?

Andrew stepped from the shadows. He signaled Kara that the coast was clear. She quickly joined him at the wall. Each block was identical to the next; except for the one with the octagon shape carved out of it.

Andrew took the key; a medallion with the VanHelsing crest etched upon it. He placed the medallion in the stone and gave it a push. The wall trembled and moaned as it opened. Andrew took Kara by the hand and at the same time removed the medallion. They quickly stepped inside the passageway just as the wall started to close. Soon the wall was back in its silent post.

The passageway was an abyss, but Andrew remembered the way, since he had used it before, to escape. Kara held tightly onto Andrew's hand as they wound their way through the passage. Soon they stopped. Kara couldn't see, but she knew that Andrew was listening for several minutes.

"Let's go," Andrew finally said.

Light peered through as Andrew opened the stone panel. They exited and now stood in the great room.

"Where is the library?" Andrew asked.

"Down the hallway, last room on the left," Kara answered.

"I want you to find Wyatt," Andrew instructed her. "Use whatever force necessary to get him to come with you." Andrew stopped and scanned the room to make certain they had not been detected. Satisfied, he continued, "After you got him, head for the helicopter."

"What about you?" Kara's eyes began to tear up. "Remember last time?"

"I will be there!" Andrew reassured her with a kiss on the cheek. "One more thing before I go. Where in the library did you conduct your interview with Ana?"

"There is a grand table in the center of the room," Kara answered. She finally got it. "That's where the book is, right?"

"Right," Andrew grinned. He gave Kara a gentle nudge to get going and he headed down the hallway. Kara watched him go. Once he was out of sight, Kara went to search for Wyatt.

The library was immense and Andrew stood there in awe, when he stepped inside. He could only imagine the great undertaking in gathering all the books that lined the towering shelves.

And there in the middle of it all was the object of his desire. A grand table of wood and stone hewed from the very mountains and forest that surround Gothica.

Andrew walked up to the table. High back intricately carved chairs, twelve in all, lined all sides of the table. The table base was solid stone, polished to a lustrous finish. Andrew ran his hand along the glossy surface of the table top and its perfectly laid edges. He stopped and knelt down to examine the octagon shapes that lined the surface of the table base. Andrew stood again and continued on. When he got to the head of the table, Andrew noticed a slot just below the edge of the table top. He removed the medallion and slid it sideways into the slot. Andrew had barely stepped back as the floor opened and revealed a hidden staircase. Andrew descended the stairs.

At the bottom of the stairs was a small room. At center of the room was a stone and wood stand. On that stand was the book. Andrew took a step forward. The stone he stepped on, sunk into the floor itself. Andrew immediately dropped down, narrowly being missed by twin deadly arrows meant for any unwanted intruder. Andrew rolled and jumped to his feet next to the stand. He took the book and made a dash for the stairs.

Andrew emerged at the top of the stairs and was immediately struck in the back. The force of the blow brought him to his knees. The book went flying from his hands and skidded across the floor. Andrew jumped up and turned around to see Ana standing there. She held a sword in each hand.

"You have become a liability," Ana was grim. "I don't like liabilities."

"Just let us go," Andrew replied.

"I can, but not with the book," Ana answered.

"I am taking the book," Andrew insisted.

Ana tossed Andrew one of her swords and he caught it. Ana rushed at him and made the first attack. Andrew blocked with his defense. He countered but Ana blocked and then brought the blade from the right. Andrew brought his blade to block. Ana spun and attacked with a kick, but Andrew anticipated her move. Instead Andrew dropped down and caught Ana in the knee with his boot. She stumbled and let go of her sword which clattered to the floor. Andrew was about to finish Ana, but she jumped up and retrieved her sword. It was as if Andrew knew her every move even before she did it. How could this be? Andrew leapt up on the table, and Ana followed right after him.

The banging of metal striking resounded across the walls as the battle raged on. For every strike that Ana made, Andrew was there with his own. His kicks and punches matched each and every one of Ana's. Her level of frustration and anger were building and building. This was exactly what Andrew wanted. He was hoping that Ana would make a mistake. Andrew knew that Ana was the one who trained all the knights. She had taught them all the same moves; her moves. So with each of her knights that Andrew had fought previously; he had learned them all.

Ana and Andrew drove each other back and forth across the table surface. They were locked in a struggle to the death; each one hoped to gain the final upper hand. Andrew sent a snap kick at Ana's face, but she blocked, spun around and caught Andrew with a blow to the chin. Andrew stumbled backwards, fell on his butt and let go of his sword. He watched in anguish as it slid across the table top and fell over the edge where the hidden room was. Ana lunged at Andrew, but he jumped up and somersaulted backwards, narrowly being missed by her blade.

When Andrew reached the edge of the table, he gave Ana a salute and vaulted off! Ana followed him and leapt from the table. Andrew had mangaged retrieve his sword and slashed Ana across both knees. Ana shrieked and let go of her sword. Like a rag doll, Ana fell to the bottom of the steps. Andrew grabbed the medallion by the chain and pulled it from the slot. The last thing he saw was the horror-struck look in Ana's eyes as the floor panel slid shut. Andrew calmly walked over to the window, opened it, and tossed the medallion into the deep snow. Andrew retrieved the book and quickly exited the library.

Wyatt was working through his moves. He wanted to impress Ana. Wyatt was hoping to impress her enough so that he could get close enough to finish his mission. He was in the middle of a swing with a wooden practice sword when the door opened.

"You!" Wyatt shrieked when he saw Kara. He instantly dropped the wood sword and bolted for the other door. Kara ran, paused to pick up the sword, and continued her pursuit. Just as Wyatt reached for the door, Kara flung the sword. It struck Wyatt in the back of the head and caused him to fall down.

"Why did you do that?" Wyatt cursed.

Kara walked away and over to the arsenal wall. She took a sword and returned to Wyatt. He cringed when Kara swung the blade and stopped with inches to spare.

"You are coming with me," Kara ordered.

Wyatt rose in submission. Kara had him lead the way as they left the training room.

Andrew finally arrived at the helicopter. Kara and Wyatt were not there! All kinds of thoughts; bad thoughts, ran through Andrew's mind. He was about to go and search for them, but suddenly stopped. Andrew saw Kara and Wyatt exit the castle and head in his direction.

"Where were you?" Andrew yelled at Kara.

"Busy," Kara nodded at Wyatt. "And you?"

"Me too," Andrew held up the book for them to see.

"What about Ana?" Wyatt looked shocked.

"Ana is no longer a problem." Andrew answered callously.

Kara gave Wyatt a shove and he stumbled towards Andrew, who caught him before he fell. Wyatt stood in front of Andrew, and there was no mistaking the expression contempt and anger on Andrew's face.

'I...I...' Wyatt began to say, but he did not get a chance to finish. Andrew knocked Wyatt out with a blow to the head. He opened the side door of the helicopter, scooped up Wyatt and put him inside. Kara took her place in the pilot's seat. Andrew climbed inside and closed the door. The engines breathed to life and the rotors picked up speed. Kara looked back at Andrew. He gave her a wink. This time was different than the last. This time they were free.

Chapter 16

A heavy glass stein filled with beer and a pack of smokes were Nick's only companions. He had sat at the same booth, the same time and the same Hoffbrau for the past four days.

Things were not good. After his arrest at the Berlin train station, he was booked and placed in a holding cell. Even his Chicago police credentials bought him no special treatment. The one phone call he got to make was to his Captain back in Chicago. When Nick talked to him, to say he was angry was an understatement. He reamed Nick up one side and down the other that day for, being so stupid. He also told Nick that if he was not back in Chicago in week, Nick was out of a job.

After his bail was paid, the Berlin police informed Nick that he should go to the hotel, get his things, and be on a flight back to the States by the end of the day. Nick did not listen, and instead used his train ticket to travel to Zwickau. It was more important for him to find out what happened to Andrew, Talia, and Kara.

When Nick arrived in Zwickau, he immediately went to the police station. The level of cooperation he got there was zero to none. They did inform him that Captain Brewster was still out and recovering from an accident. They told Nick to just return home. Again, he did not listen.

Nick raised the glass to his lips and took a long drink. The beer tasted good. He put the stein down and lit up a smoke. Nick inhaled it deep into his lungs. He coughed and exhaled.

On the second day, Nick had found a mountain guide to take him up into the Ore Mountains. When the guide learned where they were going, he suddenly changed his mind. He informed Nick that he could no longer do it. Nick even tried to find out where Captain Brewster lived, but had no success at that either. So he decided to give up for the day and return to the Hoffbrau for the evening. Nick was seated at the bar that night instead of his usual booth. There were some tourists talking about an incident with the train almost a week ago. Nick heard them talk about a police officer from Berlin, and a young woman that were found dead in the baggage compartment. They talked about seeing a black helicopter and that the local police captain had been shot with arrows. Nick continued to listen as they talked about a man being arrested and taken into custody. Nick raised the glass stein and took a long, big drink. He finished and ordered another one.

On day three and four, Nick just toured the city and all its sights. He found a park and spent most of the day there watching the people walk by. His thoughts drifted to Kara. He had never let any one get close to him like that, in a long time. Nick thought back to the day they first met when Andrew introduced her to him. She was all dark and mysterious. Here was this gorgeous creature that was interested in him. Nick gulped down his beer, grabbed his smokes and left to go back to the hotel.

The night air was cold when Nick walked out of the Hoffbrau. He zipped up his coat and started back to the hotel. As Nick walked along, from time to time he would look up at the night sky. The stars sparkled and never looked clearer than tonight. But one of them appeared to be moving. Nick rubbed his eyes and looked again.

The star was moving and it was getting closer! Nick ran in that direction and was soon at the park. Just as he got there, Nick heard the sounds of rotor blades striking the air. The snow on the ground started to swirl as the black helicopter came in for a landing. Nick covered his face as the snow whipped faster and stronger. Nick peered through his hands and saw the helicopter finally land. He ran over and when the door slid open, Nick saw Andrew emerge. Nick couldn't believe it. There was Andrew alive! Nick saw some kid lying unconscious on the floor of the helicopter. Where was Talia? Where was Kara? Nick felt a tap on the shoulder. When he turned around there was Kara. Nick picked her up in his arms and squeezed her tight. Nick kissed her for a long time. Andrew delightfully watched Nick and Kara's reunion. He missed Megan so very much. But there was one more thing he had to do. Andrew had to go back to Gothica and retrieve Talia's body.

For that he needed help. Nick and Kara drew apart and looked at Andrew. Nick walked over to Andrew.

"Where is Talia?" Nick asked.

"She's dead." Andrew was very solemn.

"Where's her body," Nick was shocked.

"We had to leave her behind," Andrew replied.

"You are going back, right?" Nick insisted.

"Yes," Andrew answered. "But we need help."

"Count me in," Nick said.

"No," Andrew ordered. "I want you to make sure that Kara and Wyatt get home safe and sound back to Bayport. I need you to do this for me, Nick."

"What about you?" Nick inquired.

"I going to see Captain Brewster," Andrew replied.

"Tonight?" Nick scoffed. "He wouldn't see me."

"He will once I show him this," Andrew retrieved a large leather bound book from the helicopter and showed it to Nick.

"What is that?" Nick asked inquisitively.

"This book contains all the names of each and every one of the Knights of VanHelsing," Andrew explained. "It also contains every person the Knights have killed over the years in the name of their so called, justice against the evil ones."

"Do they know you have it?" Nick was worried.

"Yes," Andrew answered as he closed the book.

"I will do as you ask." Nick shook hands with Andrew. "I promise."

"Kara let's go," Nick said. He climbed aboard the helicopter and closed the door.

Kara walked up to Andrew and slipped her arms around his waist. She squeezed him tightly and did not want to let go.

"You need to go now," Andrew whispered.

"I know." Kara said. Kara let go and kissed Andrew on the cheek. She walked around the helicopter and took her place in the pilot's seat. Kara closed the door and coaxed the engine to life. Andrew put some distance between him and the helicopter. He watched as it took off into the ebony sky. Now it was time to find where Captain Brewster lived. Andrew took off and did not look back.

Yuri could not sleep. The pain from his wounds still bothered him. He decided to get up and take another pain killer. He put on his robe and went downstairs. His wife was still asleep and snoring.

Yuri poured some water and opened the bottle. There was a knock at the back door. Who could it be at such a late hour? Yuri put down the glass and bottle. He walked to the back door and peered out the window first. Yuri saw a man with black hair dressed in black clothing and long leather coat. The man was holding a leather bound book tightly to his chest. Yuri opened the door.

"How may I help you?" Yuri asked looking the man over more closely now.

"My name is Andrew Knight," he replied. "I am a private investigator from Bayport in the United States. I need your help."

"You must be mistaken," Yuri scoffed. "I have a man by that name in custody. Is this some kind of joke?"

"A while ago you were contacted by Lieutenant Gunderson of the Berlin police," Andrew answered as he explained. "He told you of a joint operation between the Berlin police and yours to capture Wyatt Collins from a place called Gothica."

"How do you know that?" Yuri demanded.

"The operation was planned by an American," Andrew continued.

"Yes," Yuri added.

"There was a code name," Andrew said.

"Yes," Yuri replied. "We had a code name because this fellow suspected that there was a spy in their midst."

"The code name was 'Night Kill'," Andrew finally answered.

"Yes that was it," Yuri was in shock. "Then who is in my jail?

"The real Eric Schultz," Andrew replied. He opened the book and showed it to Yuri. "He is also a Knight of VanHelsing known as Gold Blade."

"What do you want from me?" Yuri wondered.

"May I come inside," Andrew shivered.

"Yes, yes." Yuri stepped aside. He gestured for Andrew to come inside. Once he did, Yuri closed the door. He ushered Andrew to the sitting room while he went to make some coffee.

Andrew sat down on the small, but very comfortable sofa. He opened the book to the first page; the title page. It had the date the Knight's of

VanHelsing began, and the signature of Abraham VanHelsing. Along with his signature were the ones from each and every generation that followed. Andrew paused when he came to Ana's. A feeling of regret washed over him. He couldn't believe to what lengths she had forced him to. If he hadn't defeated Ana, she would have killed him without any uncertainty. Andrew shook off the feeling and turned to the next page. Each country and city was listed alphabetically and so were the 'knights' that were assigned to them. Andrew could not even fathom the expanse of the Knights of VanHelsing. There were thousands of knights all over the world. Andrew flipped to the page for his home city of Bayport. Andrew's eyes widened with revelation. Right there in front of him were the real names of Moon Blade, Star Blade and Night Blade. Andrew slammed the book shut when Yuri walked into the sitting room with a tray of coffee and two cups. He set it down and poured them each a cup. Andrew thanked him. The coffee tasted really good after all this time. He could feel the warmth as it filled his stomach.

"What do you purpose?" Yuri asked.

"We need to go back to Gothica and retrieve the body of Sheriff Talia Delsmann," Andrew put his cup down. "We are also going to arrest Ana VanHelsing and her knights for the deaths of hundreds of innocent people."

"Do you have evidence?" Yuri asked.

Andrew opened the book for Yuri to see. Yuri could not believe his own eyes. Right there is black and white was the names of all the missing persons from the last twenty years from Zwickau. He never realized that there were these killers in their midst. They were like wolves amongst the sheep.

"I will make a call and have my men ready in the morning," Yuri stood up. He was angry.

"Is there somewhere I can get some sleep?" Andrew asked. He was drained.

"We have a guest room upstairs, second room on the right" Yuri answered.

"I'm sorry about shooting you," Andrew finally apologized.

"I am glad you are a bad shot," Yuri tapped his leg and shoulder.

"I'm not." Andrew patted Yuri on the back. "Good night." Andrew went to bed. Yuri swallowed hard when he realized that Andrew had wounded him by design, and not the alternative. Yuri put the cups on the tray and carried the whole thing back to the kitchen. He took his pill and water and headed off to bed.

Andrew set the book down on the bed. He took off his boots and coat. Andrew picked up the book and drew back the covers. He slipped into the bed and recovered himself. He placed the book on the night stand. The bed felt so comfortable and Andrew could no longer resist. He was exhausted and quickly fell asleep.

Thunder filled the valley early the next morning. A storm of retribution was coming against evil. The swift sword of justice poised to strike a blow for the innocent.

A squadron of law enforcement helicopters appeared on the horizon as the morning sun peaked over the mountains. The helicopters came in low and fast. Within minutes, they landed at Gothica castle.

The doors flew open. With their weapons at the ready, men in fatigues and body armor stormed the castle. Andrew was among them. He led a team with a stretcher to retrieve Talia's body. They quickly entered the castle and rushed up the stairs to the third floor. Andrew was bothered by the fact that they encountered no resistance. Andrew left his team alone as they prepared Talia's body for transport. There was one thing he had to know. Andrew left for the library.

Andrew had encountered no one on his way to the library. The Knights of VanHelsing had abandoned their home. Andrew shoved open the door and rushed into the room. He ran over to the grand table and to the side where the secret room was. His worst fears were realized when Andrew got there. The floor was open and Ana was gone! She was alive. Did they disappear as they had done in the past; gone into hiding at some other location? Or did they go after Nick, Kara, and Wyatt. He hoped and prayed that Ana had gone into hiding and that the fact that he had the book was enough to keep them away. Andrew did not see any sort of key in the slot. So how did Ana get out? He supposed that when the knights could not find Ana, she had to be trapped in the secret room. They must have had another medallion and used it to free her. Andrew descended the stairs. There was dried blood on the stone steps and a trail of more, leading back up. Andrew followed the trail of blood up until it stopped at one of the bookcases. There must be a hidden passage Andrew thought.

Andrew searched the shelves for the trigger. He found some more dried blood and one of the books. Andrew gave it a pull and part of the book shelf opened.

He stepped inside the passage. As soon as he had done this, the panel instantly closed. Andrew followed the winding passage, not knowing where it led to. There were no lights, only darkness. Soon he came to the end. Andrew felt with his hands and could tell it was a stone wall. Where was the trigger to open it? He continued the search with his hand and in a few minutes had located it. Andrew pushed the trigger and the stone panel opened. The light from the sun nearly blinded him as Andrew stepped outside. He was somewhere on the opposite side of Gothica castle. It was a secluded area high in the Ore Mountains. Andrew discovered another helicopter landing area. It was camouflaged and would not have been detected from the air.

If there had been a helicopter there, it was gone. Andrew had no clue where Ana and her knight could have gone. He was relieved that they were more interested in seeking refuge than an attack. Andrew had defeated them and they were going in hiding to lick their wounds. But Andrew wasn't finished. He had to make sure any Knights of VanHelsing that remained would be tried in court for their crimes. Andrew returned to the panel and found the key stone to open it. He stepped inside and the panel closed behind him.

When Andrew returned to the room, he saw them place Talia in a body bag, and then on the stretcher. He lowered his head and wept. All the frustration, all the fear, all the anger flowed out in his tears. Andrew raised his head and summoned up all the courage he had left. He led the way as they carried Talia's body to the helicopter.

As Andrew and his team returned to the helicopter, he was met by the commander of the assault team. He informed Andrew that Captain Brewster radioed that Eric Schultz escaped while being escorted to see the Magistrate. He had managed to overpower the officers escorting him. One of the officers was dead and the other was rushed to the hospital. Andrew felt sick. He had a feeling where Eric was headed.

"I need to get to Berlin," Andrew said.

"I can have one of the pilots fly you there," the commander answered. He radioed one of the helicopter pilots. He looked at Andrew once he had gotten a response. "Take that chopper," the commander pointed out the one closest to them. "Do not worry about your friend's body; we will make arrangements for it to be shipped back to the states."

"Have her transported to Berlin," Andrew replied. "I want to bring her home."

"Very well." the commander gave a salute.

Andrew thanked him and walked over and got in the helicopter. Soon they were airborne and headed to Berlin.

Nick checked the locks on the hotel room door. They were still secure. Their flight home was not until tomorrow night. They had not received any word from Andrew on how the attack on Gothic went. This worried Nick to no end. The other thing that worried Nick was that fact that Andrew still had that damn book in his possession. His gut instinct told him that Ana and her knights might try killing him and Kara and taking Wyatt into hiding with them. Nick felt it was safer to order room service. He returned to the sitting area and sat down on the sofa. Kara was asleep on the bed and so was Wyatt. The difference between them was that Wyatt was handcuffed and Kara was not. Although Nick thought it would be pretty kinky if she were. Nick picked up a newspaper and had just started to read it when there was a knock at the door. He tossed the newspaper aside and grudgingly went to answer the door. Thank goodness the food he ordered had finally arrived. Nick was starving. He never bothered to peer through the peephole and just opened the door.

A taxi cab came to a screeching halt in front of the hotel. Its lone occupant tossed the driver the fare and quickly exited the cab. He rushed through the doors of the hotel and did not even bother to acknowledge the desk clerk. He hoped that it was not too late.

Nick woke to find himself tied to a chair. Kara was next to him tied up as well. They both were gagged. Wyatt was free and talking to someone dressed in a Knight's of VanHelsing garb, right down to the deadly weapons. Nick cursed himself for not being careful and letting his hunger get in the way. Kara looked very frightened and it made Nick even sicker knowing he had let her down.

Wyatt and the other person stopped talking and walked over by Nick and Kara. Wyatt looked smug and Nick did not like it.

"We're leaving now," Wyatt announced. "Tell Mister Knight that he had better return our book to us. Otherwise Gold Blade here will take it from him." Wyatt leaned closer Nick and whispered, "You see, Gold Blade has orders to use whatever means necessary to retrieve it." Wyatt was defiant now, "Gold Blade is the best and I doubt Mister Knight is any match for him." A knock at door interrupted Wyatt's speech. He looked at Gold Blade, who nodded for him to answer the door. Wyatt went to answer as Gold Blade took up a position on the backside of the door. Wyatt peered through the peephole. There was no one there. "What the heck?" Wyatt cursed. He opened the door and stepped in the hallway to take a look.

Nick and Kara saw as Wyatt flew backwards and strike the door. He was instantly knocked out.

Gold Blade witnessed this as well and came around the door. He entered the hallway. Seconds later, Gold Blade followed the same path as Wyatt, but rolled and stood to face the mysterious attacker. Nick and Kara's hearts leapt with joy when they saw Andrew step boldly into the hotel room to face Gold Blade. Andrew was dressed in police fatigues and carried a backpack across his left shoulder. He was pointing a gun at Gold Blade.

"It's over," Andrew announced.

"Not yet." Gold Blade drew his swords.

"Then come and get it." Andrew took off.

None of them could believe what Andrew had just done, especially Nick and Kara.

Gold Blade took off in pursuit of Andrew, who had just reached the door for the stairwell. Andrew opened the door to the stairwell, paused just long enough to make sure Gold Blade was following, and headed for the roof of the hotel. Gold Blade was only minutes behind Andrew.

Nick struggled at his ropes as he tried to get free. Suddenly police swarmed in, and had the room secured it in a matter of seconds. They took Wyatt into custody and released Nick and Kara from their bindings. Nick tried to explain what had transpired, but the officer in charge informed him that they already knew. Nick and Kara found out that Andrew called ahead to the Berlin police and set up the whole operation by phone. Kara, along with Nick, suddenly realized that Andrew had planned on killing Gold Blade. Nick tried to get past to stop Andrew, but the police officers would not let him. Nick was shocked that the authorities had agreed with what Andrew was about to do.

Gold Blade cleared the open stairwell door.

"Ich weib, dass du hier bist." Gold Blade said he knew Andrew was here. He continued and asked why Andrew hid like a disobedient child, "Warum verbergen Sie sich wie ein unartiges Kind?" Gold Blade paused at the corner of the stairwell structure. "Es wird den Tod zu Ihnen und Ihrer Familie bringen." He told Andrew that the book would only bring death to him and his family." Gold Blade spun around the corner with blades slashing. He only struck air. Gold Blade crouched down and examined Andrew's boot prints in the freshly fallen snow.

"Wir haben jetzt Ende es." Andrew's voice came from above, that they finish it. Gold Blade looked up in time to see Andrew jump down off the top of the stairwell structure. Andrew struck Gold Blade in the chest with both his boots. The force of the blow sent Gold Blade sprawling down in the snow.

"We can end this now," Andrew said. "And no one has to get hurt,"

"I cannot do that," Gold Blade stood.

"I am unarmed," Andrew dropped the gun.

"Last time we met, you took advantage of me," Gold Blade rubbed his jaw. He tossed Andrew one of his swords. "But I am an honorable man and will give you a fighting chance."

"Thanks," Andrew retrieved the sword from the snow. Instantly, Gold Blade lunged at Andrew, who blocked, spun and hit Gold Blade in the back with a karate kick. Gold Blade stumbled to his knees, rolled and stood up again. Andrew did not attack, but waited for Gold Blade to make a move. Gold Blade shook off the affects of Andrew's kick. Andrew was able to anticipate his attacks. Of course Gold Blade thought Andrew must have learned how to fight from all of his battles with the Knights of VanHelsing. Gold Blade had to come up with another pattern of attacks. They circled each other for a long time, each waiting for the other to initiate an attack. Gold Blade's frustration level was about to reach a boiling point. What was Andrew waiting for? Why did he persist in this bizarre dance of theirs? Suddenly, Andrew bolted and headed for the edge of the roof. Gold Blade fought the urge to purse at first, but then took off.

Andrew jumped up on the ledge and turned to face Gold Blade.

"Wo ist das Buch?" Gold Blade demanded to know where the book was. He turned for a moment and saw the backpack lying on top of the stairwell structure. Gold Blade left Andrew and ran as fast as he could to where the backpack was located. He paused to look back and saw that Andrew was still standing on the ledge of the roof. Why did he not try and stop him?

Gold Blade retrieved the backpack and quickly opened it. The backpack was empty! Gold Blade screamed and tossed the backpack down. His rage comsumed him and Gold Blade charged at Andrew full force. Gold Blade raised his sword to strike Andrew down he as was only inches away. Andrew sprung from the ledge and somersaulted over Gold Blade, who realized too late he had been tricked. Gold Blade tried to stop, but his momentum carried him still forward. Gold Blade slammed into the ledge and flipped over it. His screams pierced the air as he plummeted to his death. Andrew walked to the ledge and peered over it. He saw Gold Blade's body lying twisted in blood. Andrew knew Gold Blade would be obsessed with retrieving the book. Andrew had counted on the fact that once Gold Blade discovered the book missing from the backpack that he would simply think of nothing else but to attack. Andrew stepped away from the ledge and he walked over to one of the air-conditioning units. There tucked safely away, was the book. Andrew returned to the stairwell structure and also retrieved his backpack. He put the book back in it and left the roof. It bothered him of what he was capable of and of what he had become. All of the bloodshed had poisoned his soul; turning it dark and vengeful. Andrew was not sure if he would ever come back. Through it all, he had forgotten the reason for it all. An innocent family had been murdered in their home. Andrew would finish what he had started. But for now he was tired and just wanted to go home.

Chapter 17

The early morning, winter gray skies, were lacking clouds. A brisk wind swirled its icy breath and drove the white powdery snow into frenzy. Browns and grays were the colors of choice of the landscape for miles around.

Peter watched as the plane circled for a landing. He had received a call from Andrew a few days ago. All Andrew told Peter was to meet their flight at the Bayport County Airport on this particular day. He said nothing else. Peter did not like all the mystery.

The plane started its descent and landed on the long black ribbon of asphalt in the material of white. A few minutes later, it came to a stop in front of the terminal building.

Peter walked up to the plane just as the door opened and a flight of stairs were moved into place. Peter watched with anticipation for the passengers to depart. He saw no one for several minutes, and then the first passenger came out. She was a woman with black and red streaked hair, dressed in black. She looked round at her new surroundings first, and then at Peter. She smiled even though he was not familiar to her. Just as she descended the stairs, the next person came out. He was a man with dark curly hair dressed in regular street clothes and a brown leather winter coat. He surveyed the surrounding before going down the steps. The next two persons to disembark were Andrew and Wyatt. Peter recognized Wyatt from his photo on file. Wyatt was in handcuffs. Peter's mouth dropped in shock at how pale and worn out Andrew looked. Andrew looked down at Peter and gave him a forced smile. Andrew was wearing fatigues and carried a matching backpack. Andrew had Wyatt head down the stairs first. Peter knew Talia had gone with them on the mission, but where was she? Peter was about to greet them, but stopped when he saw a wooden casket being removed from the cargo compartment from the plane. Peter had a bad feeling in the pit of his stomach. For some reason he could not move. He watched Andrew leave Wyatt when they got to the bottom of the stairs and go over to the casket. Andrew bent down and whispered something to the casket. He stood up and returned to Wyatt. Peter finally walked over to all of them.

Andrew greeted Peter with an embrace. Peter was surprised by how long Andrew held onto him. It was like Andrew needed it badly. Peter didn't say a word and neither did Andrew. Finally, after a few minutes, Andrew let go.

"Peter, this is Nick and Kara," Andrew introduced.

"Peter," he greeted them each in return.

"Take him into custody," Andrew shoved Wyatt. Peter handed him to one of the officers with him.

"Where is Talia," Peter asked, even though he already knew the answer.

"In the casket," Andrew was somber. "She died during the mission."

"But how?" Peter pressed Andrew. Instead, Andrew walked a short distance away. To Peter it looked like Andrew was crying. He'd never seen Andrew cry before. Peter turned to the others, "How did she die?"

"Saving Andrew's life," Kara blurted out. She broke down and sought Nick's arms. Nick held onto Kara and comforted her.

"What happened in Germany?" Peter demanded.

"I will explain everything." Andrew finally rejoined them. He grabbed hold of Peter's shoulder. "I need a few days, okay? Then I will explain everything."

"But," Peter started to protest, but Andrew and the others walked away. Peter took Wyatt and walked him over to the car. He opened the back door and placed Wyatt inside. Peter closed the door. He looked back and saw them load the casket into the hearse. Peter felt really sick inside. Andrew better have a really good explanation for all of this; a really good one to say the least. Peter opened the front door and slid into the driver's seat. He started the car and closed the door. Peter took off for the police station.

There was a city of empty, take out food containers, built in one corner of the coffee table. In another corner was a mountain range of empty soda bottles. In the middle of it all was a stack of file folders and papers scattered about.

Chloe and Roxanne were sound asleep, each respectively on the two sofas of the family room. They had spent all of last evening going over the Higgins case notes.

Chloe finally awoke from her slumber. She stretched and yawned. Chloe got up and went to use the upstairs bathroom. She had to go really bad.

Roxanne opened her eyes. At first, she was disoriented, but then remembered that she and Chloe fell asleep after hours of going over all the information in the case files. Roxanne got up. She took off in search for a bathroom.

Chloe was just coming out of the bathroom, when she bumped into Roxanne. They both laughed and went on their respective ways.

Chloe had just reached the bottom of the staircase when the front door opened. It was her dad! Chloe rushed into his open arms and practically knocked him over. She closed her eyes and squeezed him tight. Andrew whispered in Chloe's ear that he was okay, but she kept holding on for fear he would vanish once she let go. Chloe finally opened her eyes to see two strangers; a man and a woman with her dad. She gave her dad a kiss on the cheek and let go.

"Chloe," Andrew said, as he gestured to the others. "This is Kara and Nick."

"Pleased to meet you," Chloe greeted them.

"We're going to get some rest," Andrew told his daughter. Andrew kissed her and led Kara and Nick upstairs. Chloe must have looked perplexed and Andrew said, "I will explain later. Please trust me, okay?"

"Okay," Chloe smiled back. She went to clean up the family room.

Roxanne had just exited the bathroom when she saw Andrew come up the stairs with a man and woman right behind him. She immediately ran to him as he reached the top step. Andrew dropped the backpack he was carrying. Roxanne threw her arms around Andrew and squeezed him tight. Andrew hugged and kissed his friend back.

"I'm alright," Andrew assured Roxanne.

"We all missed you." Roxanne gave Andrew a squeeze and let go.

"I missed all of you too," Andrew said. He picked up his backpack.

"Who's with you?" Roxanne looked at the others.

"I'm sorry," Andrew apologized. He introduced, "This is Nick and Kara."

"A pleasure," Roxanne smiled.

"We really need some sleep," Andrew muttered. "I don't mean to be rude."

"Okay," Roxanne said. "I'll go help and Chloe clean up." She left them alone.

"Just point me to a bed," Nick moaned, exhausted.

"Me too," Kara lamented.

"Follow me." Andrew led the way, smiling. He opened the door to one of the guest rooms. Kara and Nick walked in and closed the door behind them. Andrew left for his own bedroom. Once he was there, Andrew just dumped the back pack on the floor, and climbed into bed and underneath the covers. He immediately fell asleep.

Chloe and Roxanne returned to the family room. They started to clean up their mess from the night before. Neither one of them said anything for some time. Then Roxanne finally broke the silence.

"Your dad looked bad." Roxanne was worried.

"Yeah, I know." Chloe was very concerned.

"What do you think happened?" Roxanne paused from picking up. She looked fully at Chloe, who was crying now.

"I...I don't know," Chloe sniffed back her tears. "But, I...I'm glad he is home." Chloe stopped picking up and oozed down into one of the chairs in front of the fireplace. Roxanne sat in the other one across from her. Chloe grabbed a tissue and dabbed the corners of her eyes. "Whatever happened had to be huge," Chloe cleared her throat to speak. "Really huge."

"Did you see the woman with him?" Roxanne said after making certain they were alone. "She looked like one of those vampire people we interviewed, remember?"

"Yeah, she did, didn't she," Chloe finally laughed.

"And the guy looked like a cop," Roxanne added.

"Dad said he would explain," Chloe answered.

"It must be bad," Roxanne said. "I've been getting bad vibes since they had arrived in the house."

"What do you mean?" Chloe asked.

"There are dark forces involved," Roxanne shuddered. "I feel death."

"I believe you," Chloe said. "We need to secure the house."

Both girls rose up and went to make certain that all the doors and windows were locked.

Like so many nights before, Andrew got up and went down to the kitchen for a late night snack and to think. He grabbed some food from the refrigerator to make a sandwich. He walked over to the counter and set it all down. He grabbed a loaf of bread from the bread box and opened the bag. Andrew spread the mayo on the bread and proceeded to build his creation of meat, cheese, lettuce and tomatoes. At last, Andrew declared his creation complete and was about to put it all away, when a tiny voice from the dark said, 'Could I have one?'. Andrew turned around to see his daughter standing in the doorway. Andrew grinned and went on to create a masterpiece for her too. While her dad worked on her sandwich, Chloe grabbed two glasses and poured them some milk. She put the milk back and slid into the breakfast nook. Andrew put all of the extra food away and joined his daughter.

Father and daughter just sat there, ate their sandwiches and drank their milk. Neither one said a word. But just then, as any child would, Chloe got bored.

"What happened in Germany?" Chloe blurted out. Andrew thought how direct and to the point she was. How he would answer, was foremost on his mind.

"Is it that important?" Andrew replied.

"To me it is," Chloe answered. She looked keenly at her dad, "It is just that you seem different to me; more withdrawn. You are not yourself."

"Not true," Andrew bluffed.

"You are not telling the truth." Chloe called his bluff. She stopped eating and focused on him. "I read all about what happened in Chicago. I know how you saved those kids in the park that night. I know what you had to do."

"...And," Andrew added.

"...And I want to know what happened in Germany," Chloe answered. She stretched out her hand and touched his arm. "Please tell me."

"It was worse than Chicago." Andrew stopped eating. He pushed his sandwich aside.

"How much worse was it?" Chloe choked.

"I've had to do things I am not proud of," Andrew's voice trembled as he spoke. He looked away; focused his eyes elsewhere. "I had to kill people..."

"People that wanted to hurt you or others," Chloe inquired.

"Yes," Andrew looked away, unable to face his daughter. "Others were not."

"You killed on purpose?" Chloe was shocked. In the past she knew her dad had defended others; himself, but never killed anyone on purpose. What could have brought her dad to do such a thing? Chloe demanded, "Tell me."

Andrew finally granted her request. He told her about the incident in the park in Berlin when Talia and Kara were kidnapped, how Sergeant Schindler was a Knight of VanHelsing and how he was framed for his death. Andrew further explained how he was pursued by the police on the train to Zwickau. He shared with Chloe, the fight on the train and how Lieutenant Gunderson was killed.

Chloe listened with great interest as her dad recounted all the events of the recent past. She was in awe of his rouse when he assumed the identity of Gold

Blade to gain entry to Gothica castle. She could picture it all in her mind. A chill consumed Chloe as her dad told about the death of Talia and how he took on Ana and her knights. She could not believe that Talia, who had hated her dad, sacrificed herself to save him or how her dad fought such zealous killers. Chloe had only seen her dad cry twice; once at her mom's grave and the other was the day he found out Megan was pregnant. Chloe got up and went over by her dad. She enveloped him with her arms as he wept heavily.

"What are you two doing up?" Roxanne asked as she came into the kitchen, but stopped. She saw Chloe comfort Andrew. Roxanne joined them as Andrew assured Chloe he was alright now. Chloe was not so sure, but gave him a squeeze and returned to her seat. Roxanne slid in next to her.

"What is wrong?" Roxanne asked Andrew. "Are you alright?"

"I will be," Andrew looked at his daughter. He dried his eyes.

"Did you find Wyatt?" Roxanne inquired. She eyed up his sandwich. "Are you going to finish that?"

"It is all yours." Andrew slid the plate over by her.

"So did you?" Roxanne asked. She took a bite of the sandwich.

"Yes, Wyatt is in police custody," Andrew answered. He drank some milk and went on, "I have an interview setup with him tomorrow."

"So what was in the backpack?" Chloe asked.

"It's just a book." Andrew was being vague.

"What is so important about it?" Chloe insisted.

"The book is about the Knights of VanHelsing," Andrew finally replied. "It contains the history of the knights, a list of all their names, and the people they killed."

"That is a very treacherous thing to possess," Roxanne shuddered. "What do you plan on doing with it?"

"To arrest the three knights here in Bayport," Andrew answered. He finished his milk and pushed the glass aside. "And bring them and the others to justice."

"And then what?" Chloe asked.

"Keep the book in a safe place," Andrew rose up and went the liquor cabinet above the refrigerator. He took out a bottle of scotch and returned to the table. He poured some in a glass.

"They know you have it." Chloe finally realized.

"Yes," Andrew answered. He downed the scotch and refilled the glass.

"Won't they try to recover it?" Roxanne worried.

"Perhaps," Andrew downed a second glass of scotch. "Right now Ana and the knights have gone into hiding. The rest have to maintain their secret identities and remain in the public eye. To do otherwise would draw unwanted attention to them. The three here in Bayport are probably wondering what I am going to do with the book."

"What if they come after you?" Chloe cringed.

"I will do what I have to," Andrew was blunt.

"Not like Germany," Chloe swallowed hard.

"I don't know." Andrew downed a third glass. "That will depend on them. We should go to bed," Andrew announced. He stood up and walked over to the liquor cabinet. He put the bottle of scotch back. Andrew glanced for a moment at his daughter and Roxanne. He headed off to bed. Chloe felt unsettled and afraid of what her dad might do. She left the kitchen to go after him, and left Roxanne alone at the breakfast nook. Roxanne had a bad feeling and took off after Chloe and Andrew.

Dawn approached and soon it would be too late. The hunt would have to be called off and there would be no measure of satisfaction this night. Where could the others be? Why were they not here yet? With each tick of the clock, time slipped away.

Night Blade, frustrated, waited in the shadows. Off, in the not too far distance, were the ones she hunted. They were only 'baby bats', naïve, but none the less satisfying to kill. She had received a call that these 'baby bats' had planned a blood feast at the boarded up Higgins's house. Night Blade had always been curious as to why these creatures always chose abandoned places to gather. Either way it would prove poorly for them this night. Night Blade watched as the 'baby bats' and their blood dolls broken into the house. She could wait no longer and stepped forward, but suddenly stopped when she heard a noise from behind her.

Star Blade and Moon Blade came in from the north. Each had received a call from their respective sources that there would be a blood feast at the abandoned Higgins's house. They stopped at the edge of the woods when the 'baby bats' and their blood dolls broke down back the door. Both of them wondered where Night

Blade could be. It would be morning soon and time was running out.

"We can't wait any longer," Moon Blade cursed.

"We need Night Blade to help with the attack," Star Blade growled back.

"There are only six of them," Moon Blade fired back. "Besides, we are supposed to let the blood dolls go. You know the rules of the code."

"I know the code," Star Blade fired back. "They would just become blood dolls for some other of those disgusting creatures." Star Blade watched as the last one entered the house. She removed her swords and continued, "I say we finish them all."

"Then we will do it without Night Blade," Moon Blade drew her own swords.

Moon Blade and Star Blade burst forth from the bushes and without delay entered the house through broken door.

Chloe couldn't sleep. She was very worried at what her dad was going to do about the Knights of VanHelsing in Bayport. She was afraid that he would take matters into his own hands and kill them like he had in Germany.

Chloe got up and put on her robe. She left her room and went down the hall to her dad's bedroom. Chloe wrapped on the door first and opened it. She peered inside the room. Her dad was gone! An overwhelming feeling of fear washed over Chloe. She slammed the door shut and ran back to her room. Chloe quickly put on some clothes and shoes, and grabbed her keys and jacket. She had no clue where to look, but had to find her dad before he did something horrible.

Chloe hurried down the stairs while putting on her coat. She leapt from the second step and bounded for the door. Chloe reached for the handle, the door opened and her dad entered the house.

"Where were you?" Chloe jumped on him.

"I couldn't sleep, so I took a walk." Andrew did not look at her. He closed the door.

Chloe walked up to her dad and felt his coat; it was ice cold.

"Where did you go?" Chloe was more subdued.

"Just around the neighbor hood, why?" Andrew looked and saw the disbelief in her eyes. How dare she question him about where he had been?

"I was worried that you might, um," Chloe stammered.

"You thought I was going to do something bad tonight, right?" Andrew smirked.

"Yes." Chloe took hold of her dad's hands. They were ice cold too. "Did you?"

Andrew was about to answer when there was frantic pounding at the door. Whoever it was, they seemed very much in a panicked rush. They kept knocking. Andrew left Chloe to go and answer the door. When Andrew opened the door he saw Storm standing there. Her eyeslids and face were black from the mascara. She was still crying. Her whole body was trembling. Andrew escorted her inside and shut the door. Storm was trembling so badly that Chloe put her arms around her. Andrew told the girls to go into the family room and for Chloe to start a fire. Andrew grabbed a blanket from the foyer closet and joined them soon after. Storm had taken off her coat and sat in a chair by the fireplace. She thanked Andrew for the blanket and wrapped it around herself. Storm sobbed between labored breaths. What could have upset her so much? Chloe started the fire. Andrew sat in the chair beside Storm. He knew something terrible had happened and need to find out what it was right now.

"Are you okay?" Andrew started out simple.

"Y..Yes," Storm sniffed back her tears.

"Are you hurt?" Andrew asked. He looked Storm over and bent down to pick up her coat. There was blood smattered on the right sleeve and shoulder. Andrew did not see any wounds on Storm. So whose blood was it?

"Where you at a blood feast?" Andrew took a chance.

"No, I mean yes," Storm violently shook her head from side to side. "But   it... it was much worse. He made us do it. Why...why the house?"

"Who made you do what?" Andrew grasped hold of Storm by the shoulders.

"We killed them!" Storm shrieked. She shook loose of Andrew's grip and headed to the front door. Andrew and Chloe went after her. Storm reached for the doorknob, but it was Chloe that stopped her. She put her arms around Storm and subdued her. Exhaustion finally caught up with Storm, and she passed out in Chloe's arms. Chloe struggled to keep standing, and Andrew came to her aid. He picked Storm up in his arms and carried her into the family room. Andrew laid her on the sofa and covered her with the blanket. Chloe and her dad slumped down in the chairs.

"What was she talking about?" Chloe looked at her Dad for an answer.

"Storm was part of a blood feast," Andrew explained. He glanced over at Storm who looked peaceful now. "Something went wrong." Andrew stood up and walked over to the gun cabinet. He unlocked it and took out a Glock 9mm and belt clip holster. Andrew clipped it to his belt and also grabbed extra clips. He also grabbed the pouch with throwing stars and clipped it to his belt.

"Where are you going?" Chloe stood up.

"To the Higgins house." Andrew put his coat on.

"How do you know she came from there?" Chloe inquired.

"Storm said 'the house'." Andrew looked at his daughter. "It is safe to assume Storm meant her house." Andrew took hold of Chloe's shoulders and looked her in the eyes. "I need you to stay with Storm and keep a watch on her. No one can leave the house. Make sure all the doors and windows are locked when I am gone."

Andrew looked over at Storm again. She was still asleep, which was a good thing. He went on, "I am not sure what it is yet, but I need to go and find out." Andrew now looked at his daughter, "At any sign of trouble, call the police." Andrew kissed his daughter on the forehead and left the family room. Chloe followed behind and when Andrew left the house, she locked the door. Chloe returned to the family room and checked on the fire. She lay down on the other sofa.

Andrew parked the car on the side of the road. The Higgins house was just a short trek through the woods to the south. Andrew checked his weapons and headed into the woods. He hadn't gone far when he noticed several tracks headed in the direction he was going. By the number of prints in the snow, Andrew knew it was a group of six or eight all together. Some prints were larger and others smaller. So there were both male and female in the group. By the distance of the steps, Andrew knew they were not in a hurry, but walked at a normal pace. Andrew continued on his way to the house.

When Andrew cleared the woods, he saw that the back door to the house had been forced open. Andrew knelt down and scanned the area. He did not see any movement. Whoever had been at the house was long gone just like Storm. Andrew was amazed that she had traveled several miles to Bayport. But it was not on foot, Storm had ride back to town. Who had given her that ride? He would have to worry about that later. Andrew figured the coast was clear, so he walked to the house. Andrew drew his weapon and stepped inside the house.

Andrew walked down the hallway. He swallowed hard and felt sick to his stomach. Someone had written in blood on the wall 'death to the slayers'. A shiver went up his spine. Andrew continued to the living room. When he entered, Andrew drew an exasperated breath. There were two bodies lying face down on the floor. They were Knights of VanHelsing. Their weapons lay only inches away, just out of reach. Andrew felt sick to his stomach as he knelt down beside the first one. It was Darcy, his friend from the Sheriffs Department. Her blonde hair was matted with blood and her eyes were wide open. Andrew closed her eyes. Andrew turned to the other. It was Veronica, Doctor Straussman's nurse. Her face was spattered with blood. Like Darcy, her throat had been slashed.

Andrew stood up. He left the house to get some fresh air. He walked around to clear his thoughts, but soon came upon another bloody discovery. There was another body that lay face down in the snow. Andrew knelt down. Andrew removed the hood. It was Claudia Straussman; Doctor Straussman, the one who was treating Wyatt. Andrew tossed aside the hood. Night Blade, Star Blade, and Moon Blade were dead. Andrew took out his phone and called for help.

Andrew searched the area around the body. There was a single set of prints in the snow. Andrew decided to follow to see where they led.

Andrew walked through the woods for quite some time and finally emerged on River Road. He saw relatively fresh tire tracks in the snow. The vehicle had a leak, for Andrew saw oil spots in the snow as well. It was probably and older vehicle. Andrew took out his cell phone and snapped a picture of the tire tread marks left behind. He also took a picture of the oil stains. When he had been in the woods, the majority of foot prints had been muddled due to the deep snow. But fortune must have smiled on Andrew, for there next to the tread marks were a clear and distinctive set of boot prints, along with several drops of blood. The boot impressions were set rather deep in the snow and not single flaw about them. Andrew bent down and snapped a photo of the prints. He searched his pockets and pulled out an old candy wrapper. Andrew took his pocket knife out and scraped some of the bloody snow onto the wrapper. Hopefully, the crime lab would be able to get a blood type off of the sample. Andrew closed the wrapper tightly and placed it back in his pocket. He headed back to the Higgins house. As he walked along, Andrew could hear the sirens off in the distance. Andrew looked up at the night sky. It was clear and he could see all the stars. He closed his eyes and said a prayer for the poor souls murdered this night. Andrew knew in his heart that all of this was his fault.

Chapter 18

Nick woke up the next morning to find that Kara was not there. There was a note on her pillow. Nick opened up the note and read it...

My Dearest Nick,

I had to return to Chicago to meet with my publisher. I will be back in a few days.

Love,
Kara

Nick folded up the note and went downstairs. Last night was the first in a long time that he had actually gotten a good night sleep. The bed was very comfortable and the comforter made him feel all warm and toasty inside. Nick threw back the cover and got out of bed. He put on the robe that was set out for him on the chair. Nick left the bedroom and went downstairs.

Chloe and Roxanne were already in the kitchen when Nick got there. He could smell the fresh brewed coffee. Nick saw the girls eating a breakfast of pancakes, sausages and hashbrowns. His stomach grumbled loudly. Nick was told to help himself and to join them when he was ready. Nick slid into the seat at the breakfast nook across from Chloe and Roxanne.

"Where is Kara?" Chloe asked.

"She had to meet with her publisher in Chicago," Nick went back to eating.

"In the middle of the night?" Roxanne was curious.

"Okay," Chloe shrugged.

They all heard the front door open and close. Soon Andrew walked into the kitchen. He didn't say a word, but walked over to the coffeemaker and poured a cup. Andrew never even acknowledged them and left the kitchen. Chloe and Roxanne looked at each other completely puzzled by Andrew's odd behavior. They quickly got up and followed. Nick remained and kept eating his food. He just thought Andrew was being weird and nothing more.

The girls found Andrew sitting on the sofa drinking his coffee when they entered the family room. Chloe and Roxanne sat down respectively in the two chairs by the fireplace. Andrew finally nodded his head in acknowledgment that they were there. Storm was still asleep on the other sofa.

Chloe was ecstatic at even this slight progress. She recognized the look etched on her dad's face. It was the look of him in full deductive reasoning mode. Chloe was sure her dad was pouring over all of the events that had transpired since the Higgins family was murdered.

She saw the intensity in her dad's eyes; as if he were searching for clues at that very moment. Once in a while, Andrew paused to take a drink from his cup. He still said nothing.

Roxanne sat there quietly, watching Andrew drink his coffee. She had never seen such a look of intensity on his face like that before. Roxanne hoped to get some kind of reading off of the psychic energy in the room.

She closed her eyes to concentrate. At first there was nothing, but soon psychic images in the room started to come into focus. Roxanne saw images of bodies in a house. She cringed and her heart started to beat at a quickened pace when Roxanne saw the message written in blood on the wall. Roxanne watched Andrew walk through the house as he discovered the bodies. She sensed the anger that built up inside of him; the despair. Roxanne opened her eyes again. She saw that Andrew stared at her directly. It was as if he had given her the vision.

Andrew finished his coffee and stood up. He looked at the two of them.

"Call Peter and have him put Storm in protective custody," Andrew finally said. "I have my appointment with Wyatt and will return later." Andrew gave them a look not to follow him. Chloe and Roxanne remained behind. He left the room.

The room was devoid of any bright colors. The table and chairs were of the same gray that was the room. Even the pitcher of ice water and its companion glasses looked pastey white.

Wyatt entered the room, bound in handcuffs and leg chains, and escorted by two burly looking jailers. One of them pulled a chair out and pushed Wyatt down on it and the other secured the leg chains to a hook on the floor. Wyatt would be going nowhere anytime soon. Now he had to wait.

Andrew entered the room a few minutes later. He shook the jailers' hands and joked around with them. They spent several minutes in their conversation. Then the jailers left and told Andrew they would be right outside. Andrew thanked them and took his place at the table opposite of Wyatt. Andrew placed his briefcase on the table and opened it. He took out a file folder filled with papers and set it down in front of him. Andrew stood up and removed his overcoat and hung it across the back of his chair. He retook his seat. Andrew opened the file folder.

"You are presently being treated for Renfield's Syndrome," Andrew read from the sheet of paper. "Is that correct?"

"Yes," Wyatt answered. It was an easy question, but not what he had expected.

"And who was your doctor?" Andrew asked.

"Doctor Claudia Straussman," Wyatt complied.

"How long have you been undergoing treatment?" Andrew continued.

"Since I was very young," Wyatt replied. He could no longer stand it and asked, "Why are you asking me these stupid questions. What do you really want to know? Huh?" Wyatt gave Andrew a dirty look, "I know what you want to know. You want to know if I did kill Storm's family, right." Wyatt leaned closer and folded his arms in front of him on the table. "Well, I didn't do it and neither did the Knights. But you know that already don't you? So why are you dancing around?"

"Who told you to get out of the country and go to Gothica?" Andrew closed the folder. He pushed it aside and leaned in the same way as Wyatt had just done. Their faces were just inches apart. Andrew's eyes were intense, purposeful. "Who was it Wyatt?"

"Doctor Straussman, Claudia, told me she got a call from Ana," Wyatt explained. "She told Claudia that we did not need that kind of attention for the Knights. She also said that the public had become more aware of our presence and we might have to disappear like back in the 1800's."

"Did you know about the Knights of VanHelsing's book?" Andrew switched the subject.

"Maybe," Wyatt leaned back now. He shrugged. "It was said that the only one to see the book, if it were real, would be a VanHelsing and no one else. That way only one person knew of our secret identities and the number of 'kills' we had."

"Why were you excommunicated from the clan?" Andrew switched again.

"For not following the laws of the clan," Wyatt cursed. "They were stupid rules anyway. I mean come on. One of them was we could only feed off the blood of the ones deemed acceptable by the clan. With my disease, I could not always wait for our blood feasts. Sometimes the urge came on so strong I had to have it. Well, when Ravenclaw found out this, he was enraged and so were the ruling council. They met and had me excommunicated. Storm's father was on the council.

Sure I was angry at him, but not enough to kill him or the others."

"How did you get involved with the Knights?" Andrew asked now.

"One night I was with a group and we were having a blood feast," Wyatt recounted for Andrew. "Well, all of a sudden the slayers broke in and attacked us." Wyatt stopped and lowered his head. Andrew gave Wyatt a few minutes to collect himself.

"They killed everyone but you, right?"

"Yeah, even the blood dolls," Wyatt added.

"So why did you want to become part of them, if it bothered you that they killed all of these young people?" Andrew was curious.

"I had no choice," Wyatt sniffed. "It was either join the order, or be killed. And well I was angry at Mister Higgins and the others for kicking me out of the clan. Besides, it was way cooler to be a slayer."

"Do you have any idea who else would want the Higgins family dead?" Andrew asked. He took a glass and filled it with water. Andrew passed the glass to Wyatt, who thanked him and took a drink of the refreshing water. Andrew took the other glass and poured himself some water. It tasted really good.

"I don't know," Wyatt answered. "Except for the Knights of VanHelsing, probably no one else." Wyatt stopped to take another drink. He went on. "The Knights and the descendents of Vlad the Impaler have been enemies for centuries."

"Were there any quarrels in the clan that you were aware of?" Andrew took another drink.

"No," Wyatt started, but stopped to think for a moment. He had a puzzled look as he thought deeply. Andrew sat there patiently. Soon Wyatt continued, "There was this one time when this author from Chicago came to interview Ravenclaw and the rest of us for her book." Wyatt looked at Andrew, "She was the one who flew the copter. What was her name again?"

"Kara Sadler," Andrew provided the answer.

"Yeah her," Wyatt snapped his fingers. "Anyway she wanted to interview Ravenclaw all alone, so they went into his study and shut the door. Well, the others left, but I stayed behind and listened at the door."

"What did you hear?" Andrew put the glass down and leaned closer.

"Well, she said she had just returned from Germany," Wyatt answered. He stopped to take another drink. He continued, "The problem was Ravenclaw discovered me at the door and kicked me out of the house."

"This was all before you were kicked out of the clan?" Andrew clarified.

"No," Wyatt laughed. "I had managed to sneak into the house. There were so many of us, that no one even noticed me. I pretended to do the same when the others left, but snuck back in a few minutes later."

I have enough for now." Andrew stood to leave.

"What are you going to do with the book?" Wyatt looked very worried.

"You have no 'kills' in the book." Andrew put the folder in his briefcase and closed it. He gave Wyatt a reassuring look, "And you had nothing to do with the Higgins family murders. I am going to ask the judge to dismiss the charges." Andrew smiled now, "And your mom should be very happy about that."

"What about Claudia and the other two Knights," Wyatt asked.

"I'm sorry," Andrew apologized. He had forgotten that Wyatt had no knowledge that they were killed. Andrew sat back down, "I'm sorry Wyatt, but last night Claudia and the others were killed."

"What!" Wyatt cried out in disbelief. "How?"

"Last night, they were attacked and killed at a blood feast," Andrew explained. "They were going to make a kill." Andrew stopped to drink some more water. He needed to collect his thoughts to explain the rest to Wyatt. He continued, "What they didn't realize was that it was a trap. They were tortured and killed by the group of teenagers."

"Tell me how was possible," Wyatt retorted. "You know how well they are trained. So tell me how did a bunch of kids overpower three trained killers, huh?"

"They couldn't," Andrew agreed. "You and I both know that. They had to have had help."

"I can't talk about it anymore." Wyatt shook his head. "I just want to go, okay?"

Andrew called the jailers. They quickly entered the room and released Wyatt's leg chains from the hook. "I will talk to the judge," Andrew reassured Wyatt as he was lead out of the room. "You should be home by the end of the day." Wyatt smiled and mouthed 'thank you' to Andrew, who gathered up his briefcase and left through the other doorway.

Storm yawned and stretched as she opened her eyes. She sat straight up and was confused at her surroundings for several minutes. The furniture, the fireplace, and everything else were unfamiliar. Where was she? Storm soon remembered she was in Andrew's house.

Storm tossed aside the blanket and was about to leave the room, when Chloe came in with a tray. "I hope you are hungry," Chloe smiled.

"I'm not hungry." Storm sat back down and covered up with the blanket.

Chloe set the tray on the coffee table and removed the cover. A waft of flavorful steam rose from the pancakes and sausages. It engulfed Storm with its inviting aroma. Storm eyed up the food, and in fact she was starving. Storm looked to Chloe for approval, who nodded that it was okay, so she immediately dug in. Chloe watched as Storm hungrily devoured the food. Chloe just sat there in awe. Soon Storm was done and pushed the tray away. She settled back on the couch.

"Is Mister Knight here?" Storm inquired.

"No, he went to interview Wyatt at the jail," Chloe informed her.

"What about me?" Storm worriedly asked.

"What do you mean?" Chloe asked. She got up and joined Storm on the couch. "Did you do something wrong?"

"Well, it's just that, um what happened last night," Storm muttered.

"What did happen last night?" Chloe asked.

"Something terrible," Storm confessed.

"What?" Chloe pressed for an answer.

315

"We killed those people last night." Storm buried her face in her hands, overcome with shame. "We tortured them…they begged for mercy, but…"

"But what," Chloe took hold of Storm by the shoulders and forced her to uncover her face. Chloe stared at Storm, "Who was there? Tell me, Storm."

"The members of the council were there!" Storm blurted out. She broke free of Chloe's grasp and buried her face again.

"Who is the council?" Chloe questioned.

"Ravenclaw and the rest of the heads of the households," Storm spoke through her covered face. "It was a trap and we were the bait."

"What do you mean a trap?" Chloe was sharp towards Storm.

"Ravenclaw had me call them!" Storm uncovered her face and screamed at Chloe. "He…He had me pretend to be one of their informants and tell them of this blood feast that was planned at my abandoned home. Ravenclaw knew that the Knights could not resist and would be there to attack us." Storm sobbed as she went on, "He…he knew they would come; he counted on it. He said that it was the beginning of retribution for all the centuries that the Knights had hunted our kind."

"How did he know who they were and how to call them?" Chloe was almost too afraid to ask, but had to know.

"Ravenclaw mentioned something about a book with the names of our enemies," Storm answered Chloe.

"How did he get the book?" Chloe demanded.

"I..I don't know," Storm answered back.

"Dear God," Chloe lamented.

Andrew opened the front door and walked into the foyer. He set his briefcase down and took off his overcoat. He put is coat away in the hall closet and closed the door. Andrew grabbed his briefcase and headed towards the kitchen. When he walked past the family room, Andrew saw Chloe and Storm in the middle of a conversation. He decided to join them. When Chloe saw her dad, she jumped up and walked over to him.

"How could you?" Chloe started punching her dad. Andrew dropped the briefcase and grabbed her by the arms.

"How could I what?" Andrew was confused.

"You gave him the book," Chloe broke free of her dad's grasp, turned and sat down. Andrew immediately followed her and sat down. He glanced from Storm to his daughter. They each had an accusing expression on their faces.

"What are you talking about?" Andrew demanded. "The Knights of VanHelsing book," Chloe shouted loudly. "You promised to turn it over make sure justice was done. Not any more killings!"

"I never gave any one the book," Andrew said in his defense.

"Tell him Storm." Chloe looked to her for help. "Tell him what you told me."

"What are you talking about?" Andrew was even more confused.

"Mister Ravenclaw was the one who told us he got the names of the Knights from a book," Storm recounted for Andrew. She was trembling, "He told us he was going to kill every one of them."

Andrew took off quickly and ran upstairs to the library. He kicked open the door and rushed over to the shelf on the left side of the window. The book that Andrew had hoped was there was now gone! Andrew felt sick and dropped to his knees. Someone in the house took the book.

Andrew rose and headed for the room Nick and Kara had used. He didn't bother to knock and just burst in. Nick was taking a nap on the bed. Andrew's sudden intrusion startled him. Nick bolted straight up and let loose a tirade of profanities.

"Where's Kara?" Andrew was angry.

"She had to go back to Chicago for a few days, why?" Nick explained. "Why?"

"The book is missing," Andrew bellowed.

"You think Kara took it?" Nick scoffed. "No way would she do that."

"Last night three Knights of VanHelsing were killed right here in Bayport," Andrew sat on the bed, defeated. He looked at Nick and continued, "It was a trap that they walked right into, not suspecting a thing. Storm said that Vlad Ravenclaw had gotten their real names from the book I recovered from Gothica castle."

"Holy Sh---" Nick whistled. He was defensive again, "No way that Kara took the book and give it to the creepy vampire guy. She would not do it." Nick felt sick now. He was suddenly unsettled and looked at Andrew, "She did take the book. F---."

"We need to get that book back," Andrew stood.

"How?" Nick asked.

"Dad!" they heard Chloe shout from the bottom of the stairs. "Come quick!"

Andrew and Nick both went down stairs. They went to the family room, but Chloe and Storm were not there. "In the kitchen," Chloe shouted. Nick and Andrew went to the kitchen. Chloe had the television on. She and Storm were watching the local morning news program. The news anchor came on after a commercial and announced a breaking new's story. She shared that in Bayport County, there had been suscpicious killings last evening. She added that the authorities were baffled and had no leads as to who was responsible for the slayings. Chloe and the others turned their attention from the screen and looked at Andrew. He just stared at the television with a blank expression on his face. He did not move or say a word.

"Dad?" Chloe asked softly.

Andrew turned and walked out of the kitchen. His lust for revenge and justice had gone terribly wrong. Andrew walked down the hallway. He so desperately wanted to put an end to the Knights of VanHelsing, that the Higgins family deaths took second place. Andrew ascended the stairs and went to his room. He was beaten.

The church was filled with mourners. There were civilians dressed in traditional black attire and law enforcement personnel in their dress uniforms. In front of the chapel was Talia's flag draped casket. There was a photo of Talia in her Sheriff's uniform, on top of her casket. Father Michael stood somberly at the pulpit and looked out across the vastness of tearful faces. The sun was shining brightly through the narrow stained glass windows and cast its light and warmth for all. But it brilliance and pleasurable warmth paled in comparison to the tearful and somber remorse of those in the church.

Peter and Lisa sat next to Chloe. She had on a simple black dress. Peter nervously played with his tie and played with buttons of his black suit. Next to Chloe were Roxanne and Nick. Each was dressed in solemn black attire. The one who should have been there with them, Andrew, was missing. As far as the others knew, he was still locked away brooding in his room.

As the Father Michael spoke, Peter could hear weeping from behind, which in turn caused him to wipe the tears from his own eyes. Lisa was resting her head on Peter's shoulder holding a handkerchief in one hand while holding his with the other. Roxanne was just sitting there quietly, staring at the casket. Nick sat there as if staring off into space. He was still in shock over Kara's apparent betrayal. It really pissed him off that all this time she had been able to fool them all; him especially.

With all eyes now focused on the Father Michael, Andrew slipped quietly through the doors and sat down in the back. He easily slipped into the back pew. He wore a white rose on his suit of black. Andrew smiled briefly at the woman seated next to him.

Once Father Michael was finished, he asked if anyone wanted to say something about Talia. Andrew watched and waited to see if any one was going to step forward. He waited for several minutes. When no one came forward, Andrew decided to go.

Andrew got up and walked to the front of the church. When he got to the front, Chloe and the others were shocked to see him. Andrew took his place at the pulpit. He was about to speak, when Andrew caught a glimpse of Vlad Ravenclaw slip in and take a seat in the back where he had just been. Andrew drew a deep breath.

"When Sheriff Delsmann, Talia, and I first met it was not the most pleasant meeting I've ever had," Andrew paused as a wave of respectful laughter spread across the sea of mourners. Andrew continued, "She actually despised me and was determined to put me in jail for interfering with the Higgins investigation." Andrew paused to gather his thoughts. He looked at his daughter. Like the others, Chloe waited for his next word. Andrew went on, "But over time we had become friends and there was a mutual respect for each other." Andrew stopped again, this time he looked at the photo of Talia. He remembered her that night at the hotel in Berlin. She was so thrilled to wear the evening dress. He also remembered their kiss. Andrew touched his lips. Talia absolutely hated him when they first met. But all changed when he saved her that night at JFK Prep. He also remembered Talia had saved his life that night at the park. Andrew sniffed back his tears and went on, "Talia gave her life for me. When she lay dying in my arms, Talia asked if I knew what true love was." Andrew paused. Everyone waited with anticipation for the answer. Andrew did not disappoint them, "I said no and she told me that true love was 'sacrifice'".

Andrew left the pulpit and walked over to Talia's casket. He gently caressed the cold metal with his hand. Talia had willingly sacrificed her life for his. Andrew broke down. Chloe and Peter rushed up and helped him to the pew where they were seated.

Father Michael took his place at the pulpit. He gave the blessing. Six deputies rose and took their places beside Talia's casket. Together they walked her mortal remains towards the side doors of the church and into the waiting horse drawn hearse. Peter, Lisa, Chloe, Nick and Andrew walked out and stood behind the company of Sheriff's deputies, the honor guard, the mayor and other city officials. The rest of the mourners filed out of church and joined them. Father Michael took his place at the head of the processional. The hearse driver gave his noble steed the command and the processional began its march through the church cemetery.

The funeral processional wound its way through the cemetery and finally came to a freshly dug grave overlooking the lake below. The honor guard marched in formation and came to a halt at the right side of the grave. They immediately came to 'order arms' and stood, stone-faced at attention. Father Michael took his place at the head of the gravesite as the pallbearers removed the casket from the horse drawn hearse. They carried the casket and set it down. Andrew, along with his daughter and the others, took their seats as the other mourners remained standing. It started to snow.

The snow was getting heavier now, and it soaked Andrew's overcoat as he sat there staring at the casket.

"The Lord is my Shepard, I shall not want," Father Michael began the graveside service. "He maketh me lie down in green pastures; he leadeth me beside still waters. He restores my soul. Thou preparest a table before me in the presesence of my enemies, my cup overflows, even though I walk through the valley of death, thou art with me, thy rod and thy staff comfort me, surely goodness and mercy shall follow me and I shall dwell in the house of the Lord my whole life long."

Andrew found little comfort in the words. He could not shake the image of Talia in his arms. The look in her eyes would forever be etched in his mind. His pain was reflected in the faces of the other mourners.

Father Michael stepped aside and the honor guard marched to the head of the grave. They did a right wheel and now faced the lake. The 'ready' command was given. The honor guard came to the ready position. Then the order came to 'aim', they did with expert precision. Finally the 'fire' command came. The silence was broken with the report of gunfire. Each time the honor guard fired, the rage inside of Andrew grew.

The honor guard came to shoulder arms and marched back to their original position. Two deputies removed the flag from the casket and folded it. One of the deputies presented the flag to Andrew, since Talia had no living relatives. Andrew nodded his thanks and held the flag to his chest. He and the others watched as they lowered Talia's casket into the ground. Andrew suddenly rose, handed the flag to Chloe, and walked off.

Andrew had seen Vlad standing by a tree as he watched the gravesite service. Andrew ducked behind the crowd of mourners and slipped in the surrounding woods. With great stealth, Andrew circled around to the place where Vlad was standing. Vlad, his attention focused on the service, never saw Andrew come up behind him. Andrew did not bother to even speak and punched Vlad in the back. Vlad stumbled to his knees. Andrew spun and hit Vlad with a kick to the back. Vlad fell and his face buried into the snow. He regained his composure and jumped up to see Andrew standing there. Vlad flashed his fangs and rushed Andrew, who twirled in the air and struck Vlad across the head and in the chest with his boots. Vlad tumbled and fell again. He glared at Andrew and spat blood from his mouth. Andrew walked up to Vlad and roughly grabbed him by the collar of his overcoat. He put his face close to Vlad's and growled, "I am coming for the book and you." Andrew let go of Vlad's collar and walked away. Vlad wiped his mouth and narrowed his eyes. "I'll be ready," Vlad's voice echoed through the cold winter's air. He rose a bit unsteadily to his feet and walked away.

Chapter 19

The northern wind fanned out across the land with perilous intent. Its icy breath stirred up and drove the innocent looking velvety flakes of snow into a fevered frenzy. The wind moaned and howled through the branches of the leafless trees. The snow and wind kept building until it finally climaxed and gave birth to the season's first winter storm.

From the blowing and drifting snow, a single pair of headlights pierced through it all. The road was nearly impassible, but the rider coaxed his trusty steed to continue on. When it could go no futher, the driver pulled his jeep into a wooded glen just off the road.

Andrew jumped out and trudged through the knee-deep snow to the back of his jeep. He thrust open the hatch and took out the first order of business; his shelter tent. Andrew plowed through the snow and when he got to a spot beneath two tall pine trees, he pulled the cord and the tent sprung to life. Andrew kept a tight grip for fear of losing his shelter to the hungry winds. He set his tent down now and quickly secured the lines to the trunks of the sturdy trees. Satisfied, Andrew returned to the jeep for the rest of his gear. He grabbed it all and held it tightly in his arms. Andrew returned to his shelter and while balancing his load with one hand, he unzipped the flap with the other. Andrew tossed in his gear first and then climbed in right after. He re-closed the tent flap.

The interior of the tent was pitch-black. Andrew unzipped the large bag and searched through it. He was glad and pridefully removed the lantern. He pushed the button and the electric blue light flooded the tent. Finally able to see, Andrew put down the lantern and laid out his sleeping bag. He climbed inside and zipped it shut. Soon Andrew was feeling comfortably warm. In order to save the lantern battery, Andrew shut it off.

Andrew lay awake unable to sleep. His thoughts soon drifted off to days earlier. Right after Talia's funeral, Peter along with the Sheriff's department, showed up at the Ravenclaw property with a search warrant. When they arrived, a caretaker was there to meet them. He informed them that Ravenclaw had already left to join up with friends in Illinois. Though disappointed, the authorities searched the manor and the rest of the property for the book. They could not locate it and gave up the search. Andrew knew they would never find the book there; Ravenclaw was much more intelligent than that. To make matters worse, the Sheriff's department classified the Higgins's case as unsolved and filed it away. Wyatt was released from jail as promised. Nedra, tired of the bad influences in Bayport, took her boys and just left. She also put their home up for sale. When Nedra paid Andrew for his services, she did not even tell him where they were going. Roxanne returned to her bookstore. She had suggested that Andrew seek professional counseling for his obsession with Vlad Ravenclaw.

Roxanne told him that it was unhealthy. Andrew said he would, but never intended on following through.

Chloe also told him to get help before she returned to her own private investigative business in Madison. She was concerned he would do something extreme. Andrew lied and told her he was planning on joining up with Megan and her parents. Chloe asked where they were. This time Andrew told the truth that they were going to visit family in California. Chloe must have believed him and left.

Nick had gone back to Chicago. He had with him a letter of recommendation from Peter, the Sheriff's department and the Berlin police in Germany. As a result, Nick was promoted to the rank of Sergeant. With everyone gone and back to their normal lives, Andrew was once again alone.

The wind's icy claws were scratching at the tent in search of it next victim. Andrew laid back and closed his eyes. But sleep did not come yet. Andrew suspected that Ravenclaw had Kara keep possession of the book. Her place was much more secure than Ravenclaw's. As a result, Andrew suspected that Kara was some how involved in the death of the Higgins's family. He also believed that Vlad Ravenclaw was involved too. It was all a mute point anyway, at least until he had proof.

Andrew nestled down inside his warm, comfortable sleeping bag. He did his best to ignore the howling winds. Finally, sleep did come to Andrew. He closed his eyes and drifted off into sweet slumber.

The sunlight glistened across the newly laid out blanket of snow. A light winter's breeze gently flowed across the land. The storm from the night before was gone and in its path was a winter wonderland.

Andrew woke refreshed. He had not gotten such a restful night sleep in months. He sat up and stretched the last remnants of the sandman's dust from his eyes. Andrew unzipped the sleeping bag and rolled out. He crawled on his knees to the flap and unzipped it. Andrew's gaze was immediately met with a wall of white. He would have to dig his way out. Andrew dug at the snow, shoveling it out of the way with his gloved hands.

After what seemed like forever, Andrew emerged. The sun-soaked snow blinded him and Andrew immediately closed his eyes. He reached in the breast pocket of his coat and took out a pair of sunglasses. Andrew put them on and re-opened his eyes. When he did, Andrew surveyed his surroundings.

Andrew first appraised the situation with his jeep. It was buried in the snow and going nowhere for a very long time. Andrew turned around and eyed up his tent. It looked more like an igloo now. Andrew ducked back inside and retrieved his binoculars. He walked to the edge of the hill and gazed upon the pristine landscape below. Andrew raised the binoculars to his eyes and focused on the object of his desire.

The stone block castle was impressive, but it probably was more of an eyesore amongst the more modest homes of its neighbors. Andrew scouted the fence line which was constructed of stone and electric wire. It said to intruders very loud and clear to 'stay out' or else. Andrew turned his attention to the front gate and the guard house. He saw two security personnel that carried side arms. The gate itself was a very impressive creation of an iron frame and bars. As Andrew continued to watch, a linen company delivery truck stopped at the gate. As one of the guards remained inside in the guard house, his partner approached the truck. He spoke to the driver and checked his clipboard. When he was satisfied, he waved to his partner to open the gate. Once the gate was open, the truck continued on its way.

Andrew settled down in the snow and continued his surveillance. About a half an hour later, another truck arrived. This one was from Nancy's Catering. Well, Andrew thought, Kara must be having a party. The guards followed the same procedures as earlier. There was no way he could enter the property during the daylight with such tight security. The only way was under the cover of darkness. Andrew estimated it took about five minutes for the guards to check in a vehicle and open the gate. This included the time it took to exit the guard house, walk to the vehicle, check the clipboard and open the gate. Andrew had to find a place to hide close by, and that meant he had to do that during the daylight. Once there, he could remain undetected until the time of the party. Andrew searched the area close to the gate. It was there that he found a large pine tree with its lower branches touching the snow. Andrew was willing to bet that the area beneath the branches and snow was a place to hide in. To do so, was a risk, but one he had to take. He could use the surrounding woods for cover, but the last few yards were in the open.

Andrew stood up and returned to his tent. He crawled inside and retrieved a rather large and long pack of white camouflage that matched his winter clothing. Andrew departed from his 'igloo' and started his trek towards the pine tree.

It had not been an easy hike through the knee-deep snow. Andrew was about half way and decided to rest. He took off the pack and plopped it and himself down in the snow. Andrew opened one of the side pockets and pulled out a couple of energy bars. Andrew tore open the first one and quickly downed it in a couple of bites. With the next one, he opened it and spent a little more time to eat it. As he sat there, Andrew looked around and still could not believe how much it snowed last night. Andrew stood up and slung his pack over his shoulders. He continued on his way.

Andrew had finally reached the edge of the trees. He knelt down and took out his binoculars. He focused on the guard house. The two guards had their backs to him and were in the midst of a conversation. It was now or never. Andrew put away his binoculars and dropped down on his belly. He started his approach to the pine tree. Andrew crawled along slowly and would pause from time to time to blend in with the snow and barren ground cover. By now Andrew could see the guard house and security without his binoculars. This was the critical part in his plan. This was the part where it could all go bad and he would be discovered. Andrew had to slowly inch his way towards the pine tree. What should have normally only taken a few minutes, it had taken Andrew much longer. He was never so glad when the aroma of pine filled his nostrils.

Andrew moved to the opposite side of the tree, away from the guard's view. Andrew quickly dug through the snow and as he suspected there was a 'cave' beneath the tree. Andrew took off his pack and lowered it into his 'home' and crawled in after it. He fixed the snow to make it look like it was before. Andrew left his pack and crawled on his hands and knees to the side of the tree that faced the gate. Andrew dug out a hole just big enough for him to look through and provide some necessary light. He could clearly see the security guards and the front gate. Andrew was about to go back for his pack, when a black Mercedes with heavily tinted windows, pulled up to the gate. You could not see the occupants at all. Just like before, the guard exited the guardhouse and approached the vehicle. But this time was different. As the driver lowered the window, the security guard never bothered to check his clipboard and immediately motioned for his partner to open the gate. Whoever it was, they were important. Once the gate was open, the car sped through and up its way towards the castle. Andrew went back for his pack and brought it with him to his spy window. He set the alarm on his watch and laid his head down on the pack for a pillow. Andrew was worn out and needed to rest. His eyes were suddenly very heavy and soon Andrew was snoring away.

Andrew woke in a panic. The sunlight was gone. His watch alarm did not go off! Andrew scrambled in the dark and crawled quickly to his spy hole. It was night and there were already a line of vehicles at the front gate. Andrew crawled back to his pack and grabbed it. He returned to his spy hole and shoveled the snow away like a madman. Soon the hole was big enough and Andrew climbed out. He ducked and sort of did a run crawl along the line of cars. So far he went undetected. Pretty soon Andrew was along side a black hummer. Andrew sat down for a few seconds to catch his breath, but it did not last long. The gates started to open and the hummer started to move! Andrew scrambled as fast as he could as the hummer picked up speed. If he did not move quicker, the guards would discover him. Andrew stumbled and fell as the hummer pulled away. He turned and looked. He was inside! The gate closed and with it, concealed his presence.

Not far from the gate was the groundskeeper building. Andrew scrambled to his feet and ran over to it. Andrew took out his lock pick set and bent down to examine the lock. He selected the right tools. Andrew had the lock picked and the door opened within minutes. He put the tool back in the case and back in his pocket. Andrew went inside and closed the door. Andrew removed his pack and set in on the floor. He removed his winter clothing to reveal a Knight's of VanHelsing outfit underneath. He unzipped the pack next and took the scabbards with swords along with a long leather black coat. Andrew first put on the coat and then slipped on the scabbards. He reached inside the pack for one other thing. Andrew slipped on the hood and now he was complete. Andrew hid his winter clothing and the pack beneath some lawn product bags.

Andrew left the groundskeeper's building and headed for the main house.

Andrew used the landscaping for cover as he went directly to the rear of the castle where the deliver vehicles were parked. Andrew ducked into the bushes nearby and watched. He saw a pretty steady flow of catering staff that moved from the truck to the entrance.

He at first thought it would be too risky to try and sneak in between the catering workers. The windows were out as an entry point because they probably had some type of alarm. Andrew was stumped for the moment, but then opportunity knocked; there was a break in the line of catering staff.

Andrew bolted from the bushes and in through the open doorway. He was in the hallway which led directly to the kitchen. Now what Andrew thought? There was no place to go. Great, Andrew said to himself, he would surely be discovered. Andrew leaned against the wall, and before he could react the wall seemed to swallow him up! Andrew stumbled backwards and landed on his butt. The secret panel closed and a light immediately illuminated the area he was now in. It was a narrow passageway.

Andrew stood and walked to the end, since he had no other choice. It was there that he saw a set of stone step that spiraled upwards. Andrew ascended the stairs and finally came to another wall. He felt around for the trigger device. Just as his right hand hit a raised section of the wall it opened. Andrew was on the second floor of the castle. The area was familiar to him. He had been here the last time he was at Kara's. Her bedroom chamber was just a short walk down the hallway.

Andrew strode at a quickened pace and was soon at the door of Kara's room. He listened first and upon not hearing a sound, opened the door. Andrew immediately stepped inside and shut the door again. Andrew stood there and surveyed the room. Now where would Kara have hidden the book? It was probably in a safe. But where would the safe be?

The main hall was brimming with Kara's invited guests. They were all there to celebrate a victory; a victory against their age old enemy.

The room-length table was adorned in deep red linen with gold accents. Crystal fountains cascaded with tuica, a plum brandy usually enjoyed before a meal along with some appetizers. It varies in strength, dryness and smell according to the region. But if you attempt this drink, beware it does have a kick to it! The table was also filled with Romanian national dishes not to be missed, such as Coirba, a sour soup made from fermented bran, bacon, potatoes and beef or chicken. Then there were also Mititei, minced meat rolls with aromatic herbs, along with Tochitura, a hearty meat stew seasoned with onions and/or spices. Also served was muschi poiana, which consisted of mushroom- and bacon-stuffed beef in a puree of vegetables and tomato sauce. Guests could also sample the traditional Romanian fish dish of grilled carp called saramura. And Kara did not forget the dessert lovers. There were plenty of apricot ice cream, merengue layered cake, cherry compote turkish baklava and apple strudel.

Kara wore a red velvet flowing gown accented with a gold lace bodice and diamonds. Her hair was swept up and held in place with a gold hair comb, which complimented the features of her face.

Kara milled about the room as she greeted her guests. She was the perfect hostess. Once in awhile, Kara would glance across the room to make sure he was still there.

Vlad also greeted his honored guests; members of not only the Ravenclaw Clan, but other clans across the country and from Europe. Tonight, Vlad would share with them the prize he had finally won; the book of The Knights of VanHelsing.

Vlad walked across the room and came up behind Kara. He caught a whiff of her essence and it drove him insane. But no, he would wait until the blood feast later this evening. Vlad drew Kara closer and tenderly kissed the back of her neck. He desperately wanted to partake of her lifeblood, but again there would be time for that later.

"It is time for you to get the book," Vlad whispered his command.

"Yes my love," Kara murmured.

Vlad released his grasp of Kara, and she left to go upstairs to her bedroom chamber. Kara ascended the stairs as Vlad watched. A smile of fulfillment was on his face.

Kara reached the top of the stairs and went to her room. She opened the door and went inside.

Kara walked directly to the painting on the wall next to her bed. She swung the hinged painting aside.

Kara entered the access code on the safe key panel. Once the safe was open, Kara took out the book. She re-closed the safe and turned to leave. Kara was about to scream, but Andrew quickly silenced her with a blow to the head. As Kara fell, she let go of the book. Andrew ignored Kara and grabbed the book before it hit the floor. As Andrew held the book in his hands, a realization suddenly hit him; one he had been afraid to admit. The book was far too dangerous for any one to possess. Andrew had to destroy it.

Vlad wondered where Kara could be. She was gone far too long. He excused himself and went to go and bring her back. He hurriedly ascended the stairs to the second floor and to the door of Kara's bedroom. Vlad did not bother to knock since the door was open. He boldly stepped into the room and immediately saw Kara lying unconscious on the floor. Vlad sensed another presence in the room. He scoured the room; there was someone in the shadows.

"Come out," Vlad hissed. He cringed when a Knight of VanHelsing stepped forward with the book in his hands. "How did you get past security?" Vlad angrily demanded. There was no response. This infuriated Vlad and he screamed, "Give me the book. It will do you no good to have it." Still there was no reply. Vlad kept his eyes on his adversary as he walked over to Kara. Vlad knelt down and checked on Kara. She was still alive. Vlad rose again to his feet.

"What is your name?" Vlad inquired. His lips curled into a satisfied smile, "For I know them all."

Instead, his adversary drew the twin blades of death.

336

"Will you strike me down as you cowards have always done?" Vlad opened his arms in a gesture of submission. "Or will you give me a chance to defend myself?" His adversary tossed one of his swords. Vlad caught it by the handle. He swung the sword to see how it felt in his hand. "I have killed many of your brethren," Vlad confessed. "As I am sure you have killed many of mine." Vlad took up his stance. His eyes narrowed, "I believe it is your move." Vlad expected an attack, but instead his advesary grasped his hood and removed it.

"You!" Vlad was taken aback.

Andrew bowed gracefully, with his gaze on Vlad.

"I want the truth," Andrew demanded.

"Are you certain of that?" Vlad's top lip curled to reveal his fangs.

"Tell me," Andrew said, his sword at the ready.

"The plan was simple," Vlad began his tale. "We wanted the book you hold in your other hand." Vlad walked backward and closed the door. He locked it. Vlad continued, "Kara and I became lovers soon after she interviewed me for her book. It was actually her idea to go to Gothica and retrieve it. She setup the interview with Ana VanHelsing. Unfortunately, Kara was not successful. So we had to come with a new plan. We had to get someone on the inside Ana would trust. Wyatt was more than eager to help us retrieve the book. We suspected that Doctor Straussman was a Knight of VanHelsing. So I went to the council of elders and told them that Wyatt violated the laws of the coven. They voted to excommunicate Wyatt from the clan for not adhering to our bylaws. The next part of the plan was up to Wyatt. In one of his sessions with Doctor Straussman, Wyatt confessed his excommunication. He also confessed his desire for revenge. Wyatt later told me, that Doctor Straussman was in fact, one of our most hated enemies. She took Wyatt under her wing to train him, but did not take him to Gothica." Vlad kept his place by the door; there was no way he was going to let Andrew simply walk out of the room with the book.

"Why were the Higgins's murdered?"

"They never agreed with my plan to obtain the book," Vlad was practically giddy. "And I knew we needed something that would force our enemy to protect Wyatt. A sacrifice had to be made. Because of Higgins's lack of courage, the choice was easy." Vlad laughed out loud. "Wyatt even volunteered to do it, but I would not let him. The honor was mine."

"You spilled innocent blood," Andrew held up the book and spewed forth his disgust. "And you killed them all because of this?"

"It was worth it," Vlad was solemn. "Every life."

"Even Talia's?" Andrew cursed.

"The authorities believed Wyatt was responsible for the killings, because of evidence I planted at the house," Vlad continued. "He had the motive and the opportunity. Because of the chance of their order being exposed to public knowledge, Doctor Straussman sent Wyatt to safety at Gothica."

"But things did not go as planned," Andrew surmised. "Did they?"

"No," Vlad said with bitterness. "He could not find the book either." Vlad eyes fixed on Andrew, "That's where you came in."

"Me?" Andrew scoffed at Vlad's suggestion. "I was part of your plan?"

"Yes," Vlad nodded. "You were a very important part indeed." Vlad switched his sword back and forth front of him. "I long knew of your reputation as an investigator. Actually, it was quite impressive."

"Really." Andrew was sarcastic.

"The trouble was we had to convince you to get involved," Vlad was full of pride. "It would have to be an authentic performance. And what better way to accomplish that than a very worried and desperate mother. She even convinced Father Michael by confessing to him the dire situation Wyatt was in. It was joyous news when Nedra told me you accepted the case." Vlad took a few paces closer to Andrew, who immediately raised his sword. Vlad stopped. He went on, "From there we just let you do what you do best, use your skilled deductive powers to look beyond the ordinary. Unlike the bumbling authorities, who focus on the usual, you can see beyond the usual. When you contacted Kara to interview her about her book and how it related to the case, my heart lept for joy. If not, the plan was for her to use a cover story to contact you. The only loose cannon were Sheriff Delsmann. I never suspected she were a Knight of VanHelsing. We did not count on her hatred for you. We were very concerned the plan was dead when you were nearly killed, and suffered from amnesia." Vlad took a step back, as if he were anticipating an attack. He eyed up Andrew and continued. "It was a glorious day for us when you recovered it."

"Why would Nedra or Wyatt be willing to help you?" Andrew came back sharply. "What kind of hold did you have on them?"

"You mean by now you, the great detective, has not figured it out?" Vlad broke out for a few moments in a loud, boisterous laugh. He stopped once he had caught his breath, "Nedra and I met when I was younger. We were married, but later separated and soon divorced. Out of the fear of my enemies, we agreed to have the children take her last name of Collins. Wyatt and Chad are my sons."

Andrew was numb. He never suspected any of this. How stupid and inept could he have been? Andrew was so focused on solving the case, and then championing the downfall of the Knights of VanHelsing, that he was blind to the brilliant mastermind of it all. There was only one thing left to do.

Kara awoke from unconsciousness. With her eyes wide open now, she saw Andrew with his back to her. He and Vlad were in the midst of a stand off. Kara lay down and slithered across the floor to the other side of the bed. Once she was there, Kara reached under the pillow and pulled out a semi-automatic handgun. She stood up and looked at Vlad first. He saw her, but did not acknowledge, for fear of giving her away to Andrew. Kara raised the gun and capped off the first round!

Andrew flinched as the first bullet slammed into his back. He let go of the sword as two more bullets struck. With each one Andrew's body jerked. He dropped to his knees and turned towards Vlad with a look of despair. Andrew fell face down and did not move. He slowly closed his eyes.

Vlad put down his sword and applauded Kara. They rushed into each other's arms and their lips came together in a fervent kiss of victory.

"Get the book and let us be on our way," Vlad said as they parted.

Kara walked over to get the book. When she turned around, Kara's face drained of color. Vlad's back shivered with fear and he turned to see that Andrew had risen from the dead. Vlad scrambled for his sword, but Andrew spun and hit him with a kick to the back. Vlad skittered across the stone floor and right past the sword. Kara rushed at Andrew, but he hit her with a combination of kicks. Kara dropped to the floor, beaten. Andrew picked his own sword up, just as Vlad jumped up and finally got hold of his own. Andrew charged at Vlad, who was ready. Vlad thrust his blade and caught Andrew in the leg. Andrew howled as Vlad withdrew his blade. Andrew stumbled and fell to the floor with blood seeping from his wound. Vlad lifted the blade to his lips and tasted Andrew's blood. Soon he would have more.

Kara jumped up and rolled across the bed. Andrew never saw her. She was after her gun.

Andrew stood and tore off his overcoat. He hobbled over to the bed and with his blade, cut off a strip of the sheet. Andrew tied it around his wounded leg to slow down the bleeding. From the corner of his eye, Andrew caught a glimpse of Kara. With his left hand, he reached in the pouch on his belt and then let loose a deadly pair of throwing stars. The first one struck her in the chest;

the other her neck. The gun flew from Kara's grasp as she fell backwards to the floor.

Vlad eyes flashed in horror at seeing his lover get struck down. Vlad howled and bared his fangs. He switched his blade back and forth like a cat's tail and charged towards Andrew, who also obliged the same. But this time was different. This time Andrew dropped the very last moment, slid on his knees and thrust his blade into Vlad's chest and severing his heart. Vlad coughed and blood ran down from the corners of his mouth. He looked down at Andrew with a cold, soulless stare. Andrew stood and withdrew the sword and tossed it away. Vlad collapsed face down in his own blood.

Kara pulled the throwing stars from her chest and neck. She used the bed to pull herself up. She cleared the edge of the bed in time to see Andrew kill Vlad. Kara screeched and bound over the bed. She instantly picked up one of the swords. Kara charged at Andrew. He tumbled, rolled on the floor and picked up the other sword. Andrew turned just in time to block Kara's attack. Kara withdrew and attacked from the right, but Andrew blocked it again. He hit Kara in the chest with a fore fist punch. Kara backpedaled a bit, as Andrew stood up. Kara charged once more and attacked from the left. Andrew countered. Kara raised the sword above her head in an attempt to drive it into Andrew from above. Andrew blocked, gave his sword a twist which ripped the sword from Kara's hand. Andrew spun and drove his blade into Kara. She stared down in disbelief at the metal blade protruding from her bellie. She grasped hold of Andrew and drew herself closer. As Kara moved, the blade penetrated deeper and deeper into her body. When Kara was face to face with Andrew, she cupped his face with her hands and leaned in closer. Kara paused. She stared at him for a moment. Kara leaned in and kissed Andrew with her blood stained lips. When Kara withdrew, Andrew recoiled at the sight of Kara's hollow eyes. It was the same look Talia had. Kara silently mouthed the word 'sacrifice'. Her eyes closed. Andrew let go of her and Kara slid to the floor.

Andrew walked over and picked up the book. Andrew strode past Vlad on his way to the door. He stopped and cast a disgusted gaze upon the fallen mastermind and his tragic lover. Andrew unlocked the door, opened it and silently walked out.

About the Author...
R.L. Edinger lives in Northeast Wisconsin
with his wife and their three children

8600347R0

Made in the USA
Charleston, SC
25 June 2011